THE CLOVER CHAPEL

A Jamison Valley Series Novel

DEVNEY PERRY

THE CLOVER CHAPEL
Copyright © 2017 by Devney Perry
All rights reserved.

ISBN: 978-1635761221

No part of this book may be reproduced, distributed or transmitted in any form or by any means, including photocopying, recording or other electronic or mechanical methods, without the prior written permission of the author except in the case of brief quotations in a book review.
This is a work of fiction. Names, characters, places and incidents are the product of the author's imagination or are used fictitiously. Any resemblance to actual events, locales or persons, living or dead, is coincidental.

Editor: Elizabeth Nover, Razor Sharp Editing,
www.razorsharpediting.com

Cover Artwork © Sarah Hansen, Okay Creations,
www.okaycreations.com

Proofreader: Julie Deaton www.facebook.com/jdproofs

Formatting: Champagne Formats,
www.champagneformats.com

Other Books

Jamison Valley Series

The Coppersmith Farmhouse
The Clover Chapel
The Lucky Heart
The Outpost
The Bitterroot Inn

The Birthday List

PROLOGUE

"I AM NOT A SPOILED BRAT!"

The man sitting next to me huffed. "You're sitting in the corner glaring at the rest of us. You haven't said a word until now. Every time someone mentions doing something fun, you roll your eyes. Yeah. You're a spoiled brat."

He was right. I was glaring at everyone and hadn't said a word for over an hour and I may have rolled my eyes a time or two. I definitely had at the mention of going to a male stripper show.

But this weekend was not going at all as I had planned and, thus, my grumpy mood.

"I am not a brat. I'm just not having any fun."

My friends and I had planned this big spring break trip to Las Vegas to celebrate my birthday tomorrow and our upcoming graduation from Yale. Since all of our previous spring breaks had been spent studying or doing

v

internships, we had decided that for our last, something adventurous and crazy was long overdue.

I was supposed to be having an amazing time with my girlfriends, making memories that would last a lifetime.

Instead, I was miserable.

The last thing I wanted was to be sitting in our stretch limo, crammed into the back corner because now there were four guys crowded in with us.

My friends, unlike me, were overjoyed to be hanging with this group of strangers. Steffie was sandwiched between two of the men, both of whom were staring at the ample cleavage pouring out of her barely there silver dress. Marian and Alice were hanging off the bad boy, a man wearing a sleeveless shirt to showcase his enormous muscles and plethora of tattoos.

That left me in the corner, next to a guy who clearly had no issue insulting a stranger.

"It's your own fault if you're not having fun," he rumbled. "Your friends aren't afraid to have a good time. It's not like it's hard to find. We're in Vegas."

"I'm aware of our location."

He was right again. The girls were genuinely having a good time, making the most of this night in Sin City, letting themselves go wild. Why couldn't I? Sad and defeated, I slumped further into the seat.

"This was supposed to be our last adventure," I said. "A crazy weekend together that we'd remember for the rest of our lives. This trip was for us to spend time with each other, but last night, they all found different guys to hook up with and ditched me. And since I didn't want to have a one-night stand or get plastered by myself at some skeezy bar, I watched TV in our hotel room."

"If you want to have a crazy night, you're going to have to fucking relax. You're uptight."

"I am n—" I started, ready to defend myself again, but stopped. Instead, I turned to the window and muttered the truth. "I know."

I expected him to ignore me now and leave me in my corner alone, eventually trying to steal Marian's or Alice's attentions away from his bulky friend. So when he wrapped his arm around the back of my shoulders and turned me away from the window, I gasped, surprised both by his touch and his closeness.

And then I froze.

When the men had climbed into the limo, I'd been so busy glaring at Steffie for inviting them along that I hadn't really looked at him. And because he'd sat next to me, I'd only glimpsed his profile.

Wow, had I missed out. He was striking.

The vision made my heart pound so hard, its rhythm echoed through my whole body. His hazel eyes were framed with thick, dark lashes. His jaw was covered with a short, dark brown beard. I bet it was soft and would tickle if he kissed the side of my neck—or other places.

His nose was straight with a small bump at the bridge. His hair was shaggy and overly long, but the messy look didn't make him look sloppy. It was sexy and carefree. He didn't give a shit if his hair was a mess.

I gripped the hem of my dress to keep my hands from reaching up and threading my fingers through the thick strands. Then I forced myself to inhale. His gorgeous face alone had made me dizzy. He was by far the most handsome man in his group, which was saying something because my friends were not fawning over the other guys for no reason.

"I can help with that," he said, his mouth turning up at one side in a crooked grin that made my belly dip.

"What?" I was so taken by his magnificent features, I'd forgotten what I'd said.

At my question, his mouth widened into a full-blown smile. Beneath his full lips were perfectly straight, white teeth. I wanted to kiss that mouth. I'd never kissed a man with such a beautiful smile before.

"If you keep looking at my mouth, I'm going to kiss you," he said.

I studied his lips as he formed the words, unable to pull my eyes away from his mouth. I wanted that. I wanted him to kiss me so badly, my body started trembling. The attraction I felt for him was the strongest, most intense feeling I'd ever had.

"Not yet," he whispered.

I tore my gaze from his mouth and looked into his beautiful eyes. Rimmed with a circle of dark gray, the centers were sage green flecked with golden brown. Even in the muted limousine light, the colors were vibrant and bold.

"Do you still want an adventure?"

I blinked a couple of times, forcing myself out of my trance. "Yes," I whispered, surprised at both my answer and that I was actually able to get the word out.

His smile got bigger. "I can do that."

He might be a stranger, but I felt safe by his side. No matter what we did tonight, it would be amazing just because it was with him.

"What's your name?" he asked.

"Emmeline Austin."

"Emmy. I'm Nick Slater."

"Have you ever been on a roller coaster?" Nick asked as the limo sped away from the curb.

"Once, when I was younger. It scared me though and I didn't like it." I hadn't been scared of the heights, but the insane speed and violent spins had brought me near to tears.

"Roller coaster it is then."

"Did you not just hear me tell you that it scared me?"

"Sure." He shrugged. "But this is an adventure. And any adventure worth having is a little scary."

"How about drinks instead? Or we could catch a show?"

He grabbed my hand. "Come on, Emmy. We're going for a ride."

I didn't miss his cheesy innuendo so I gave him my best eye roll while trudging along behind him.

With a hard tug, he pulled me to his side. Never letting go of my hand, we walked side by side along the crowded sidewalk. My small hand fit in his large grip perfectly and my fingers naturally laced through his.

"Up there. That's our ride," he said, raising our linked hands to point out the Stratosphere hotel.

I looked way, way up. A roller coaster car circled the top of the skyscraper. "No. No way. Roller coasters that start at ground level are scary enough. I don't need to experience one thirty stories up."

"I dare you to do it."

"A dare? We're not in middle school, Nick."

He stopped walking and stepped right into my space, his minty breath hit my cheek. "A dare's a dare, Emmy. No matter how old you are. You can tell a lot about a person by their reaction to a dare."

A flush of warmth spread through my cheeks at his intimate tone and closeness. My heart started to race again. His vibrant eyes were looking down at me with such intensity, my worries and reservations all disappeared. As long as I could look into those eyes, everything would be okay.

"Fun?" Nick asked, helping me out of the roller coaster car.

"Yes." The second the ride had ended, a huge smile had broken across my face.

"Good. Up next we're going to a strip club."

"Absolutely not. I have no desire to watch you ogle perfectly plasticized, naked women as they dance around in front of you."

A crooked grin stretched across his mouth. "Dare you."

"Oh for the love . . ." I muttered and stomped past him, dragging him along behind me. "Let's go."

Nick took the lead when we hit the sidewalk and maneuvered us to our show. I was so happy to be with him, still on a high from the roller coaster, I blanked out the world around us and stuck tightly to his side. When we got close, he asked me to close my eyes and to trust him.

"Okay. Open your eyes, Emmy," he said against my ear, sending a shiver down my neck.

The smile on my face vanished when I opened my eyes. Somehow he had managed to shield me from the casino signs because, had I seen where he was taking me, I would have vehemently protested.

"What?" My feet refused to step further into the room.

We had just walked through the doors to Thunder From Down Under. "I thought you said we were going to a strip club."

"We are. You just assumed I meant female strippers."

"I am not watching greased-up men dressed like the Village People gyrate on stage."

"Too late. Show starts in three minutes. Let's grab a quick drink and then go to our seats," he said, dragging me to the bar.

Nick lifted his chin, summoning the female bartender, who ignored the masses of women surrounding us and came directly to him. She was probably glad to have a break from the estrogen and serve the one and only man at this ridiculous show. It didn't hurt that Nick was smoking hot.

"Four lemon drops. Two shots of Jack straight up," Nick ordered. One minute later, all six shots were lined up in front of us.

"Here you go, Emmy. Get to it." He pointed to the lemon drops.

"I can't take four shots! I'll puke!" That comment got me strange looks from the horde of women close by.

"Hurry up," he said, drumming his fingers on the bar. "You're going to want those."

"What about you?"

He answered by taking the whiskey shots and throwing them back, one right after the other.

If I didn't "get to it," he would just dare me again, so I reluctantly picked up one glass and set the sugar-covered rim on my lips.

After a fortifying breath, I tipped my head back and let the sweet liquid roll straight down my throat, burning all the way to my belly. I grimaced but managed to repeat the process with the other three shots.

"I didn't even have to dare you that time. You're relaxing, Emmy." Nick grinned, leading me away from the bar and to our VIP section seats.

I sank into a moderately cushioned, straight-backed chair, then leaned over to whisper in Nick's ear. "No judgment if you are, maybe I've been misreading things between us, but is this your way of telling me that you're gay?"

He threw his head back and laughed into the air above us. His laugh was amazing. Rich. Deep. Honest.

And long.

He kept at it until the show started and his sound was masked by the thumping music and the audience's catcalls. When he finally stopped laughing, he turned and placed both hands on my jaw. His large hands framed my face completely.

I stared at his mouth, waiting to see what he was going to say, but instead of speaking, he licked his lips, sending tingles straight to my center. Then his mouth came crashing down on mine, his soft lips taking over, coaxing my mouth open so he could dip his tongue inside for a taste.

Before I could kiss him back, he pulled back an inch.

"Does that answer your question?" His hands were still framing my face but I managed a nod. He leaned in and kissed the tip of my nose before turning back to the stage.

I stared, unblinking, at his profile, only seeing the show peripherally. A half-naked man had just stripped off his shirt and was parading around in a fireman's hat and baggy pants.

I barely heard the screams when the stripper started unbuttoning his pants. The beat of my own heart and the rush of blood in my ears were deafening. I was in shock. The way Nick's lips had moved on mine and the gentle caress of his tongue had been like no other kiss I'd ever had.

So preoccupied, I jumped when a hand landed on the back of my chair. I turned to see what was happening a millisecond before a man's arm pulled me from my seat and out of the VIP section.

"Have fun!" Nick called before I was whisked up on stage by a stripper dressed as a police officer.

"No way!" I shouted, pulling away from the fake cop. My feet were pointed toward the exit, but I didn't get two steps into my escape before the nearly naked fireman and the now-shirtless police officer pushed me down into a chair, center stage.

I sat, mortified, as both of them started shaking their manly bits in my face and dry humping my legs. The laughter and the shouts from the audience rang loudly in my ears as my face turned violently red. And above all of the female noise was Nick's booming male laugh.

Squinting through the bright stage lights, I searched for him in the audience. I lost sight when a third stripper joined the show, this one dressed in a cowboy hat and brown briefs printed with horseshoes.

Nick had been right. I had needed those four shots.

After an eternity, I was released from that torturous chair but I didn't go back to Nick. I marched straight to the now-deserted bar, where I promptly ordered another two shots.

"You did good, Emmy," Nick said when he reached my side. "But I think that's enough crazy for a while. Feel like gambling?"

"If that means we get to leave here, then absolutely, yes."

He bent down and placed a short, sweet kiss on my forehead. "Let's go."

Hand in hand, we walked out of my first and, hopefully, only male strip show to continue our Vegas adventure.

The desert night air had cooled but it was still warm enough that walking in my little black dress was comfortable. I'd bought this dress special for the trip, hoping it would be sexy enough that I wouldn't look like a librarian compared to Steffie's wardrobe of slinky dresses and midriff-baring halter tops. It had capped sleeves and a plunging neckline that framed what little cleavage I had. Its short and tight fit gave my petite frame the illusion of curves.

Most of the men around us were dressed in full suits. Just the type of men my father would have expected to see me walking with. If he saw me now, strolling along with Nick, his face would give me that look of disapproval I was all too familiar with.

Nick was dressed in a solid black T-shirt that was strung tightly across his broad chest. When he crossed his arms, it cinched around his large biceps, displaying all the contours of his chiseled frame. He wore a pair of faded jeans that sat perfectly on his hips and muscled thighs. Not to mention the wondrous things they did for his ass.

He looked better than any of the suit-clad men we passed.

Wanting to know more about my handsome new acquaintance, I asked, "Where do you live?"

"Colorado."

"Oh." I frowned. Colorado and Connecticut were on opposite sides of the country.

"What are you studying?" he asked.

"Marketing and public relations."

"That's what you want to do?"

Taking a deep breath, I told him something that only

out

Gatsby

It

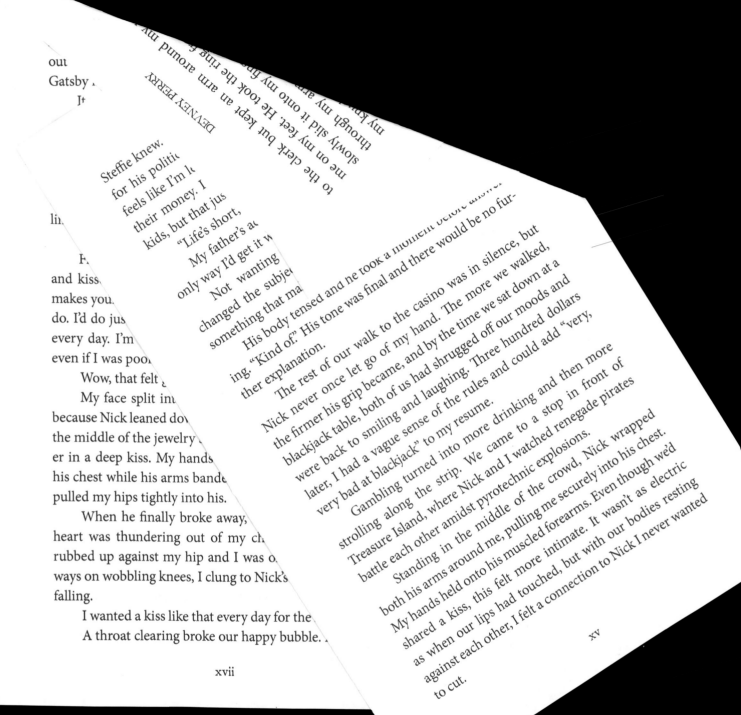

to the clerk but kept an arm around my
me on my feet. He took the ring the
slowly slid it onto my fin
through my arm

Steffie knew.
for his politi
feels like I'm l
their money. I
kids, but that jus
"Life's short,
My father's a
only way I'd get it w
Not wanting
changed the subje
something that ma
His body tensed and he took a moment before answ
ing. "Kind of." His tone was final and there would be no further explanation.
The rest of our walk to the casino was in silence, but

and kiss
makes you
do. I'd do jus
every day. I'm
even if I was poo

Wow, that felt

My face split in
because Nick leaned do
the middle of the jewelry
er in a deep kiss. My hands
his chest while his arms bande
pulled my hips tightly into his.

When he finally broke away,
heart was thundering out of my ch
rubbed up against my hip and I was o
ways on wobbling knees, I clung to Nick's
falling.

I wanted a kiss like that every day for the
A throat clearing broke our happy bubble.

Nick never once let go of my hand. The more we walked,
the firmer his grip became, and by the time we sat down at a
blackjack table, both of us had shrugged off our moods and
were back to smiling and laughing. Three hundred dollars
later, I had a vague sense of the rules and could add "very,
very bad at blackjack" to my resume.

Gambling turned into more drinking and then more
strolling along the strip. We came to a stop in front of
Treasure Island, where Nick and I watched renegade pirates
battle each other amidst pyrotechnic explosions.

Standing in the middle of the crowd, Nick wrapped
both his arms around me, pulling me securely into his chest.
My hands held onto his muscled forearms. Even though we'd
shared a kiss, this felt more intimate. It wasn't as electric
as when our lips had touched, but with our bodies resting
against each other, I felt a connection to Nick I never wanted
to cut.

...waist to steady ...om the clerk's hand and ...ger. Tingles spread from my hand ... when it was positioned perfectly against ...ckle.

I admired the jewels and how perfectly they looked on my finger. How perfectly my hand looked in Nick's.

Gazing up into his vibrant eyes, I knew Nick was the only man for me. I had found the one. Fate, something I hadn't believed in until tonight, had brought us together. We'd only been with each other for hours but I was undeniably in love.

"When are you two getting married?" the clerk asked.

"Tonight," Nick said, not taking his eyes from mine.

"Oh, congratulations! Which chapel did you choose?" she asked.

"We haven't picked one yet."

"Well, if I may offer a recommendation . . ."

One hour later, Nick helped me climb out of a town car in front of The Clover Chapel.

"Wow." My eyes raked over the charming, square building.

The white stucco walls were dotted with intricate, stained glass windows made of blues and greens. A small steeple at the peak of the roof held a brass bell. Vines with small, white flowers climbed over the walls, covering the stucco.

The clerk had not been wrong. It was incredible.

I felt Nick's heat at my side and my fingers naturally found his. I rushed to pull him inside, barely containing my excitement to see the chapel's interior.

The air evaporated from my lungs the instant we

Being with ...
...ectations.
easy grace were c...
ever I wanted. Say ...
relaxed. Happy.
"Let's get married,"
"What?" I gasped, tur...
eyes. Where had that come f...
"Let's get married. You sai...
is crazier than two people who j...
Las Vegas."
"We can't get married!"
His vibrant eyes gleamed as his mo...
crooked grin. "I dare you."

"You don't need to buy me that ring. It's too much m...
I said.
I turned my eyes to the jewelry. Sitting on a velvet cl...

crossed through the pale wooden doors with a tiny four-leafed clover tacked to the top of its frame. The beauty of this chapel was beyond any of my wildest dreams.

Through an arched opening directly in front of us was a short aisle lined with small, wooden pews. At its end was a pergola threaded with greenery, glittering twigs, fairy lights and white magnolia flowers. Hanging white wisteria blooms filled the open ceiling.

We had just walked into a garden wonderland. Someone had reached into my mind and created the setting for my dream wedding.

Magic.

"Hello! Welcome to The Clover Chapel," the receptionist said. "How can I help you?"

"We'd like to get married tonight," Nick said.

"Congratulations! Clover will be so excited." She flipped open a three-ring binder to show us their wedding packages. When we made our choice, she left to find the officiant, Clover herself.

"Are you going to regret this?" Nick asked, pulling me into his arms. His question was sincere. He wouldn't hold this against me if I chose to call a quit to this dare.

But this wasn't a crazy adventure for me anymore. It was real.

We were real.

It didn't matter that I wasn't wearing a designer couture gown and my hair wasn't in an elaborate updo. I had no desire to spend a fortune on my wedding. I hated the pretentious and over-the-top fiascos my engaged friends were all planning. All I wanted was to marry a man who was the only one for me.

Nick was that man.

I didn't know all of the mundane details of his life or his past. I'd learn those in time. For now, I knew what was important. Nick was kind, generous and affectionate. He looked at me like I was the only woman in the world.

"No, I won't regret getting married. Will you?" I hoped with everything I had that his answer was no.

"Abso-fucking-lutely not."

My breath hitched and I fought to swallow past the lump in my throat. Never in my life had that ridiculous saying sounded so wonderful.

"We're ready for you," the receptionist said, popping her head out into the entryway.

Nick held out an elbow and I looped my arm through his before he escorted me down the aisle. Step by step, we strolled together to Clover standing under the arch.

Ten minutes later, we were husband and wife. We had repeated traditional vows, promising to love and cherish one another until death parted us.

With permission to kiss his bride, a smile spread across Nick's face as he hoisted me up into his arms.

"Hi, Wife."

"Hi, Husband."

The light in his eyes was dancing. I imagined that mine looked much the same.

I dropped my lips to his for a kiss that I would never forget. The moment our lips touched, the world around us melted away.

There was only us.

Leaving the chapel, we barely spoke as the receptionist handed us our marriage certificate and wedding photos. The smiles on our faces were so wide they couldn't be broken for words. Never in my life had I been so deliriously happy.

"Do you believe in fate?" I asked Nick as we rode back to the Bellagio.

"Yeah."

"Are we going to make this work?" I whispered.

"Fuck yes we are."

Any lingering anxiety in my stomach vanished. "How?"

"We just are. We belong to each other. Tomorrow, we'll figure it all out. Tonight, let's just be us."

"Okay. Let's just be us," I said, thanking all the angels in the heavens that I was lucky enough to have him as mine.

"Nick?" I called through the sitting room of the hotel suite.

I'd just woken up alone, and after searching the bedroom and bathroom, I'd walked out to the common area, hoping to find him with coffee. The shots from last night had given me a mild headache and I needed caffeine.

He wasn't on either sofa or in the kitchenette. I turned back toward the bedroom for some clothes but stopped when a shiny object on the foyer table caught my eye.

The closer I got to the table, the heavier my steps fell on the polished marble floor. I knew that shiny object. It was the platinum band I had placed on Nick's finger at The Clover Chapel last night.

I reached out and let my fingertips brush the cool metal. Sliding it to the side, I read the one-word note underneath.

Sorry

CHAPTER 1

Nine years later . . .

"**E**MMELINE?"

"Hi! Come on in, Rich," I said, smiling at the school's principal and my boss. Rich Garcia, a short Hispanic man in his forties, walked across the linoleum floor into my classroom.

"I just wanted to check in and see how your first day of parent meetings was going."

"It's been great! I only have three more families left to meet. Everyone has been so welcoming and kind. I'm really looking forward to starting with the kids next week."

"Oh, good." His frame relaxed. "Sometimes these parent-teacher introductions can be difficult. I didn't want anyone to scare you off. We're so glad you've moved to Prescott and joined our staff."

I smiled wide. "There's no scaring me away. This is my dream job. It's been a long journey for me to finally get here and I'm not giving it up."

"Good. Let me know if you need anything. Anything at all," he said before walking out of the room, sidestepping the couple coming in.

"Sheriff Cleary. Gigi. Good to see you both," Rich said. "Rowen starting school this year?"

The sheriff shook Rich's hand. "Yeah. She's excited. Georgia's not. Cries every night thinking about it."

"No judgment, Jess," Gigi said. "I'm allowed to be sad that my baby girl is growing up and starting kindergarten. And I haven't cried every night because of this. I'm hormonal. I cry about everything. Last night I was crying because you ate all the cookies."

"I'm not judging, Freckles," Jess said. "Just stating the facts. And I saw you with your face in the fridge last night, scarfing down that last chocolate chip when you thought I wasn't looking. You cried because *you* ate them all."

She narrowed her eyes at her husband, who stood a good seven inches taller than her.

I bit my lip to keep from laughing as they bantered. Most of the marriages I had witnessed growing up had been awkward and fake. The couples wouldn't dare tease one another in public. But this is what I secretly wished I had for myself. Something natural and light. Something real.

When she finished scowling, Gigi turned to me and extended her hand. "Hi. I'm Gigi Cleary. The sheriff there is my husband, Jess. We're Rowen Cleary's parents."

"Nice to meet you. I'm Emmeline Austin. I'll be your daughter's teacher. I've got a few things to go over with you if you'd like to have a seat?" I said, swinging my hand to the chairs in front of my desk.

Gigi was probably five or six months pregnant. Her

bulging belly was slightly hidden behind a draping tunic but it was starting to take up a good portion of her midsection. And she was stunning. Her long, wavy brown hair was shiny and rich. Freckles dusted her nose and her eyes were a beautiful shade of deep blue.

Her husband, Jess, was not only a large man but also a very good-looking one. He had a strong jaw and broad shoulders. He wore a tan shirt with a shining badge on one hip. His gun was tucked in a holster under his arm.

As he pulled out his wife's chair, his bright, light blue eyes sparkled down at her. Here was a man completely in love with his wife.

"I'm looking forward to meeting Rowen next week," I told them. "Before school starts, I wanted to take the opportunity to meet with you both and find out if you have anything special you'd like me to work on with her this school year."

I'd practiced my introduction speech so many times in the mirror that I'd almost rushed the words. Even though I'd given it to ten other couples so far today, I was still nervous. I desperately wanted to make a good impression on my soon-to-be students' parents.

I took a breath before finishing. "Also, if you have any concerns, we can discuss those too."

Jess and Gigi shared a look. *That couldn't be good.*

"We had some drama earlier in the year," Jess said. "Georgia got kidnapped and it shook up Roe. I think she's over it but every now and again she gets a nightmare. I doubt anything will come up at school, but we thought you should know."

"Oh my god," I gasped. "I'm glad you're okay."

"I'm fine," Gigi said while rubbing her baby bump.

"Rowen's fine too. Jess here is just a little overprotective and Roe knows how to manipulate her dad. He stays home with her the mornings after these quote, unquote *nightmares*."

"She's not faking them, Georgia."

"She totally is, Jess."

"I can watch for signs of distress or anxiety with Rowen. Just in case," I said.

"Thanks," Gigi said. "She's so excited for school, I'm sure she'll be fine. So what about you? You just moved here, right? How are you liking Prescott?" Her smile and easy nature settled my nerves.

"Yes, I did and I like it here very much. I had never been to Montana before and only heard stories about how beautiful it is. I haven't been disappointed. I've only been here for a couple of weeks but am completely lovestruck."

"Rowen and I moved here just a year and a half ago and we fell in love with it too. Where did you move from?" Gigi asked.

I smiled. "New York City."

Her eyes got big. It was the same reaction I'd gotten from all of the parents today.

"I finished getting my teaching degree at NYU last spring and decided I needed a change of pace. After I started looking for jobs, I stumbled across Prescott's ad for a kindergarten teacher and I just went for it. I mean, what's a bigger change of pace than moving from Manhattan to small-town Montana?"

"I thought my move from Spokane was a big one," she said. "Well, I guess, welcome! If you need anything, feel free to call us. The local sheriff is great at moving boxes." She winked and patted Jess's arm.

"Thanks." I added a mental tick to the tally in my head.

In one day, seventeen different people had welcomed me to Prescott and offered their help with whatever I needed.

And with every offer, my doubts about the decision to leave my former life behind were disappearing. At thirty-one years old, I had started over. It was a huge risk but one I was glad to have taken.

I didn't know if I'd stay in Prescott for more than this year, but for right now, it was the perfect place for me.

"Hi, darling," I said into my phone as I drove home in my cherry-red Jeep.

"Hi," Logan said. "How was your first day?"

"So good. I can't stop smiling. The kids were all great. My lesson plan worked perfectly and they all stayed engaged for that math exercise I was worried about. It couldn't have gone better."

"I'm glad, sweetheart," he said, "though I was secretly hoping it would be horrible and you'd come home to me."

I took a long, deep breath. "You know why I had to do this, Logan. It isn't forever."

"I know," he said, "but that doesn't mean I like the fact that my girlfriend lives across the country."

"We talked about this," I reminded him. "You said you understood why I needed to make this change."

Logan had promised that he supported my decision to take a year away from New York. He knew that the city I'd once loved had started to suffocate me, that I'd felt exposed and constantly under a microscope of public scrutiny. Escaping the city had seemed like my only option.

"I just miss you," Logan said. "I hate that you're out there on your own and I'm here. Just promise me after this school year you'll consider coming home?"

"I promise."

"What are you doing tonight?" he asked.

"Reviewing my lesson plan for tomorrow. I want to be prepared in case things don't go as well as they did today. Then I'm going to keep unpacking. What about you?"

"I'm still at the office. I need to put in a few more hours on the civil suit we're filing next week against that pharmaceutical company."

Logan had just gotten a promotion at his law firm, and this lawsuit would be his first as a managing partner. His career was at a pivotal point and I understood why he couldn't step away to head out West to try a simpler lifestyle.

And even though Logan had been supportive of his live-in girlfriend leaving for Montana, I suspected he thought my relocation was just a whim and I'd change my mind soon and come back. But he didn't realize how miserable I had been. How lonely and sad. He worked so much between his job at the law firm and his family's foundation. We rarely had time to spend with one another outside of social functions, sex and sleep.

I was hoping our long-distance relationship would actually bring us closer. That even if it was over the phone, we'd find the time to connect that we hadn't in the city. I wanted to get back to the place we had been at the beginning, desperate to soak up as much time together as we could squeeze in. To spend long nights talking about anything and everything.

"Do you want to call me when you get home?" I asked hopefully.

"It'll be late," he said.

"I'm two hours earlier than you are. I'll be awake. You could tell me good night. We could talk for a while. Catch up."

"Uh, maybe, but don't wait up." Papers shuffled in the background. "I might put in a long night and crash here on the couch."

"I'm worried about you." He sounded stressed and exhausted. "Don't use my leaving as a reason to work yourself into the ground."

"What the fuck else am I supposed to do, Emmeline? You left."

"Logan, don't," I whispered.

"Sorry. I'm going to let you go."

"Okay," I sighed. "I love you."

"Love you too," he said quickly and hung up.

I stared at my phone for a second before tossing it onto the passenger seat. I hoped that call wasn't indicative of others to come.

Logan and I had been together for the last five years. We'd met at a fundraising gala where I had been working for my father and he had attended as a guest, representing the extraordinarily wealthy Kendrick family.

I had been dancing with my father when Logan approached and asked to cut in. My father had gladly handed me over after telling me that I "wasn't to fuck up his setup."

I'd felt so confused at that moment. I hadn't wanted to be with someone because he'd passed my father's criteria as suitable boyfriend material, but I also hadn't been able to walk away from Logan.

His white smile and handsome face had been irresistible. I'd been mesmerized by his deep brown eyes and the sight of his lean muscles wrapped perfectly in an expensive

Italian tux. So I'd spent the rest of the night dancing in his arms, laughing as he'd told me embarrassing stories about some of the gala's guests.

My separation from Logan was the only thing I regretted about moving to Prescott. He was an important part of my life and I didn't want to lose him. I just hoped that after I got some space from New York, I'd have a better idea of which direction my life was headed. Until then, I needed to balance living in Montana and holding onto my relationship.

I'd work to find those small ways to connect with Logan. I'd call and text often, then email him when I could. And for myself, I'd focus on my students. I'd spend my nights in the peace and quiet of my new home, and I'd explore this new-to-me part of America.

I'd search for that elusive happiness I had been missing lately, hoping to find a piece of it here in Montana.

Two months had passed since my first day of school and I was preparing for another meeting with the Clearys. Sitting in my desk chair, I took a minute to look around the classroom, making sure everything was put away for the evening. Books and counting blocks would be strewn all over the alphabet carpet as soon as the kids arrived in the morning, but for now the room was neat and tidy.

A knock at the door stopped my inspection and I stood as the Clearys walked in.

"Hi, Gigi, Jess," I said, smiling as they took a seat. "Thanks for coming in this afternoon."

"No problem, Emmeline. Is something wrong with

Rowen?" Gigi asked, nervously patting her protruding belly. Jess reached out and grabbed his wife's hands.

She looked so much bigger than the last time I had seen her. She was either closing in on her due date or her baby was going to be huge.

"It's nothing serious," I told them. "Rowen is a wonderful and bright little girl. She's full of energy and is so positive. But I did want to make you aware of a situation."

Jess nodded as Georgia's face paled.

"This really is nothing serious. Please don't be worried. She's been such a joy to have in my classroom these last two months. I just wanted you to be aware that I've had to reprimand Rowen a few times these last couple of weeks."

"Oh, no," Gigi muttered.

"I've had to get after her recently for using inappropriate language in school. I understand that children these days are exposed to cursing at home and from media outlets. I'm not trying to change what you say at home, but as it is kindergarten, I don't want to let hints of bad language into the classroom."

"I knew it!" Gigi cried before I could continue. She twisted to glare at Jess. "I knew this would happen, Jess! I've been telling you over and over again to watch the effing language in front of her. But you just keep on cussing. Saying you two have an understanding and if she repeats those words you'll have to arrest her. Now look at where we are! If she's not cussing, then she's not even scared of jail anymore! What's next? Drinking? Drugs? Look what you've done!"

"Georgia, relax and breathe," he said. "You're working yourself up and we don't need you going into labor."

I waved my hands to get their attention. "Actually, if I could interrupt . . ."

"Sorry," Jess said as Gigi huffed and crossed her arms on top of her belly.

"No, I'm so sorry. I should have been more specific. Rowen is not cursing. She's just using replacement words. And though they aren't actually bad, I don't want the kids getting in the habit of adding curses or placeholders to their sentences. We're working on expanding their vocabulary and crafting complete phrases. Rowen adds one word in particular quite frequently. She says 'eff' a lot."

Gigi's jaw fell open.

Jess's head tipped back and he roared with laughter.

The longer he laughed, the harder I fought the urge to laugh along with him. The guilty look on Gigi's face was hilarious.

"You feel like telling me you're sorry?" Jess asked Gigi with a smug grin after his laughter subsided.

"No," she mumbled.

"We'll have a talk with Roe," Jess told me with a huge smile. He stood, then reached down to help Gigi from her chair.

"I'm so sorry, Emmeline," Gigi said embarrassed. "This is my fault. I'll be sure to tell Roe not to say it anymore."

"I'd appreciate that. Again, it isn't a huge deal but I wanted you to be aware that I've asked her to at least stop saying it in school."

"Of course. I'm sure that she'll stop just because you asked her. She adores you and has learned so much already. You're a wonderful teacher."

"Thank you." I didn't try and hide my smile.

My heart swelled at her compliment. I so badly wanted to be a good teacher. Her praise made all of the recent changes in my life worth the stress and anxiety. It reinforced that

I'd done the right thing by choosing to pursue my dreams despite all of the protests from my family and friends.

And I loved hearing that Roe adored me because I cherished her too. Rowen Cleary was a bright, beaming light.

"Do you have any plans on Friday night?" Gigi asked before they reached the door. "We're having a Halloween party at our farmhouse. I kind of go crazy on Halloween."

"Kind of?" Jess muttered.

Gigi elbowed him in the ribs but smiled. "We'd love to have you over if you don't have any plans. It's nothing fancy. No costumes or anything. Just a bunch of us getting together after trick-or-treating on Main Street. Seven o'clock?"

My weeknights since moving to Prescott had consisted of reheating a frozen meal, unpacking a few boxes, infrequent phone calls with Logan when he could spare me the time and reading alone in bed until I fell asleep. Weekends had been spent doing much of the same, though I had been spending my Saturday afternoons exploring the downtown area.

For the first three weeks, I had thought that the quiet, restful evenings and weekends were amazing. But now that it had been over two months, I was getting lonely.

I'd had a hectic social calendar in New York. There had always been something to attend at least four or five nights a week. The weekends had usually been full of charity dinners and galas. I didn't miss the hectic and crazy schedule, or the uncomfortable ball gowns, but I did miss being around people. Spending my days with five- and six-year-old kids wasn't satisfying my craving for social interaction.

So it was easy to answer Gigi's question.

"I'll be there."

A night away from my house in the presence of other adults sounded like magic.

Nick

"What's up, man?" Silas asked, handing me a bottle of beer in the farmhouse kitchen.

"Nothing much. Looking forward to getting Gigi all riled up about something tonight and watching Brick squirm trying to calm her down. He's fucking freaked she's going to go into labor early."

My normally hard and stubborn friend, nicknamed for his size and solid mass, was falling completely apart over his very pregnant wife.

"Jess will kick your ass if you piss her off," Silas warned.

"Worth it."

I loved teasing my friend about the overprotective streak he had when it came to his wife, daughter and un-born son.

But joking aside, I was glad for Jess. He deserved all the joy that Gigi and Rowen had brought into his life. It had been nearly a decade since I'd met Jess and never once had I seen him as happy as he'd been since meeting Gigi.

That happiness was something I envied but had no de-sire to try and create for myself. The dream of having a fam-ily of my own had died a long time ago.

Silas nudged my shoulder. "Jess said they got called into the school today by Rowen's teacher. Guess Roe has been saying 'eff' just like Gigi does. Teacher said she didn't want the kids pretending to cuss."

I burst out laughing. "That's my angle then. Where's Gigi?"

Silas tipped his chin and lifted his beer in the air. "She's upstairs with Rowen and the teacher. Have you seen her yet?"

"Who? The teacher?" I asked as Silas nodded. "No. Why?"

"I know you don't go for redheads but she's fucking hot," Silas said. "I'd make an exception to your rule. Has all this auburn hair. Beaming smile. Petite, little body."

"No can do. No redheads for me. If she's so hot, you go for her."

Silas scoffed and shook his head. My friend had some issues when it came to women, or one woman in particular, so I wasn't surprised that he preferred to stay out of the dating pool.

After taking a long pull of my beer, I wandered into the living room. The entire place was covered in decorations, inside and out. Gigi lost her mind on Halloween but at least some of them were funny. When I'd arrived earlier, I had laughed at the tombstones in the front lawn. One said "Hugh Jass – A Well Rounded Man" and another read "Bea Yotch – A Nice Lady".

Stepping into Jess's huddle, I clapped him on the shoulder then shook his hand. "Where's your wife, Brick? I need to talk to her about her language."

"Fuck you, Slater. Mention that to her and I'm kicking your ass."

"Fine," I said, holding my hands up in surrender. "I'll leave it alone. Where's Roe? I need to give my princess a kiss." If I wasn't razzing Jess about riling up Gigi's temper, I was teasing him about Roe, who had a little-girl crush on me.

When Jess's jaw clenched tightly, I laughed and turned

to the stairs, hearing Gigi and Rowen coming down.

"Nick!" Rowen yelled and dashed over.

Bending at the waist, I looked into her blue eyes. "Hey, princess. Love the costume. Who are you this year?"

Twirling around in a blue dress, she said, "Princess Elsa from *Frozen*."

"Hey, Nick," Gigi said.

I stood to give her a hug but froze solid. The second I recognized the woman next to Gigi, that beautiful face, my heart stopped beating. Was she really here?

When her eyes hit mine, she inhaled sharply, her face paling as she clutched a hand to her heart.

Silas had described a lot of Emmy's good features in the kitchen. Her hair. Her figure. He hadn't mentioned her flawless, porcelain skin or her full, pink lips. Most importantly, he'd neglected to mention her eyes. Her best feature.

Gray with a hint of green in the centers. The circles rimming the irises were so dark they were almost black. I'd memorized the colors when she had been locked in my arms and I'd been buried deep inside her. Just hours after she had become my wife.

"Nick, this is my teacher, Ms. Austin," Rowen said, tugging on my arm.

It took a few seconds of staring to process that she was standing right here in front of me. She wasn't an illusion I'd dreamed up like so many times before.

Emmy hadn't changed much. She'd only become more beautiful with time. Her hair was slightly longer and her face a bit thinner. Years of fantasies, and none had ever come close to the beauty before me.

Not once had I given into the temptation to Google her or find her number. I had stayed true to my vow to set her free. That and I knew I'd risk my own sanity by checking in on her. Learning that she'd found that life I had wished for her, one with a husband and kids, would have blown my already broken heart to smithereens.

"Nick?" Gigi asked, but I didn't speak or take my eyes off Emmy. She was frozen just like I was.

Finally, Emmy broke away. "Sorry. I have to go," she mumbled before racing to the door.

"What was that? Do you know her?" Jess asked.

None of my friends had ever learned about Emmy and what I'd done to her. Marrying her had been something I'd always kept a secret. Partly because I'd wanted those memories as my own. Partly because I was a fucking asshole and had abandoned her, even if it had been for her safety.

Yeah. I knew her.

"She's my wife," I said and then sprinted out the door, ignoring the shocked faces and surprised gasps coming from my friends.

CHAPTER 2

"E MMY, WAIT!" NICK SHOUTED, BUT I didn't stop jogging toward my Jeep.

Just as I reached for the door handle, his hand grabbed my elbow and spun me around.

"Don't," I said, jerking my arm free. The night was pitch black except for the lights coming from the house and garage. But even the dark couldn't dim the light shining from his eyes.

"Sorry," he said, holding up his hands. "What are you doing here, Emmy?"

"Emmeline," I corrected. He was the only person who had ever called me anything but my full name, and as much as I had loved it all those years ago, hearing it now was painful.

He frowned. "Emmy. What are you doing here?"

"I live here. What are *you* doing here?"

"*I* live here. Have for years."

I swallowed an exasperated laugh. What were the chances? Of all the small towns in America, I had moved to the same one where my long-lost husband lived. A husband my private investigator had spent nine years unsuccessfully searching for.

Years had gone by and all I'd ever gotten were reports stating Nick's whereabouts were unknown. A paid professional couldn't find him but, here I was, standing in his space because I happened to pick Prescott as my home.

Shit.

Nick stared down at me, unspeaking. I was so shocked to see his face I didn't know where to start or what to say. Apparently, he was having the same problem. Twice he opened his mouth to say something but then clamped it shut before words came out.

"Emmy—" he finally started but my ringing phone cut him off.

Scrambling to find it in my bag, I pressed the phone to my ear. "Hi, darling," I told Logan. "Can you hold on one second?" I pinched the phone between my ear and shoulder, opening the car door to climb inside.

"We need to talk," Nick said, reaching out his hand.

I flinched right before his fingers could touch me. I glared and shook my head furiously. He frowned but didn't push.

My conversation with Nick was over for the night. I needed to regroup and get my head together before we had a discussion. I didn't want to hear anything he had to say.

Not tonight.

"Emmeline," Logan called after I slammed the car door.

"Sorry. I'm here," I said, backing out of the gravel lot, seeing Nick sidestep my car.

"Where are you?" Logan asked.

"I was at a Halloween party."

"Did you have a good time?" A hint of disdain colored his voice. He was probably mad at the idea of me going to parties and making friends here in Prescott. Friends meant I was building a life here. Something he did not want.

My gaze traveled to Nick in my rearview mirror. He stood in the middle of the drive, legs planted wide with his arms crossed over his chest.

"No. I didn't have a good time."

I stood by my dark bedroom window, staring out into the black night.

The Montana nights were remarkably different from those in New York. Though, the same was true about almost every aspect of my life here in Prescott.

In the city, it was never really dark. Somewhere a light from a building or street lamp illuminated the shadows. But here there were no lights. Nothing interrupted the blackness.

Some people may have found it a bit frightening, but I loved that I could see up into the starry sky. I'd never known there were so many stars. My first night in Prescott, I'd stood outside for an hour, gazing up into the Milky Way.

But tonight, all the stars in the universe couldn't light the blackness.

Nothing could have prepared me for seeing Nick tonight. The emotion was crippling.

I vaguely recalled my short conversation with Logan as I had sped home from the farmhouse. I had given him a quick account of the Clearys' party but hadn't mentioned Nick. I wasn't ready to discuss the subject with Logan yet. First, I needed to get my own head wrapped around the concept.

Logan knew I had been married but he didn't know any of the details. He also didn't know that I was still legally bound to another man. That fact was not going to go over well.

What was I going to do?

Swiping my phone from an end table, I pulled up my friend's number.

"Hey!" Steffie answered. "Meet any hot cowboys yet?"

I laughed. She knew I was in a committed relationship with Logan but that didn't stop her from wanting me to find a mountain man to climb. Steffie was quite open with her sexuality. In college, her antics had been amusing and . . . enlightening. When she'd started dating my father, I had told her in no uncertain terms to never bring up her sex life to me again.

"No cowboys, though I did run into my husband." I held the phone away from my ear, waiting for the shriek I knew was coming.

"What!" she shouted. "You're fucking kidding me!"

"Not kidding." For the next ten minutes, I filled her in on the details from the party and how I had reacted to seeing Nick.

"What are you going to do?" she asked.

I sighed. "I don't know. I have to tell Logan all the details even though he's going to be so angry. But keeping it from him feels like a betrayal." I had only given Logan a vague account of my marriage, blaming my decision on youth and alcohol. No one but Steffie ever knew the truth about that night and why I'd married Nick: that I'd fallen in love with him in only five hours.

"Yeah, Logan's going to flip. So is Trent."

I winced at the mention of my father. "I know this isn't fair of me to ask, but please don't tell him. Not yet. I'm not ready to deal with him."

"I get it. Consider my lips sealed."

I didn't have a loving father-daughter relationship, but even with my father being her boyfriend, she never wasted effort pushing for us to get closer.

Trent Austin had never had any interest in his daughter. I wished I could pinpoint when it had started, identify that trigger and fill in the missing pieces, but as far back as I could remember, he just . . . didn't like me. He tolerated my brother, Ethan, and at times made some effort in his son's case. But I had never been much more than just another person living in his house.

After I was born, his marriage to my mother had started to deteriorate. Maybe he blamed me, instead of himself, for chasing her into the arms of another man. Regardless of the reason, my father and I had never been close.

And I had never been quite good enough.

It was only a couple of years ago that I'd finally stopped trying to meet his unreachable standards.

It was acceptable for him to parade around with younger women and for my brother to get divorce after divorce, but being embarrassed by his daughter was deplorable. My marriage was an embarrassment of unfathomable proportions.

On the flight home from Las Vegas, I had debated not telling my father about my marriage. Had I not needed to discuss my divorce options with his attorney, I would have kept Nick a secret. As it was, an Austin marriage without a prenuptial agreement put our family at financial risk and I'd been forced to have an extremely unpleasant conversation with my parents.

I had disparaged our family's reputation by acting like a stupid whore, those having been his exact words.

At the time, he had been screwing his twenty-two-year-old secretary.

"So? What are you going to do about Nick?" Steffie asked, pulling me from my thoughts.

"I don't know. Go back in time and not be so stupid?"

Not fall in love.

Was it love? Nine years was a long time to dissect every bit of one night, but in all that time, I still couldn't come up with the right answer. Deep down, a part of me still believed that my connection to Nick had been real and he must have had good reason to leave.

"It's been a long time. Talk to him. Go from there," Steffie said.

"You're right. I'll take a few days to pull myself together and then approach. Thanks. And thank you for not mentioning this to Father."

"Chicks before dicks."

I rolled my eyes before laughing.

"What are you going to tell Logan?" she asked.

"The truth," I said. "He deserves the full story. But before I do anything, I need a plan and I need to talk to my attorney about a divorce."

"Good idea. Logan will take it much better if he knows you've just been waiting to find Nick so you could settle the divorce."

I hoped she was right and that after Logan learned I was still legally tied to Nick, he wouldn't be too mad. That maybe he'd understand why I had refused his two proposals.

I hadn't denied him because I didn't love him. I just wasn't free yet. A part of my heart still belonged to Nick and I couldn't marry Logan until I had taken it back.

"Thanks for listening," I said.

"That's what I'm here for. And to give your dad—"

"Stop. Immediately," I interrupted.

"You're no fun anymore." She laughed. "Keep me posted."

"I will. Bye."

I stared into the black night, processing everything that had happened tonight. Thinking about everything that had happened back then.

Tossing my phone on my bed, I walked to my dresser and pulled out the small box I had kept hidden behind my underwear for years, its sole purpose to hold two rings, a tattered photo and a CD.

I went for the ring first, slipping it on my index finger and twirling it around like I had so many times. Never once had I put it back on the intended finger.

Next I went to the photo.

There was no light in my bedroom but it didn't matter. I could see the picture as if it were day.

Nick and I were in profile under the chapel's pergola. The officiant had just stepped away to give us a private minute. It was the moment Nick had hoisted me up with his big arms wrapped around my lower back and hips. My heeled feet had dangled in the air and my fingers had been threaded through the hair at the back of his neck. Our foreheads rested together and we both had huge smiles spread across our faces.

Then, love had been written on my face.

Now, it was wrecked with tears and anguish.

Five minutes spent in Nick's presence had cracked open the gashes in my heart that I'd spent years stitching together.

If Nick's life was in Prescott, I couldn't stay here. But I wasn't leaving until I had some answers to the questions swirling in my head. Questions I'd asked myself over and over again. Somehow, I would find the strength to ask Nick why.

Why had he left me that morning? Had our night together meant so little to him that he could leave me behind, never bothering to look back? Why hadn't he found me for a divorce or an annulment?

My nose started to sting as tears pricked the backs of my eyes. Nick was responsible for rivers of my tears. Tears over the crushing disappointment that I'd been so wrong about him. Tears because everything he'd told me that night had been a lie.

I inhaled a ragged breath, trying to swallow the lump in my throat.

"I wish I didn't feel like this," I told his picture. "I wish that you looked different. Not like the man I've been imagining for years. I wish you weren't real and that it wouldn't hurt so much."

Mostly, I wished that I could just let him go.

"Emmeline, I'm sorry but there isn't much else we can do."

"I just don't understand. Why can't we get the divorce papers drafted this week?" I asked Fred Andrews, my family's attorney. I had called him first thing on Monday morning before heading into work.

"Like I've told you, we're in a precarious position here. My advice is to proceed with caution, and that will take some time. At a minimum, a month. I know you'd like to have this done as quickly as possible but rushing a divorce at this point may position you and your family for an unjust financial claim."

"How can that be? I haven't seen Nick in nine years."

"Correct, but during your marriage your trust fund limitation expired and all of the money from your grandparents was fully released. He could claim a portion of those funds with no prenuptial agreement in place before your union."

"That is ridiculous, Fred," I scoffed. "We were together for less than twenty-four hours."

"True. And if this does get taken to court, I doubt any judge would rule in his favor. But I need time to draft the appropriate papers. I could have processed an annulment within a week. A divorce settlement that ensures your assets are protected will be much more involved."

"Okay," I said. "Is there anything I should be doing while you work on the papers?"

"There's nothing else for you to do. You might get some unwanted publicity, even with you no longer living in the city, but I doubt it. I'll notify you and your father before the settlement is filed, as this work will go against his retainer fees."

"No. Please bill me directly. Thank you, Fred," I told him before we said our good-byes and ended the call.

I let my head fall into my hands as I sagged in my desk chair. "Stubborn and stupid," I muttered to the empty classroom.

Years ago, Fred had told me that he could have my marriage to Nick dissolved on the grounds of abandonment.

Had I listened?

No.

Because I had been stubborn and stupid.

I had been too angry and upset to let Nick off the hook so easily. I had insisted that my private investigator would track Nick down in no time and I'd get the chance to look him in the eyes and watch as he explained why he'd lied and left.

Desperate for closure, I'd refused to get divorced until I got my explanation.

I'd had no idea that Nick Slater would be a ghost, impossible to find. That my stubborn streak would run so deep that, years later, I would still not have gone through with the divorce.

Now, looking back, I should have swallowed my pride and forgotten the idea of a standoff with Nick.

I should have gotten my divorce.

"Okay, class. That's the lunch bell. You can all get your coats for recess and *walk* to the cafeteria."

Shouts of glee filled the classroom as fourteen five-year-old kids rushed into the hallway.

We had just finished the story circle and I was shelving books, thinking about how much I was going to miss the kids and my classroom when I left Prescott.

I had no idea where I would move but with Nick living here, I couldn't stay.

The idea of disappointing my colleagues and abandoning my students gave me a sharp stomachache but the thought of running into Nick on a regular basis, or seeing him with another woman, felt even worse.

Was he with someone now? Did he have kids? Just the thought sent my heart into my stomach. I needed to get away from here before he ripped me to shreds. Maybe I could make it through to summer and finish up the school year. If I lived as a hermit, sticking close to the school and home, I could probably avoid seeing Nick.

Lost in thought, I jumped when a rumbling voice sounded in the room.

"Emmy?"

Avoiding Nick was going to get really hard if he barged into my classroom.

I drew in a labored breath before spinning around, my eyes raking him from head to toe. He was as gorgeous as ever. Not much had changed about him over the years. His beard was a bit shorter and he had more muscle on his frame.

"Emmeline," I corrected. "What are you doing here, Nick?"

"I told you Friday. We need to talk."

"I'm not ready to talk yet."

"Nine years wasn't enough time to think of something to say?"

I winced at his joke. "Is that supposed to be funny? Because it's not."

"Sorry," he muttered. He looked me up and down. "Fuck, Emmy. Is that what you wear every day?"

I dropped my chin to inspect my clothing. What was wrong with this outfit?

I wore wide-leg black pants with patent nude pumps and a cream blouse with a mandarin collar. Because the blouse was sheer, underneath was a lace-trimmed camisole. At my wrist was the rose-gold, oversized Chanel watch my mother had given me for Christmas the previous year.

I wore this type of clothing almost every day. It was classy and professional, exactly the image I wanted to portray as a teacher. Nothing about my clothing was inappropriate for a kindergarten setting, though it may have been a bit dressy for rural Montana.

"What's wrong with my outfit?"

"Nothing. You just look beautiful," he said.

I closed my eyes and took a deep breath. "Please don't say things like that to me."

"I can't give you a compliment?"

"No. Not anymore."

"Emmy," he said softly. "We need to talk about us."

"Emmeline. And there is no us. Even if there were, we are not talking here," I said and sat behind my desk.

I did everything I could to avert my eyes. It was too hard to look at him. First, I busied myself by organizing pens. Then I restacked the papers on top of my desk. Lastly, I grabbed my coffee mug and gave it a thorough inspection.

I was obsessed with clever mugs and over the years I had collected many. Today's was a simple white mug that said "Oh for fox's sake," but instead of the word "fox" there was a cartoon fox wearing reading glasses.

"Emmy," Nick said. "Will you fucking look at me?"

"No," I told my mug.

Two hands slapped down on top of my desk. "We're talking. Now."

"No," I snapped and shot out of my chair. "We are going

27

to talk when I'm ready. This time around we're going to do things my way. On my timeline. And right now, I need to get some lunch so I can be ready when my kids get back to class. I will not get into this with you. I need to speak to my attorney about our interactions, and depending on his advice, I will *consider* talking to you at a later date."

"Your attorney?" he asked. "Why do you need to talk to your fucking attorney before having a conversation with me?"

"Stop cursing. You're in a school full of impressionable children."

"Answer the *fucking* question."

I crossed both arms over my chest. "My attorney is getting the ball rolling on our divorce proceedings. I need to find out if he thinks we should limit our interactions to those supervised by legal counsel." I had forgotten to ask Fred that this morning, mostly because I wasn't sure which answer I wanted him to give me.

Nick leaned away from the desk and blinked a couple of times. "Divorce?"

How was this a surprise to him? What did he think would happen? "Yes. Absolutely. Now that I've located you, we can officially end our marriage. And when this disaster is finally over, there will be no reason for you to think we need to talk or ever see one another again."

"No. No divorce. Abso-fucking-lutely not." All of the shock on his face was instantly replaced with anger.

This time it was my turn to be shocked. "I hate that saying! And what do you mean 'no'? I haven't laid eyes on you in over nine years. You left me the night of our wedding after you spent hours lying through your teeth. I've been together with another man for five years. On what planet do you actually think our relationship resembles a marriage worth keeping? So yes. We are getting divorced. As soon as my attorney has a chance to draft the papers."

"I never lied to you, Emmy," he said gently.

"I asked you if we were going to make it work and you said we were. That was a lie. I deserve an explanation from you and you're going to give it to me. But not right now. When I'm ready to talk, you'll be the first to know. Then after I've gotten my answers, I'll finally be free of you. Now, you can leave."

"Dinner."

"Excuse me?"

"Dinner. You want answers, you can have them over dinner. Tonight."

"I am not eating with you," I said through gritted teeth. "My timeline. Remember?"

"And I don't give a fuck about your timeline. We're eating tonight. You want answers. You'll get them. And I won't be waiting for legal counsel."

"Fine," I clipped.

"I'll pick you up here at five," he said, turning to walk out of the room.

"No," I said to his back. "I'll drive myself. Where shall I meet you?"

He grumbled something under his breath before answering. "The Black Bull Steakhouse."

"Fine. I'll be there at six."

He didn't say anything else as he strode through the door.

I scoffed. *At least this time, I got to watch him leave.*

And tonight, I would finally get my answers.

CHAPTER 3

THE BLACK BULL STEAKHOUSE WAS LOCATED about five miles outside of Prescott. The exterior of the building was covered in distressed barnwood with dark amber glass windows. The restaurant's sign was made of branded wood with longhorns mounted on top.

Exactly what I would have expected for a Montana steakhouse.

As I inspected the building, an idea popped into my head for my restaurant in Manhattan. I quickly made a few notes on a scratch pad before grabbing my phone to run the idea by Logan.

But my fingers paused before I could bring up his number.

My attorney had warned that there could be some publicity surrounding my divorce, though I doubted people would care now that I wasn't living in New York. But the last thing I wanted was for Logan to learn of my marriage from the gossip rags.

The restaurant conversation would have to wait. I couldn't delay telling him about Nick any longer.

Steeling my spine, I pressed his name and waited for his answer. "Logan?" All I could hear were people laughing and talking in the background. "Logan!"

"Hi," he finally answered. "One second, sweetheart."

I listened to him maneuver through what sounded like a large crowd. What was he was doing at a party on a Monday night? I had talked to him yesterday and he hadn't mentioned any social plans.

"Sorry," he said after finding a spot away from the noise.

"It's okay. Where are you?"

"A cocktail party in Midtown benefitting the Kohlberg Foundation. I ran into your friend Alice today at lunch. She's working for them and invited me to come along with her."

"Alice Leys?" I asked.

Alice and I hadn't stayed close after graduating from Yale. Though we had both moved to New York, we'd been busy trying to jump-start our careers and had lost touch. Our paths had crossed occasionally when I'd been at Austin Capital, but I hadn't seen her since I'd quit.

I was actually surprised that Logan remembered her. They'd only met a couple of times and I recalled being a bit put off with how forward Alice had been toward him. At the time, I had thought it was only to gain access to the millions of dollars the Kendricks donated each year. But now I was wondering if her interest was more personal.

"Yes, that Alice," he said. "She's been inviting me for years to her events. We always had conflicts in our schedules. But now that you're in Montana, I was available."

"Well. Isn't that convenient for her," I muttered.

"Jealous?" he asked.

"Yes," I admitted.

"Good. That means you haven't forgotten about me."

I smiled as he teased. "Will you be out late? I need to talk to you about something important."

"Probably. They've brought in a speaker from the foundation to try and separate us all from our money. I doubt I'll make it home before midnight."

"Okay. Call me later? Tomorrow?" I asked as the background noise picked up.

"Sure. Talk then," he said and disconnected.

I had really wanted to tell Logan about my marriage before my dinner with Nick. No such luck.

Five minutes later, I was sitting across from my future ex-husband.

And I was doing everything I could think of to distract myself from his handsome face until I could get my nerves to settle.

"What are you doing?" Nick asked.

"Well, this contraption is what they call a smart phone," I said. "You aim this little circle thing around and then push this other little circle thing here and it takes this newfangled thing called a picture."

"Funny. Why?"

"I'm going to email these and some of the exterior to my restaurant team. This would be a great theme for a New York City steakhouse." I hoped that the photos would turn out in the dark setting.

This was going to be the next theme for my Manhattan restaurant. I could already see my pretentious friends dressing up in their imposter cowboy boots and designer pearl-snapped Western shirts to eat a hundred-dollar steak.

The interior was a dimly lit space with walls paneled in the same barnwood as the exterior. Chandeliers made of animal antlers hung from the wood-beamed ceiling and gave off a soft, yellow glow.

We were seated at a booth upholstered in a deep maroon vinyl and the table was covered with charred cattle brands. I was glad for the high-backed booth seat, which would provide us privacy from eavesdropping neighbors.

"Is that how you make your money? Through restaurants?" Nick asked.

"No. I make my money from teaching." My attorney's warning was still fresh and I didn't want to talk about money should our divorce get nasty.

"Right," he said, not believing me.

We sat for a few moments in silence until our waitress arrived to deliver my red wine and Nick's Coors Light. I was grateful to have the glass to hold and occupy my twitching fingers.

"That guy who called you on Friday. Who is he?"

"My boyfriend, Logan."

"Are you two serious?" he asked.

"Yes. We lived together in New York."

"If you're serious, why'd you leave him?" he asked.

"It's a long story, but it basically boils down to me needing to get out of the city. Logan just made partner at his law firm and he couldn't jeopardize his career to follow me to the Wild West."

"Hmm," he muttered.

We sat in uncomfortable silence for a few minutes. I dutifully sipped my wine and studied the designs on the tabletop, avoiding eye contact with Nick.

"Did you talk to your lawyer again?" he asked.

"No, but I'll touch base with him as he drafts our divorce papers. Once they're complete, he can work directly with your attorney if you'd like. I'll just need his or her name and phone number."

That got me another "hmm" before he drained the rest of his beer. He must have been a regular at The Black Bull because the waitress didn't bother asking if he wanted another, she just brought it over.

"Why'd you wait?" Nick asked.

"Wait for what?"

"To get a divorce," he said.

I pulled in a deep breath. Admitting to Nick why I had held onto our marriage for this long was not going to be easy. "I didn't want to dissolve the marriage on terms of abandonment. My foolish pride wouldn't let me. So I hired a private investigator to track you down. Did you know there are 723 Nick Slaters living in Colorado and not one of them is you?"

He didn't respond. He just tipped his head down to study his fresh beer.

"And I wanted to know why," I said. "Why you put on such a convincing show. All those dares and sweet words. I've never met a man who could let lies roll off his tongue so easily. And that's saying something, considering my father and all of his associates are world-class deceivers."

He flinched and his eyes snapped to mine. "I told you earlier today, Emmy. I didn't lie to you."

I took a deep breath. *Stay strong.* This hurt act of his was just that. An act. I was the wronged party here and the last thing I needed was to fall for more of Nick's lies. To lose my nerve.

"Then why have I spent tens of thousands of dollars

on a private investigator to find you? You were not living in Colorado."

"When we met, I was," he said. "Shortly after, I wasn't. I moved here a few months after Vegas."

More lies. The blood started to boil in my veins. "I started looking for you immediately, Nick. You. Weren't. There."

"Calm down," he said.

"Calm down?" I hissed. "Explain why they couldn't find you. Now."

Though I was seething, Nick kept his composure. In fact, the madder I got, the more his face gentled.

"My first name isn't Nick. It's Draven. My father is Draven Sr., and I've gone by my middle name, Nicholas, my whole life. I'm sure your investigators didn't look for a Draven Slater living in Colorado. If they had, they would have found me."

"Then we're not even married. If you didn't put your legal name on our marriage certificate, all that time spent looking for you was for nothing."

"I did put my legal name on the certificate. You just weren't paying attention. You were too busy looking all over the chapel."

Shit.

My private investigator had swindled me. There was no way he wouldn't have been able to find a copy of our marriage license.

Nick had left his ring, maybe so I could sell it, but he'd taken the certificate with him when he'd abandoned me in the hotel. But even without the paper, my investigator should have found him. Draven was too unique a name. A little effort and he would have earned all that money we'd paid him. Instead, he'd been content to sit back and lie to me. Tomorrow I was stopping payment on his last check, not that it would make me feel any better.

My gullibility made this entire situation even more embarrassing.

Because I couldn't blame the investigator entirely. I'd had the choice to hire someone else. Instead, I'd just chosen to push the whole thing deep down and try to forget it. Another mistake.

When the waitress delivered our steaks, I took the welcome interruption as a chance to calm down. I needed a few minutes to pull myself together and to muster the courage to ask him the question I was dreading.

Why had he left me?

We ate our meals in silence. While Nick cleared his plate, I picked at my food. It was delicious but I'd lost my appetite. With every minute that went by, I told myself to ask but the words wouldn't come together. Why couldn't I get them out?

After the waitress removed our dinner plates, Nick reached across the table and captured my hand with his. I tried to jerk it away but as I tensed, his grip firmed and my hand remained trapped.

"I want a chance," Nick said.

"A chance for what?" I asked.

"A chance to start again."

My mouth fell open. Was he serious? "What? Why?"

"You asked me back then if I believed in fate. I didn't until I met you. And I've spent nine years thinking I'd never see your face again. But fate brought you back into my life and I'm not going to mess it up again."

I struggled to swallow the lump in my throat and speak. "You left me."

"Please believe I did it for a good reason. And not a day has gone by when I haven't regretted it." He stroked the side of my trapped hand with his thumb.

"Why?" My eyes filled with tears the second the word passed my lips.

"I promise I'll explain. Just not tonight," he said.

My heart sank and I sagged into the heavily padded bench seat. This was his test and he had failed miserably. I didn't want a deflection, a promise to explain later. He could disappear tomorrow for another nine years for all I knew.

"No," I said. "No chances. You could have found me. You could have explained. You've lost your chance."

His jaw clenched and the muscle on his forehead twitched. If he actually thought a couple of sweet sentences—which lacked an apology, I might add—would have me falling all over him again, he was sorely mistaken.

"I stayed away from you because I figured you would have moved on. But you're not happy. I can see it plain as day. Give me a chance?"

I looked to the table. "No. I want a divorce."

"You won't get one."

"What?" I gasped, my eyes snapping up to his.

"No divorce. I'll contest it."

"Do you really think challenging me and my legal team is a good idea, Nick? You'll be wasting both our time and money."

"I don't care. I'll do whatever it takes."

"Is this about my money? Is that what you want? Then fine. Name your price. Just let me go."

"It's not about your fucking money. It never was. But I'm not letting you go until I get my chance."

"I'm in love with another man. Your chances are over."

His body flinched so violently that it almost caused me physical pain. "A month. I want a month. And then I'll let you go."

I sat for a minute, weighing my options. I could dig in my heels and tell him to go to hell. Or I could let him think he had a chance. The only way I was getting my answers was with the latter. And I needed those answers desperately.

I needed to move on with my life.

"A month is too long and I'm not dragging this out. I'll give you a week."

"Fine. But I want five dates. You're not going to blow me off for a week and then say I had my chance."

"Okay," I grumbled. "Five dates. One week."

"Good. We start tomorrow."

After exchanging phone numbers, I collected my purse and slid out of the booth, making our way to the restaurant's exit.

But just before Nick could push the door open for me, a blond, skinny woman came rushing over and started fawning over him.

"Oh, Nick!" she said, grabbing his arm and petting his bicep. She leaned so far into his space that her surgically enhanced breasts rubbed up against his side. "I've been wondering when I'd see you again. Small world that we'd both be here for dinner."

"Good-bye, Andrea," Nick said, yanking his arm free.

"Don't leave! Not yet! I came here with a friend but I was hoping you could give me a ride home," she begged.

With Nick distracted by this Andrea woman, I slipped out the door. The last thing I wanted was to witness my soon-to-be ex-husband being hit on.

Practically sprinting to my Jeep, I shut the door and

sagged against the steering wheel.

Five dates.

I just had to get through five more encounters with Nick and then I could put this all behind me. And tomorrow, I could talk to Logan.

Driving home, I tried to concentrate on the beautiful scenery around me but my mind kept drifting back to dinner. Had Nick been sincere? Or was this just another one of his games?

I had left dinner with more questions than answers. I was *sick to death* of the unanswered questions.

And I was sick to death of how much Nick had consumed me these last few days.

Even now, when I should be worried more about Logan and arranging my divorce, I couldn't shake the unwelcome chills that traveled down my spine at the mental image of that Andrea woman rubbing against Nick at the restaurant.

I was annoyed that Alice was paying too much attention to Logan but that jealousy was just a pinch compared to the gut-wrenching twist I was feeling over Nick. The thought of him having sex with her, or any other woman, was making me nauseous.

This had to end before I went mad.

"Five dates. One week," I said to myself. "Then this will all be over."

CHAPTER 4

PRESCOTT'S MOVIE THEATER WAS LOCATED IN the middle of Main Street, sandwiched between the deli and a fly-fishing shop. Main Street was Prescott's hub, filled with locally owned shops and stores. It ran right through the middle of town, eventually connecting with the highway. The highway had other businesses, including the motel and grocery store, but so far, I'd spent most of my time wandering downtown.

Walking down the sidewalk, I spotted Nick standing outside the theater's ticket window. His canvas jacket showcased his broad shoulders. His jeans molded perfectly to his thighs and highlighted the perfect shape of his ass. He was wearing a hunter-green baseball cap and the longer hair at his neck was hanging free, curling at the ends.

My feet teetered and I almost fell down. After all these years, the sight of him still made my knees weak. I cursed myself for letting his looks get to me, but on the bright side, at least he wasn't looking and had missed my stumble.

"Hi," I called out.

"Hey," he said. A crooked grin spread across his face as his eyes raked over my body.

His eyes were hungry and I was glad that I'd been able to swing home after school to change into something less flattering than the dress I had worn to work. I was in jeans and a tan sweater with camel suede elbow patches. Because I always got cold in theaters, I had pulled on a slouchy, brown beanie.

The first of our five required dates was a movie. Nick had wanted dinner but I'd managed to convince him (via a lengthy text message exchange) that I'd been dying to check out Prescott's Rialto Theater. Though it hadn't been a lie, my real motivation had been because we wouldn't be able to talk.

I had four more nights to get his explanation. Tonight was all about avoidance and getting this over with quickly.

Handing me my ticket, he asked, "Snacks?"

"Popcorn. Skittles. Junior Mints. Diet Coke," I ordered. "What? Don't give me that look. It's my dinner."

The lobby of the theater was packed full of people. Next to the small ticket box was a long concession counter where four high school kids frantically filled food and drink orders.

"Is it always this busy?" I asked.

"Tuesday night they run a special where everything is half off," he said.

We waited our turn in awkward silence. This was not the place for a serious conversation but casual chitchat wasn't an option either. We had too much baggage. After what felt like hours, we had our snacks and shuffled into the theater.

The two-story room was much larger than I would have guessed from the outside of the building. A small balcony hung above the main floor. The walls were draped in maroon curtains tied with gold, tasseled rope. The wood trim was carved in intricate swirls.

"This place is amazing," I said, following Nick to a pair of open seats on the lower level.

"Yeah. A couple of years ago they renovated the place, but this has been the theater in Prescott since the early 1900s. Back then they used to do vaudeville shows. The stage beneath the movie screen is the original."

"Very interesting. Do you come here often?" I spread my snacks around me for easy access during the movie.

"No."

I jumped in my seat when I felt his breath on the side of my face. I'd been so busy arranging my popcorn that I hadn't realized he'd gotten so close. The seats in the theater were squished so closely together that my arm would be rubbing up against his all night.

Shit.

Maybe the movie wasn't such a good idea after all. At least with dinner, I'd have had a table separating us.

The movie started and though my eyes stayed locked on the screen, I wasn't absorbing the film. All of my focus was on the man sitting next to me and the arm he'd draped around my shoulders. For two hours, Nick drew circles on my shoulder with his fingertips.

I should have pulled away and told him to stop. The words were right on the tip of my tongue but I just couldn't get them out. Why had I let him touch me?

Because I was bat-shit crazy. That's why.

When the crowd stood to leave, I breathed a sigh of relief that the night was over.

"Good night," I said when I was safely on the sidewalk,

but before I could escape, Nick captured my elbow and spun me around.

"Tomorrow night. Dinner."

"I can't tomorrow. Thursday either. I need to spend some time finishing my lesson plans," I lied.

My prep work for school had been done since the weekend, but I had to get some space from Nick. My mental stability was at stake. Spending last night with him at The Black Bull and then tonight at the theater was too much.

"Lesson plans? Don't you teach little kids?" he asked.

"After you spend a day attempting to keep fourteen kindergarteners entertained *without* a lesson plan, you can question their necessity. Until then, trust me when I say they are vital."

"Fine," he said with a smug grin. "Friday. Dinner. Prescott Café. Six o'clock."

I nodded and rushed away before he could say anything else. What was with that arrogant smile he'd given me? Had I missed a joke?

It wasn't until I was sitting in my driver's seat that I realized why he had grinned. We had four dates left to fit into six days. If I delayed date two until Friday, it meant that I'd be seeing him Friday, Saturday, Sunday and Monday.

A whole weekend of Nick.

"Oh for the love . . ." I muttered before banging my forehead against the steering wheel.

"Ms. Austin!"

"Fuck," Nick muttered.

My eyes scanned the room, looking for the child who had just called my name. In the middle of the restaurant, Rowen Cleary was wildly waving.

"Hi, Rowen." I waved back, overjoyed that I could use her as an excuse to get some space from Nick.

We were on date number two at the Prescott Café. Nick had been waiting for me outside the café when I'd arrived, and as soon as I had been near enough, he'd bent to kiss my cheek. I was sure the left side of my face was still bright red because my skin was on fire.

When I reached the Clearys' table, Jess stood to greet me and shake Nick's hand while I gave Rowen a hug.

"Hi, Gigi," I said.

"Emmeline! Great to see you! Sorry I can't get up." She frowned, rubbing her stomach. "Jess has to practically lift me out of chairs these days. We couldn't even sit at our regular booth over there by the window because I don't fit."

"Well, you look radiant. Pregnancy absolutely agrees with you." Her skin was glowing and her hair was thick and shiny.

"Thanks." She smiled.

"When are you due?"

"December tenth." She giggled as my eyes widened.

She looked like her due date was yesterday but she still had over a month to go. That baby was going to be a giant.

"Mommy, can Ms. Austin and Nick sit with us?" Rowen asked.

"Great idea, sweetie!" Gigi said. "We just got here and haven't ordered yet. Please eat with us. It will make me feel like less of a behemoth if you take up some of the extra space at this big table."

I felt Nick at my back. "Thanks, Gigi, but we can—"

"We'd love to!" I interrupted his protest. I took the end seat so Nick couldn't sit at my side and touch me again like he had at the theater.

I got settled and quickly scanned the restaurant. The café had an old-fashioned diner feel. Blue vinyl booths ran along the edges of the room. A long counter with matching stools lined the back and behind it was an open view of the kitchen and cooks.

"How's teaching going?" Gigi asked. "Is my baby girl behaving herself?"

"She's perfect," I said.

Rowen's face split into a beaming smile.

I started to review the menu but looked up when Nick asked, "No pictures tonight? You don't want to recreate the Prescott Café in downtown New York?"

"Funny," I deadpanned. "And no. The Black Bull is just what I'm looking for."

"The Black Bull?" Jess asked.

"Emmy is going to create a Montana steakhouse in Manhattan," Nick said.

I stared at three skeptical faces. "I have a restaurant space in Manhattan that I turn over every year," I explained. "We redesign and redecorate the space while my chef creates a brand-new menu. All of the proceeds go to charity and I thought a Montana-themed steakhouse would go over well. Last year, we did an old-fashioned Italian bistro and gave away three point four million dollars."

I had always chosen authentic and classic restaurant themes. Most restaurateurs would choose something trendy, like molecular gastronomy or ramen burgers or a poke bar, but comfort foods have always appealed to me more. Large portions of simple, delicious food. Given the huge response we had gotten over the years, I knew I wasn't alone in my desire for something unassuming.

"That's impressive," Gigi said while Jess and Nick looked at me in surprise.

"Thanks. This will be the seventh year my team has made the flip."

"Which charities do you donate to?" Jess asked.

"I alternate every year but I always pick one whose main beneficiaries are children."

"Why kids?" Gigi asked.

"My grandparents were devoted to the children of New York City and spent a lot of time volunteering at inner-city organizations. I used to go with them and found a passion for it."

Those had been some of my best experiences growing up. I had adored my grandparents, and that time spent with them had been precious. They'd given me a different perspective on life and I tried to honor their memory with the restaurant and continuing their work.

"That's remarkable, Emmeline," Gigi said.

"For sure," Jess added.

"Thank you." I ducked my head to hide my blushing cheeks.

The restaurant had taken a lot of time and energy to get going, but each year, it became more and more successful. Outside of getting my teaching degree, it was my proudest accomplishment. I was glad to know that kids were getting hot meals and warm clothing all because I was able to convince the snobby socialites of New York that an unpretentious meal was worth four hundred dollars a plate.

"You didn't tell me any of this the other night," Nick said.

"You didn't ask."

We stared at each other for a moment until our waitress arrived and our table conversation split. While Nick and Jess were visiting, Gigi leaned toward me. "So, uh, you and Nick are what exactly?"

"Old acquaintances," I said at the same time Nick said, "Married".

I guess he wasn't as deep into his conversation with Jess as I'd thought.

"Right." Gigi grinned.

"It's complicated," I said as Nick nodded in agreement.

"Why'd you move to Prescott? Not for this asshole, I hope," Jess teased.

"Uh, no." I shook my head. Not wanting to delve into the drama that was my marriage, I told them how I'd come to find Prescott. "I graduated from NYU last spring and started looking for kindergarten teacher positions around the country. It's actually silly how I landed in Prescott. I chose the mascot I liked best."

"Seriously?" Gigi giggled.

"Yes, and let me tell you, there were some interesting choices. Snapping Turtles. Sugarbeeters. Blue Ponies. I wanted something other than Lions, Tigers or Bears so when I saw that Prescott had the Mustangs, I liked it and . . . here I am." I laughed.

Jess and Gigi both laughed with me, but Nick scowled.

"What?" I asked.

"You said you were at Yale," he said.

"I was. Nine years ago. I haven't been in school this whole time." I rolled my eyes. "After I worked for a few years, things changed. I went back to school at NYU to become a teacher."

47

An awkward silence fell over the table.

"Sounds like you two have some catching up to do," Gigi said, finally clearing the air.

"It's complicated," I repeated.

Conversation lightened as Rowen took over, telling us stories and asking questions. By the end of the meal, all of the awkwardness from earlier had vanished and we all cheerfully exited the café.

I was glad things hadn't been uncomfortable with the Clearys. I hadn't seen them since I had so rudely bolted from their Halloween party and was relieved they were reserving judgment.

After bidding farewell to Jess, Gigi and Rowen, I stood on the sidewalk, waiting as Nick said his good-byes. There was no escaping a discussion with Nick about date three, so I stayed put rather than disappearing to my car.

With one last wave to my student, I turned to Nick.

"Tomorrow night, I'm coming to your house. No more distractions or public places, Emmy."

I didn't argue about the date's location because he was right. Plus, a private setting would give us time to talk.

"Emmeline," I corrected. "Are there any toppings you don't like on pizza? I'll pick one up for us."

"Mushrooms. Everything else is fine," he said.

"See you tomorrow." I nodded and walked away.

Two dates down. Three to go.

"Shit!" I yelled as I flew forward.

Since the day I'd moved in, I had been tripping on a

small wrinkle in the living room's tan wool carpet.

Normally, I'd land on my hands and knees. But tonight, I was hauled backward by a strong arm banded around my waist.

"Gotcha," Nick said into my hair.

Squirming to get loose, I stepped out of his space.

"The evil living room carpet fairies have been tripping me in that spot for months," I blurted, trying to shake off how good it had felt to be pressed up against his hard chest. "I usually come in through the kitchen and avoid this area altogether."

"Want me to see if I can stretch the carpet? Get that ripple out?" he asked.

"No, that's okay. I just need to remember it's there. I might replace it all with hardwoods anyway." I took another step away. "We still have about fifteen minutes until the pizza is ready. Shall we continue the tour?"

My modern, yet rustic house was nestled into the forest at the base of the mountains. Other than a small lawn out front, the whole place was surrounded by large evergreens.

There were three levels in the house. The two upper floors sat on top of the garage and wine cellar. Outside, a set of wide stone stairs curved its way from the driveway to my front door.

"Big place," Nick muttered as we moved further into the living room.

"It's more space than I need but I love all of the windows and balconies."

I had pictured myself living in a quaint Montana cabin; unfortunately, none had been on the market. So I'd settled for this place, knowing I'd be surrounded by trees instead of high-rises.

The living room was made mostly of floor-to-ceiling windows except for a wall with a huge stone fireplace. I stayed inside while Nick inspected the deck that ran the entire length of the room.

I skipped the upstairs tour so I could avoid showing Nick my bedroom. The idea of him standing by my bed was unsettling and far too intimate.

"Would you like a beer?" I asked as we entered the kitchen.

"Sure. This is quite a kitchen," Nick said.

I went to the fridge and got myself a glass of chardonnay and him a Coors Light. "You are not wrong."

The kitchen spanned almost the entire back length of the house, running behind the dining room and joining with the living room. Rich brown alder cabinets lined the walls. The Sub-Zero refrigerator was almost five feet wide, the gas range had seven burners, and there were two sets of stacked convection ovens. In the center was an enormous butcher-block island.

Most nights, I ate at one of four stools bordering the rectangular island. It felt too lonely to sit at my eight-seat dining room table.

"Do you like to cook?" Nick asked.

"I don't have a lot of experience. When I was growing up, my family had a chef so I never learned. Logan and I ate out for most meals." I didn't miss the way his jaw clenched at the mention of Logan's name. "I've been trying to teach myself since moving here but it's hit or miss."

"Bet you're going stir crazy up here in the mountains all by yourself."

"A little. I miss being around adults, but I don't miss all of the forced smiles and small talk. That scene was always my father's. After I quit working for him, I would have stopped going to those types of events completely if it weren't for Logan's responsibilities."

"What are those?" he asked.

"Logan oversees his family's foundation. The Kendricks give huge sums to charities every year, and either Logan or the foundation's CEO tries to personally attend the larger events."

"Hmm." He took a long pull from his beer.

This was miserably uncomfortable. I had decided earlier that I would take any opportunity to mention Logan tonight. Nick needed the reminder that I had a boyfriend, and if I were being honest with myself, so did I. But now that the room was filled with tension, I was rethinking my plan.

We both stood at the island in silence until the timer on the oven dinged. We ate quietly opposite one another. Nick was deep in thought and I focused on my food.

"Is that the life you want, Emmy? Chefs. Charity dinners. Money," he asked when we'd finished our meal.

"Emmeline. And that's the life I know. Not necessarily the one I want."

"Okay," he sighed.

Had I just given him permission to help me find the life I wanted?

Shit.

"Sorry. I didn't think of picking up anything for dessert," I said, clearing our plates.

Without answering, Nick walked into the pantry and took inventory. He emerged with his arms loaded full of supplies.

"What are you doing?" I asked as he set down sugar, chocolate chips, Rice Krispies and some other ingredients.

"Teaching you how to make one of my favorites," he said.

"Which is?" I asked.

"Scotcheroos. They're like Rice Krispie treats on steroids."

For the next twenty minutes, Nick hovered by my side as he gave me step-by-step instructions on how to make a sugar and peanut butter mixture for the rice cereal that we topped with melted chocolate and butterscotch chips. It was only by chance that I had the necessary ingredients. I had gone crazy at the grocery store a couple of weeks ago then failed spectacularly at making myself cookies.

When the bars were cooling in the fridge, we sat in the living room and visited about nothing serious. I was too tired for a conversation about the past. It could wait until date four or date five.

"What do you do?" I asked, sipping my wine.

"I'm the chief at the fire department."

"Does Prescott have a large station?" I asked, ignoring the rush of excitement I got from learning that Nick was a firefighter.

"No. I'm the only full-time paid employee. The rest of my crew are all volunteers. There's not enough fire activity here to have a big staff. Mostly, I make sure the volunteers are up on training in case we do get a call. In the summer, we help the Forest Service with the smaller forest fires that burn too close to town."

"Do you like it? Your job?"

"Yeah. I like the variety and I've got a great volunteer crew."

"That's good."

"Glad you got to be a teacher like you always wanted."

I smiled. "Me too."

My phone rang, interrupting our conversation. Logan. I'd tried all week to get ahold of him and tell him about Nick, but every time we had connected, he had been rushing off somewhere. Of course he'd pick this moment to call me back.

"Sorry. I need to take this." Putting the phone to my ear, I made my way out of the living room when I tripped again on that menacing wrinkle. "Shit! Damn you, evil fairies!"

"Emmeline?" Logan asked.

"Hi, I'm here. Sorry. I just tripped."

"Do you have people over?" he asked, Nick's laughter echoing in the background.

"Oh, uh, that's just the TV," I lied. "What are you doing?"

"Just pulling up to the Waldorf. I'm meeting my parents for dinner."

"Oh." That meant that in less than two minutes, he was going to hang up on me. Again, he was too busy for us to have a conversation.

"I really need to talk to you. Can you please call me tomorrow?" I asked.

"I'll try. But I'm planning on brunch with Tom so we can catch up on the case. And then I'm going into the office."

"Fine. But if you don't call me tomorrow, I'm going around you and talking to your assistant so she can block off time on your calendar."

"Uh, sure. Whatever you want," he said. He was distracted and this phone call wasn't a priority.

"Good night, Logan," I said and didn't wait for his reply.

Our relationship was deteriorating. Or maybe I was now realizing that it already had. We weren't a priority in each other's lives, not like we used to be. And, aside from moving home, I didn't have a clue what to do about it. The thought of losing him was depressing but living in the city wasn't an option.

Chocolate. And more wine. That's what I needed. I walked into the kitchen and found Nick cutting the scotcheroos.

"You okay?" he asked.

"Great!" I lied. He didn't buy it and strode right into my space, placing his hands on the sides of my face.

"No lies, Emmy." He leaned down and kissed the tip of my nose. The second his lips connected with my skin, all the muscles in my body tensed.

That touch was painfully familiar. I remembered every one of Nick's caresses and kisses from Las Vegas. Back then they had meant the world to me, but now they hurt my heart.

No matter how much I hated it, I was still drawn to him. Our connection was magnetic. The stronger I pushed it away, the harder it pulled back. We needed more distance if I was going to come out of these five dates in one piece.

"Please. Don't do that," I begged.

His forehead rested against mine for a brief moment before the heat from his body was gone and my face was freed from his grasp. Taking a large scotcheroo from the pan, he said, "See you tomorrow."

I stood on the porch and watched the taillights of his massive red truck disappear into the trees.

Another date done and I was still without answers. It had been a mistake not to press and wait for tomorrow, because tonight I'd felt a shift.

Maybe I didn't want an explanation. Whatever Nick had to tell me might make me hate him all over again.

And deep down, I dreaded that thought.

"Three dates down. What does he have planned for the next?" Steffie asked.

"I'm not sure. He just said, 'See you tomorrow,' before he left."

"You can make it. Stick it out through these last two dates. When you know more, you can start making decisions."

I'd called Steffie for advice not long after Nick had left. Other than Nick and myself, Steffie was the only person that knew every sordid detail about Las Vegas. I had been so broken that she'd had to practically carry me through the airport the morning he'd left.

"You're right. I can endure two more evenings with Nick." *I can endure.* I had been enduring for a long time.

"Do you ever wonder?" she asked.

"Wonder what?"

"Wonder what if? What would have happened if he hadn't left you in Vegas?"

"No." My answer was definite and true. I had always guarded against picturing what our nine years could have been.

"Don't start now," she warned.

Damn it, Steffie. Her words had the exact opposite effect.

In a flash, unwanted images assailed my mind.

I saw Nick at my graduation from Yale, standing in the crowd next to my family, clapping loudly and whistling as I walked across the stage and received my diploma.

I pictured him dropping me off at the small college in

town every morning where I was getting my teaching degree.

And I saw a beautiful little boy chasing a German Shepherd puppy. His dark hair was the exact color of Nick's but he had my gray eyes. The boy's little sister played on the grass, her auburn hair curled at the ends, just like her daddy's.

The clarity of the images made them almost real.

And just that more painful.

"I'm going to let you go," I told Steffie, choking out the words past my tightening throat.

I hung up the phone, then squeezed my eyes shut, clutching a hand to my heart. Using every bit of mental power I had, I pushed out those wistful images until all I saw was black.

There were some things I couldn't endure.

CHAPTER 5

THE CHIME OF MY DOORBELL WOKE ME FROM A dead sleep.

Shooting out of bed, I glanced at the clock. It was only six in the morning. Considering I knew very few people in Prescott and even fewer knew where I lived, my early morning visitor was likely Nick.

After shrugging on my black floral-print silk robe, I stomped down the stairs and threw open the door. "It's six in the morning. You said you'd see me tomorrow. It's not tomorrow yet. Go away."

He chuckled, then pushed his way inside.

"You could have at least brought coffee," I said, following him to the kitchen.

Heading straight to the counter, he wordlessly grabbed a scotcheroo and took a huge bite.

Last night after he had left, I'd gone crazy and eaten three. The butterscotch chocolate layer on top of the peanut-butter-coated crispy cereal was delicious and addicting.

But consuming that much sugar at six o'clock in the morning could not be good for you. Though, Nick didn't seem like the type of guy who really cared about health foods and fad diets. With all those muscles to burn off the calories, he could probably eat as many sweets as he wanted.

"Breakfast of champions?" I asked.

His mouth formed a crooked grin while he chewed.

"I'm making coffee," I said.

Perusing my extensive mug collection, I picked one of my favorites. It read:

DO NOT READ THE NEXT SENTENCE.
You little rebel. I like you.

Grinning, I moved to my Keurig. I was so focused on the filling coffee mug that I almost missed Nick's footsteps as he invaded the space at my back. My muscles locked in place, not needing to turn around to know he was close.

Too close.

The space around me warmed and his amazing scent filled my nostrils. He must have just showered because the spicy, fresh scent of his soap lingered all around him. It was the perfect mixture of nutmeg and orange peel.

Nick's smell, combined with the fragrant coffee, was re-laxing. So relaxing that I almost leaned back into his chest. Almost. I snapped out of my trance. What was wrong with me? Why had I just stood there and let Nick invade my space?

Because it was six in the morning. That and I was bat-shit crazy. That's why.

Ducking around him, I went back to my cabinet to get him a coffee mug.

"Coffee?" I asked.

He nodded and I felt his hazel eyes on my back as I made him his coffee. After I handed him his full mug, I walked around the island, using it as a barrier between us.

His mug was black with nothing on the outside. The only decoration was inside at the bottom, where it read *You've been poisoned* in small white letters. I was looking forward to seeing his reaction when he reached the bottom.

I had used that mug on my father many times, always enjoying the nervous look he'd give me when his cup had been finished.

After taking a few sips, Nick finally spoke. "We're going on a hike."

"A hike? I've never hiked before," I said.

"Today's your day. The weather is going to change soon so this is one of the last weekends to explore the mountains. I figured you probably haven't done much of that, city girl. But don't worry, you'll like it."

"Shouldn't we wait until it gets a bit warmer? It's barely light out. To me, a hike says 'afternoon.' Not predawn."

"We've got things to do first," he said. "We're going to breakfast at the café. Then we need to pick up a couple of sandwiches for lunch. After that, we'll hit the mountain." I opened my mouth to protest but he talked right over me. "No arguments. You've got time to shower and get changed. Make sure you wear something warm. It will be colder up where we're headed than it is down here."

"Fine," I grumbled.

After refilling my coffee mug, I walked up the stairs. Just as I was stepping off the top step, Nick's rich laughter filled the floor below me. My heart stuttered and I smiled at the sound. He must have seen the bottom of his cup.

I really liked that mug.

My future ex-husband was evil.

The bastard had probably used this hiking ploy as a way to get women into bed countless times over the years. Because at this very moment, I was so turned on I couldn't do much more than put one foot in front of the other.

I had been trudging after Nick on the mountain trail for over an hour. Every time I looked up, my eyes immediately landed on his sculpted behind.

For years, I had thought that no man's ass could look as good as Logan's did in his tailored suits.

Well, I had been quite wrong.

Nick's ass kicked Logan's ass.

The Carhartt pants he was wearing weren't tight, but their cut highlighted all of the rounded and muscled contours of his butt. Who knew tan canvas pants could be so sexy?

Just staring at his ass had my whole body buzzing. All I *wanted* to do was reach out and grab a handful. But what I *needed* to do was stop thinking about Nick's ass.

I hated that I was still insanely attracted to him.

"You doing okay back there?" Nick called over his shoulder.

"Great!" I lied, looking up into his smirking face. He had totally just caught me checking him out.

Shit.

"How much farther?" I asked, trying not to appear guilty.

"We're just about there. Ten minutes, maybe?"

"Is this place a favorite of yours?"

"Yeah. It's got a great view of the Jamison Valley. And the hike itself is fairly easy. Didn't want to take you on anything too difficult this first time."

"Easy. Right." I had been huffing and puffing for twenty minutes. My thighs were burning and my calves were balled tight. My body hadn't worked this hard in years.

I was lucky to have a petite frame and fast metabolism, which meant that I hadn't stepped into a gym since college. And even then, it had been to ogle the football team with Steffie. As long as I didn't go crazy with junk food, I was able to maintain my figure without much exercise.

True to his word, Nick soon veered off the trail and we maneuvered through the trees to a large opening in front of a rock cliff.

When my eyes took in the sight before me, tingles traveled through my limbs.

Magic.

Jamison Valley was located in southwestern Montana, and from this position we could see forever. Nick even showed me where Yellowstone National Park started in the distance.

Prescott's brown buildings were tiny from up here. The aerial view allowed me to see how the town filled the space along the Jamison River. Miles away was another indigo mountain range towering over the golden plains between us. The evergreens around the rock cliff stood tall. Their green color provided a stunning contrast to the cloudless, light blue sky above.

"Pretty view," Nick said.

"Montana is not ugly."

Chuckling, he asked, "You want some coffee?"

I nodded and followed him to a bare spot on the ground where we both sat, facing the breathtaking view. From his backpack, he produced a large thermos and two cups. With coffee in hand, this had just become my favorite place on earth.

I pulled out my phone and snapped a few photos. They were good but no picture could do the scenery justice.

Taking a few deep breaths, I thought of all the words to describe the incredible mountain air. Clean. Stony. Light. There was nothing else like it.

"Are you cold? Your nose is a little red," Nick said, reaching out a finger to gently touch my face.

"No," I said, leaning away. "I'm good."

The steaming coffee was doing wonders to warm my nose and cheeks, the only cold parts of my body. The air was cold and crisp but the added layers of my clothing were definitely keeping me warm. Almost too warm. My sweaty hair was sticking to my scalp under my fleece hat.

We sat quietly, enjoying the view, until Nick started asking questions about my past. "You told me that you weren't going to be able to be a teacher. That you had to work for your dad. What changed?"

"After I graduated from Yale, I went to work for him for almost seven years," I said.

"What did you do?"

"My job was to make connections with potential high-dollar donors and convince them that they should give to whichever political candidate we were promoting at the time."

"Hmm. How did you do that? Make connections," he asked.

"I spent a lot of time researching them and their families. Basically, I had to act like a stalker. I would befriend their personal assistants so I could have access to their private schedules. Then I'd casually bump into them in restaurants or at other charity events. If their kids had programs or concerts, I would be sure to go, then lie and say I was there for my nonexistent nieces and nephews."

"That doesn't sound like you, Emmy."

"Emmeline. And it wasn't. It was my father. I was his puppet. Whatever he needed me to do, I did. Until he betrayed me and I quit."

"He betrayed you? How?"

Only two people knew this story. I'd kept it a secret from everyone except my mother and Logan. Steffie and I never talked about Austin Capital, and my other friends weren't to be trusted, but I felt safe telling Nick. He wouldn't leak it to the press for a quick buck or gossip about it behind my back.

"An important donor called my father to lodge a complaint about one of my employees, Tiffany. The donor told my father that she had promised sexual favors in return for a significant donation. When I confronted her about it, she confessed but told me it was at my father's personal instruction. That he had told her to do it."

"Did he?" Nick asked.

"He swore up and down that Tiffany was lying. To this day, I can't believe I actually thought he was telling me the truth. But I did believe him and I cleaned up the mess. Tiffany agreed to a large severance in return for her promise never to sue or slander the company."

"That's why you quit? You found out he was lying?"

"No," I said. "He *was* lying but that isn't why I quit. A month later, I was at a gala with Logan. The donor that had complained to my father walked up and started accusing me of basically being a whore. I remember standing there speechless, stunned and having no idea what he was talking about. Thankfully, Logan jumped in and got the whole story."

"Which was?"

"My father had blamed the entire Tiffany incident on me. He said that I was the one encouraging her to make sexual advances and that he knew nothing about it. He had even hinted that I started dating Logan to gain access to the Kendrick fortune. But that's why I quit. He saw a situation where his professional reputation might have been tarnished, and instead of owning his mistake, he falsely blamed it all on his daughter."

His personal reputation was questionable but professionally, my father had always been the epitome of a respected businessman. Lies. All lies, but he was good at telling them. He had to be in order to make the money he was so grossly fond of.

"But there's a bright side," I said. "It was the push I needed to break free. I hated it anyway. The best day I ever had at Austin Capital was the day I packed up my office and turned in my security badge."

"Then you went back to school?" Nick asked.

"Yes. I started classes the next semester. Since I already had my undergraduate degree, I only had to go for two years. Then I happened upon the Mustangs and here I am."

After a few moments of silence, Nick said, "Not a fan of your father."

"Me either." I laughed.

Growing up, I had always tried to please him. But

no matter what I did, he had always been disappointed in me. Nothing had ever been good enough. Not my perfect grades. Not my exemplary volunteer work. Nothing. It took me a long time to realize that I wasn't the disappointment. He was.

"Is he the reason why you left New York? Couldn't you have just gotten a teaching job there?" Nick asked.

"I wouldn't say my father was the reason but he was certainly the catalyst. I'm sure I could have found a job there, but it was time for a change. Time for me to just be me. Emmeline Austin. Not *the* Emmeline Austin, everything there is about money and prestige. You're measured by your social standing and the number of times you hit the society pages. I didn't want to live that life anymore."

"Do you miss it? The city?" Nick asked.

"I miss a few things. Logan, mainly. I miss my restaurant. Twenty-four-hour dry cleaning. Hot dog street vendors. But other than that, it feels good to be living a simpler life. New York can be a cold place for those in the spotlight."

"You don't miss your friends?" he asked.

"No," I scoffed. "Most of my 'friends' haven't spoken to me since I left."

"What about those girls you were with in Vegas? What happened to them?"

"Marian moved to Los Angeles and we lost touch. Alice lives in the city, but we were both so career focused after Yale, we lost touch too," I said. "Though, apparently, she's been keeping tabs on Logan."

"What about the other one? The one with the, uh, implants?"

I choked on my coffee. "Steffie? We're still friends. Our relationship is . . . different. About six months before I quit working for my father, I went over to his penthouse unannounced. Guess who he had naked and bent over the back of his couch?"

"Steffie?"

"I still gag when I think about it. Things were awkward at first but we've been able to stay friends regardless of her relationship with my father."

"Interesting," he said sarcastically.

"Things have always been a bit unconventional at the Austin estate."

"What about your mother?" he asked.

"She lives in Italy. Shortly after I graduated from high school, she moved there with her Italian boyfriend, Alesso. She started having an affair with him when I was sixteen. When his work visa expired, she decided to move to Italy with him permanently."

"She was cheating on your father?"

"Oh, yes," I said. "For as long as I can remember, they were married while both carried on blatantly public affairs. They only just got divorced five years ago."

"Fuck. That's a lot of drama," Nick said when my storytelling was over.

"You are not wrong."

We sat quietly for a while, then wandered slowly down the trail and ate sandwiches in the back of his truck before Nick drove me home.

"Thanks. I enjoyed the hike."

We were standing by my front door and I was pulling out my keys, mentally preparing to ask him why he had left me. I had decided on the drive back that his time was up. He had promised me an explanation and had yet to give it.

All day long we had visited and not once had he

broached the subject. He'd learned plenty about my life today but shared little about his.

So this afternoon I was demanding answers. And I wanted it to happen here in my home, my own private place where I felt safe to have whatever emotional reaction I needed.

"Nick, I need you to—" I was interrupted by the soft brush of his lips on mine.

For a second, all of my thoughts were consumed by how wonderful his lips felt. How, for years, I had longed to feel them again, even after swearing to hate this man for breaking my heart.

But that second passed. I could not allow Nick to kiss me. I wasn't his. I belonged to Logan. A loyal, handsome, brilliant man who had not broken my heart.

Turning my head to the side, I broke contact before planting one hand on his chest and shoving him back. "No."

"Emmy."

"Emmeline!"

"Emmy. You'll always be my Emmy."

"I'm not your anything, Nick."

"You're my wife."

"A paper certificate does not make me your wife," I said.

His frame deflated and his eyes filled with regret. "Forgive me. Give us a chance. We have something here and you know I'm right."

"There is no us. And how can I forgive you? You haven't even told me why."

"And if I do?"

"I don't know. I may forgive you but that doesn't erase the pain. I gave you my heart and you betrayed my trust. Your explanation may heal some of those past wounds but we have no future. Logan is my future."

His gentleness evaporated. "He's not your future. I am. Because your heart still belongs to me."

"What? Are you crazy?" I gasped.

"You are *mine*. You are my wife."

"You are crazy."

"You don't want him. It's all just in your head because you're mad at me. Your face doesn't light up when he calls, not like it does when you look at me. You talk about what you two do but not how he makes you feel. And if you really loved him, no way in hell you'd stay married to me for nine years. You could have gotten that divorce a fuck of a long time ago."

I blinked at him, astonished. How could he stand there and criticize my relationship with Logan? How could he think that three dinners and a movie would make up for his actions in Vegas?

But he was right. I should have gotten that divorce a hell of a long time ago. Something I would remedy immediately.

"We're done. My lawyers will be in touch. Leave. Now." I pointed to his truck.

"I'll be here tomorrow after work to pick you up. We're not done."

"We. Are. Done. You've played your game and it didn't work. No more dates. No more avoiding the truth. Just go!" I shouted.

"You think this is a game?"

"What else would it be? That's all you've ever done. You're playing me again but this time I'm not going to be the stupid idiot that falls for it."

"You seriously think I'm fucking playing you?"

"Yes!"

68

Tipping his head to the sky, he roared, "Fuck!" His chest heaved and his eyes closed as he worked to calm down. "Tomorrow night. You'd better be here when I show up. You're not, I'll find you," he threatened. "You want to know everything? Fine. You'll get all the answers you want. Maybe see that this isn't a fucking game to me. This is my fucking life!" he yelled and stormed down the stairs.

Rushing inside, I sagged against the front door the second the latch clicked. His truck rumbled to life outside and sped away. Gripping my belly, I sank to the floor.

I couldn't do this. I couldn't be around Nick anymore. It hurt. But even with the pain twisting at my sides, I had to know the truth.

Whatever he had to say would likely crush my heart all over again but the thing I feared the most was that everything he had just said was true.

Nick

"Fuck!" I shouted at my dashboard. The speed of my truck matched the rhythm of my frantic heartbeat.

Emmy wasn't going to forgive me. I could see it in her eyes.

I had foolishly hoped that by spending time together, we could get back to where we had been once. That maybe she'd let go of the past and I wouldn't have to tell her the truth.

But that was just a fucking pipe dream.

My only chance was by laying it all out there. Years ago,

I had made the decision to leave her for her own safety. We hadn't talked about it the night we'd gotten married, but I'd known she had money. Money that would attract the evil and soul-destroying demons that were my family.

So I had ripped out my own heart to save hers.

The image of her the morning I'd left was burned into my brain. Her naked body sleeping peacefully, draped over the place where I had been lying. Her beautiful hair spread down her bare back and all over the pillows. A small smile playing on her rosy lips.

I remembered gently lifting a strand of hair off her porcelain face before whispering that I loved her. Words she had never heard me say. And then with an aching hole in my chest, I'd silently crept from the hotel suite, leaving behind the only person who could bring warmth to my cold heart.

Nine years and I could still hear the click of that fucking hotel room door.

She had been better off without me. Back then, I had been too deep into my family's dangerous life to keep her safe.

I had vowed to stay far away but things were different now. She was here. And I had learned that living a life without warmth was no life at all.

The moment I had laid eyes on her again, the heat had spread like wildfire through my chest. And I'd known I would fight to the death to win her back. Every minute that I'd spent with her this week had reinforced my desire to keep fighting.

The boyfriend could go fuck himself. She was mine.

Emmy had been an incredible person nine years ago, but somehow time had managed to make her even better.

She was so fucking smart and witty. Never once had

she flaunted her wealth. If anything, she took extra measures to ensure those around her weren't intimidated or threatened by it. She was kind and loving. The way she beamed at Rowen Cleary made me desperately want to see that light shine on kids we made together.

And beautiful. She was breathtaking.

Today on the mountain, with her flushed cheeks and pink nose, it had taken every ounce of my willpower not to take her right there in the trees.

"Fuck the secrets." No matter what it would take, I was getting my wife back. My Emmy.

Even if that meant telling her things I'd sworn never to reveal.

CHAPTER 6

"**D**ID YOU MOVE THERE FOR HIM?" LOGAN asked.

I clenched my phone tighter. "No, I didn't move here for him. I just told you, I didn't even know he lived here. If you need the private investigator's reports to prove I didn't know, I'll send them over tonight."

"I don't know if I can believe you."

Tears dripped down my cheeks. Wow, that hurt. "How can you say that, Logan? I have never lied to you."

"Really? You don't think that not telling me you were still married was a lie?"

"No, I mean, yes. I just . . . I don't know why I didn't tell you. But it wasn't to hurt you."

"Did you call Fred Andrews?" he asked.

"Yes. I talked to him right after I found Nick. He's working on the divorce papers." I waited on the phone, listening to Logan breathe.

"I don't know what to do here, sweetheart." His soft voice caused a fresh wave of tears.

"Believe me when I tell you I didn't expect him to be here. And that I regret not getting a divorce nine years ago."

"I need some time."

"Okay." I sniffled, trying to pull myself together.

"I hate that we are having this conversation over the phone."

"Me too. I love you, Logan," I added before he could hang up.

"I love you too. I've got to go."

Today had been a wreck and the worst was yet to come. Date five.

After Nick had left yesterday, our conversation had replayed in my mind over and over again. Sleep had eluded me and I'd finally gotten up at three thirty and cleaned. Even though I had gone to school utterly exhausted this morning, at least my house was spotless.

The only break I'd caught today was with my students. They'd been angels, like they could sense I'd been on the edge of a meltdown and instead of pushing me over, they'd clung to my feet and kept me anchored.

When I'd gotten home, I had reluctantly called Logan. Not letting him brush me off again, I had forced the inevitable conversation. Now that was over and I had to mentally prepare for another evening with Nick.

It was only five thirty. I was guessing Nick wouldn't get here until after six, which gave me at least thirty minutes to sit on my couch and cry.

And that's just what I did.

"What's wrong?" Nick asked when I answered the door.

"Nothing," I lied. "What are we doing tonight?"

Nick crossed his arms over his chest. I mirrored his stance and we went into a stare-down.

I didn't owe him any explanations. If I was upset, that was my problem. Not his. And there was no way in hell I was going to tell him that I'd been crying over my phone call with Logan. My relationship, my business.

"Fuck, you are a stubborn woman," he muttered.

I raised my eyebrows and stuck out my chin, silently reminding him that he had yet to answer my question.

"We're going to my place."

"Fine. Let's go," I said and pushed past him, slamming the door behind me.

We rode to Nick's house in silence. The sun was starting to set behind the mountains, the orange and yellow sky slowly fading into bright pinks and purples.

I had assumed that Nick lived in town but he actually lived quite close to me. After turning off the highway, we started winding up a narrow gravel road lined with tall trees.

The end of the lane opened into a small, round clearing in the forest. In the center was a two-story log cabin. A covered porch ran the length of the house, and two large dormer windows jutted out of the roof on the second story. Behind the cabin was a large brown metal shop.

This was the quaint Montana cabin I had wanted. Seeing this place made me regret buying my house. It was too big and ostentatious. But a place like this would have been just right.

The front door opened to a large, open space. The glow from the soft white lights created a warm and cozy atmosphere. The floors were made from a rough-cut tan wood, and when I looked closely, I saw the circular grooves made from the saw blades.

One corner of the main room was a square kitchen filled with dark cabinets. A tall counter separated it from the rest of the living room. A stone fireplace was surrounded by brown leather furniture aimed at a large television in the corner.

Opposite the living room was a dining room table surrounded by six chairs. Both the table and chairs were made in the same log style as the living room's coffee table.

As I inspected the inside of the house, I regretted my extravagant home purchase even more.

"You want something to drink?" Nick asked.

"What do you have?"

"Beer. Whiskey. Water."

"Whiskey, please." There was no way I was going to make it through tonight's conversation without alcohol, and since I wasn't a huge beer drinker, whiskey would have to do.

As Nick moved to the kitchen, I walked toward a set of bookshelves at the back of the room, next to the wooden staircase that led to the second floor.

Nick's book collection surprised me. I hadn't figured him for a reader but the shelves proved me wrong. He had quite a few classics as well as some more recent thrillers. I also noticed a couple of thick automotive texts on the bottom shelf.

A long shelf in the middle was completely dedicated to framed photos. All of the pictures were small, but there were so many packed onto the shelves, I couldn't see the ones in the back.

A few of the pictures showed a younger Nick. In one, he was with a group of men all wearing leather vests and standing next to a line of big motorcycles. In another, he was on a bench with a beautiful brunette woman, another boy at her other side.

The remaining pictures were of the Nick I knew, with his messy hair and full beard. In one, he and three other men were wearing green jumpsuits. Behind him were the remains of a completely burned forest with black trees sticking out of the scorched earth.

Sliding some of the pictures to the side, I started examining the ones hidden toward the back. My eyes caught on a small, unframed picture tucked into the corner joint of the shelf. I grabbed its edge and pulled it free from the wood.

I gasped when the light hit the photo. It was a picture of me from Las Vegas.

I was sleeping on a white pillow. My hair was a wreck, sticking out all over the place. I was still in makeup from the previous night and it was smudged on my eyelids. My lips were red and puffy from a night of kissing Nick. I looked like a mess. But even in sleep, I'd looked happy.

Tears filled my eyes and the picture blurred.

Nick had taken a picture of me the morning before he'd left me alone at the Bellagio. And he'd kept it all this time. The edges of the photo were worn and wrinkled, like he had held it in his hands and studied it countless times. It showed the same wear and age as our wedding photo that I'd kept tucked away.

"Why?" I whispered to the picture.

"Because you're my wife," Nick said behind me.

"What does that mean?"

"It means we belong to each other."

He had said those exact same words right after we had been married, right before his most blatant lie. When he had promised that we'd make our relationship work. The fact that he would throw them out there again made me instantly angry.

I spun around. "You said that to me once before. I liked it the first time. Now, not so much. Word of advice? Don't reuse your Vegas material."

His jaw clenched and he took a deep breath through his nose. "Drink this," he clipped, shoving a glass of whiskey in my face. "And calm the fuck down."

I huffed and rolled my eyes. This was going to be a long night.

"Come sit down," he said, walking to the living room couch.

I sank into an oversized leather chair opposite the couch and took a long sip of my whiskey, grimacing as the amber liquor burned a path down my throat.

"Would you like me to cut that with some water?" Nick asked, resting his elbows on his thighs.

"No," I coughed. "It's fine. Explanation, please. Let's get this over with."

"Fine. Did you see that picture with the woman and two kids on the shelf?"

I nodded.

"That was my mom with me and my younger brother," he said. "She died when I was sixteen."

I closed my eyes. "I'm sorry."

I couldn't imagine how painful it would be to lose your mother at such a young age. My mom wasn't the most outstanding role model, but she was still my mom. She was always there for me.

"She was murdered because of my father," Nick added.

The muscles in my frame locked. "Your father killed your mother?"

"He didn't pull the trigger but it was because of his

fucking selfish choices that she's dead."

"What happened?" I asked.

Nick leaned forward and took a drink of his own whiskey before sitting back. "My dad is the president of a motorcycle gang. And it *is* a gang. Everyone calls it a club, they pretend like it's just a group of guys taking weekend rides on their Harleys, but it's a gang. They use violence to intimidate people who don't do as they want. They have little respect for the law. And they charge their clients a fucking fortune so they can rake in a wad of cash every month."

"What kind of clients?"

"Mostly they provide protection services for whoever will pay. Some local businesses in Clifton Forge. That's where I'm from. They run an underground fight circuit around the state and take a rake from every fight. But their biggest clients are drug smugglers. The club provides protection for shipments coming down from Canada. They make sure the drugs don't get hijacked or caught by the cops."

"Canada?" I asked. "I thought most imported drugs came across our southern borders."

"Drugs made from plant extracts do. Marijuana. Cocaine. Heroin. But a lot of meth is brought down from Canada. It gets made way up north and then driven down. Border security is tight at the official crossings but Montana's a big state. There's a lot of border that doesn't get watched."

"So I'm guessing that somehow all of this illegal activity led to your mother's murder?" I asked.

"Yeah. Dad's operation was expanding and they pissed off a rival gang. They retaliated by going to our house in the middle of the fucking day and executing my mother while she was gardening. My brother and I found her when we got home from school."

A sharp pain traveled from my heart and settled in my stomach. "I don't know what to say."

"Nothing to say, Emmy. Just need you to understand what my life has been like."

"Okay." I nodded.

"When I was little, I couldn't wait to be in the club. Then after Mom died, I couldn't wait to break free. Dad got his revenge, brought an end to that other club and then acted like everything was okay. He kept expanding and digging deeper into the underground. He never once admitted that his need to be the most powerful club in the Northwest is the reason why I don't have a mother."

I shook my head but remained silent.

"It caused a lot of tension between Dad and me. He had always planned for me to take over the club but I made it clear I wasn't going to prospect. I turned eighteen the week before graduation, got my diploma and left for Colorado. I started going to school down there to be a diesel mechanic. I got my certification a couple of years later and started working in a garage."

"That's when you met me?"

"Yeah," he said, "that's when I met you. Me and those guys I was with all worked at a garage in Colorado together. We decided on a whim to take a road trip to Vegas for the weekend."

I sipped my whiskey. "Why did you leave Colorado?"

"My younger brother was just graduating high school. I thought if I lived in Montana, maybe I could convince him to live with me and not join the club. The job at the fire station was open and I decided to give it a try. Gave up being a mechanic and came to Prescott."

"Did he join the club?"

"Yeah." He frowned before swallowing the rest of his drink in a huge gulp.

We sat in silence but my heart beat louder and louder. I took a few jagged breaths and ignored the nervous energy pooling in my belly.

Because this was the end.

I had held onto Nick, or the *idea* of Nick, for almost ten years. After tonight, it would all be over. I could move on with my life. I would have no reason to think of him again. To look at our wedding picture. To secretly wear my ring.

"Why did you leave me?" Just asking the question hurt.

"I got a call from Dad after you fell asleep. He was in a fight with another club. Again. One of the younger guys in Dad's club got shot and killed. He was my age and we'd grown up together. Anyway, Dad said they were getting threats against family members. That both my brother and I were at risk. Told me to watch my back."

My nose started to burn and I felt tears.

This was his excuse? That his leaving had been for my own good?

Men had been making decisions on my behalf my whole life. Decisions without communication. Always saying afterward that it was for the best and never once bothering to ask how I felt.

"I never meant to hurt you, Emmy," he said. "But you weren't safe with me. Not back then. They would have come after you and your money. And I couldn't risk your life. I wouldn't risk having you killed like my mother. So I left."

I closed my eyes and let the tears fall down my cheeks.

I didn't want this explanation. I wanted a different one.

One where he had been forced out of the hotel room at gunpoint and held prisoner for nine years. An explanation like that would have made the ache in my heart go away. Instead, his choice to leave without talking to me made it hurt even worse.

He knelt next to my feet before setting aside my whiskey and taking my hands in his. "I'm sorry. I am so fucking sorry, Emmy," he whispered, peppering my hands with kisses.

"Why didn't you tell me any of this?" I asked. "You could have told me back then. We could have worked something out."

"Because I knew that if I looked into your eyes again, I would never let you go. And you were too good for that life. You needed someone who could give you so much more than I ever could."

He had me completely confused. If I was too good for his life, then why had he been pressing so hard this week? Why did he say that my heart still belonged to him? Just minutes ago, he had declared I was his and he was mine.

"Then what was this past week about? Your chance?" I asked. "I don't understand how I was too good for you back then—which I wasn't, by the way—but now everything is different."

His hazel eyes stared deeply into mine. "You've always had my heart, Emmy. I know I fucked up by leaving but I thought it was my only choice. It took me a long time to realize I had other options. And by then, I was afraid it was too late. That you'd moved on with your life. But the moment I saw you, I knew I had a chance to make it right. No man can ever make you happy because no other woman will ever make me whole. We're it for each other."

As good as those words sounded, and felt, he was wrong. It was too late.

"Take me home," I ordered and stood from the chair, forcing him out of my space.

He stood with me but before I could turn away, his hands framed my face and turned up my chin so I was forced to look at him. His eyebrows were pulled together. Clearly he had, expected a much different reaction to his speech.

"Take me home," I said.

"No." His lips crashed into mine before I could protest. They were firm and determined. His tongue stroked my lower lip until I finally opened for him. Then it was inside, sliding against my own as he took control.

My hands latched onto his flannel shirt so I wouldn't fall down on my shaking knees.

The past came flooding back as I remembered how amazing it was to kiss Nick. How he was the only man that could make me ignite in seconds.

Our lips moved frantically back and forth as we erased nine years of history and went back in time. Right now, it was just us.

His hands traveled down my face, down my body, rubbing and squeezing down my sides. When they reached my hips, his fingers gripped my flesh tightly and he lifted me off my feet. My legs automatically wrapped around his waist as he crushed me to his chiseled body. One of his arms banded around my lower back while the other kneaded my ass.

He carried me backward but I didn't open my eyes. All I could focus on was my mouth fused to his. The feel of his tongue sliding against mine. My throbbing core pressed firmly against the hardness in his jeans.

My back hit a wall, and as Nick's mouth traveled down my neck, I opened my eyes. He had carried me to a wall directly across from one of the cabin's large front windows.

I could see his back in our reflection and my legs around his waist.

On my feet were a pair of Sperry duck boots. The tan leather contrasted brightly against the dark blue of Nick's jeans.

Logan had given me these boots before I'd moved. He had told me to wear them so my feet wouldn't get cold. He knew my feet were always cold.

Ice coursed through my veins. Here I was, making out with another man, when just hours ago I had told Logan that I loved him. Which I did.

"Stop," I said and unwrapped my arms and legs from Nick. "I'm sorry. I can't do this. I won't do this. I'm not this person."

"What? What's wrong, Emmy?" Nick asked.

"What's wrong? I have a boyfriend! That is what's wrong! I need to go." Pushing my way around him, I ran to the door and jerked on my coat.

"Emmy," Nick started but I closed my eyes and furiously shook my head.

"No. Please, Nick. Please take me home," I begged, my voice cracking as I fought back tears.

What kind of a person had I become? I didn't cheat. I had vowed never to become like my parents. How could I do this to Logan? My sweet, wonderful boyfriend, who was having trouble adjusting to the fact that his girlfriend was now living in Montana while he stayed at home in New York.

"I am a terrible person. How could I do this to Logan?" I asked myself. Hearing my own words caused a new wave of tears.

"You're not, Emmy," Nick whispered to the top of my head as he wrapped his arms around me.

"Let me go, Nick. Please," I sobbed into his chest.

"Never again," he said, pulling me tighter into his warmth.

For a moment, I let him hold me while I cried. I let his soothing smell and his strong arms comfort me until I found the strength I needed to push him away and ask one last time.

"Take me home."

CHAPTER 7

"RICH?" I CALLED INTO THE PRINCIPAL'S office.

"Emmeline! Come in, please," he said, standing from his desk. "What can I do for you?"

"I'm not sure what to do about a student and I was wondering if I could get your thoughts," I said as we both sat.

"Of course. Which student?"

"Mason Carpenter."

He frowned. "I wondered if there were going to be problems with Mason. What's happening?"

"It's been almost a month since he moved here and he hardly speaks. I'm getting worried that his behavior isn't just because he's shy. He doesn't make eye contact with me. If I get too close, he flinches. He won't have anything to do with the other kids except Rowen Cleary. He'll whisper to her and then she'll tell me what he says."

"That is a bit extreme. I've seen some kids act like that

85

for the first few days, maybe even a week, but then they get used to the new setting. Has he gotten at all better over the last month?" Rich asked.

"No. I worry about his behavior, but on top of that, his appearance is throwing up all these red flags. Every day this week he's come to school dirty and he's been wearing flip-flops to school. I haven't seen him with socks or a pair of sneakers yet. It's much too cold for flip-flops."

My worries over Mason Carpenter had grown significantly, especially after this morning. His normally brown hair had been almost black with grease and he had been clouded with a foul odor. His poor little toes had been almost blue. If something wasn't done, and soon, he'd be at risk for frostbite.

"Let me do some checking around," Rich said. "He transferred here from Bozeman. I'll give his previous school a call and see if they can share anything. I'll also poke around a bit and see if I can learn more about his home situation. You might try and ask him about it too."

"Okay. I doubt he'll tell me but it's worth a try."

"Let's start documenting all of this. Can you jot down some notes and email them to me? We'll want dates and specific examples in case we need to involve Child Protective Services."

"Yes. Absolutely. I'll do that this afternoon when the kids leave. Is there anything else we can do? What about his shoes?" I asked.

"Unfortunately, there's not much you can do."

"What if he doesn't have any warm shoes? Could I buy him some?"

"I'd be careful. Your offer is very generous and I'm not saying that you can't, but there's a fine line between getting your students gifts and providing things that parents and guardians should be responsible for. Especially if you are buying for only one child," he said.

"Understood. It's just heartbreaking. How long will it take for the authorities to get involved if there is some type of abuse or neglect happening at home?"

"Depending on the severity of the situation, it could be months. Let's concentrate on building a thorough file, and when it's enough, we can contact social services. But even after we involve them, this could be a lengthy process. Unless we can irrefutably prove that Mason is in immediate danger, he'll likely stay where he is for a while."

"That's not okay. Not if he is being neglected."

"I agree. It shouldn't take that long. But, right now, the most important thing for you to do is to keep Mason safe while he is here. Be there for him in case he does decide to talk. Provide him with a safe learning environment."

I nodded and sagged in my chair. I felt hopeless and helpless. Going above and beyond for Mason while he was in school was good advice. But what about when he wasn't with me? Who would take care of him then? Because whoever was supposed to be doing that job was clearly shirking their duties.

"Have faith, Emmeline. As a teacher, you can do a lot to change a child's future. It just might not happen overnight."

"Thank you. I appreciate your time."

"You are most welcome." He relaxed into his chair. "Are you looking forward to Thanksgiving next week? Do you have plans with family or friends?"

"No major plans this year. I think I'll just lay low and get caught up on some house work." As if Mason Carpenter's situation weren't depressing enough to talk about, discussing my holiday plans was sure to put me in a somber mood. This year I would be alone. No Thanksgiving Chinese takeout feast with Logan. My plans included a Netflix binge while working my way through two pizzas and a gallon of ice cream.

"You are welcome to join me and my family. We always have plenty of food and my wife would love nothing more than to tell you embarrassing stories about me," he offered.

"Thank you, Rich. That is so nice of you. I'll keep it in mind."

I'd almost made it to the door when a thought crossed my mind. "Do teachers typically buy holiday gifts for their students?"

"Most do. Why?"

"I was just curious. I was thinking of getting them all something but didn't want to be the only teacher who bought gifts," I said.

"Whatever you'd like to do for them, I am sure they would love it."

Rushing back to my classroom, I mentally rearranged my lesson plan for tomorrow. And tonight I was going to brainstorm a new art activity where somehow I would learn each kid's shoe size.

If getting Mason Carpenter a new pair of shoes meant that every one of my students got a new pair, fine by me.

A week later, all of my students were opening their holiday gifts.

"Are these for me?" Mason whispered.

While all of the other kids were shouting wildly and showing each other their new tennis shoes, I knelt next to Mason, who was staring at his with wide eyes.

Thanksgiving was tomorrow, so today school was only going until noon. I was sure that once all the kids made it home, my afternoon would be spent listening to numerous messages from parents concerned about my extravagant gift.

But I didn't care. As long as Mason Carpenter had something warm to put on his feet, I'd take whatever flak got thrown my way.

"Do you like them?" I asked.

He nodded and, for the first time ever, looked me in the eyes. His beautiful, big brown eyes were filled with tears of joy.

"Do you not have any other shoes, Mason?"

He looked down and shook his head.

"Then I guess it's a good thing that the Thanksgiving shoe pixies stopped by today."

A small grin spread on Mason's face, revealing a dimple on his left cheek. No matter what I had to do, I was going to make it my mission in life to see that adorable dimple every day.

"You've reached Logan Kendrick. Please leave a message."

"Logan. It's me again. Please call me back." I was driving home for Thanksgiving break. It had been over two and a half weeks since I had told Logan I was still married, the same night I had kissed Nick, and I hadn't talked to either man since.

When Nick had dropped me off that night, I'd asked him to give me some space. He'd immediately rejected my plea, but after I'd begged him to give me time to process everything, he'd reluctantly agreed.

Though, my time was coming to an end. Before driving away, he'd declared, "You've got until Thanksgiving to get your head together. I am not letting you go, but I'll give you some time."

It wasn't for a lack of trying that I hadn't spoken to Logan. I had called him every day but he hadn't answered my calls. We had become so distant these last few months, we hadn't even made holiday plans. I was tempted to charter a jet back to New York so I could see him on Thanksgiving tomorrow and we could talk face-to-face.

Could our relationship be repaired? The guilt I felt for kissing Nick was crushing and I would never be able to keep it a secret. But if I told Logan about it, that would be the end. He would never forgive me for kissing another man.

And though it was heartbreaking to think of my life without Logan, I wouldn't blame him. This was all my fault.

I pulled into my driveway, which was currently occupied by a large, black Cadillac SUV parked by the garage. The driver's door opened and a tall man stepped out, wearing a black wool dress coat and jeans.

Logan.

I had no idea what he was doing in Montana but it didn't matter. Whatever his reasons, I was just glad to see him.

Jumping out of the Jeep, I walked right to him and wrapped my arms around his waist, burrowing my head into his chest.

I held my breath, waiting for his reaction, hoping he

wouldn't push me away.

When his arms closed tightly around my shoulders and his cheek dropped to my head, the air rushed out of my lungs.

"I missed you."

"I missed you too," he said, kissing my hair.

"Are you here to break up with me?"

He chuckled. "I wasn't planning on it."

"Good," I said, squeezing him tighter.

I took a few deep breaths, inhaling his Armani cologne, before pulling away. Logan always smelled good.

Nick smells better.

That unwelcome comparison ran right through my mind without control. Silently scolding myself, I looked into Logan's brown eyes. My brain unwillingly conjured up the image of Nick's vibrant hazel ones.

Nick's eyes are better too.

What was wrong with me? Why was I standing here with my amazingly handsome boyfriend thinking about Nick Slater?

Because I was bat-shit crazy. That's why.

"You okay?" Logan asked.

"What? Oh. Yes. I think I'm still in shock that you're actually here," I lied.

"Sorry. I should have called, but I just needed some time. I'm tired of having phone conversations."

"Me too. We need to talk."

"We do, but not this second. I was thinking we could barricade ourselves in your house and camp out in the bedroom. We can talk in there, among other things." He grinned.

"I like that plan. But we're going to need provisions. Otherwise, we'll starve to death. All I have left in the house

91

is Diet Coke and a half-eaten bag of Swedish Fish."

"Is there a Chinese place in town where we could get some takeout for Thanksgiving tomorrow?" he asked.

A huge smile took over my face. I'd been terribly depressed, thinking of spending my first Prescott holiday alone. But now with Logan here, it would be like normal. "You're in luck, darling. Along with one take-n-bake pizza place, there are exactly four restaurants in Prescott, one of which is Peking Garden Chinese."

"Excellent. Show me this town of yours, sweetheart. Get us our Thanksgiving feast."

Five minutes later, we were driving the Jeep into town. "When do you have to go back?"

"Friday evening," he said.

"Right." I frowned. That meant we weren't going to get all weekend together. Instead, we'd have less than forty-eight hours.

"I'm behind as it is, Emmeline. Taking a couple of days off right now isn't helping. I'm just hoping if I check in today and work for a couple hours tomorrow, I won't go home to a disaster."

It hadn't been my idea for him to fly out here. If this was such an inconvenient trip, why had he even bothered to come? We could have talked on the phone. Was he here to make me feel guilty for two days? Because I didn't need his help for that.

I kept my eyes on the road and bit my lip. I didn't want to get into an argument with Logan twenty minutes into his visit.

"I thought it would be prettier. Greener maybe," Logan said.

"What do you mean?"

"Montana. I thought it would be prettier. Everything is brown."

"Are you crazy? It is pretty," I said. "I think the contrast between the flat land down here and all of the mountains and forest around us is breathtaking. And the grass is *golden* because it's winter."

"Don't be offended. I just had a different image in my head," he said and looked at his phone.

I used the rest of the drive to calm down.

Why were we snapping at each other? We had never fought when I'd lived in the city. We'd been short with one another lately but I had assumed it was because we'd been adjusting to a long-distance relationship. Maybe there was more behind those calls than I had wanted to admit.

"Let's walk around Main Street a bit," I said. "It's really cute and I could show you some of my favorite spots."

I loved the quaint feel of Main Street. Maybe Logan would too. All of the stores had character. Nothing matched but everything went together. And it came together naturally, not forced like it was on so many of the Manhattan streets where I had once lived.

The window displays weren't professionally designed. The signs weren't expertly coordinated. Prescott wasn't fancy or elaborate, but it had real charm. Its allure was in the people who took pride in their work and town.

Logan held my hand as we strolled down the street. I occasionally pointed out different stores that I liked, but instead of finding anything positive about them, he made a few comments about the plethora of Western apparel and the abundance of horseshoes.

I brushed off his remarks and kept walking, hoping he wasn't going to be so judgmental during his entire visit.

As we passed the sporting goods store, I caught a glimpse of our reflection in the glass door and laughed.

"What?" Logan asked.

"We look out of place. I'm still dressed up from school. You're perfectly styled as always. The only thing about us that goes with Prescott is your jeans."

"That's because we are out of place, Emmeline."

My laughter stopped immediately at the sight of his serious face. "It was a joke, Logan. Why are you acting like this?"

"Your joke wasn't funny and I'm acting like I always do. I apologize for not being overjoyed to spend Thanksgiving in Montana, walking around a little town with my girlfriend, who has somehow convinced herself that she fits in here."

"Then why did you come?" I asked, stopping on the sidewalk.

"Because we need to have a conversation about your marriage. I've got a conference call scheduled with Andrews on Friday morning before I leave. I need to be better informed about what he's doing but he won't discuss the divorce proceedings with me unless you are present."

"Logan, tell me you didn't go around me to Fred Andrews. Not after I told you I was getting it taken care of."

"You had nine years to get it taken care of and you didn't. So yes, I went around you."

"Why?" I asked.

"Why? Maybe because I had hoped someday you would be *my* wife. That the ring I've tried to give you twice now might actually go on your finger."

My anger was immediately replaced with guilt.

Shit.

I had been so consumed with getting an explanation

from Nick, I hadn't taken enough action for Logan. When I found myself living in the same town as my lost husband, I should have immediately gotten my ass back to New York, explained everything to Logan and then personally picked up my divorce papers. Instead, I had spent a week going out on dates with Nick and then made out with him, plastered against a wall in his house.

I was not a good girlfriend.

Just as I was opening my mouth to apologize, a familiar voice rumbled from behind me.

"Not happening, pal. She's mine."

"This is not happening," I muttered and turned around to face Nick. "Stay out of this, Nick."

"No," he said.

"The husband, I presume?" Logan stepped into the space beside me and threw his arm around my shoulders, his whole frame rigid.

"Yeah. And since I'm her husband, how about you get your fucking hands off her?"

"I'll touch her whenever I please. I have for the last five years."

"Enough!" I said, ending this ridiculous macho man show before it got carried away. "The only person that gets to decide who touches me and when, is me. Stop acting like Neanderthals."

"Time to go, Emmeline," Logan declared and grabbed my hand, pulling me behind him as we marched back to the Jeep.

The sound of boots thudded on the pavement behind us. I slipped my hand free from Logan and spun around, again facing Nick.

I was desperate for him to leave me be. The last thing

I wanted was for Nick to mention that we had kissed. That was my story to tell Logan, on my terms, but Nick's eyes were determined. He was going to do whatever it took to keep me apart from Logan.

"Stop," I whispered. "Let me go."

"Never." His face gentled and he looked down at me with his own desperation. "Emmy, don't do this. Don't stay with him just because you're still holding onto the idea that life will go back to how it was. Everything has changed. Be honest with yourself, and with him. We're it for each other. You walked back into my life and I won't leave you again. And deep down, you don't want me to let you go."

"Emmeline," Logan called.

I choked down the lump in my throat and blinked away my tears. "Coming."

The drive home was silent, but the moment I parked in the driveway, Logan reached for my hand.

"You love him." He wasn't angry and yelling. He sounded defeated and sad.

I shook my head. "No. But I did once."

"It's still there, sweetheart," Logan said, stroking the back of my hand with his thumb.

I wanted to protest but I couldn't. I was too confused about my feelings for Nick. In one night, I had fallen in love with him. I thought that years of anger and hatred had erased all of that love. But spending time with him, kissing him, had brought it all back. Only, the hatred was still there too. How could I get rid of one without the other?

"When you walked away from him, I've never seen pain like that on your face before. Not even when your father was at his worst. I want to be the man to take it from you, Emmeline, to carry that pain so you can live a life of happiness. But it's never going to be me."

"What? What are you saying, Logan?" I asked.

"I never even stood a chance. Nothing I can ever do will be enough. He'll always have that piece of you."

I shook my head. "You're reading too much into this. He just upset me. And you and I had been arguing. There was a lot of emotion flying around. Let's just forget it and have a nice Thanksgiving together. Please?"

"He calls you Emmy."

"He always has. What does that matter?"

"When we first met, I called you Emmy once. You corrected me and said you hated that nickname. But that wasn't true. You didn't want me to call you Emmy because it was already his."

He was right. There were things I wouldn't give him because Nick had been there first. I'd convinced myself I hated nicknames and kisses on the tip of my nose. I didn't, really, but I'd told myself I did. Because it hurt too much to be reminded of Nick.

He had been right.

Everything had changed.

Living in Montana had shed light on the problems Logan and I'd had before Nick had ever gotten thrown into the mix. Logan and I wanted different lifestyles. I had found a home in Montana and he loved New York. I was happier living a quieter life while he thrived on busy workdays and a hectic social calendar.

"It's not just Nick, is it?" I whispered. "It's me here. You there. I'm not coming back. And you'll never leave."

"No. It's not just him."

We sat in silence for a few moments until Logan spoke. "I think I had better change my answer to your previous question. I believe I am here to break up with you."

I knew it was coming but that didn't make it any less painful to hear. My breath hitched and I struggled to get it back.

When I twisted my neck to look into his eyes, the ache in my chest grew so fierce I feared my heart would stop beating. "I'm so sorry, Logan."

"Me too." Reaching across the console, he cupped the back of my head and pulled me in for a kiss.

I let our good-bye kiss convey all of the things I didn't say. That I was grateful for every moment we'd had together. That I would never be able to thank him enough for all the wonderful things he had done for me these past five years. That I would always remember him and care for him deeply.

"Be happy," he said, then climbed out of my Jeep and got in his SUV, backing out of my driveway and out of my life.

When he was no longer in my rearview mirror, I collapsed into the steering wheel with body-wrenching sobs.

CHAPTER 8

"**Y**OU KNOW I LOVE SEEING YOU, DEAR. Especially around the holidays. But I think you'd better tell me why you called to say 'Merry Christmas' and fourteen hours later you're here in Italy."

My mother and I were sitting side by side in the spa at the CastaDiva Resort on Lake Como. My body was wrapped in a white plush robe and my feet were getting an elaborate pedicure.

Yesterday morning I had been home in Montana. Today I was in Italy for an unplanned but necessary vacation.

"It's a long story, Mom," I said.

"Then we'd best get a bottle of wine while you tell me what is going on."

"You'd better make it two."

An hour later, she was caught up on my complicated love life and we were both tipsy.

"What happened after Logan left?" she asked.

"I drove to the grocery store and loaded up on junk food. Then I camped out on the couch for the rest of the weekend, binge-watching old episodes of *Friends* for four days."

"Have you talked to him?"

"Logan? No. I sent him a text saying Merry Christmas but that was it." I left out the part where he had responded by asking me not to text him again because he needed to put some distance between us. Apparently, two thousand miles weren't enough.

"And Nick?" she asked.

"He came to my school the Monday after Thanksgiving. I said I wasn't ready to see him yet and asked him to stop pushing. He agreed, but I think it was only because I told him Logan and I had broken up."

The look of relief on Nick's face was burned into my brain. I'd wanted to slap him for being so glad that I had been heartbroken. But at the same time, that look had been honest and pure. Everything that he had been telling me had been true.

He wasn't playing a game. He wanted another chance and he had been genuinely scared that I would choose Logan.

"I haven't seen him, but he sends me text messages every day," I said. "Usually just says hello. Tells me what he's up to. They're thoughtful."

"Hmm. And why did you come here?" she asked.

"I was lonely," I confessed. "I poured myself into work after Thanksgiving. There is this boy in my class that I've been trying to get to open up to me, so I spent a lot of extra time creating special activities he would like. But school is on break right now and I was sitting at home, alone, and needed to get out of there. The whole town of Prescott was decked out in Christmas. I didn't even have a tree. It was depressing."

"Sounds like you are running away to pout."

"I am n—" I started but clamped my mouth shut. "I know," I sighed.

"What do you want to do about Nick?"

"I don't know. What would you do?"

"It's not my decision, Emmeline. But in my opinion, there's a reason why you didn't get divorced. And it has nothing to do with your father's absurd logic or pride. It's the same reason why you turned Logan down when he asked you to marry him. The fact that you moved to the same town where Nick lived is . . . unbelievable. It's fate. If it were me? I would see where it goes. You two might not make it. But at least you finally have that chance to try."

"What if I can't ever get over it, forgive him for leaving me?" I asked.

"Darling, your heart already has," she said. "You just need to give your brain a chance to catch up."

The society rags loved to portray my mother as snobbish and shallow. In many ways, she was. Her affairs had always made Page Six and she had never tried to hide her wealth.

But she had a softer side, one she mostly reserved for her children and loved ones. One she kept hidden from the public eye as a means to keep the vultures at bay.

Collette Austin was incredibly smart and kind. And when it came to me, she had the uncanny ability to read my suppressed emotions. Mom often knew how I was feeling even before I did. For a New York socialite turned permanent Italian tourist, she was incredibly wise.

"Thanks, Mom. And thanks for letting me barge in on your holiday plans. Is Alesso going to be put out?" I asked.

"I love to have you here any time. Pouting or not." She smiled. "And Alesso's fine. He loves you. I think he was relieved, actually, when I told him we were going to spend the whole day at the spa. His family is visiting, and whenever they're around, he has to interpret for me. They talk too fast for me to keep up."

"You know, you could learn his language."

"Ridiculous." She waved her hand in the air to dismiss the idea. "How long are you staying?"

"Through New Year's. I need to get back a few days before school starts again to prepare."

"Excellent! I want to go on a lake tour to see all of the Christmas lights but Alesso is scared of boats. You can go with me."

"Sounds wonderful," I said.

Cruising around the Lake Como coast would be frigid but taking in the gorgeous, snow-covered Italian buildings trimmed with sparkling Christmas lights was worth braving the cold.

"I've missed you, dear," she said. "We're going to plan a trip to Montana. I need to see what the fuss is all about."

"I've missed you too. Visit anytime before summer."

I didn't expand on my timing request. Instead, I relaxed into my seat and closed my eyes. While one technician manicured my fingernails, another started a facial.

If I decided to move away from Prescott this summer, Lake Como, Italy, was quickly climbing up my list for potential new hometowns.

Nick

Fuck space.

I'd tried to respect Emmy's wishes and give her time to herself, but that shit wasn't working for me anymore. Now that she was back from wherever she'd gone for the holidays, her space was as good as gone.

It had been over a month since I'd seen her, and though I'd kept in touch, sending a text message every day wasn't the same as looking at her beautiful face.

I needed to touch her. To smell the coconut in her hair. To look into her eyes.

So, fuck space. I was switching tactics.

I had pushed her hard in Vegas with my dares and challenges. And since I'd had much better results then, I would try that again now.

Raising my fist, I pounded on her front door.

I watched her march my way through one of the five rectangular windows that filled the front door, rolling her eyes when she realized I was at her house.

Christ, I loved that eye roll.

"What are you doing here?" she asked.

I didn't answer. I just bent down to pick up the bags resting at my feet and pushed past her into the house, walking straight to the kitchen.

"Nick!" she called but I ignored her again. I deposited the groceries on the island while she scowled at me from the kitchen doorway. My teeth clenched together and I fought back a curse. She'd lost weight and there were dark purple rings under her eyes.

"Come on, Emmy. We're making dinner. From the looks of it, you could use a decent meal."

DEVNEY PERRY

"What the hell is that supposed to mean?"

"It means you look like shit. When's the last time you ate? Those clothes are hanging off of you." The black dress she wore looked more like a rectangular bag than a fitted dress. Though, her legs still looked smoking hot in those tall-ass shoes.

Her eyes got wide and her mouth fell open an inch. "Excuse me? Insulting me is not doing you any favors."

"Emmy, even exhausted and miserable, you're the most beautiful woman in the world so don't get too bent out of shape. Now get in here so we can start cooking."

Her face flushed and I turned away to start un-bagging groceries, smiling to myself.

I gave her a few moments and then ordered, "Emmy. Get in here. Find a cutting board and a knife."

"You're not going to leave me alone, are you?"

I spun around to look her directly in the eyes. "Abso-fucking-lutely not."

"Oh for the love . . ." she muttered and stomped into the kitchen.

"Get out a frying pan too. And a big wooden spoon."

She opened cupboard after cupboard to get my tools. Coffee mugs were in every one. She must have a hundred of them tucked away.

"What are you making?" she asked.

"Fajitas," I said. "And you're making them."

"I assume you'll be helping me?"

I smiled.

Her eyes moved to my mouth and her breath hitched. She was just as affected by me as I was by her. I just needed to get her to admit it so we could move forward.

Five minutes later, she was at the island attempting to

chop a green bell pepper.

Holy fuck, she was bad at this. "You're doing great."

Her slices were six times too wide, nothing like the example I'd shown her. Not only were her cuts uneven, making them took forever. If I didn't step in to help, we wouldn't eat until midnight.

"I'll just do a few of these too," I said, reaching for an onion. I wanted to tease her but decided to save it for a different day when we were on better terms.

When she'd finally finished with one pepper, I'd sliced the other three, the onion and the chicken.

"Spices next. Sprinkle a teaspoon of all three over the meat and vegetables," I said, handing her three small jars.

After finishing her task, she hopped up on the counter to drink the glass of wine I had handed her.

I took a deep breath and summoned all of my willpower to keep from walking into the space between her legs and taking her mouth. Someday soon I was going to have her again. She would be right here in the kitchen, in that exact position, moaning my name.

"Where did you learn to cook?" she asked.

"Mostly from experimenting on my own. After Mom died, Dad tried to cook for my brother and me but his food was shit. He gave up and would just take us to McDonald's or Taco Bell. I got sick of eating fast food so I started to mess around in the kitchen. I wasn't good at it at first but then I started to get the hang of it."

"I'm sorry."

"Don't be. Other than Mom not being there, I enjoyed it." I went to the fridge and grabbed one of the beers I'd brought over. "Where'd you run off to?"

"I decided to go see my mom last minute," she said.

"Wait. How did you know I was gone?"

"I came by to give you your Christmas present and saw you'd left. I checked on the house a couple of times while you were gone."

"Oh. You didn't need to do that, but thank you. You really got me a Christmas gift?" she asked.

"Isn't it customary to buy your spouse a present? Does that mean you didn't get me anything?" I feigned surprise.

"You are not funny."

I smiled. "You say that now, but just wait until you get my present."

I'd gotten her a coffee mug for her collection. I thought it was hilarious and hoped she'd like it too. But now, after seeing the insides of her kitchen cabinets, I was concerned that she already had it.

"I thought you said your mom lived in Italy. Is that where you went?"

"She does. And yes, they live in Milan but usually spend the holidays at a resort on Lake Como. I spent a couple weeks with her and Alesso there."

"I'm glad you could go see her."

"Me too. What did you do?"

"Nothing much. Took a few days off work. Spent some time chopping firewood. Read a book."

"You didn't go anywhere for Christmas?" she asked.

"I did. I came here."

Her shoulders fell. "Sorry. I just needed some time away."

I walked from the island to stand at her side and leaned down into her face, gently taking hold of her chin. "I get that, Emmy. But no more running away. I told you I'm not letting you go, so you need to get used to having me in your life. Every day. No more space."

"I am not ready. I just ended a five-year relationship."

"Get ready," I said. "I thought about you every day for nine years, wondered what you were doing. I had questions I wanted to ask but couldn't. Those nine years are on me. It was my mistake to walk away from you but I'm not doing it again. And I won't let you do it either. All I'm asking for is time. I'll prove to you that you can trust me again."

"I can't promise to forgive you, Nick. It still hurts."

The pain behind her words was like a punch to the gut.

I was such a fucking asshole.

"I don't need a promise. Just a chance to erase that pain," I said and leaned all the way down to brush my lips across hers. She was frozen stiff but that didn't stop me from keeping my lips against hers for a few perfect seconds.

When I leaned back, tears glistened in her eyes.

"Don't cry, my sweet Emmy."

She sniffled and blinked away the tears. "Can we change the subject?"

"Yeah. What to?"

"Which book did you read over Christmas?"

I walked to the stove. "*The Count of Monte Cristo*. It's a favorite."

For the next hour, we talked about books and ate dinner. Emmy relaxed and we were able to enjoy each other's company without drama or stress. It was the best meal I'd had in years. Because I was finally with my Emmy.

Emmeline

"What's wrong?" Nick asked.

"Nothing," I lied, erasing the scowl on my face.

Nick had just sidestepped the stream of children rushing out the door. He smiled at each of them, but when Rowen Cleary had run up to him, he had picked her up and tossed her in the air, calling her "princess" and asking about her day.

Nick would make a great dad.

It was happening again. Spontaneous Nick thoughts.

That one had come out of nowhere and caused my face to scrunch up. My bat-shit craziness was getting worse.

"What are you doing here?"

"Picking you up for dinner," he said.

"It's only three thirty. I prefer to put at least six hours between meals and I ate lunch at noon."

"I'm not here to take you now, Emmy. But I'm giving you a heads-up that I'll be back at five thirty. Don't drive home."

"You could have texted me all of this," I said.

"Yeah. But then I wouldn't have been able to do this."

He crossed the space between us in a millisecond and captured my mouth, wrapping his arms around my waist. His lips pressed roughly against mine as his tongue swept my lower lip. Over and over he stroked until my mouth fell open. When his tongue found mine, I melted. Heat erupted throughout my body and my knees gave out.

When I started to sink to the floor, he stopped kissing me but tightened his grip on my waist.

"I've got you." A crooked grin formed on his lips.

I took a moment to steady my legs and stand tall before

stepping back a foot. The skin around my mouth was surely pink from the contact with his beard. But at least it would match my flushed cheeks.

"Five thirty," he said and walked out the door.

Shit.

Thinking clearly was not an option after a Nick kiss but I really needed to pull myself together. I'd spent last night tossing and turning, replaying all the things Nick had told me these last few months.

You've always had my heart, Emmy.

We're it for each other.

I thought about you every day for nine years.

And I thought about what my mother had said. That my heart had already forgiven him and I just needed to get my head straight with that concept.

Sinking into my chair, I let my head fall into my hands. "What am I going to do?"

I tried to picture what our life could be like. Me happy. Nick and I living a normal life. But every time that image popped in my head, it was immediately followed by the vision of me waking up alone to a note that said he was sorry.

Time was ticking away and I needed to make some decisions. My attorney had emailed me while I was in Italy to say he'd have my divorce papers drafted by the end of the month. Nick was not going to stop inserting himself into my life unless I made it clear we were over.

Were we over?

For nine years, I'd thought we were. But so much was different now. He was everything that I remembered. Kind. Affectionate. Intelligent.

And stubborn. Every time I tried to push him away, he just pushed back harder. But honestly, I really hadn't put up much of a fight against his advances.

"Ten seconds ago, you let him stick his tongue down your throat with no fight at all, Emmeline," I mumbled into my hands.

"Ms. Austin?"

My head flew up. Mason Carpenter was standing in front of my desk. "Mason. I'm sorry. I thought all of you kids had gone home. Are you okay?" I asked, standing up, then kneeling by his feet.

Ever since I had bought the children shoes, Mason had started opening up to me. He still wasn't speaking to any of his fellow students, with the exception of Rowen, but now he would talk to me as long as I was kneeling down with him and no other students were listening.

"I was wondering if I could eat lunch inside tomorrow with you," he whispered.

"Sure," I said. "Can you tell me why you don't want to go outside with the other kids?"

"It's really cold outside. And today Rowen gave me her extra coat but the other kids were making fun of me because it was pink."

How had I not noticed Rowen bringing him another coat? Or that he hadn't been wearing one when he'd arrived at school? I made a mental note to email Rich again, hoping this would be enough to start digging further into Mason's home situation.

"You know? This will work out perfectly. I was just going to ask if you wouldn't mind helping me over lunch. I'm really having a hard time getting all of my work done and the classroom set up for our afternoon activities. Maybe you could help me?"

He nodded and gave me a small smile.

"Maybe we can check to see if Rowen wants to help out too."

This time, I got the dimple.

"Where are we going?"

"The fire station," Nick said, driving along the highway.

Past two gas stations, Main Street merged with the highway that led out of town. Other than my trips to the grocery store, I hadn't explored the businesses in this area, so I stared out the window, taking them all in.

We had almost reached the hospital when Nick turned left and followed a side street to a tall, narrow building made of gray concrete blocks. In its center was a large white garage door. A Prescott Fire Department sign arched above it.

Nick parked alongside the building and climbed out to open my door. He captured my hand and tugged me behind him as he unlocked a tinted glass door and walked inside the station.

"Wow." My eyes traveled around the large, concrete room. "It's much bigger on the inside than I would have guessed."

"The tour's pretty easy since you can see everything from this spot. But that's the fire truck," he said, pointing out the obvious. The red truck occupied half of the long building, other than some tools mounted on the walls.

"That far wall has all the volunteer lockers where we stow the gear. My office is over there," he said, indicating a room made mostly of glass panels in the back corner. "Behind it is the bathroom. And over here is the on-call pit."

He pulled me toward a lounge area at our left.

The space was filled with two old couches and three beat-up recliners, all of which were pointed at a huge TV. Under the television was a cabinet filled with every gaming console imaginable and a pile of action films.

"What's an on-call pit?"

"A place for the on-call volunteers to hang out. This time of year, we don't have the volunteers stay at the station. Whoever is on-call just has to make sure they're in town and can be reached on their pagers. But during forest fire season, we have them stay here. I take the day shifts since most of them have regular jobs, but they come in and spot me at night."

"Do they get paid? Or are they truly volunteers?" I asked.

"They get paid. It's not enough to make a living but it makes their time hanging out here worth it. And we all make serious cake if we get pulled in on a fire."

"Interesting. So what are we doing here? Are you on-call or something?"

"No. Thought I'd show you the station and make you dinner."

"Here?" There was a kitchen behind the lounge area but it was tiny.

"Yeah. Spaghetti okay?" he asked.

"Sure. Though, I shouldn't have worn a white top today." Somehow I always managed to spill red sauces on myself.

He smiled. "You can borrow a sweatshirt."

I climbed up on a stool by the kitchen and visited with him while he did his cooking, admiring the way he moved in the small space. For a man with such muscle and size, Nick was graceful, and in the kitchen, it made him sexy as hell.

Thankfully, he asked me about my day, so rather than

sit and ogle his body, I launched into my whole story about Mason.

"Have you talked to Jess?" he asked.

"Jess? No. Why?"

"I'm sure he'd look into it for you."

"I would but I don't want to go around Rich. I don't know if that would be professional. Though, I'd love to move this along a little quicker. It's really cold out right now. What if Mason doesn't have heat at home? Or food?" The thought of cute little Mason Carpenter freezing or starving to death made my stomach ache.

"Just ask the kid, Emmy. If you think he's at risk, then talk to Garcia again. If he still delays getting Jess involved, go around him. The last thing you want is for something horrible to happen to this kid because you were hesitant to push."

"You're right." I frowned. I didn't want to alienate Rich or worse, risk my job, but if that's what it would take to get Mason through the winter, that's just what I would have to do.

"I'll cheer you up," Nick said after putting a handful of noodles into a pot of boiling water.

I gave him a sideways glance and raised my eyebrows.

He smiled and pulled a square box from a bag on the counter. It was wrapped in green foil with a red and white ribbon on top.

"My present?"

"I hope you don't have it already."

Carefully opening the paper, I unfolded the top of the box and lifted out a white ceramic coffee mug. In swirly black script, the cup read *Sorry I'm late . . . I didn't want to come.*

My nose started to burn and I rapidly blinked the tears away.

It was perfect.

Logan had always made fun of me for my coffee cup obsession and discouraged me from buying such "witless trinkets." He would have never bought me one.

Nick frowned. "You don't like it."

"No! It's wonderful," I said. "Thank you."

"It wasn't much. But I saw it and it made me think of you."

"It's just the type of mug I would have bought myself. I'm sorry I didn't get you anything."

"I only need you, Emmy," he said and went back to the stove.

Wow, that felt good.

Twenty minutes later, I was sitting on one of the on-call pit's leather couches, wearing a huge red Prescott Fire Department sweatshirt and scarfing down the best spaghetti I had ever tasted.

If being married to Nick means I get to eat meals like this on a regular basis, I might have to call Fred Andrews and cancel those divorce papers.

Another spontaneous Nick thought.

CHAPTER 9

I WAS MIDGULP WITH A CAN OF DIET COKE PRESSED to my lips when a dark figure walked into my living room. I tried to scream but choked instead. The soda lodged in my throat and I started to panic.

The figure walked through the foyer and into the light. It was none other than my current, maybe future ex, husband.

"Fuck," Nick muttered, rushing to my side. "Breathe, Emmy."

Diet Coke was dripping down my chin and coming out my nose while he patted my back. "Tissue," I choked out.

From his pocket, he produced a red bandana and shoved it in my face. "Here."

I cleaned off my face and took a few deep breaths, savoring the oxygen.

"What the fuck, Emmy?" Nick yelled.

"What? Don't 'What the fuck, Emmy?' me! What the fuck to you? Why are you breaking into my house? You scared the shit out of me!"

"Why is your security system off?"

"It's five thirty. I just got home."

"You need to set it all the time. They only work when they are fucking turned on."

"Relax," I said, rolling my eyes. "I highly doubt that at five thirty on a Friday night in Prescott, Montana, someone is going to attempt a break-in. Even if it is dark out."

"Yeah? Maybe ask Gigi Cleary what time she was kidnapped."

My anger deflated when I realized he was mad because he was scared.

Logan had been the same way, overprotective and quick to anger when he thought I was being careless. So as much as it annoyed me, I gave in. I didn't have the energy to debate his ridiculous request and rub his male ego the wrong way.

"Okay." I raised my hands in surrender. "I'll set it all the time. Now what are you doing here? I thought you wanted to eat in town."

Earlier today, he had texted me, asking if we could eat dinner at the café. It had been two weeks since Nick started having dinner with me and he hadn't missed a single night.

Mostly we would eat at my house, but a couple of times he had collected me from school and had taken me to different places in town. On the weekends, he had come over early, and instead of cooking for me, he'd cook with me, my culinary lessons lasting all evening.

"Jess called me and said they are having a last-minute party at the farmhouse."

"And my attendance is required?" I asked. Part of me wanted to get out and do something social but the other was content to lounge at home in yoga pants.

"My attendance is required, therefore yours is too," he said.

"Okay. Let me get changed." Fifteen minutes later, I was ready to go. I had pulled on a pair of super-stretchy skinny jeans, because they were almost like yoga pants, and an oversized black sweater. But since I didn't want to be too slouchy, I'd dressed them up with a pair of black suede, over-the-knee boots.

Clicking down the stairs, I scanned the house to find Nick. I loved that from the floating steps I could see almost all of the main floor and kitchen.

Nick was pacing along the back windowed wall of the living room, his phone pressed to his ear. When he heard my heeled feet hit the landing, he quickly hung up his call.

"Is everything okay?" I asked.

"Yeah. Ready?"

"Yes. But do we need to bring anything?"

"Beer. I picked it up on the way here so we wouldn't have to drive all the way into town."

As we drove through the darkness, Nick reached out and captured my hand. He brought it to his lips and spoke against my skin. "Those are some boots."

"What?" I asked. "What's wrong with them?"

"They're sexy as fuck. Sometime I'm going to see what you look like wearing them and nothing else," he said.

I was glad the truck's cab was dark and he couldn't see my cheeks flush. A shiver ran through my body and my sex started throbbing at the mental image he'd conjured.

Nick and I hadn't done anything but kiss these last few weeks and he'd kept them all PG-rated. He'd brush his lips quickly against my cheek or my temple, his soft beard giving me tingles. More often, he would lean down and kiss the tip of my nose.

And that's exactly how I had wanted it. I wasn't ready to take things any further. But my body was protesting my brain's decision. At this very minute, it was running hot.

I rationalized it as a lack of sexual activity. I hadn't had sex since moving from New York, five months ago. Back then, Logan and I'd had a great sex life. My feelings were all just a result of going cold turkey. Right?

Nick laughed. "Stop thinking about sex, Emmy."

Shit.

The sexual tension in the truck was stifling. Of course he knew I was thinking about sex, so there was no use denying it. Luckily, the drive was short and soon we turned down the gravel lane that led to the Clearys' home.

The farmhouse was outside of town and not all that far from mine. Their place was set further into the prairie but the back of their property butted up against the same forest that surrounded my house.

As we walked toward the enormous garage, which was perpendicular to the farmhouse, all of the sexual energy I'd been feeling was replaced with anxiety.

Nick must have felt my nervousness, that or heard my pounding heartbeat, because he shifted the six-pack he was carrying and grabbed my hand.

His hand-holding should have been comforting but it was actually making things worse.

The last time I had been here, I'd bolted right after the Halloween party had started. I'd seen the Clearys since but no one else from that night. Prescott was too small for Nick's friends and acquaintances not to know who I was. What did they think of me?

Usually I didn't care much about what people thought,

but here things were different than they had been in the city. I wanted to *fit* in Prescott and I worried that I didn't.

But that wouldn't stop me from trying.

I wanted to be a beloved member of the community, like Gigi Cleary. Everyone talked about her with admiration. Even though she wasn't a Montana native, she was one of Prescott's adored citizens. I wanted to be the adored kindergarten teacher. At least for as long as I was living here.

All of the people here tonight were Nick's friends and long-time Prescott residents. What were they going to think of me waltzing into a party, holding Nick's hand?

"Don't stress, Emmy," he said.

"Easy for you to say. These are your friends. I'm just the estranged wife."

Nick stopped us a few feet away from the garage door. "These are good people and they won't judge. Besides, they all know that the reason we were *previously* estranged was because of me."

"What? You told them?" I asked.

"Yeah. I didn't go into specifics but I let them know that any anger or hostility you had toward me was well deserved. They all know that I was the one in the wrong."

"Why would you tell them that?"

"Prescott's a small place. I didn't want gossip flying around and getting out of hand," he said.

He had protected my reputation without being asked. He'd never know how much that meant to me, but it was the world. "Thank you," I whispered.

"We're going to walk in there and the women are going to steal you away."

"I'm sure I'll be fine."

"*You* will be. I won't. I've liked having you all to myself these last couple weeks."

He could be so unbelievably sweet. "I'd be lying if I said I didn't feel a little of the same."

"We're going to make it, Emmy." He pulled me inside before I could respond.

The garage was decked out with balloons, streamers and crepe paper. Across the back wall was a huge banner that read *Happy Kidnap-versary!*

"Ms. Austin!" Rowen called at the same time her mother exclaimed, "Emmeline!"

Nick was not wrong. I hadn't been inside for more than five seconds before Gigi pulled me into the huddle of women standing next to the snack table. It was filled with so much food that it rivaled some of the spreads I'd had catered for my father's fundraising galas.

"Emmeline, meet Maisy Holt," Gigi said, introducing me to a beautiful blond woman with doe-shaped gray eyes and a warm smile. A cute brunette baby with dark brown eyes was perched on her hip. "And this is her son, Coby. Isn't he the cutest thing?"

"He's adorable," I said, leaning in to coo at the baby. "How old is he?" I asked Maisy.

She smiled. "Five months."

I knew about Maisy Holt from the news archives I'd dug up last fall. Coby's father was the drug-dealing whacko that had kidnapped both Gigi and Maisy with the intention of murdering them.

"This is my mother-in-law, Noelle." Gigi continued with the introductions. "And this is Sara Phillips. She works with me at the hospital, and her husband, Milo, is one of Jess's deputies." Sara was a young woman with strawberry-blond hair and green eyes.

"Where's your baby?" I asked Gigi when the introductions were finished. "I've been dying to meet him."

Every day, Rowen had come to school and given me a report of what baby Ben had done the previous night. He'd been born two weeks before Christmas and his proud big sister talked about him nonstop.

"I'll go steal him from Jess. He's a Benny hog." She smiled and went to the other side of the garage where the men had congregated.

"Ms. Austin, do you want to see my kitties?" Rowen asked, yanking on my hand.

"Oh, I'd love to," I said as she led me to a small alcove. I met all of her cats before Gigi came over with a bundled, sleeping baby in her arms.

"He's big, isn't he?" I asked as she placed him in my arms. I hadn't been around a lot of babies but I was surprised at how heavy he was for only being six weeks old. Ben wasn't all that smaller than Coby Holt, despite the age difference.

"He's huge. Ninety-fifth percentile on the growth charts."

"Oh, my," I said. "So, what's the party for? I didn't get a chance to ask Nick when we got here." The unique banner had me wondering.

"Maisy and I were kidnapped a year ago and we decided that instead of hiding out at home, we'd throw a party."

Nick's overreaction to my unarmed security system made more sense now.

She gave me a mischievous grin. "Jess was none too happy with our party idea. Ever since Ben was born, he won't hardly let me do a thing. But I've been going stir-crazy on maternity leave so Maisy and I just planned the party while he was at work. Then this morning I went to the station and told him to bring home some drinks and tell his friends."

I giggled. The way that she'd outmaneuvered her husband's overprotectiveness was entertaining.

"Emmeline," Jess said at my side.

"Hi, Jess. Congratulations on little Ben here. How are you?"

"Doing good. Be even better if my wife would listen to me."

"Not happening, Sheriff," Gigi said.

"Been meaning to swing by the school and talk to you. Care if we do it now?" he asked.

"Not at all."

"Gotta talk about those shoes," he said.

My nose scrunched up and I didn't try to hide my grimace.

As I had expected, I'd received many, many calls from concerned parents after giving my students shoes before Thanksgiving. Other than Mason's parents, the Clearys were the only ones who I hadn't talked to yet.

With every call, I had told the parents the truth. Or a vague version of the truth.

That a wealthy friend from New York donated them for my first class of students. It had actually been Principal Garcia's idea not to admit that I had personally purchased the shoes. He hadn't wanted to create any animosity with other teachers or draw attention to Mason's home life. I had been glad for his advice, and so far, my story had worked.

But I had a feeling that a vague half-truth would not satisfy the Jamison County sheriff.

"I'm sorry if it offended you," I told them.

"Not offended. I figured there was something going on when Rowen came home and told us about her friend

Mason. The stuff she's been telling me isn't good. Talked to Nick today and got the scoop," Jess said.

"I think you buying all the kids shoes just so he could have a pair was wonderful," Gigi said.

"Thanks. No one knows that was the real reason. I've kind of lied to everyone else. I just don't want people prying into Mason's life. He doesn't need that."

"I'll start digging," Jess said. "But before I do, wanted to see what you know."

"Not much." I frowned. "He's probably told Rowen more than he has me. I asked him a couple of weeks ago what his house was like and he shut down."

"Hmm," he muttered.

"Principal Garcia said that before we could go to the authorities, we needed to have a good foundation of documentation. That's why I haven't come to you yet."

"I'll make sure he knows you didn't come to me. That I approached you," Jess said. "But Garcia forgets we don't live in LA. He doesn't need to build a case before I'll look into a situation. Especially when it comes to kids."

"Thank you. I can't tell you how worried I've been about Mason."

"You're a good teacher, Emmeline," Gigi said. "I'm glad Rowen has you."

A huge smile spread across my face and I turned it on Ben still sleeping in my arms.

I wasn't sure what would happen, but a part of me hoped that I would still be in Prescott by the time he was old enough to be in my class.

After our conversation about Mason, Gigi and I went back to visit with the women and snack from the abundant food trays. Maisy and I hit it off right away. She was sweet and energetic and I loved hearing her stories from the Fan Mountain Inn, Prescott's one and only motel, where she worked as the manager.

The Clearys' garage party ranked in my top five best social events, and it wasn't even over yet.

Gigi was just finishing a story of how the garage was built to replace an old barn where she had been bitten by a rattlesnake when I felt Nick's heat at my back.

Craning my neck over my shoulder, I asked, "Are there snakes by my house?"

"Nope. You're too far up into the mountains. It's too cold."

"Good." Just hearing Gigi's story gave me chills. I was not a fan of reptiles or bugs.

"Come on, Emmy. We're playing pool," Nick said. "You too, Maze. You're Silas's partner."

"I don't know how to play pool," I said as we walked toward the table at the back of the garage.

"That's okay. Maisy isn't any good so me and Silas will carry you ladies."

"Hey! I'll have you know that I'm getting better," Maisy said.

"Sure you are. That's why Silas told me to beg Gigi to play with him and only take you as a last resort."

"He did not," Maisy said.

"He did."

"Silas Grant!" Maisy shouted. She took off to where all the men were talking and smacked a blond man in the arm before transferring Coby to a mountainous man with dark hair and a thick brown beard.

He was the only man in the group who stood taller than Jess, and his size was intimidating. The square angles of his jaw gave him a stern look, but when he settled Coby on one bulky bicep, his whole face relaxed.

When Nick and I reached the group, he started introductions.

"Emmy, this is Beau Holt," he said. "Beau works for the Forest Service and leads the Search and Rescue team in Jamison County."

Maybe it was the three glasses of wine I'd already had, I don't know, but my normal polite greeting didn't immediately come out of my mouth. Instead, when I tipped my head way, way back to look at Beau's face, I said something out loud that was meant to stay inside my head.

"You are not small." I slapped my hand over my rude mouth and stared at Beau with wide eyes. "Sorry!" I said through my fingers.

A huge smile broke out over Beau's face and the entire circle erupted in laughter.

Nick chuckled. "This is Silas Grant." Silas was the blond man that Maisy had smacked. His lean, muscled frame was similar to Nick's though Silas stood an inch or two taller.

After shaking his hand, I turned to the last man in the group. I didn't need Nick to introduce me. After hearing Sara's story about meeting her husband in a burn unit, I knew this was Milo. He had a wrinkled burn scar on the top of his forehead and another under the side of his jaw.

"Milo Phillips," he said.

"Emmeline Austin."

"Emmeline, I heard you went temporarily insane a few years back and married this asshole," Silas said, jerking his chin toward Nick.

"You're so fucking funny," Nick muttered.

"Are we playing pool or what?" Maisy asked.

"We're playing," Silas said.

"Coby, can you stay with Uncle Beau?"

"Yeah," Beau answered for him.

My eyes darted back and forth between the Holt siblings. I never would have guessed that tiny, blond Maisy was the dark-haired giant's sister.

"What are we betting?" Nick asked Silas.

"Dinner?" Maisy suggested. "We could all meet up at the café one night. Loser pays?"

"Deal," Nick and Silas agreed simultaneously.

Five minutes later, the balls on the table were spread out everywhere and Nick was leaning over my shoulder, teaching me how to line up a shot.

Fifteen minutes later, I was getting annoyed at Nick's incessant hovering. Every time I got ready to shoot, he'd interrupt me and tell me to hit a different ball. I'd been slowly hinting for him to let me try but he wasn't hearing it.

Finally, I'd had enough. "Would you leave me alone? You're driving me crazy. You are a rotten teacher!"

"What? No, I'm not. I'm an awesome teacher. You're just a bad student. That's not the best shot."

I felt the temper rise in my chest, but before I could snap again, I took a couple of deep breaths and reminded myself that the entire party was watching our game. "Your ego is overinflated. Can you just let me try my own way? Who cares if I miss?"

"I do. We're winning."

"Go away."

"Hit the green stripe. Not the blue one."

"No."

"Emmy," he growled. "Green stripe."

"You are pushing me, Nick. You won't like it when I

push back."

"Oh, yeah? What are you going to do?"

I turned my gaze to our audience. "Did you guys know that Nick has an obsession with male strip shows? His favorite Las Vegas show is *Thunder From Down Under*. He loves it so much that he made me go to it before we got married."

The garage exploded with laughter. Silas moved to Nick's side and clamped onto one of his shoulders as he bent over howling, shaking Nick's body.

"I love her!" Silas yelled.

I aimed a smug smile at Nick as he glared down at me. "Blue stripe. Or they learn about how you squeal like a little girl when you're riding a roller coaster."

The laughter in the room got even louder as Nick fought a grin. He bent to speak into my ear. "That's just not even true, Emmy."

"Blue stripe," I repeated.

"Fine. Hit whatever ball you want," he said

I missed the shot but didn't care. With a smile on my face, I leaned against the back wall while Maisy took her turn.

"You two spar more than Jess and Gigi. It's pretty fucking entertaining. I can't wait for dinner," Silas said.

"Thanks," I said.

Silas's words confirmed something I had begun to realize these last few weeks. Nick and I had that easy banter I had longed for. Something I had envied about Jess and Gigi. Being with Nick was comfortable. We fit together and I could be myself around him.

I'd had years of practice pretending to be the Emmeline Austin that New York high society had expected me to be. That Emmeline only said what was proper and polished. Her manners were impeccable. Her proclaimed opinions were never too strict or off-center.

My father had expected me to be that Emmeline. My friends. Even Logan to some extent.

I did not like that Emmeline.

But not once during the last two weeks of dinners with Nick had I felt the need to mask my emotions or stifle my opinions. He liked me just as I was. No pretense. And the real me flourished around him.

Everything I had ever wanted in a relationship I had with my husband.

How ironic.

The same day that I realized maybe Nick and I had a future was the same day my divorce papers had arrived in the mail.

CHAPTER 10

BLARING SIRENS FILLED MY EARS. THE SOUND was so loud, I shot out of bed and immediately scrambled for my phone on the nightstand, wincing as the light illuminated the dark room. Fumbling to dial 9-1-1, I rushed to my walk-in closet and closed myself in.

"What is your emergency?" the dispatcher answered.

"My alarm system just went off," I whispered.

My heart was thundering in my chest and I was having trouble breathing. Going from a dead sleep to instantly awake, and terrified, was wreaking havoc on my body.

"What's your name?"

"Emmeline Austin," I said.

"Hold on. Let me get a patrol car dispatched." His voice was in the background but I couldn't make out his words.

A beeping rang in my ears and I pulled my phone away to see I had another incoming call. Most likely it was my security company. Their protocol was to try and reach me first and then notify the police if I didn't answer.

Not long after the beeping stopped, the dispatcher came on the line. "Ms. Austin, I've got your security company on the other line. Are you in a safe location?" he asked.

"I'm hiding in my closet."

"Good. Stay there. The patrol car is on its way and should be there soon. I'll let the officer know where you are hiding. Don't leave the closet. When the deputy gets there, he'll come to you. His name is Sam Eklund."

"Okay," I whispered.

"Hold on while I let your security company go," he said. I was glad he didn't hang up on me. It made me feel like I wasn't totally alone during one of the scariest moments of my life.

The adrenaline coursing through my blood was making my body shake. I wrapped my free arm around my knees to keep them from knocking together while my mind started racing, thinking of all the possibilities for my alarm going off.

Was someone trying to break into my house? What if the intruder was making his way to my bedroom?

Huddled in the corner, I closed my eyes and focused on listening. If I could hear my intruder before he reached the closet, maybe I could at least tell the dispatcher before something bad happened to me. The blasting alarm, the dispatcher's typing and labored breathing were all I heard.

Every passing minute felt like an hour. Any minute now, I imagined that a dark figure would throw open my closet door and find my hiding place. I mentally started preparing myself to fight. Maybe if I put up enough of a struggle, I could delay my attacker long enough that the sheriff's deputy would arrive in time to save me.

When footsteps sounded in my bedroom, I held my breath and stared through the darkness toward the door, hoping that on the other side was a police officer and not my intruder.

"Ms. Austin? This is Deputy Sam Eklund." Two short knocks came on the closet door.

Sagging further to the floor, I blew out the breath I'd been holding. "He's here," I whispered and hung up on the dispatcher.

"I'm coming out," I said, picking myself up off the floor. The light from my bedroom was blinding after having been in the pitch-black closet.

"Can you get that alarm off?" Sam asked, yelling over the sirens.

Nodding, I disarmed it using the app on my phone.

"You doing okay?" he asked.

"Not really," I said. "What's going on? Did someone try and break in?"

"No one is here but the sensor on your basement door tripped. I'm going to call in an update to the station. How about you get dressed and come downstairs? Give me a chance to look around more closely."

When I realized just how sparse my attire was, I wrapped my arms around my chest to try and cover up my nightwear.

I had on a thin-strapped maroon silk camisole and matching shorts. With all of the excitement, one of the straps had slipped off my shoulder and I was centimeters away from flashing Sam one of my breasts.

"Okay. I'll be right there," I said, turning back to my closet. I pulled on a floor-length robe lined with faux fur. My mother and I had each gotten one from the spa in Lake

Como. It had been an extravagant purchase, but as I slid my arms into the plush cream garment, I didn't regret a single penny.

My feet carried me quickly down the hall, but when a familiar voice called out, I started jogging to the stairs.

"Emmy!" Nick shouted.

"Up here!"

Nick didn't wait for me in the foyer. The second he saw me hit the top stair, he was racing toward me, taking two steps at a time. He reached me at the top of the staircase and enveloped me with his strong arms. "Are you okay?" he asked the top of my head.

"No," I whispered.

"I've got you."

I let my body relax and fall into his. The smell from his flannel shirt was a mixture of Nick and laundry soap. I breathed it in deeply, savoring the safety and warmth of Nick's embrace.

"Nick," Sam called from below us. "Better come see this."

Grabbing my hand, Nick led me down the stairs and into a tan leather chair in the living room. "Stay here. I'll be right back."

He rounded the kitchen corner and disappeared into the small hallway at the back of the house. If the alarm had been tripped by the sensor leading to the basement, then whoever broke into my house did so through the garage and then tried to come inside from the interior staircase.

As the minutes passed, my eyes wandered back and forth over the windowed walls. Was my intruder lurking outside watching me? The thought gave me chills. I hated being alone up here, feeling exposed and vulnerable. Where were Nick and Sam? What was taking them so long?

Footsteps on the marble kitchen floor captured my attention. Nick came directly to me as Sam walked to the foyer and pulled out his phone.

"Did you find something?" I asked, standing from my seat.

"Yeah," Nick said. "We're going to call Jess over. Hang tight. We'll run through it all with you once he gets here."

"The waiting is wrecking me, Nick."

His large hand wrapped around the nape of my neck as he leaned his forehead down to mine. "I'm sorry, Emmy. But it will be better if we talk when Jess gets here. That way we only have to do this once."

"Okay," I whispered. Nick's warmth and gentle voice soothed my nerves. "I'm going to make myself a cup of tea."

"I'll do it," he offered.

"I need to do something other than sit and worry. Keep me company?"

As my Keurig brewed, I hopped up to sit on a counter. "How did you know to come?" It was almost two o'clock in the morning. He had probably been dead asleep.

"Heard the call come through dispatch."

"Oh. Were you awake?" I asked, confused why he'd be monitoring 9-1-1 calls on a Tuesday night.

"Nope. I have a scanner by my bed. When I don't have a volunteer on call, I monitor dispatch from home."

"Right," I muttered. I sipped my hot tea, hoping it would calm my nerves, but it wasn't helping. "I'm freaking out."

Nick crossed the kitchen and pulled me off the counter, into his arms. "I'm freaking out too. Worst ten minutes of my life, driving here not knowing what I'd find."

"I'm okay," I said, hoping the words would comfort us both.

"I never realized how Jess must have felt when Gigi was taken," he said. "Not until tonight. I don't know how he managed to keep his shit when he came home and she was gone. I don't know what I would have done if you hadn't been here."

"I'm okay," I repeated.

Headlights flickering outside caught our attention and we broke out of our bubble to rush to the door. Five minutes later, Jess and Sam had finished examining the back hallway again and we were all sitting in the living room.

"Thanks for being patient, Emmeline. Sorry for making you wait. But we wanted to go through this once. That way we all get the same story," Jess said.

I nodded.

"Someone did get into the garage," Jess said.

Tears pooled in my eyes and I sucked in a jagged breath.

A part of me had hoped this was all just a false alarm. That my state-of-the-art security system had just malfunctioned and tomorrow we would all laugh about how we had overreacted. Instead, the reality was that a stranger had invaded my home.

"They managed to get past your alarm sensor on the garage's side door. Must not have been expecting the one at the top of the stairs. From what we can tell, as soon as the alarm sounded, the trespasser took off," Jess said.

"I dusted for prints on both doors," Sam said. "Didn't find a thing. Means the burglar wiped both doors clean."

"So what do we do? How can we catch him?" I asked.

"I'll come back tomorrow and look around the property in the daylight," Sam said. "Might find some tracks or clues outside that can help. But for tonight, we've done all we can."

"Do you think he'll come back?"

"Not likely. But no one would blame you if you didn't stay here tonight. I could call the motel, get a room for you," Jess offered.

"I'm staying," Nick said.

"Figured as much," Jess said.

I relaxed a bit into Nick's side, the tension in my shoulders lessening, knowing that I wouldn't be alone tonight.

"Can you give us a quick rundown of your security system, Emmeline?" Sam asked.

"Sure. I had a company from Bozeman come over and install it. They said it was their best system. The front and garage doors have panels for me to arm and disarm the system. I can do it from my phone too. They put sensors on all of the sliding glass doors to the balconies. If the system is armed, I can't open any of them. I have motion sensors in the living room, dining room and kitchen. But I haven't been setting them when I'm at home."

"At night when you go to bed, start setting the motion sensors. I don't care if we get some false alarms at the station. Rather you have them on at night," Jess said.

I nodded.

"Any ideas who might want to break in? Any enemies?" Jess asked.

"No. I don't know that many people in Prescott yet. Certainly no one I would consider an enemy."

"What about outside of Prescott? Anyone from the city?" he asked.

"No one I can think of."

"What about potential stalkers? Anyone seem overly interested in you? It'd be someone that you'd know. Could be a frequent visitor to the school. Or coworker that you've run into by 'accident' more than two or three times."

"No one here comes to mind. Though, about a year ago, I did have a situation in New York. I started noticing a guy from one of my NYU classes around me a lot. He'd be at my favorite coffee shop or at a restaurant where I was eating lunch. I didn't think much of it until he started showing up to charity galas that Logan and I were attending. He was giving me a creepy vibe so Logan and my father both insisted I have a bodyguard with me at school and during the day. Shortly after that, I stopped seeing the guy anymore. And then one day he quit coming to our class."

"Did you request a restraining order?" Sam asked.

"No. Since he stopped following me, I didn't think it was necessary."

"What's his name?" Jess asked.

"I don't know. At class or when I'd see him around, he never spoke to me. He was just always a little too close and was constantly watching me. That's what freaked me out."

"Who is Logan?" Sam asked.

"My ex-boyfriend. We broke up before Thanksgiving."

"Any chance he isn't taking the breakup so well and would come here to scare you?" Jess asked.

"No. Absolutely not. He's in the city and would never do such a thing."

"You mind if we contact him? Rule it out?"

"I'd prefer if you didn't but understand if you must."

"It's not the ex, Brick," Nick said. "Guy isn't the type. You'd be wasting your time."

"Okay. We'll see what we can find tomorrow and go from there. Let you two try and get some rest," Jess said, standing up from the couch. "We'll be in touch."

Nick escorted Sam and Jess to the door as I started

turning lights off in the living room and kitchen. We walked upstairs together and I stopped outside the door to the guest bedroom.

"There should be an extra toothbrush in the bathroom. And there are extra blankets and pillows in the closet if you need them."

"I'm not staying in there, Emmy," he said.

"You can have the couch but the bed in here is far more comfortable."

"I'm sleeping with you."

"No. This is the guest bedroom, Nick. And you are a guest." If he thought he could use tonight's ordeal as a way to get into my bed, he was mistaken.

"I'm not a guest. I'm your husband."

"A husband that sleeps in the guest bedroom." He closed the distance between us in a flash and before I could step back, his mouth was slamming down on mine. The intensity of his kiss completely took me off guard. My knees wobbled and I clutched his flannel shirt.

His tongue tangled with mine as his beard tickled the sensitive skin on my face. Though he was only touching my mouth, it felt like sparks were going to start shooting out of my fingers and toes at any minute.

Breaking our kiss, he whispered against my lips. "I'm not leaving you alone until we find out who broke in tonight. Scared me to fucking death to hear that call come in. I need you close. And that means I'm going to sleep in your bed."

Nick's kiss, along with his gentle pleading, broke my resolve. If he hadn't been here for me tonight, I don't know what I would have done. Because he was staying with me, I felt safe sleeping in my own bed. If sleeping next to me tonight would help some of his fears, I could give him that.

"Just for tonight," I said and walked to my bedroom.

My room sat at the back of the house above the kitchen. The two exterior walls were made entirely of glass and a balcony wrapped around the corner of the room.

With the open view of the forest, my bedroom was styled to match. Dark walls. A deep green duvet. Espresso wood furniture. It felt like a cave.

Without saying a word, I shrugged off my robe and climbed into bed, facing away from Nick. I listened to the rustle of his clothes and the thud of his boots as they hit the floor. With every dropping article, my heart beat faster.

What was I thinking a minute ago? I couldn't sleep next to him. I was crazy for agreeing to this.

When his weight hit the mattress, I stopped breathing.

Thankfully, my bed was wide, and even if I moved a bit in my sleep, it would be unlikely that we would touch. I just hoped that Nick would respect the imaginary boundary line between us.

No such luck.

As soon as his body sank into the memory foam, he shifted and reached for me. His strong forearm wrapped around my middle and he hauled me into the center of the bed. His arms locked around me as he buried his face in my hair.

"Sleep, Emmy," he said, sliding one of his large legs between mine.

The hair on his chest pressed against the bare skin of my back and his heart beat against my spine. No way in hell was I sleeping.

Plus, I hated spooning. Whenever Logan had tried to curl into my back, I would always twist so that I was facing him.

Nick had ruined spooning for me in Vegas. The memory assaulted my mind. I remembered falling asleep in his arms, thinking that if this was how I went to bed for the next fifty years, I'd die a happy woman.

I couldn't do this.

I couldn't stay here with him like this. The familiarity of our position created an overwhelming ache in my chest. All I could do was close my eyes and try to breathe through the pain. I desperately wanted to escape Nick's embrace but didn't have the energy for another discussion.

So instead I waited. And waited.

Finally, when his body relaxed into sleep, I slipped out of bed and silently crept downstairs.

Sinking into a living room couch, I could breathe again. But when the air filled my lungs, the emotions I'd been holding in came pouring out. My body curled into a tight ball as sobs rocked my chest.

It wasn't just tonight's events causing my meltdown. It was a buildup from months and months of stress and anxiety. Moving across the country to start a new job. Finding Nick after years of searching. All the memories and heartache that came with seeing him again and ending my relationship with Logan.

It was too much.

So I did my best to cry quietly, hoping I could get control again before morning.

"Let it all out, my sweet Emmy," Nick whispered as his arms circled me, pulling me into his lap.

I didn't fight him off or try to stifle my tears. I burrowed completely into his bare chest and let him hold me. When I'd finally cried myself dry, I raised my chin and stared into his vibrant hazel eyes.

His hand moved to my jaw and his thumb stroked my cheek, wiping away the wetness.

"Sorry," I whispered.

"You don't have to apologize, Emmy. Ever. This is all on me."

"No. It's not just you," I said. "This has been building for a while now."

"You wouldn't be crying if I'd stayed in the first place."

I didn't have a response to that. What could I say?

Yes, you're right? We could have had nine wonderful years together? We could have been blissfully happy and in love? You threw it all away because you were too much of a coward to talk to me about your fears?

"I don't know if I can ever get past it, Nick."

His forehead dropped to mine. "What can I do?"

The answer was simple. "Stay."

"I'll never leave you again," he promised. Maybe if he said it enough, I'd start to believe it was true. "Does this mean you're going to give us a chance?"

I nodded.

His arms squeezed me tight and he sighed against my temple.

Relief washed through me too. Admitting to him how I was feeling and agreeing to give us a chance allowed me to give up the fight. I hadn't realized how much energy I had been using to keep up my guard.

Exhaustion settled into my body. It was only a Monday night, or Tuesday morning now. I had no idea how I was going to make it through my day tomorrow.

"We need to get some sleep. We've both got work to-morrow," Nick murmured.

I nodded but otherwise didn't move. All my energy

was gone.

Nick knew it too, because I didn't have to summon the power to move. He lifted us both off the couch and carried me upstairs to bed.

When he'd situated me in his arms, my back to his chest, he took a few deep breaths against my hair.

"Good night, Wife," he whispered.

My heart swelled at his endearment. I managed to swallow the lump at the back of my throat. "Good night, Nick."

CHAPTER 11

THE SATURDAY AFTER THE BREAK-IN, NICK and I were walking downtown toward the café to meet Silas and Maisy.

After we'd lost the pool game last weekend, Nick and Silas had insisted we settle up on the bet quickly. Silas hadn't wanted us to renege and Nick had wanted to lock in another date.

Not that he needed to coerce me into dates anymore. I meant what I had told him. I was giving us a chance.

So here we were. Dating.

I had shoved my divorce papers in a kitchen drawer and decided I'd get them out again if and when the time was right.

Since the break-in, Nick had been glued to my side. He'd been at my house for dinner every night. Afterward, we would curl up on the living room couch and watch a movie. He had declared that my exposure to Westerns was sorely lacking now that I was a Montanan, and he had taken it upon himself to remedy the situation.

Nick hadn't let me sleep alone, despite my initial protests. Sleeping next to Nick each night was still difficult. I would lay awake for hours, wondering if he'd be gone when I woke up. Nick had sensed my unease because he hadn't pushed. Not once. We had slept close but that had been all. Not once had he made a move for sex.

But it was coming.

This morning, Nick had suggested we go snowshoeing. And by suggested, he'd shoved a pair of snowshoes in my hands and ordered me to go change. When I'd come downstairs wearing a pair of black insulated leggings, Nick's eyes, filled with lust, had locked on my legs and ass.

It wouldn't be long and Nick would make a move to end our sexual hiatus. I just hoped that when the time came, I would be ready.

But I wasn't worrying about it now. Instead, I was excited to be having dinner with Silas and Maisy. Mostly, I was looking forward to getting to know Maisy better. I missed having girlfriends close to home and I envied her relationship with Gigi. Maybe one day I could consider them both good friends. If I stayed in Prescott, that is.

"So are Silas and Maisy a couple?" I asked Nick. At the party, they'd seemed close but I hadn't seen them touch and I didn't want to make any wrong assumptions.

"They're just friends," Nick said.

I didn't get the chance to prod for more because the second we crossed the threshold into the café and joined Silas and Maisy in a booth, they jumped right into questioning me about the break-in.

"They didn't find any tracks or anything in the woods?"

Maisy asked.

"No." I frowned. "Sam looked all over the next day and didn't find a thing. He thinks that someone must have walked to the house along the driveway where the snow had been plowed. There weren't footprints anywhere except right by the edge of the garage."

"Creepy," she said. "And you don't have any idea who might have wanted to get into your house?"

"None."

Jess had stopped by yesterday to tell me that they were at a dead end. I was deflated and scared. It terrified me that the criminal was still at large.

"What do you think?" Silas asked Nick.

"I don't know. Jess, Emmy and I did some guessing but didn't come up with much. It might be a random burglary, someone breaking into a fancy house on the mountain to score a load of pricey pawn items. Though, I doubt a common thief would come at night when someone was likely to be home or have the skill to disarm her security system."

"What about kids?" Silas asked. "Some of those high schoolers are fairly tech savvy. Could it have been a prank?"

"Maybe. I could see some of them getting past her security panel. But to leave no trace, wipe prints, think about footprints? It seems a bit too sophisticated and way over the top for a prank. We're thinking this was professional," Nick said.

"Like a professional thief?" Maisy asked. "Why?"

"Money," I said. "I'm from a well-off family and someone may have broken in hoping to get a big payday. Scare me into handing over a wad of cash and fancy jewelry."

"Oh my god!" Maisy yelled. "You can't stay there then! What if someone wants to kidnap you for ransom? You're in danger, Emmeline!"

"Maze, calm down," Nick said.

"Calm down? How can I calm down? How are you not taking this more seriously?" she asked.

"We're all taking this seriously," he said.

We were so wrapped up in our conversation that none of us heard a woman approach our booth. "Nick Slater *and* Silas Grant. It's my lucky day."

I looked up to see the woman who had pressed herself up against Nick months ago when he had taken me to The Black Bull.

"Go away, Andrea," Nick said.

"Blech," Maisy said.

Silas ignored her presence completely.

"There's no reason to be rude, Nick. I just wanted to see how you two were doing. See if you needed anything? Anything at all." Her words were filled with innuendo and her breasts were thrust out as far as she could manage.

This woman was an absolute wench. "He doesn't need anything," I said.

She laughed. "Do you think that just because you're eating dinner with Nick and his friends that he'll actually be interested in you? It's a well-known fact around here that Nick doesn't go for redheads. I hope you haven't gotten your hopes up."

"I think you're mistaken. He doesn't think redheads are repulsive. After all, he married me."

The smug grin fell off her face as her eyes darted between Nick and me. "You're married?"

"Yes. Go away, Andrea," Nick repeated.

This woman was not only a wench, she was also a bitch because she didn't do as Nick asked. Instead, she opened her mouth and out spewed pure venom.

"That's okay. I think Silas is more my type anyway," she said. Bending down and shoving her fake cleavage in Silas's face, she whispered, "You can do better than Maisy Holt. Don't forget, she killed the last man she fucked."

Maisy's head flew up in utter disbelief as the men shot out of the booth with clenched fists, forcing Andrea back a few steps.

"You need to leave. Immediately," I said, my voice firm and loud. I slid out of the booth and stepped between Nick and Silas, getting directly into Andrea's space.

I'd dealt with my fair share of skanks before; I was a former New York socialite after all. So if this slut wanted to be a bitch, she'd met her match.

"You reek of desperation. Find someone that appreciates your brand of fake and leave us alone. What did you actually think would happen tonight? You'd come over here, jiggle those implants and one of these two men would fawn all over you?" Reaching back for my purse in the booth, I yanked out my wallet and pulled out the first bill my fingers touched. "Here," I said, shoving a one-hundred-dollar bill in her face. "Buy yourself a clue."

Andrea stared down at the money in my hand with wide eyes. Her shock soon turned to anger and she gave me an evil sneer. But I stood my ground. Her snarl was like a warm caress compared to those my father doled out. She could give me that look all day long and I'd never budge.

A slow clap started in the background. I glanced over my shoulder to see that Maisy had a huge smile on her face and had started the clap.

Before my head could swivel back around, the entire café burst into applause and laughter. People were standing up from their chairs, roaring hysterically at Andrea's now bright red face. She didn't stick around long before turning on her designer imposter heels and stomping out the door.

The second she was gone, Nick spun me around and slammed his mouth down on mine.

The noise in the restaurant vanished as my whole world became about Nick. His lips were hard and rough against mine. His hands cradled my face, pulling me toward him. As quickly as it started, it was over.

"That was fucking awesome, Wife."

I pulled in a deep breath and smiled. "It absolutely was."

I'm sure he was talking about Andrea. I was referring to the kiss.

We left the café not long after eating our meals as Maisy needed to pick up Coby from her parents' house. After buying dinner and saying our good-byes, Nick decided to stop at the grocery store for breakfast supplies.

So now we were strolling the aisles of Jamison Foods at eight o'clock on a Saturday night, picking up eggs and a plethora of vegetables for his "fucking awesome" quiche.

"Is it necessary for you to replace all of the items I put into the cart with the exact same thing? It seems quite inefficient," I said as Nick lifted out the onion I had just grabbed and chose another. So far he hadn't liked my tomato, avocado or pepper selections.

"Yeah. When you get the wrong thing," he said.

"That onion looks exactly like the one I just had."

"The one you picked was a yellow onion. I want a sweet

onion. They look the same but taste different."

"How about I push the cart?" I suggested. "Then you can pick out whatever you want."

"Works for me," he said.

I took his place in front of the cart and started to push but stopped when he pressed against my back. His hands rested on the handlebar outside of mine as he trapped me between the cart and his hard chest.

"Really?" I asked.

He smirked. "Let's go."

I gave him an eye roll but started walking. "I could do without seeing your friend Andrea ever again."

"Me too."

What was she to Nick? Had he slept with her before? Was that the reason she was so desperate to get his attention? Or was it all just a game to toy with me?

She had jumped at the chance to intimidate and embarrass me, even if her attempt had backfired. She was a complete stranger but I knew her type. Possessive. Jealous. Shallow.

"I hate to ask," I said. "What's the history with you and her?"

Nick abruptly stopped the cart, forcing my stomach into the handlebar. His hands grabbed my shoulders and spun me around in the tight space.

"I wish I could tell you there weren't women in my life these last nine years, but I can't. I can tell you that there wasn't anyone serious. And never once did I go there with Andrea."

I wasn't dumb. There had to have been women in his life, just like there had been men in mine. But thus far in our second chance, I'd been able to pretend he didn't have a past.

Since we hadn't talked about it, his history wasn't real.

Now it was and I did not like the way my stomach twisted at the thought of Nick with another woman.

"Okay," I said. "The grocery store is not the place for this conversation. Can we go?"

"You asked, Emmy."

"I know." I nodded and looked to the floor. "And I shouldn't be upset. But I am."

Nick's chin dropped to the top of my head. "And that shouldn't make me feel good, but it does. I about crawled out of my skin that day I saw you on the street with your ex. Thinking you took him home and were kissing him. That you might be fucking him. I drank a whole bottle of whiskey that night just so I could sleep."

Somehow his statement eased the sickness in my stomach. It wasn't that I was glad he had been upset about me and Logan. It was that we could both openly admit we were jealous.

And I was elated that he hadn't been with Andrea and she couldn't throw a past sexual encounter in my face.

I lifted my arms from my sides and wrapped them around his waist, giving him a brief squeeze before I tipped my chin way back to meet his eyes.

"Come on. Let's get out of here," I said. "Maybe you can make me cookies when we get to the house."

Without a word, he steered us to the refrigerator aisle and grabbed a long tube of premixed cookie dough. Peanut butter, chocolate chip. My favorite.

"We've got eight minutes before those are done," I said after sliding a cookie sheet into the oven.

I was proud of myself for taking over the cookie baking while Nick unloaded the groceries. Not that making pre-made cookies was difficult, but still, a year ago I wouldn't have had a clue what to do with that tube of dough. I was making slow strides toward one day becoming a decent cook.

Nick's hard chest pressed against my back and startled me. "Then we've got seven minutes to do something else."

The feel of his warm breath against my skin and the pressure of his fingertips at my hips had my body instantly trembling.

"Nick, what are—" His mouth dropped to my neck and his soft lips traveled up and down my skin.

"Nick." I inhaled as one of his hands moved around my hip and to the front of my jeans. My stomach dipped as his fingers lightly caressed under the hem of my sweater.

My heart started pounding as his fingertips slid under the waistband of my jeans.

"Nick, I don't think—" I couldn't finish that sentence either. My mind was torn. I should put on the brakes but at the same time, I really wanted to see what Nick was going to do.

"Shh, Emmy," he whispered. "Stop thinking. Just feel it."

A small moan escaped my mouth. I was feeling, all right. I was feeling Nick everywhere. His strong chest against my back. His lips behind my ear. One hand kneading my hip. The other's fingers unbuttoning my jeans and sliding down the zipper.

When his hand slid into my purple lace panties, I groaned and closed my eyes. I laid my head against his shoulder so he had better access to my neck.

His mouth latched on while his fingers moved further into my panties.

"Oh my god," I gasped when his middle finger found my center. It circled around and around, spreading my wetness.

Nick's arm banded across my stomach when my legs started to shake and buckle. His mouth and hand never once paused as he kept me from falling.

His finger at my core dipped inside and pressed against my inner walls. In and out, over and over.

"Nick, please," I begged.

His finger stopped plunging and went to my swollen clit. His strokes started soft and slow, my hips rocking back and forth to match his movements. I started panting as his finger worked faster and harder between my legs.

When my orgasm hit, a loud moan came from deep in my chest, filling the kitchen as my body trembled. Nick kept working his finger until I was limp in his arms.

I took a few ragged breaths and put pressure back on my feet. The beeping oven timer caused my eyes to fly open.

I had just let Nick finger fuck me in my kitchen. Even though he had once explored every inch of my body, I was embarrassed. We had just crossed the sexual boundary. How was I supposed to act?

Pushing at his arms, I tried to get out of his embrace but the more I struggled, the tighter he hugged me.

"Emmy," he said. "Stop fighting me."

"I'm not. I just need to get the cookies out of the oven before they burn," I lied.

"We can make another sheet."

"Let me go. Please."

He didn't let me go but his frame relaxed and his

forehead dropped to my hair. "You're not ready yet."

I let out a long breath and my shoulders fell. "No. Can I get the cookies?"

He let me go and grabbed a beer from the fridge.

Shit.

Transferring cookies onto a cooling rack, I got my head together. I didn't want to hurt Nick's feelings or lead him on and I wasn't trying to push him away or bruise his ego.

I just didn't want to go too fast. We still had so far to go. Adding sex into the mix was bound to make this harder than it already was.

"I'm sorry," I said to the cookies.

The beer bottle hit the island and his footsteps came my way. "Don't be sorry," he said, wrapping his arms around me. "That was the hottest moment I've had in nine years. We'll go as fast or slow as you want. I can wait. Even if it takes another nine."

Wow, that felt good. Nearly as good as the orgasm he'd given me.

I smiled and lifted my hands to his forearms. "Thank you."

"You're welcome, my sweet Emmy."

CHAPTER 12

"HELLO," I SAID INTO MY PHONE WHILE curled up in a living room chair.

My father had been calling me repeatedly for the last week and I had yet to take his calls. He had called mostly while I had been teaching and hadn't been able to talk. And I had ignored one of his calls because Nick and I had been watching another Western.

Presumably, he wanted to scold me about breaking up with Logan, so I hadn't been in a big hurry to call him back.

But it was now an early Sunday morning and I had no good excuse for dodging another call. Nick was still sleeping in my bed upstairs and it was better to get this call over with sooner rather than later.

"It is extremely rude not to return a phone call, Emmeline," my father said.

"I agree and apologize. This has been a busy week but I understand that is not a valid excuse."

"It is not. Your manners are dwindling. Likely because of your new environment. Are the uncivilized rural country folk rubbing off on you?"

Normally, I would let that insult slide but I was still half asleep and had yet to consume any caffeine, so my retort slipped out easily.

"Now who has forgotten their manners?"

"Do not speak to me in that tone!"

I winced and held the phone away from my ear. "May I please ask the reason for this early morning phone call, Father? It is, after all, barely six in the morning in Montana. Surely, you recall I am in a different time zone."

"Mind your attitude, Emmeline," he said. "I am calling because I ran into Logan last weekend at a benefit for the Met."

My intuition had been correct. He had called because of Logan. I was surprised it had taken him this long. It was early February and we had broken up back in November.

"And?"

"And he was with a friend of yours from college. An Alice Leys."

That stung a little, but I wasn't terribly surprised. I had no doubt that when Alice had learned Logan was once again single, she'd immediately moved in. I just hoped that she had genuine feelings for him, not just his wallet.

But I certainly wasn't going to let my father in on any of this. I just hoped that his call was only to berate me about Logan and that Steffie hadn't slipped and told him about Nick.

"And?" I asked again.

"And!" he yelled.

I don't know why I'd jumped. It shouldn't have surprised

me that he was shouting.

This time I didn't put the phone back to my ear. He kept on screaming and for the sake of my eardrum, I listened to it from a few inches away.

"How could you be so foolish? You've chosen to live in a backwoods hick town for what? To teach the dunce children of adult halfwits? You get your ass back here and make this right with Logan. That alleged friend of yours was hanging all over him. If you're lucky, you may still have a chance to get him back. I am sending a plane. Now, Emmeline."

"I'm not returning to the city," I said. My voice was steady though my pulse was racing and my fingers were shaking.

"You are," he ordered.

"I am not."

The shouting stopped, which meant things were about to get much worse. Whenever Trent Austin wanted to make a point with his children, he did it with vicious, but quiet attacks. When he was shouting, I stood a chance.

"I'm surprised at you, Emmeline." His tone was normal, likely the same one he used with his yachting buddies or his suit tailor. "Even when I think you can't possibly disappoint me further, you sink so far beneath my expectations it's a wonder I set them at all. It's no surprise that you had to trade sexual favors to be a successful fundraiser. Tell me. Is that why your team was always so far ahead? Because you were fucking our wealthiest contributors?"

I closed my eyes and sank further into the chair. He knew that I would never prostitute myself for campaign donations, but he was throwing the lie out there as a reminder that he could still smear my reputation.

Why did his insults still hurt? For the majority of my

life, I'd done everything I could to please him. I thought I'd set that all aside after his betrayal. That since I had quit my job and moved to Montana, it wouldn't hurt when he told me I was a disappointment.

But it did.

Just like it hurt that he'd tell vicious and filthy lies about his own daughter simply because I didn't marry the man of his choice.

The little girl inside me was still hoping that one day she could make her father proud. I needed to have a heart-to-heart with that little girl and tell her to wise up. It was never going to happen.

"You know I have never slept with a client. That's a lie, Father."

"According to you," he said. "Get on that plane."

"No."

"Get on that fucking plane and make this right!"

This time when I flinched, my phone didn't stop two inches away from my face. Instead, it traveled up to Nick's ear in the hand that had ripped it from my own.

Nick's face turned to stone and the muscle in his forehead twitched as my father continued his rant.

"Shut the fuck up," Nick growled. "You won't talk to her like that again."

Straining my ears, I barely made out my father's reply, "I'll talk to my daughter any way I see fit."

"You're done, pal. Call her again and say anything other than how beautiful, smart or kind she is and you'll be talking to me," he said and hung up the phone.

Nick and I both took a few moments to compose ourselves. His chest heaved with deep breaths and I assumed he was trying to calm his temper.

My chest did the same but it was to keep myself from crying happy tears.

This was what it felt like to have someone who stood up for me without question or restraint? Incredible.

As a child, my mother had always played mediator but her tactics against my father had always been to change the subject. She'd distract him from whatever rampage he was on and I'd sneak away. Unfortunately, he'd usually find me again when she wasn't around to act as the buffer.

And because it took so much relentless energy, I'd rarely stood up for myself.

But not Nick. Standing in my living room, wearing only a pair of flannel pajama pants, he was infuriated. Whatever he'd heard had been enough. Without hesitation, he had defended me to the one person who had always made me feel like I was less.

Nick managed to collect himself before I did and knelt down in front of my chair.

"Fuck. I'm sorry, Emmy. He's an asshole. Are you okay?"

My blurry eyes looked into Nick's and I nodded. Reaching out, my fingers slid into the soft hair on his face while I leaned forward and pressed my lips against his.

I wanted to be as close to Nick as I could get.

I was ready.

I softly kissed Nick's mouth until he caught on and took over. I opened and his tongue slid inside, stroking back and forth while his lips pressed deeper and deeper into mine. His taste invaded my mouth, and as I dragged in a ragged breath, his scent filled my nose. Every one of my senses was consumed by Nick.

His hands came to my waist and he picked me up out of the chair. The robe I was wearing fell open as my legs wrapped around his hips and my ankles locked together at his back. I gave his beard one last stroke before wrapping both arms around his neck.

His mouth never broke from mine as he carried me upstairs and toward my bed. As we walked, Nick pushed the thin cotton fabric of my pajama shorts up and slid his hands underneath them and into my panties.

I gasped when his palms squeezed my ass and he pulled my core into the hardness under his flannel pants.

Feeling how much he wanted me sent sparks all over my skin. Every inch of my body was tingling. My sex was throbbing and I ground my hips into his, trying to get some friction to ease the ache.

Nick lowered us down into the bed and his weight settled on top of me, pushing me deep into the mattress. I cradled his hips with mine and gazed into his vibrant hazel eyes full of lust and heat.

Without breaking eye contact, his hand reached out to the nightstand and came back with a condom. When had he put them in there? It didn't matter. I was just glad that he had.

As he eased off the bed, I lifted my head so I could watch his movements. His chest was lean and cut, the muscles of his pecs and abs perfectly defined. I couldn't wait to trace the strong lines at his hipbones with my tongue. My fingertips were itching to run through the dark sprinkling of hair at his chest and lower belly.

I was so primed and ready for him that my whole body twitched when he put two thumbs into the waistband of his pants and slid them off. The sight of his hard cock sent a fresh wave of tingles to my core.

With the condom on, he came to me and pulled the

robe from my shoulders and the tank off my top. Both went sailing to the floor, followed shortly by my bottoms and panties.

Nick's hands spanned my ribs as he picked me up, setting me farther up the bed. Then with one powerful surge, he sank deep. My eyes squeezed shut as I savored the burn and stretch, my body molding to him.

"Emmy," he groaned as his hips pushed hard into mine.

For a moment, neither of us moved. When I opened my eyes, his were fixed on me.

A memory flashed. Of us in this exact position, not long after we had been married. Nine years hadn't dulled that memory in the slightest.

Reaching out, his hands found mine and our fingers naturally laced together. He brought our entwined hands above my head and bent down to kiss the tip of my nose.

The ache in my core was overwhelming me and I needed Nick to move.

"Nick," I pleaded, pressing my hips up against his.

Without pause, he started making love to me. His cock moved in and out with a steady, unrushed rhythm. The hair on his chest brushed against my pebbled nipples with every stroke.

I savored the feel of us connected together. Being with a man had never been as good as with Nick. And time hadn't changed that.

My orgasm built slowly but with force. Long and hard, my body shook as my inner walls clenched around his cock. The moans escaping my mouth were loud and unfiltered. Everything about that moment was pure and real.

Not long after I started to come down, Nick's muscles bunched and he dropped his head into the crook of my neck, groaning as he came.

We stayed locked together for a few moments while we both worked to regain our breaths and calm our thundering hearts.

"I missed you, Wife," Nick whispered into my hair.

"I missed you too."

He lifted off me, then gave me a light kiss at the base of my collarbone before going to the bathroom to deal with the condom.

I let the warm happiness of the moment flow through me before shifting back into the pillows and covering myself with the soft blankets.

It was still early and I wanted nothing more than to take a nap. Then we could start this day all over again. This time around, without the rude phone call from my father.

Though, I would lobby for a repeat of the unbelievable sex.

His weight hit the bed, then he hauled me into his chest and wrapped me tightly in his arms.

My theory about why he always wanted to spoon was because it put him in the best position to smell my hair. He always took a few long breaths when he settled. With every inhale and exhale, his body relaxed until he was asleep.

I took my own breaths and smiled again.

Sex, a morning nap and Nick. It was shaping up to be an awesome Sunday.

After our nap, Nick and I had gone at it again before coming downstairs to start breakfast. While sex the first time was slow and sweet, our second experience had involved much more foreplay and had ended with Nick driving into me from behind.

I was ravenous by the time he pulled the egg pie from the oven.

"This is really good." My rear was on an island stool and I was inhaling an enormous piece of quiche. The crust was golden and flaky. The eggs were light and creamy. The vegetables gave the dish a variety of flavors and colors.

I was famished. The only thing I didn't love about the quiche was that it took nearly an hour to bake.

He grinned. "Better than Lucky Charms?"

"Say what you must about my cereals, at least they are quick to prepare."

All week long he had been making fun of my cereal selection. It wasn't until I'd gone away to college that I had been introduced to cold cereal. Now I couldn't get enough of it. In my pantry, there were currently eleven boxes, all different varieties of sugar-filled kids' cereals.

"What do you feel like doing today?" he asked.

It was nearly noon and the only productive thing I had done so far was shower.

"I've got to work on my lesson plan for tomorrow. It's almost done so I just need thirty minutes or so. You?"

"I was thinking we could drive out to the hot springs. They shouldn't be too full of tourists this time of year, and it's fun to get all hot in the water and jump in the snow," he said.

"Sounds good. But I'll leave the snow jumping to you."

Chuckling, he reached for his ringing phone. "Brick."

I really hoped that Jess was calling to tell Nick they had found my burglar. I felt safe with my alarm system and Nick staying the night, but it would be a considerable weight off my mind if the criminal was at least identified. Then maybe we could learn why my house had been targeted.

"Yeah. We'll be here," he said and hung up. "Jess is coming over in about ten. He wants to talk to us about a few things."

"Okay. I'll run up and get dressed. Do you think we'll still have time for the hot springs?" I asked.

Even though he'd just mentioned the idea, I was attached to it. An hour sitting in a hot pool sounded amazing. My muscles were starting to get stiff from the snowshoeing yesterday. Bonus, I could check out Nick's amazing body in a pair of swim trunks.

"If Jess's business doesn't take too long, we should still have time. Just wear your suit under your clothes. There isn't a great place to change there."

Nodding, I went upstairs, hoping Jess had good news.

Fifteen minutes later, we were all huddled around the kitchen island.

"Sorry for barging in on your Sunday," Jess said. "But I thought you'd want an update as soon as possible and I didn't want to bother you at school."

"No problem. Is it about the break-in?" I asked.

"I've got nothing new to tell you. We're at a dead end." He frowned. "I'm here about Mason Carpenter."

It had been a week since the "Kidnap-versary" party and I hadn't heard back from Jess. He had promised to look into Mason's home situation, and if he was here, it meant he'd found something. Hopefully, something to get my student some help.

"I had a meeting with Garcia this week. Told him I was concerned about one of Rowen's classmates. He gave me the info you've been sending him these last few months," Jess said.

"Did you tell him that I approached you?" I asked.

"No. But I did remind him a prebuilt case file wasn't necessary before he could call me. He actually seemed relieved. I think he was worried I'd tell him to take a hike," he said.

"Thanks." I didn't think my boss would have cared about our conversation, but at the same time, I didn't want him to think I didn't respect his authority.

"So what'd you find out?" Nick asked.

"Not much. But it's a start. Kid moved over from Bozeman to live with his aunt, Kira Robertson," Jess said.

"Don't know her," Nick said.

"You wouldn't. She doesn't run anywhere near the up-and-up crowd. Ran a background. Before Prescott, she got busted on two counts of marijuana possession and one drunk and disorderly. Lays low here so far, but I asked around the station and she's been seen out with some of Wes's old acquaintances."

"Fuck," Nick muttered.

"Sorry, I'm a little lost. Wes?" I asked.

"Wes Drummond. He ran the meth trade in Jamison County. Died a little over a year ago. Murdered by the same people who kidnapped Maze and Georgia," Jess said.

"What is Mason doing living with her then?" If his aunt had problems with controlled substances, there should be cause to remove Mason from her care. A knot was forming in my stomach as I thought about what could be happening in that house.

"Called the Bozeman PD and had them pull the kid's file. Mason's mother got sent to prison a few months ago. That's why he's with the aunt. Mason's mom makes Kira look like a saint. Could see why a judge would send him here. Anything was better than where he was at," Jess said.

"What happened with the mother?" Nick asked.

"Five-year minimum sentence for prostitution and possession. Her record was a book. The final arrest that tipped the scales was right before the kid got placed here. They busted her high as a fucking kite, giving some guy a blow job while Mason was huddled in the corner. Found her apartment loaded with about every drug imaginable. Looks like she was storing it for her boyfriend, who was a junkie and small-time pimp."

I felt sick. At any moment, the quiche in my stomach was going to come back up. What kind of horrific things had Mason seen in his short life? He was probably lucky to be alive. No wonder he kept to himself.

"This keeps getting worse," I said. "Mason went from a terrible situation to a better one. But it still isn't acceptable. There has got to be a better place for him."

My voice cracked at the end of my tirade and my lip was quivering.

Nick wrapped an arm around my shoulders, pulling me close.

"I talked to the county social worker," Jess continued. "She's been making routine visits and says every time she's stopped by, the place checks out. Their place is old but she told me it's been clean and Mason seems cared for. The kid was quiet but when she asked him if he liked living there, he said he did."

"That can't be!" I yelled. "He's filthy most days when I see him. And he looks miserably unhappy."

"When I showed your reports to the social worker, she was shocked," Jess said.

"What is she going to do about it?"

"She's going to do a random check sometime in the next week or ten days. Stop by unannounced and see what it looks like."

"Can she do that?" Nick asked.

"Yeah. The aunt is still under probation as Mason's guardian. Any fuckup and the kid is removed. Kira loses her bimonthly checks from the state. Not surprising that when the social worker had appointments, everything was in order. But I agree with Emmeline. Something is happening. We just need to prove it. Hopefully before the aunt gets wind that Mason's teacher is suspicious," Jess said.

"And if the random inspection works? What happens next?" I asked.

"He'll go to a foster family in town."

"And will that be better or worse than his current situation?"

Jess smirked and fought a smile while Nick's chest started shaking against my back. Clearly I had said something funny. I just didn't have a clue what it was.

"What?"

"Emmy, this isn't New York. Ninety-nine percent of the families that live in Prescott are good, honest people."

"Okay. Then foster care would be an improvement."

"Yeah," he replied.

"What can I do?" I asked Jess.

"Same as you have been. Send your concerns to Garcia. He'll route them to me. Hang tight until the social worker does her check. I'll let you two get back to your weekend." Jess waved a hand as he turned to the front door.

"Thanks, Brick," Nick said.

"Jess?" I called before he left. "Thank you for sending a

blue coat to school with Rowen. Mason was overjoyed that he could play outside at recess without being teased."

"I'll pass it along to Georgia," he said and walked out.

"Do you think Mason is going to be okay?" I asked Nick.

"With you as his teacher, it's the best chance he's got."

CHAPTER 13

"**F**RED, I APPRECIATE YOUR CONCERN BUT I haven't decided what to do about my divorce. Rest assured, when I do, I will inform you."

My lawyer had called me this afternoon, wondering why he hadn't received my signed divorce papers. Given that during our last conversation I had been frustrated at a delay on his part, a delay on mine had been unexpected.

"I must warn you, Emmeline, the longer you wait, the more probable a redraft of the decree or settlement agreement will be required. I would hate to see you incur that unnecessary cost," he said.

"Understood. If it comes down to that, I will be happy to pay you and your team the fee to have the papers reworked."

"Your father will not be pleased to see a repeat cost against his retainer."

"Fred, I told you last fall that these charges are not to be put against my father's retainer. I will pay you personally.

This is not Father's business."

"Yes, of course," he backpedaled. Either he had forgotten my instruction or he had ignored it. I was really hoping for the former but I suspected the latter, since he and my father often golfed together.

"I will notify you when I've made my decision. Goodbye," I said and hung up.

It had been a month since Father's irate early morning phone call and I hadn't heard from him since. Though, Steffie had called. Apparently, she'd caved and told him the man that had yelled at him that morning was none other than my husband.

But if Fred told him that I was delaying the divorce, my father would get much more intrusive, and even Steffie's charms wouldn't keep him from plotting something nasty.

Shit.

I needed to decide what to do. Not just so I had an answer to my father's inevitable questions, but for my sake. And Nick's.

I enjoyed being with Nick. Our relationship was normal. It satisfied the cravings I'd had my whole life for something genuine and real.

But it didn't feel like we were married. It felt exactly like it was: two adults who were dating. We were seeing how the other fit into our everyday life with no long-term promises.

Someday I wanted what my grandparents had had in their marriage. Love. Honor. Commitment. Trust. Friendship.

Did Nick and I have those? In small pieces, but not as a whole.

Part of me wondered if we could ever move forward if we didn't do something drastic. Truly start over. Both of us were content with how things were going. But what was next? If we were already married, what could we look forward to? Maybe one day living under the same roof?

I wanted more. I wanted Vegas back. All of that passion and excitement. To know I was the luckiest woman in the world. To be utterly consumed by love.

And over these last few weeks, I'd started thinking a divorce might be our best option.

I didn't want to give Nick up. I just wanted to keep *dating* Nick. Then I could look forward to the day when we could get married again. And the second time around, it would be without ignorance or secrets.

Nick was going to go ballistic when I brought up the topic of divorce. It would disrupt the normalcy we had just found, which is why I had kept the papers hidden.

And they would stay tucked away until I could muster the courage to talk to my husband about a title change.

Scratch husband. Scribble boyfriend.

I pushed the phone call aside and finished up my tasks at school. Then I drove to Nick's house for our new normal nightly routine.

"I'm here," I called into Nick's house.

"Kitchen, Emmy."

I shed my coat and shoes by the front door and padded through the main room. This was becoming my favorite part of the day. Walking barefoot through his cozy house. Savoring the warmth from the fire ablaze in the hearth. Smelling whatever meal he was cooking for dinner.

Two minutes in the cabin and I was completely relaxed.

This is what all homes should feel like. I would have traded my enormous childhood mansion any day of the week to come home to a place like this.

When I reached the kitchen, Nick was standing in the middle of the room with his hands planted on his hips and a frown on his face.

"What?"

"I didn't see you this morning," he said.

"Yes. You did. If you recall, we had sex before I got in the shower. How can you not remember?" Tapping my index finger on my chin, I asked the ceiling, "Am I losing my touch?"

He grinned. "You left when I was in the shower. I didn't see what you were wearing."

"And?" I asked.

In two long strides, he crossed the room and plastered his body to mine. The hardness in his jeans was like stone against my hip. "And had I seen this dress, I would have fucked you again while it was bunched up above your ass," he said before taking my earlobe between his teeth.

A shiver ran from the nape of my neck, down my spine and to my sex.

Dirty talk. Another favorite part of coming to Nick's house at night. His verbal foreplay would continue all evening until I couldn't take it anymore and either I dragged him upstairs to bed or I attacked him on the couch.

"You have my permission to try that later."

With a groan, he ground his erection into my hip before lightly kissing my cheek and turning back to the stove.

My dress was a pale gray, form-fitted sheath with long sleeves. This morning it had been an article I rarely wore. Tonight it had just become a staple.

"What are you making?" I asked, boosting myself up on the counter.

"I did a pot roast in the Crock-Pot today."

"Sounds delicious. What can I do?" I asked.

He set out a couple of plates and turned to me. "Nothing. Do you want some wine?"

"Is my name Emmeline Austin?"

After my first visit to his house, I'd made sure he had wine stocked so I wouldn't be forced to drink whiskey again. I might not know my way around a kitchen, but a corkscrew was a different story.

The last two weeks had been spent mostly at Nick's cabin when I wasn't at work. He had asked if we could stay at his house instead of mine so he could monitor the fire station dispatch.

Apparently, his system was wired into the house, and moving it would have been a big hassle. Really, I think he missed his kitchen, where the cupboards were full of actual kitchen gadgets, not coffee mugs.

My place was still tainted by the break-in so I had been more than happy to get out of there. I went home every day to pick up wardrobe items but then came to Nick's for dinner and sleep.

"How was your day?" I asked.

"Good. Quiet. You?"

"Wonderful. I love my kids. They had so much fun doing that full moon art project I told you about."

Today, I had taught my class all about the moon. During the month of March, I was planning on introducing them to the entire solar system. We were slowly putting together a large model as we learned about the sun, moon and planets.

"Knew they would. Kids and finger paint. You can't go wrong," Nick said.

"True. I let them go crazy too. There was paint everywhere. Some of the kids even had it in their hair. And obviously I couldn't send them home that way. So the dirty ones had a field trip to the high school locker rooms."

"Right. And by some kids do you mean *only* Mason Carpenter?" he asked.

"That poor kid was just covered in paint," I lied. Mason was spotless, unlike his classmates. "I just *had* to get his hair cleaned. Unfortunately, while I was washing, I accidentally spilled water all over his clothes. Clumsy me. Good thing I had some extras handy."

For the last month, I had been manipulating my lesson plans so that I could get Mason washed at least once a week and into some clean clothes. Messy art projects. Spills during snack time. Whatever it took so that while the other kids were at recess, I could work some of the smell off him.

"Emmy, be careful. Don't step on the social worker's toes," Nick said.

"I don't know why it should matter. She's not getting any results. Two random inspections and she hasn't found anything. I'm not paranoid about this, Nick. Something is going on in that house. If she can't do anything about it, I'm going to."

"Don't get defensive," he said, coming to me at the counter. "I'm not saying what you're doing is wrong. I just want you to be careful. If other parents notice Mason getting special treatment, it could cause you problems."

My shoulders sagged. "I know you're right. But I hate this. I hate feeling helpless. It's like I'm the only one he has."

He reached out and rubbed my arms. "Jess will take care of it. Trust him. If the social worker doesn't get some results soon, he'll start going there himself. If the aunt doesn't start taking her guardianship seriously, he'll make her life miserable. That shit doesn't fucking fly in his town."

"Okay," I said. "Something to know about me. Patience is not a strength."

He chuckled. "Figured that one out already. I thought you were going to take my head off the other night when my pork chops needed more time in the oven."

I rolled my eyes.

With a light kiss on the tip of my nose, he went back to cooking.

An hour later, my tummy was full of the best pot roast I'd ever had. It was tender and juicy. When Nick described the few easy steps it had taken to prepare the meal, I decided that maybe Crock-Pot cooking could become my forte.

While our stomachs settled, we curled into the couch to watch TV.

Tonight's Western was another John Wayne classic, *The Man Who Shot Liberty Valance*. We were only half way through it but I expected it to be an absolute winner. I was a big James Stewart fan and his character's name, Ransom, was a top contender for any future son that I may have.

Ransom Slater.

Another spontaneous Nick thought. They'd been coming over me regularly for months now. Ever since my breakup with Logan. I needed therapy. "Oh for the love . . ." I muttered to myself.

"What was that?" Nick asked.

Bat. Shit. Crazy.

"Nothing," I said.

Nick leaned forward and grabbed the remote, pausing the movie. "I need to talk to you about something, Emmeline."

My body was instantly on alert. He'd used my full name. Nick never used my full name.

I gave him a sideways glance. "Okay?"

"Do you feel comfortable here?" he asked.

"Here?" I asked, pointing to the floor. "In your house? Or do you mean in Prescott?"

"Both."

"Then yes to both. Why?"

"You know why I left you in Vegas," he said. "Your money. My lifestyle and family. The combination put you in a dangerous position."

I sat up straighter in the couch, my stomach rolling. Where was he going with this? The pause he took before continuing made my heart pound. The crackling fire echoed in the silent room.

"Your money still worries me. Not for the same reasons but . . ." He shifted in the couch. "I don't give a fuck about money but I can't . . ."

His fingers were fidgeting and his foot was bouncing on the floor. Nick was always so calm and collected. His nervousness was unsettling.

My eyes searched his face for some kind of clue as to what he was struggling to say. "What?"

He pushed out a loud breath and blurted, "I need to know if you're going to eventually leave me because I don't have any money." Standing from the couch, he raked his hands through his hair. "At least not the kind of money you're used to. What happens when you decide Montana life in a log cabin isn't enough? That you'd rather be back in the city? Are you going to leave when your father cuts you off because you stayed out here with me? He's a fucking dick, Emmy. He'll take it all away from you just because you didn't fly to New York and beg your ex to take you back."

There was a lot in his rambling speech to take in so I

sat unmoving, formulating my response, while he paced in front of the fireplace.

"Can you come back to the couch?" I asked.

"No."

"Nick. Get over here," I ordered.

"Just tell me. Yes or no."

"Yes or no to what?"

He stopped pacing and threw his arms out wide. "Yes or no that you are going to leave me because I don't have any fucking money!"

"Where is all this coming from?" I asked, shocked by how upset he was. Not long ago we were laughing over dinner and chatting about our days.

"That man's success was all based on a lie, Emmy," he said, pointing to the TV, paused on a still of James Stewart.

I had no idea what he was talking about. I mentally tallied the number of beers Nick had drank with dinner. He shouldn't be drunk after two. Right? Maybe my bat-shit craziness was rubbing off.

"Start over, please," I said. "James Stewart lied? When?"

"He didn't shoot Liberty Valance. John Wayne did. But he took all the credit."

"Spoiler alert," I muttered. Moving on. "Tell me how you got from that movie," I said, pointing to the screen, "to me leaving Montana. And while you're at it, you had probably better explain why you think I'm some spoiled brat that only cares about money. And why you think I would throw my life here away and go running back to the city if I had a zero balance in my bank account."

Up to this point, I had mostly been confused by his freak-out. But as the words flew past my lips, the hold I'd had on my temper fell apart.

Did he honestly find me that shallow? Had I not made it clear how much I despised my greedy father? That I was nothing like him? And how could he not understand how much I loved living outside the city? I talked about it constantly.

"That's not what I meant," he said. "I don't think you're a spoiled brat."

I stood from the couch. "Then explain. Now."

"In the movie, James Stewart lived his life with regret. I don't want that for you. Or for me. I thought I'd be clear of it when you came here. That I could stop regretting the choice I made to leave you in Vegas. And I don't anymore. But I've been thinking about this for a while. What if you wake up one day and realize the life you had was better? I can't give you that, Emmy."

My temper fizzled when Nick sagged into a chair and his head fell into his hands. "I told you I wouldn't leave you and that I wouldn't let you go. But I will. If that's what it takes for you to be happy. I'll let you go."

I walked around the coffee table and stood above Nick. Running my fingers through his hair, I said, "You're freaking out."

"I know." He sighed and looked up at me. "I just don't want to lose you again."

"Then stop being an absolute moron."

When he opened his mouth to respond, I pressed my fingertips to his lips. "My turn," I said and pushed his shoulders back so I could straddle his thighs. My fingers played with the hair at the base of his neck and I started picking apart his concerns.

"Let's start with you thinking I will want to move back to the city. Please believe me when I say that I won't. Ever.

Prescott might not be the last place for me, but I won't call New York home again. And if you've been listening to me at all during the last few months, you'll know it's true. Understood?"

"Yeah."

"Next up, my father. From the time I graduated from Yale, he has had not one thing to do with my personal finances. His only influence was on my salary while I worked for his company. He could offer me billions and I would never take it from him. I do not want his money and I never will."

He nodded.

"Lastly, money. If all I had was my teacher's salary to live on, I'd be happy. I don't need riches and fancy things. Yes, I've had them my whole life. But I don't need them."

"You've never been without, Emmy. How do you know?"

"I don't," I said. "But I know to the bottom of my soul that it's true. You'll just have to trust me when I tell you that money doesn't matter to me. Yes, it makes life easier. No, it does not guarantee that life will be good. I've seen rich people miserable and poor families happy. I know what's important." When he didn't acknowledge me, I asked, "Do you believe me?"

He nodded.

"Crisis averted?"

He nodded again.

"I'm not going to leave you because you don't have money. I will leave you if you spoil the endings to all the movies we watch."

His quiet chuckle brought a smile to my face.

"I'm getting more wine. Then I'll give you the full

money story so you know."

As I poured my glass, I laughed to myself at how paranoid I had been just months ago, thinking Nick could be out for my riches. Mr. Andrews had been certain Nick would contest our divorce without the promise of a large payday.

Absolutely silly.

Nick did not care about money. At all. He just needed to know that I didn't either.

"My paychecks are important but not because they fund my lifestyle," I told Nick when we were seated again in the couch. "It's because every cent of those checks was one I earned for myself."

It made me proud that that money came from my efforts. My ideas. It wasn't money handed to me because I was born into the right family.

"My father's family was well off, nothing extravagant, but he was able to use his parents' money as a foundation to become the rich man he is today. My mother's family, on the other hand, was extremely wealthy. They were extravagant."

"How come?" Nick asked.

"My grandfather was a career investor. He poured money into small, startup companies and helped them become billion-dollar corporations. When he died, he had considerable stock in most of today's well-known tech giants."

"Your money is from him?"

"Yes. My parents supported me as a child, obviously. And I needed my father to pay for college. But after that, I received a large sum from my grandfather. My inheritance was contingent upon getting my degree," I said.

"It didn't go to your mom?"

I shook my head. "Just a portion. My grandmother passed before my grandfather. I think if he had died before her, its entirety would have gone to Mom. But it didn't work out that way. To say that my grandfather and father hated each other would be an understatement. Grandpa didn't want Father to get his money so my mom got their liquid savings and their properties. But the bulk of their fortune was split between my brother and me."

"I didn't know you had a brother."

"Ethan," I said. "I haven't spoken to him much this last year. He lives off of his trust fund in the city. His current wife, Number Four, is an absolute witch so I avoided them both when I lived in New York. He's emailed me a couple of times since I moved here but we don't talk much."

"Hmm," Nick muttered and sat silently in thought. "I can see why you'd want to teach. It was your dream. But why didn't you just use the money from your grandpa after Yale? You could have avoided working for your dad. Why'd you work at his company if you didn't need the money?" he asked.

I shrugged. "Habit. Hope, maybe. Neither of those are good reasons, but I've done a lot to try and win my father's approval. It was hard for me to break out of that cycle."

"I get that," he said.

After college, I had thought that by working at Austin Capital, we might finally break the barriers between us. That we could bond over his beloved company. It took me a while to figure out that no matter how much I excelled or how many donations I brought in, he'd never be proud. When he'd sacrificed my reputation for his, I'd known it was time to give up. So I'd used my trust fund for the first time to pay for NYU.

"Do you want to know how much money we're talking about?" I asked. It was a large number and I didn't discuss it with anyone. But if he wanted the amount, I'd tell him. If we stayed together, he'd eventually have to know.

"Not really."

"Okay." I was relieved we could delay that conversation for a different day.

"What now?"

"Now you let me apologize," he said. "I could have handled that better."

It was almost comforting the way he overreacted, scared I would leave him. We both had the same fear. "You can make your official apology in bed."

His embarrassment was replaced with a sexy smirk. He moved in a flash, standing from the couch and hauling me up over his shoulder. My face was upside-down with an up and close view of his amazing behind. With both hands I gave his butt a firm squeeze.

"You'll pay for that," he rumbled.

Using the hand that wasn't locked around my knees, he slid it up and under the hem of my dress. His palm slipped right beneath my panties and kneaded one cheek before slipping across to do the same on the other. Then he dipped his thumb down and teased my clit.

"Nick," I gasped and squirmed.

He circled his thumb again before throwing me down onto his bed.

One swift movement and my dress was riding up my waist and my panties were somewhere on the floor. Nick's mouth was latched onto me and one finger was stroking inside.

My legs were quaking and I was almost there when he lifted his head an inch and murmured, "I'm sorry, Emmy."

He didn't wait for my reply before getting back to it,

making me come hard and long with his mouth and then again with his cock.

When we were both spent and curled in for sleep, I whispered his reprieve. "You are completely forgiven."

Smiling, I fell asleep with the sounds of his laughter ringing in my ears.

CHAPTER 14

"**L**ET'S GO, EMMY!" NICK CALLED FROM THE foyer.

"Three minutes!" I yelled back.

Shit.

I needed *thirty*-three minutes.

I was running late to Rowen Cleary's birthday party because I'd been so consumed with wrapping her gift that I'd lost track of time and had hopped into the shower an hour behind schedule.

"Shit, shit, shit," I muttered to myself, swiping on my makeup. On the bright side, at least I was dressed. Picking an outfit was often my most time-consuming process.

"Sorry," I told Nick after I climbed into his truck, thirty minutes later.

Grabbing my hand, he laced his fingers with mine and brought them to his lips. I loved the soft scrape of his beard against my skin. "It's okay. We don't have to be there until three."

"What? You told me two thirty!"

He just kept grinning. "You're notoriously late, Wife. And it's going to take us a while to get there."

"The drive is five minutes. Do we have to go into town for something?" I asked. We had already bought the beer and wine. Rowen's present was in the back. What else did we need?

"We'll need the extra time to walk. You'll see," he said.

Nick was not wrong. We parked and had to walk down the entire length of the gravel drive to the farmhouse. Cars were lined up along both sides all the way back to the paved county road. Apparently, the whole town of Prescott had been invited to a six-year-old's birthday party.

"Wow," I said as we reached the house. The garage was open and full of people, and through the farmhouse's windows I saw that the house was packed too.

"Gigi has a tendency to go overboard," Nick said. "Jess told me yesterday that she's been decorating all week. He's pretty happy she's going back to work soon. Then the parties will go back to their normal level of over the top. Not this fucking insanity."

I wouldn't classify the party as insane but it was certainly festive. The party was princess themed with an abundance of pink and purple decorations scattered throughout the house and garage. Balloons. Streamers. Banners. Gigi had even found a couple life-size princess cardboard cutouts to set up by the present and cupcake tables.

The guests were decorated too. All of the women were wearing crowns or tiaras and the men were given pink beer cozies. Rowen was in a full princess costume complete with plastic heels and satin gloves.

Wandering through the house and garage, Nick and I

made our way through the crowd while he introduced me to the many guests. Thankfully, years of galas and parties had prepared me for just this moment. I could finally put my name-memorization skills to use in Prescott.

Unlike the kidnapping anniversary party from a month ago, Nick stayed close to my side all afternoon and evening. If we were walking around, he'd hold my hand. If we were standing, his arm was around my shoulders so that I could wrap my arm around his lower back and tuck my hand in his back jeans pocket.

Jess and Gigi had both visited with us briefly, but with the chaos of the party, we mostly stayed in the kitchen with Silas, Maisy and Beau. The birthday girl herself darted around the house, smiling brightly and leading around the puppy Jess had bought for her.

"How do you do it? Teach a whole room full of kids like her all day, every day?" Beau asked.

"I drink a lot at night." I laughed.

"She's got a gift. Some of the stuff she thinks up to do with those kids is fucking brilliant," Nick said. "Those kids are lucky to have her. Wish I would have had a teacher like that."

Pride swelled in my chest and a wide smile spread across my face. "Thanks, Nick," I whispered.

He pulled me closer into his side and leaned down to kiss the top of my head.

"You know, I used to come in and teach forest fire safety classes. I haven't done one yet this year. We could plan a visit for your kids," Beau offered.

"That would be amazing!"

"I bet you could talk Nick into joining me too. Bring out the old 'Stop, drop and roll.' Make a bigger class of it. Fire safety at home and outdoors," Beau said.

Nick nodded. "Good idea. Just wish I would have thought of it first. She's going to be all pissed later that I didn't."

"If you come to teach my class, I promise to only be mad for a day or two," I said.

"Deal." The smile on my face was giant. I couldn't wait to see the look on my students' faces after spending an afternoon with Nick and Beau.

"So when are you two gonna have kids?" a man asked.

I didn't recognize the voice so I searched the room, trying to determine who had just asked an extremely personal question to a stranger. My eyes landed on an older man standing on the other side of the kitchen. He was staring at Nick and me, waiting for a response.

"Oh, Seth. Butt out," Maisy told him.

I was instantly grateful for her interjection. It gave me time to think of a way to politely dodge his question.

The Prescott residents were *all* about one another's business. Prying came with the territory, and at times it felt more intrusive than the New York paparazzi and gossip columnists.

Nick and I still had a lot to overcome. We were a *long* way from adding children to the mix.

"Ignore him, Emmeline," Maisy said quietly. "He means well but he's one of the meddlesome old men in town. They thrive on gossip and drama."

"I don't know why you're even asking, Balan. You and all your retired buddies will just make up a story when you meet at the café next week for coffee," Nick said.

"You young kids." Seth chuckled. "So sensitive these days. All right, all right. I get the hint. I'll just tell everyone you've got ED and the Viagra isn't working."

The people in the kitchen burst out laughing and even Nick couldn't keep a straight face.

Hours later and my smile hadn't faltered. As a teenager, I'd loved attending social gatherings with my parents. But things were different now. Those fancy parties and pretentious dinners paled in comparison to a casual gathering with good people and honest friendship.

"You're lucky to have such good friends," I told Nick as we drove to his house.

"They're your friends too, Emmy."

I didn't agree but I wasn't going to argue. Maybe someday I would consider them friends. It wasn't that I didn't *want* them as friends, but right now, they belonged to Nick.

Though, I was excited to spend some time with Maisy and Gigi next week. Maisy had invited me to join them for their monthly girls' night at the Prescott Spa. We were getting pedicures and drinking wine while they enjoyed a few hours of adult conversation without their kids interrupting. I couldn't wait.

"Do you want kids?" Nick asked.

It wasn't out of the blue but his question still managed to surprise me. During the party, I had been grateful when he'd dodged Seth Balan's question. But it was one of those that once asked, it was difficult to ignore.

"Yes," I said. "Do you?"

"Yeah. How many?"

"At least two. My mother was an only child and she always complained about how lonely her childhood was."

"Let's go for three," he said.

What? Let's go for three? Wasn't this a hypothetical discussion? I didn't realize we were talking about how many kids we were having together.

This divorce discussion couldn't be stalled any longer. We were on different pages as to where our relationship was headed. Maybe not the end goal, but certainly the speed in which we were getting there.

I took a few deep breaths and worked up the nerve to start this discussion. This was going to cause a miserable fight.

"Nick, I've been wanting to talk—"

"What the fuck's he doing here?"

I followed his gaze down the driveway to an enormous black truck sitting in front of his house. The vehicle was massive. Tinted windows. Chrome plating. Lifted frame. I would have to be hoisted into the passenger seat it was so tall.

"Who is that?"

"Stay here," he said, parking the truck and jumping out. The door slammed shut behind him as he marched up to the man standing on his steps.

He was dressed completely in black. A chain hung from his front jeans pocket to his back. On top of his T-shirt, he wore a black leather vest covered with embroidered patches.

This had to be someone from his father's motorcycle gang.

Given what Nick had told me about them, I was instantly nervous. I assumed that his association with the club was limited to family members but maybe I had been mistaken and this visit meant trouble.

As they talked, the visitor came down the steps to stand on equal footing with Nick. He was about the same height and had the same brown hair. Could this be his younger brother? It was too dark for me to compare their faces.

After another minute of talking, Nick relaxed and

embraced the man with a quick hug and back slap. While Nick came to me, the man grabbed a duffel I hadn't noticed and walked through the front door.

"It looks like we've got company for the night?" I asked when he opened the passenger door.

"Yeah. Sorry."

"Don't be sorry. It's your house. Should I go home?" I asked.

"Abso-fucking-lutely not," he said and helped me down. When we got inside, the man had already helped himself to a beer from the fridge and was waiting for us in the living room.

"Dash, meet Emmeline Austin," Nick said. "Emmy, this is my brother Kingston Slater."

Brother. Right.

"Hello. Nice to meet you, Kingston," I said, extending my hand.

"Dash. Everyone calls me Dash. Except Nick here when he wants to be a dick. Nice to meet you too, Emmeline."

The similarities between Nick and Dash were many. Even if he hadn't been introduced as Nick's brother, I would have made the assumption. They had the same hair and body shape, though Dash had numerous tattoos on his forearms, and his face was covered with light stubble, unlike Nick's full beard.

"What's with the crown, princess?" Dash asked.

"Oh." I blushed and yanked the tiara from my hair. "We were at a princess-themed birthday party."

"A princess party? You sure know how to live it up, Nick."

"Fuck off," Nick said. "You know you could find somewhere else to stay tonight, asshole. There is a motel here."

"No way. Me and *Emmy* have a lot to talk about," Dash said, sinking into the couch.

"Emmeline," Nick and I both corrected.

"I'm getting a beer. Do you want something?" Nick asked me.

"Wine, please."

"What brings you to Prescott, Dash? Nick said you live in Clifton Forge, right?" I asked, sitting in the chair across from him.

"Yep. Came 'cause I thought Nick might want to help me with a car. And I haven't seen the fucker in months. He didn't even come back for Christmas this year."

I frowned, feeling guilty that I had kept Nick from his traditional holiday plans. That he'd stayed in Prescott for me, even though I had been in Italy. I hated that he'd missed time with his family because I had run away.

"What car?" Nick asked from the kitchen.

"Got a 1970 Plymouth Road Runner I'm restoring for a guy in Washington. I haven't worked on one before but remembered you did back in the day. Thought you could help me get the timing right," Dash said.

"I can do that. Where'd you leave it?"

"Hauled it up with me. Trailer's by your garage."

"Dash is a shit mechanic." Nick grinned as he handed me my wineglass.

"Compared to you, everyone is a shit mechanic," Dash scoffed. "Don't listen to him, Emmeline. I'm fucking awesome. I'd change your oil any time." He winked.

"Are you hitting on my wife?"

Beer sprayed from Dash's mouth all over himself and the couch. Nick muttered, "Fuck," and ran to grab a towel from the kitchen. "You're married!" Dash shouted after patting himself dry.

"Yeah," Nick said.

Dash stood from the couch and threw the towel in his brother's face. "What the fuck, Nick? How could you not tell us? At least me? I would have come to the wedding."

"Chill, Dash," Nick said and sat down on the couch.

Dash muttered a curse under his breath and sat too, taking a few long gulps from his beer.

"Our wedding was nine years ago," Nick said. "In Las Vegas. You were in high school. Don't get all bent out of shape. I didn't tell anyone, okay?"

"And in the last nine years, you didn't think to mention you had a wife? Maybe bring her home to meet your family?"

"We were estranged," I said. "I've been living in New York where I grew up. I only moved to Montana last fall, and now that I'm in Prescott, we've reconnected."

"Uh-huh," Dash muttered.

Nick gave me a puzzled look but I just shrugged and smiled, silently urging him to let it go. He would have admitted to leaving me in Vegas but I didn't want him to have to explain our whole ordeal to his brother. He was off the hook for once. Some of those old wounds were starting to heal and I didn't want them scraped open by hearing our history again.

"May I ask? Why does everyone call you 'Dash'?"

Both men looked to one another and smiled. "My mom started calling me Dash when I was a little kid. Nick built me a soapbox go-cart and I may have disabled the brakes."

"It was all we could do to get the little shit to wear his helmet." Nick chuckled.

Dash shrugged. "I've always been an adrenaline junkie for speed."

"Tell me more about this car," Nick said.

For the next hour, the brothers talked about cars while I sat quietly, listening and enjoying my wine. I learned that the motorcycle club had a successful garage in Clifton Forge where Dash worked as a mechanic and Nick's father was the manager.

I noticed that throughout the conversation, they always managed to steer clear of discussing club business. Dash mentioned their father briefly but Nick didn't acknowledge it or ask more about his well-being.

But it was Nick's passion for cars and mechanics that surprised me most. I rarely saw him this animated. When he talked about Dash's projects and gave his brother advice, there was a fire in his eyes. I imagined I had that same light when I talked about teaching.

"Emmy," Nick whispered, putting his hand on my shoulder and startling me awake.

"What? Oh. Sorry."

"Don't be sorry. Let's go to bed," he said, picking me up.

"I can walk," I told him but closed my eyes and rested my head against his shoulder. I loved how Nick often carried me around. It made me feel like I was precious.

"Night, Emmeline," Dash called.

"Good night, Dash," I said. "Let's get Nick to make us his quiche in the morning."

"She's a smart woman, Brother. Not sure why she married you," Dash told Nick as we went upstairs.

"Me either," he said. "But fuck I'm a lucky man because she did," he added quietly, so only I could hear.

"Morning," Dash said, joining Nick and me in the kitchen.

"Good morning."

"Coffee." Nick held a mug out to his brother.

"I forgot how comfortable that bed is in your guest room," Dash said. "Might have to extend my trip by a few days."

"Stay as long as you want," Nick said.

After a delicious breakfast of quiche and fried breakfast potatoes, I followed the men outside to the garage.

In all my time at Nick's, I hadn't been in the building, and much like his fire station, the garage was pristine. Red tool cabinets and black metal shelves bordered the walls and there was a hydraulic car lift in the middle of the cement floor.

Sipping my coffee, I watched the men work from my perch on a tool bench. Dash was an apt student and Nick was in his element.

"I think you got it," Dash said, giving Nick a clap on the back a couple hours later.

"Yeah," he replied, wiping the grease from his hands with a red rag. "Do you want to take her out and see?"

"Fuck yeah!"

The engine roared to life as Dash eased the yellow Plymouth through the tall garage door. When he hit the road, the noise spiked as he sped off.

"What's 'Slater's Station'?" I asked Nick, pointing to the huge sign that hung on the wall opposite me.

"Nothing. Just an old dream."

"Tell me."

"You know how I was working at that garage in Colorado?" he asked.

"Yes." I nodded.

"Before that, I worked for my dad at the club garage where Dash works now. I learned early and it came naturally. So when I started in Colorado, the owner didn't have much to teach me that I didn't already know or I hadn't learned from my certification classes. So instead of teaching me about cars, he taught me about running a business. Encouraged me to start my own shop. When I told him I was quitting to move home, he gave me that sign."

"It's a remarkable piece." The huge stainless steel sign was shaped as a wrench and hung from the ceiling by two thick chains. The letters were cut into the metal in solid blocking.

"Yeah. He was a nice guy. Passed a couple years ago from cancer," Nick said.

"I'm sorry. Why didn't you start your own garage?"

"Money, mostly. Security. When I came up here, I was hoping Dash would come live with me and avoid the club. I wanted to have the stability of a paycheck. Starting a garage can be risky, especially in a small town where there's already a good shop."

I could see his point. The Prescott populace was nothing if not loyal. And if there was a garage in town where people trusted the owner, they would be reluctant to move their business to someone new.

But Nick wasn't a stranger in town anymore. He was loved in this community. Prescott's residents would support him if he started his own garage.

"You love it, Nick. I've never seen you this excited about your work. Why don't you try it now?"

"I like the fire station. It feels good to be part of something that protects the community. My whole childhood was spent with guys who avoided the law and any type of authority. It feels good to embrace it instead of fight it. Plus, I get paid well and it's fairly low stress most of the time."

"But it's not your passion."

"No, it's not. I enjoy the challenge of working on a car. It's like putting a puzzle together. Making all the pieces fit."

"Then do it."

He shrugged. "Maybe someday."

His deflection told me that he'd given that dream up ages ago. But I wasn't going to stop encouraging him. I had abandoned one career path for another so I could pursue my dreams, and not once had I regretted my decision. It might take some time, but I was going to keep pushing until he had his dream job too.

Dash returned and we enjoyed the rest of the afternoon and evening together. I enjoyed the time getting to know Dash and seeing Nick interact with a family member. He was caring and affectionate and it was obvious he would like to see Dash more often.

"Thanks, Brother," Dash said, shaking Nick's hand as he was leaving.

"Any time. It was good to see you."

"Glad to have met you, Emmy. Get this douche bag to bring you up to Clifton Forge one of these days," Dash told me.

"Thank you." The chances of Nick taking me to his hometown were slim at best.

"Dad's always bitching about having too much custom work to keep up with. Bet he'd ship a few cars here if you wanted a project to tinker with," Dash told Nick.

I was pressed against Nick's side with my arms wrapped around his belt. With the mention of their dad, tension radiated through his body.

"No thanks," Nick said.

"That's what I thought. Maybe one day you two can work through your fucking shit so I can see you more than once a year."

"You know how I feel about all your club business. My stance hasn't changed."

"I think you don't know shit about my club."

"True. Let's keep it that way," Nick said. "Drive safe."

Dash shook his head and strode to his truck.

As he roared down the drive, I thought it was such a shame to end his visit on a sour note. We'd had such a nice Sunday together, working on his car, grilling steaks for dinner, laughing and sharing stories. Now the day felt tainted.

"Are you okay?" I asked as we watched his brother leave.

"No. I shouldn't have snapped. He always plays the middleman between Dad and me. I wish he'd realize that I can't be around the old man. Just give it up."

"I think he just misses you."

"Yeah," he sighed. "I miss him too."

"He seems nice. I guess when you told me your family was in a motorcycle gang, I pictured a much scarier version of a brother. Someone dark and menacing."

He scoffed. "That's what's scary, Emmy. Everything in their lives appears normal until the minute they're taking a pipe wrench to a man's body or holding a gun to your head."

I shuddered at the mental image and Nick knew he had me freaked. "Sorry."

"It's okay," I said.

"Come on, Wife. Let's watch a movie. It's time you were introduced to *Butch Cassidy and the Sundance Kid*."

I had actually heard of that film before. Paul Newman and Robert Redford? He'd get no objections from me.

CHAPTER 15

THE SECOND MY CELL PHONE STOPPED RINGING downstairs, Nick's dispatch radio kicked on.

"*Milo, this is dispatch. Got another call from Emmeline Austin's security company. Her alarm's been tripped and she didn't answer when they called.*"

"*Roger. I'll go over now. Gimme the address.*"

"Fuck," Nick cursed and shot out of bed.

"Oh my god," I gasped. "Do you think it was another break-in?"

"I don't know, Emmy. But we need to get over there."

"Right. Should we call the station so they know I'm not home?" Nick's phone was already at his ear. Following him to the closet, I threw on some clothes and mentally prepared for whatever I might find at home.

"Why is this happening?" I asked Nick as he sped to my house. The clock on the dash read 3:16 a.m.

"I don't know but it'll be okay," he said, lifting my hand

to his lips.

"I hope you're right."

Milo had beaten us to the house. The lights on his cruiser were flashing and he was standing in the drive watching our approach.

"Fuck. I hope he didn't come racing down here with those lights on and fuck up any chance of catching this guy," Nick clipped.

"I'm sure he knows what he's doing."

He grunted. "I wish we would have been here tonight. I would have loved to catch this guy in the act."

I felt exactly the opposite but kept quiet. Wishing we'd been here was asinine. A dangerous and potentially armed criminal had been here not long ago. I felt lucky we *hadn't* been here.

Two break-in attempts just a month apart could not be random. Someone was targeting my house. Maybe they were targeting me. Who knows what could have happened if we had been here?

"What'd you find?" Nick asked Milo as we congregated by the cruiser.

"Nothing. The front door was wide open when I came up. Whoever broke in was long gone by the time I showed," Milo said.

"Did you check the area?" Nick asked.

"Yeah. Tracks in the snow lead around the side of the house and then south into the trees. I didn't follow them far. Jess is on his way. He might want to hike out there tonight. I'm guessing he'll wait until first light," Milo said.

"Fuck," Nick hissed. "I'm going with you guys when you check them out."

"Sure thing, Nick."

"Did you clear the house?"

Milo nodded. "First thing I did. Place is empty."

"Emmy, go ahead and disarm that thing."

I used my phone to silence the blaring alarm.

"Come on. Let's get inside before you get too cold," Nick said, grabbing my hand and pulling me up the front steps.

Nothing was like the first break-in. Whoever came in had not been careful and quiet. The handle on the front door was broken and hanging loose. My table in the foyer was knocked over. Snow was tracked in past the entryway and up the stairs.

"Fuck me," Nick muttered. "Are these tracks yours, Milo, or were they here?"

"They aren't mine." Milo pulled out his phone. "Before you guys go too far, let me get some pictures."

"I'm scared," I told Nick while Milo worked.

"I've got you," he promised, holding me close.

An hour later, I was back in an all-too-familiar position: huddled next to Nick on a couch while Jess informed me of the break-in.

"I'm sorry, Emmeline. Wish we could have caught this guy the first time around. Hate that we're here again," Jess said.

"It's not your fault," I said.

"Least this time we've got some leads," he said. "Footprints Milo found show him leaving through the trees. Either he didn't leave any tracks coming to the house or we just haven't found them yet. We'll know more in the morning. First light I'll hike up behind the house."

"I'm coming with you," Nick said.

"Okay." Jess nodded.

"Do you think it's the same guy from the first

break-in?" I asked.

"Most likely. Alarm didn't scare him away, which tells me he knew it would trip when the door popped. And he wasn't wasting any time. Tracks up the stairs look like he took them two at a time, coming and going. Like he knew exactly where he was headed."

"My bedroom is upstairs. Do you think he was coming for me?"

Nick must have been thinking the same thing because the grip he had on my hand became painfully tight.

"I don't know," Jess said. "It could be that's where he suspected jewelry or valuables would be. Could be about you. Either way, don't plan on staying here by yourself until we know what's going on."

"Not to worry. She's been at my place for weeks. That's where she's staying for the foreseeable future," Nick said.

"Do you think it could be a stalker? Am I in danger?" I asked Jess.

"Can't be sure," he said. "Have you noticed anything strange lately? Anyone give you the creeps?"

"No," I said. "Everything has been normal."

"Good. I doubt someone's stalking you. If they were, they would have known you weren't here tonight. My guess is your intruder saw your vehicle missing and thought they could make a quick score. That said, be diligent. Pay attention to folks around you."

"Okay."

"You're not to come here alone anymore, Emmy," Nick said. "If you need clothes or something, you wait for me to come with you."

I nodded.

"I've gotta swing back to the farmhouse. Then I'll be

back. You guys staying here or heading back to Nick's?"

"My place," Nick said.

"Hike out at seven?" Jess asked him.

"I'll be here."

Nick and I went back to his place but sleep was pointless. We both sucked down cup after cup of coffee before he insisted on driving me to work.

It was the worst Monday in history.

I was exhausted. Keeping focus was a struggle. Everywhere I went, I looked over my shoulder. If Jess didn't find the person or persons breaking into my house, I was going to reach an all-time-high level of crazy.

The minute the students left the building, I texted Nick to come and get me. Even though Jess had said I wasn't likely in danger, the idea of staying in my classroom alone had me scared.

With a pizza in the truck, we stopped by my house to pack a couple of weeks' worth of clothes. The minute we got to Nick's house, I was pulling on yoga pants, eating half of our pepperoni special and going to bed.

"I can't believe you didn't find anything," I said, tossing a stack of sweaters into my suitcase.

"Me too," he said. On the drive over, he'd told me that he, Jess and Milo had followed the tracks through the trees but when the footprints circled back to the paved highway, they'd lost the trail.

My shoulders sank. "Now what?"

"Jess is pulling footage from the stoplight camera on Main Street. That was an odd hour. If the guy drove back through town, we might be able to identify a license plate."

I threw a pair of pants on the bed. "This is so frustrating!"

"I know," Nick said, pulling me into his arms. "But

we'll catch them. Tomorrow we're going to put some security cameras up around the house. If the stoplight footage doesn't get us anywhere, hopefully the guy will be stupid enough to come back."

"What if it's different people? We don't even have a clue!" I cried into his chest.

"Let's not worry about it anymore tonight, okay?" he asked. "We're both exhausted. Let's go home, eat dinner and get some fucking sleep. Tomorrow we'll meet with Jess after work and start brainstorming next steps."

I huffed out a breath. He was right. Nothing was going to get solved tonight and I was too tired to think straight.

"Did you pack the gray dress?" he whispered into my hair.

I tipped my head back and looked into his hazel eyes. Today the brown flecks were more pronounced than the sage green.

"And a fancy green one so you can take me to dinner at The Black Bull. I think you'll like it. I can't wear panties or a bra."

"Change of plans, Wife. Home. Sex. Pizza. Sleep. Tomorrow after we meet with Jess, we're going to The Black Bull."

A shiver traveled down my spine as I walked back to the closet. I wasn't all that tired anymore.

Sex with Nick did not disappoint. He always took care of me, usually more than once. He loved making me come with his mouth. If I went down on him, he made sure to thoroughly reward me for my efforts.

And my man had stamina. He could go forever, hence his ability to dole out multiple orgasms every night.

With a smile on my face, I finished packing and sent

Nick to the truck with my suitcases while I thumbed through some mail in my kitchen.

"Emmy, are you expecting company?" Nick called.

"No. Why?"

"Two black Escalades are coming up your drive."

"What?" I gasped, running to the front door. My mother and Alesso climbed out of the first SUV. Her assistant and personal chef emerged from the second.

"Not today," I muttered, closing my eyes.

"I take it you know them?" Nick asked.

"That's my mother and her entourage." We stood together at the door and watched as the crew hustled their way up my stone steps.

"Emmeline, darling! Surprise!" my mother said and threw her arms around me.

"Hi, Mom," I said, hugging her back. Even though her visit was a shock, it was nice to have her here after such a rotten day. "What are you doing here?"

"We were bored and I missed you. When we talked on the phone last week, you sounded so relaxed. I thought we could visit and ruffle your feathers a bit. Is this my son-in-law?" she asked, abandoning me and crowding right into Nick's space for a hug and double-cheek kiss.

"Nick Slater," he said.

"Nice to meet you, Nick Slater. I'm Collette Austin," she said. "This is my fiancé, Alesso Nespola."

"Fiancé?" I asked, shocked. My mother agreeing to marry Alesso after fifteen years together was news. Page Six news.

"Oh, yes. We've finally decided to get married. Another reason for our visit. We need to celebrate!"

"Congratulations, Mom!" I gave her another hug,

then turned to Alesso. "I'm so happy for you!" I said as we embraced.

Alesso was younger than my mother by a few years. His black hair was liberally streaked with gray, and the olive skin on his handsome face was creased with laugh lines. He kept himself in good shape but wasn't bulky. He was Mom's silver fox.

"Me too," he said, squeezing me tight. "Sorry we barge in, *bella*."

"You're always welcome. I'm glad to see you both."

Nick and Alesso exchanged greetings and I introduced him to Mom's assistant, Frannie, and chef, Samuel.

The pair had been with my mother for years, long before she'd moved to Italy. Frannie and Samuel were married with no children and were the closest thing I had to an aunt and uncle. When Mom had decided to move with Alesso, I hadn't been surprised when they'd followed her across the Atlantic.

"Are you going somewhere?" Mom asked when she spotted my suitcases.

I grimaced. The thought of rehashing the break-in stories, both of them, was daunting. I had omitted the first one from our biweekly phone calls and knew she would not be pleased that I had kept it from her.

"Come on into the living room," I said. "We've had a bit of a situation."

After a brief recap of my troubles, numerous gasps and a thousand questions, we left my house and all drove up to Nick's.

"I love this place, dear. It's so comfortable," Mom said, wandering through the main room. Nick, Alesso, Frannie and Samuel were all in the kitchen, laughing and talking, while the four of them supervised the baking of one pizza.

"I think so too," I said. "Are you sure you don't want to stay with us?"

"No. No. No," she said. "We are not going to put you out. Frannie found us this wonderful rustic chalet for the week and Samuel won't stop talking about experimenting with Montana bison and trout. It's all decided."

"Okay. If I can, I'll try and find a substitute for the end of the week."

"No you will not!" she scoffed. "You go to work and shape the minds of the future. Don't worry about us. Frannie has planned activities to keep us busy all week while you teach. You and Nick can plan to join us for dinner in the evenings and then this weekend we'll all do something together."

"Thank you. That sounds wonderful," I said, grateful that my mom was so supportive of my teaching career.

"What a lovely picture," she said, lifting up Nick's photograph of me from Las Vegas.

At some point between my first visit and my return from Italy, Nick had found a frame, and the photo was now front and center on his bookshelf.

"This isn't recent," Mom said.

"No. It's not."

She gave me a smug grin and continued snooping. "I'm worried, Emmeline. I don't like the sound of these troubles you're having. Should I call your father? For all his faults, he did always make sure we were safe. Remember that awful bodyguard we had your senior year? What was his name?"

"Dale. And no, I don't want Father in the middle of this. I decided when I moved here that I wasn't going to have someone following me around anymore. I want to live a normal life. Besides, I need some time before I can speak to Father again. When he found out that Logan and I had broken up, he said some things to me that were uncalled for."

"I'm sorry, dear. I wish I could say I was surprised." She frowned. "Have you spoken to him lately?"

I shook my head. "No, but I talked to Steffie a few days ago."

Her eyes swung to mine. "I heard that Alesso and I aren't the only ones engaged."

"I wasn't sure if you had heard."

"Your brother called me this morning to deliver the news."

"Sorry, Mom. I should have told you."

She reached out and patted my hand. "Don't be sorry. Your father and I were over many, many years ago. I'm glad he's found someone, even if she's a bit of a tart."

"That's my future stepmother you're talking about," I teased. "Ugh. That's not something I ever thought I would have said about my college roommate."

We both laughed.

"Let's discuss a much more normal union," I said. "I'm glad for you and Alesso."

"Thank you, darling. So am I." She smiled. "It's time. Years of battling and I finally managed to divorce your father, and Alesso never faltered through it all. He's always been by my side and I do love him very much."

"He's a good man."

"One of the best." She hugged me and I rested my head on her shoulder.

"I'm happy you're here, Mom." I smiled when she didn't let me go. Her tight embrace and the laughter coming from Nick's kitchen worked miracles to soothe my troubled mind.

Hours later, we waved good-bye from the porch. I felt Nick's heat at my back a second before his fingers slipped under the hem of my sweater and started drawing circles on my hip.

"Upstairs, Emmy." Two words and I was hot.

Without delay, we both rushed inside and to his bedroom. My clothes started flying through the air as I raced to undress first so I could watch Nick.

I loved the way he tore off his T-shirt, grabbing it from the nape of his neck and whipping it off his body. That one fluid motion flexed all the muscles of his arms and stomach. When he unfastened his belt, his jeans dipped to just the right place, clinging perfectly to his chiseled hipbones. Teasing me with what was beneath.

But the best part was the way he hooked his thumbs into the band of his boxers and slowly pulled them down. It was magnificent torture.

I held my breath as he pushed the black elastic lower and lower, revealing his thick cock inch by glorious inch. When he finally sprang free, I was practically drooling.

"On your back, Emmy. Spread wide."

My whole body was aching to be touched. The cool cotton on my back did nothing to dim the fire in my blood.

I needed Nick. He had become as vital to my body as water.

When the condom was in place, Nick kneeled on the bed. His hand was wrapped around his cock and he stroked it slowly. Seeing him touch himself almost pushed me over the edge. He'd have me writhing beneath him in seconds.

While one hand stroked, his other came to me, lightly brushing my skin with his fingers. They trailed up my torso, belly button to sternum. Twice they circled my breasts, carefully avoiding my nipples.

I was squirming and desperate for more. When his fingers finally rolled over a nipple, I inhaled a sharp breath and let it out with a pleading moan.

"Patience," Nick whispered.

His fingers again started traveling, this time working down my ribs, tickling my side. I closed my eyes, savoring the trail of tingles they left as he dragged them across my hip.

With just the right amount of pressure, Nick's thumb took over and started circling my clit. Heat erupted through my body as he coaxed the first orgasm out of me. A scream tore through my lips and sound filled the room.

"Fuck, Emmy. That's so fucking hot," Nick said. "I love it when you scream."

My head was pressed back into the bed and my eyes were squeezed shut as every inch of my body vibrated. Just when I felt myself start to come down, Nick grabbed the backs of my knees, jerking my hips into his as he thrust his cock inside.

A second orgasm exploded long and hard as Nick pounded into me with a steady rhythm. Over and over his hips moved like pistons until he planted himself deep and repositioned us. One at a time, he moved my legs up and over his shoulders, the new angle allowing him to sink as far inside my body as he could go.

"Oh god, Nick," I gasped when he ground his hips against my ass.

He started his thrusts again. It didn't take either of us long to come together. My orgasm wasn't as hard or long as the other two had been, but it still left me limp.

Gently lowering one leg and then the other, Nick kept

our connection and brought his chest down on mine. The sweat from our bodies mixed as we both panted to calm our racing hearts.

Nick chuckled. "Fuck of a lot better end to the day than the beginning."

I laughed. "You are not wrong."

Laughing with Nick after hot sex? Absolutely better.

He settled me on my side and took care of the condom before joining me in bed.

"I like your mom," Nick said into my hair. His naked body was cradling mine. "I pictured her differently. Not as down to earth."

"She wasn't always that way. In the city, she played her part as the wealthy heiress. But Alesso mellows her."

"He's a nice guy. That name he calls her, *la mia vita*, what's it mean?" he asked.

"It's Italian for 'my life.' "

"And *bella* is 'beautiful'?"

I nodded. Alesso had started calling me *bella* when I was a teenager. Though it had been strange, getting introduced to my mother's boyfriend while she had been married to my father, I had adjusted quickly to Alesso being in my life. He was so different than my father. Calm. Patient. Affectionate. He didn't let my mother get carried away and it was obvious that his love for her ran deep.

"Accurate endearment," Nick said.

"He's a bit biased since I look so much like my mother."

"No. He's just got eyes."

I smiled and relaxed further into his arms.

It felt like a lifetime ago that we had been at my house dealing with the break-in. My mom's visit was perfectly timed. Having her here helped put everything into perspective. If someone was determined to steal my jewelry or fancy heirlooms, what did it matter? I had wonderful people in my life, and the material things were just not important.

And she had been right about my father. He had always made sure we were safe. Maybe calling him and getting his advice wasn't such a bad idea.

"Never met the guy, but I can't see your mom with your dad," Nick said. "Not after everything you've told me about him."

"They never fit. I can't remember a time when they seemed to enjoy one another's company. I think she married him because he was ambitious. I know he married her for the prestige of her family name. Why they *stayed* married is the mystery."

"At least now she's found a better fit," he said.

"Much better."

"I'm glad they could be here today. Too bad they live so far away."

"It is. Although Frannie told me in confidence tonight that Mom and Alesso are scoping out the area for potential real estate purposes. When they get married, his immigration status will change and they won't need to spend so much time in Italy."

I left out the part of my conversation where Frannie had also mentioned the word "grandchild." Apparently, Mom and her crew were wagering how long it would take for me to get pregnant. Though it would be nice to see my mother more often, I could do without her pressure to procreate.

"Let's hope for no drama tomorrow," Nick said.

"Absolutely. We'll have to postpone our visit to The Black Bull but at least we can relax tomorrow night. Samuel is making a big dinner so you won't have to cook for me."

"I like cooking for you," he said. "But I am interested to see how he makes that trout. I've never gotten the hang of fish."

"Well, after you learn, you can start adding salmon into the rotation. It's a favorite."

"Whatever your heart desires, my sweet Emmy."

You. Just you.

Another spontaneous and unguarded Nick thought. Though I had yet to figure out how to stop them, at least they were all true.

CHAPTER 16

"**W**E COME BACK AGAIN SOON, *BELLA*."
Alesso pulled me into his arms and I smiled against his chest, enjoying the sound of his thick accent and the smell of his rich cologne. "I like your Nick."

"Me too."

"Give her up, Alesso. It's my turn," Mom said.

Rolling my eyes, I gave him one last squeeze, then let my mother smother me before her crew departed for the airport and returned to Italy. We'd had a wonderful week with them, and despite my mother's attempts, their visit hadn't ruffled my feathers. I was sad to see them go.

Every night for dinner, Nick and I had gone to their chalet. Samuel had gone all out experimenting with the local foods, and every meal had been delicious.

Mom, Frannie and I had spent a lot of time visiting. They had listened intently to stories about my students and my worries for Mason Carpenter.

Alesso had instantly taken to Nick. He'd been enamored with how much Nick knew about the mountain trails. Each night, Nick had drawn him a map for his next morning's snowshoeing adventure.

Frannie had a packed agenda for the trip. Every afternoon, the group had explored the area. They'd soaked in the hot springs, strolled downtown and even drove over to Bozeman to visit a whiskey distillery.

And one afternoon, the four of them had surprised me with a visit to my classroom. I was not the only one who loved Alesso's accent. The kids had practically attacked him. They'd peppered him with questions about where he'd come from and why he'd sounded different.

Yesterday, we had all enjoyed a Saturday traveling through Yellowstone. Frannie had arranged for us to take a private snow coach to Old Faithful for their last excursion in Montana. I had never visited a national park before and the experience had been like none other.

The landscape was spectacular. Glittering snow had blanketed the hills. Hot pools and small boiling streams melted the valleys. We'd spotted elk, buffalo and a token grizzly bear in the open fields between evergreen forests. Old Faithful, named for its predictability, had been right on time. The geyser's water had sprayed tall and white against the cloudless blue sky.

The next time Mom visited, we were planning on going again.

"Stay safe, Emmeline," Mom said before one last hug.

The only shadow on an otherwise perfect week was Jess's update about the break-in. No vehicles had passed the downtown stoplight's camera and he was out of leads.

Nick had arranged for my door handle to be repaired

and deadbolt locks put in on all the exterior doors. He was also installing cameras around my home and property. But the added security did little to erase my fears.

"Are you going to call your father?" Mom asked.

"No. I thought about it but decided against it. I trust the local sheriff. He's doing all he can and the last thing he needs is Father sticking his nose into the investigation," I said.

"All right, dear. If you think it's for the best," she sighed.

"I'll be fine."

Her head swiveled to Nick and then back to me before smiling. "Yes. You will."

"Love you, Mom."

"Love you too. Call me next week."

As my family drove away, Nick pulled me into his side. I concentrated on breathing in the fresh mountain air so I could fight back tears.

"You okay?"

I nodded. "I'm glad they decided to buy that chalet. It will be nice to see them more often."

Luckily, the chalet that they had rented was also for sale. Mom and Alesso had immediately jumped on the purchase, and within a month, the place would be theirs. After they built a home on the property for Frannie and Samuel, they would be back for an extended stay.

"What do you feel like doing today?" For the first time in weeks, we had no plans. No six-year-old birthday parties. No family visitors. No Montana explorations. Nothing.

So I had the perfect answer to his question. "You."

Two weeks later, I was rushing to the spa to meet Gigi and Maisy for our girls' night. Maisy had postponed our original date because Coby had been sick, and unfortunately, they'd rescheduled for a night where I wasn't going to be good company.

Tomorrow was Nick and my anniversary and it was consuming my headspace.

I sank into a massive black chair between Gigi and Maisy and plastered a smile on my face. Maybe this was just what I needed to get my mind off Nick.

And ten years.

I had been legally married to a man for ten years and had only spent months in his presence. How could I possibly act normal tomorrow? I considered faking sickness and hiding out in the motel.

"Emmeline? Are you okay?" Gigi asked. She had been visiting with Maisy while I'd been lost in my own thoughts.

"Oh. Yes. I'm so sorry. I've been an unfocused mess all day."

"Want to talk about it?" Maisy asked.

"That's okay. I hate to burden you both with my trivial problems."

"That's what friends are for. Besides, we're out of juicy gossip. Spill," Gigi said.

This was probably the best place as any to get advice. "Did Nick tell you how we met and got married?" I asked.

"Some of it but he probably left out all the good stuff," Maisy said.

Twenty minutes later, they knew the whole Vegas story.

"What a jackass!" Gigi yelled. "You know, Nick told Jess and me about what happened, but he definitely gave us the abbreviated version. Now that I know the whole story, the next time I see Nick he's getting a smack in the head."

I laughed and genuinely smiled for the first time all day. It felt nice to have her on my side.

"So why have you been a mess today?" Maisy asked.

"Tomorrow is our anniversary. It feels weird to celebrate and I don't think Nick even remembers. He's been completely normal all week and hasn't mentioned a thing or brought it up. Which is actually making it worse. What should I do?"

"You guys are finally back together! You have to do something. It doesn't have to be fancy. Go out to a nice dinner, maybe? No, the theater! That's where you guys had your first kind of date, wasn't it? How perfect! Go there," Gigi said.

"You can't listen to her," Maisy said. "She's become a hopeless romantic since meeting Jess. You should have seen her before they got together. Like, totally content without a man in her life. Now she's on a mission to make sure her friends are all set up."

"She might be right," Gigi muttered.

"I'll think about it. Thanks for listening," I said.

Even though I wasn't any closer to sorting out my head, it was nice to share my burdens with friends. Besides, if Nick and I just spent a normal night together, it would be better than the last nine anniversaries.

This anniversary, I could at least have sex with my husband.

"Nick!" Rowen Cleary shouted from her desk. The kids were supposed to be tracing the letter T but now they were all staring at Nick in the doorway.

"Hey, kids," Nick called. "Are you guys learning a lot today?"

"Yeah!" they all shouted in unison.

"Hello, class," Rich called, following Nick into the classroom.

"Hello, Mr. Garcia," they said in chorus.

"What's going on?" I asked Nick. "Is everything okay?"

He leaned down and gave me a quick kiss on the cheek, which elicited a chorus of "Ohhs" and "Ewws" from my class. "Everything's great. Mr. Garcia is taking over for the rest of the day. You're coming with me."

"What? Why? Is this about the break-ins?"

"Nope."

"Ms. Austin, would you mind running through your lesson plan with me? I'll try to keep on track until you get back Monday."

"Oh, sure, Mr. Garcia," I said and outlined the rest of my Friday afternoon lesson plan.

"I think I can manage. You two have a nice weekend," he said before Nick dragged me from the room and to his truck.

"What's going on, Nick?" I asked after fastening my seatbelt.

"Patience," he said.

His cavalier attitude was annoying and I hated secrets, but nothing was wrong. He wouldn't be so smug if there were a problem. "Is this why you insisted on driving me to work this morning? So you could kidnap me?"

"Yep."

"Another one-word answer. Do you think you could string a few more of them together and actually respond in a full sentence? Preferably one where you tell me what's going on?" I asked.

"Enjoy the suspense, Emmy."

I frowned as butterflies started flying in my belly. This had to be about our anniversary, right? Why else would he be trying to surprise me?

I despised surprises and the angst that came with them. Nervous energy made me queasy, not excited. I was the type of person who read the last chapter of a book before the first, just to make sure it had a happy ending.

My stomach swirled as Nick drove out of town. After a few miles of highway, he pulled off and onto a dirt road that cut through an open field. The snow on the ground had started to melt but there were still large patches of it in the dips and curves of the plains.

"Nick." I gasped when he turned past a grove of trees and I realized our destination.

In the middle of a large clearing was a hot-air balloon tethered to the ground. The balloon was made of red fabric with large orange and yellow suns patterned into the center row. The pilot was standing in the basket, monitoring the burner.

Nick parked the truck and leaned over the center console, kissing me lightly on the lips. "Happy anniversary, Wife."

"You remembered?" I asked. "I wasn't sure if—" I started but couldn't continue. My nose started to burn and I closed my eyes so I wouldn't cry.

This was so romantic. Nick hadn't just remembered our anniversary, he'd gone all out to surprise me with something special.

"Worth the wait?" he whispered.

"Yes." I nodded before pressing my lips against his.

The kiss I laid on him was rough and desperate. My hands were threaded into his beard as my tongue took over his mouth. When we were both breathless, I leaned away and whispered, "Happy anniversary, Nick."

"Now I need a minute before we can leave." He grinned. "I doubt the pilot wants to fly me around with a hard-on."

"It would probably be best if you saved that just for me."

"Only you, my sweet Emmy."

We sat with our foreheads pressed together for a few moments until he pulled away. "We need to get bundled up. It's going to be cold as fuck up there," Nick said. "Clothes are in the backpack."

Fifteen minutes later, we were floating.

It was magic.

Nick had been right, the air was sharp and cold. But it didn't matter. The happiness in my heart kept me warm.

The beginnings of spring were starting to show. Green buds were coming to life on the trees and wildflowers were in bloom. Rivers and streams were rushing with water from the melting snow. The Jamison Valley was alive with new life and color.

"This is amazing," I told Nick.

After an hour ride, the hot-air balloon pilot set us down in another open field across the valley. Nick was up to something else because not far from our landing pad was my Jeep.

"Are you going to tell me what we're doing or do you plan on continuing this torture?"

"Torture. I like making you squirm." He winked.

We said our good-byes to the pilot and took off on the next part of Nick's surprise. The sun was setting and the sky was alight with vivid color.

Nick drove through a maze of gravel roads until we started up an incredibly steep hill. When the Jeep plateaued, we faced a wooden A-frame chateau built into the side of a mountain. The large front windows were a golden beacon.

"Are we staying here?" I asked, not even trying to contain my excitement.

"Yeah. Rented it out for the whole weekend."

"Wow," I whispered.

Nick pulled me inside so I could explore while he brought in our bags and the groceries he'd stashed in the car. The interior of the house had a similar feel to Nick's cabin. Rich woods mixed with rough stone. Cozy furniture. Enormous fireplace.

"You like it?"

"It's beautiful. Thank you," I said. "Do you want a drink before dinner?"

"Yeah. I'll start cooking in a few," he said.

"Okay. I'll get you a beer. Did you bring wine?" I asked.

"Is your name Emmeline Austin?"

That meant yes.

I smiled and walked to the kitchen, where an abundance of food items was resting on the counter next to two bottles of my favorite wine.

Nick was a romantic. Some of his declarations over the last few months still took my breath away. But this was beyond my wildest dreams.

While Nick bustled around in the kitchen cooking dinner, I relaxed in front of the fireplace and enjoyed my wine. Delicious smells filled the house, and by the time we were seated at the table, my mouth was watering.

"You made me salmon?"

"I made sure to ask Samuel how you liked it before

they left." Forking off a flaky bite, a moan escaped my throat when the flavor burst on my tongue.

"Good?" he asked.

"Amazing. You've outdone yourself. And Samuel."

We ate mostly in silence, both content to enjoy the meal and the peaceful setting.

"I'll clean up," I offered.

Part of our nightly routine was Nick cooking and me cleaning the dishes. He must have suspected that I'd volunteer because when I walked into the kitchen, I came to a stop at the sight of two wrapped boxes sitting on the island.

Why hadn't I gotten him something? I should have known he would remember our anniversary. Nick remembered everything from Las Vegas. Obviously, the date hadn't slipped his mind. Instead of searching for the perfect gift, I had been busy doubting him.

"I didn't get you anything. I should have. I'm so sorry," I blurted.

"I don't want anything. All I need is you." He kissed the tip of my nose. Taking the plates from my hands, Nick set them aside and went to the boxes.

"You shouldn't have. The balloon. This house. Now gifts? This is too much."

"Whatever your heart desires, Emmy. That's what I'll give you. If you want a quiet weekend together, it's yours. You told me a while back you wanted to go on a hot-air balloon ride. Done. I've got nine missed anniversaries to make up for and I promise to do it."

My vision blurred. I wanted nothing more than to have those nine years with Nick back. To go back to Vegas and start over. But that wasn't possible.

"Thank you," I whispered. "For everything."

"Don't thank me. Just be happy."

"I am." I nodded. "Can I open them?"

"This one first," he said, handing me a rectangular package. I knew by its weight and shape, Nick had gotten me a book.

"This is for our first anniversary. The traditional gift is paper," he said.

I carefully unwrapped a tattered yellow book. When I examined its worn cover, my eyes stared at it, unblinking. Nick had bought me a first edition of *Rebecca* by Daphne Du Maurier, my favorite book. It had to have cost him thousands. Thumbing through its yellowed pages, I inhaled its unique musty smell.

"Oh, Nick. This is incredible! Imagine where it's been, who's read this before me? I love it. Thank you!" I hugged the book to my chest.

"How'd I score with that one?" he asked.

"Off the charts." I smiled.

"Good. Next up. Ten years," he said. "Tin or aluminum. But the more modern gift is diamonds. So I designed you something with all three."

Inside a small, square box sat a simple banded ring. The circle was made with rose gold, inlayed with metal stripes. I assumed the silver threads were tin and aluminum from Nick's preface. The metals in and of themselves were unique but with the diamonds in the center, this ring was one of a kind.

A wave of rough-cut diamonds was inverted into the band. The gold above the gems was jagged, like mirrored mountain ranges, with the jewels beneath the surface.

"You designed this? It's . . . I don't know what to say," I whispered. Nick's talents never ceased to amaze me.

He took the ring from my hands and placed it on the ring finger of my right hand. I was glad he hadn't gone for the left. He had already bought me a ring for that hand. I hadn't told him that I still had our wedding rings. Until I knew what our fate would be, those rings were staying a secret.

"Yeah. Thought it would be kind of cool to have the diamonds below the metal. Kind of like how you'd find them in a mine. You like it?"

I nodded. "Love it."

"Off the charts?"

"Out of this world." As I admired the ring on my finger, I thought about all of the things I should have gotten Nick. A John Wayne movie collector's set. A new pair of snowshoes because his were getting old. A new flannel shirt to replace the one I had borrowed with no intention of returning.

"I wish I would have gotten you a gift."

Pressing his lips to my temple, he chuckled. "An anniversary blow job wouldn't go unappreciated."

I licked my lips and got to work. When I was done, he hauled me up to my feet.

"Out of this world." He smiled.

We did the dishes and Nick shuffled me into the master bedroom for anniversary sex that did not disappoint.

"Thank you for a wonderful day," I whispered to Nick lying next to me. Abandoning our normal position, we were facing each other, inches apart. A sheet was thrown over his legs and I had it pulled to my chest.

"You're welcome. I enjoyed it too."

"It sure beat my normal anniversary ritual," I teased.

Nick winced and his face tightened. "I'm so sorry, Emmeline," he whispered. "I am so fucking sorry. It eats at me. I'll never make it right."

Reaching out a hand, I gently stroked his beard. "Is that what today was about? The surprise. The gifts. You were trying to apologize?"

"No. Maybe a little," he said. "I wanted it to be special for us this time. Ten years."

Ten years.

We hadn't been married for ten years. Not the type of marriage I wanted anyway. Today had been wonderful but it felt like our first anniversary, not our tenth. I wanted a diamond anniversary with the man who had slept by my side every night for a decade. Not months.

This was exactly the reason why I wanted us to get divorced.

But first Nick needed to stop punishing himself.

"You have to forgive yourself. Nothing you can do will change what's happened."

"How can I forgive myself when you can't?" he asked.

I already did.

Somewhere along the road, my brain had caught up with my heart. I had forgiven him. I was over his leaving me in Vegas.

Did I like to think about it? No. Did talking about it sting? A little. But that was all residual feeling. Any resentment or anger I had felt toward Nick was gone.

I had finally moved past it.

"I do forgive you."

Confusion replaced the pain on his face. "You do?"

I nodded. "I don't need big surprises and fancy gifts. I know you regret what happened in the past. We both need to let it go and stop bringing it up. Let's just be us now. Okay?"

"Okay," he said. "Let's just be us."

I didn't like the space between us, so I shifted to my other side and waited for Nick to pull me into his chest.

"My dad always went all out for Mom on their anniversary," Nick said into my hair. "Every year she'd flitter around the house, anxious to see what he'd done for her. I loved that he did that. At least once a year she got to see how special she was. I promise to cool it on the gifts, but I can't promise I won't do the surprises. It means something to me. The big show. I want that for you."

I kissed his arm closest to my lips. "I can live with that."

We slept curled together until the next morning when Nick woke me up and dragged me into the kitchen.

"What do you want for your birthday breakfast?" Nick asked.

Remembering it was my birthday was impressive. In Las Vegas, I had only mentioned it in passing, so either he had a steel-trap memory or he'd recently snuck a peek at my driver's license.

I suspected the former. My man was smart. Either way, I was going to enjoy being spoiled.

"Were you going to make me a cake today?" I asked.

"Yes."

"Then cake, please."

"It's going to take a while."

"That's okay. I want to read my book," I said, snagging my first edition from the counter. Two hours later, he interrupted my reading and handed me an enormous piece of cake.

"Funfetti cake with rainbow chip frosting?" I yelled. "How did you know it was my favorite?"

"I called your mom."

A huge grin spread across my face. He was good.

"Thank you," I said. My mouth was full of cake so it came out more like "Fane oo."

Laughing, he went back to the kitchen, likely to get a breakfast not made entirely from sugar.

We enjoyed a wonderful weekend together. One of the best I'd ever had.

"Is it bad I don't want to see my students? I like our happy bubble here," I told Nick as I loaded up my suitcase.

He had struggled with the packing but I gave him kudos for trying. But for the next surprise trip, I had hinted he should enlist Gigi or Maisy to help.

"I like it too. We'll plan a trip to come back," he promised.

As we pulled out of the driveway, I waved. "Good-bye, chateau." I had a sinking feeling that I'd never see this place again.

And I was right.

CHAPTER 17

"THAT WIND IS COLD! WOULD YOU MIND IF I left you for a minute? I want to run inside and get my heavier coat," I asked Prescott's fifth-grade teacher. We were paired for bus duty this week, supervising the children as they loaded up for their journeys home.

"Just head on in and stay there." She smiled. "The kids are almost all loaded up and I can finish up here. You go inside and warm up."

"Thanks!" My teeth chattered as I ran inside.

My short steps turned into long strides when a frustrated scream echoed from my classroom. My heels ground to a stop when I rushed through the door and saw Mason Carpenter frantically digging through the trash can by my desk.

How did he get back inside without a teacher noticing? And what the hell was he doing in the garbage?

"Mason?"

He spun around with wide eyes.

Giving him a gentle smile, I crossed the room and knelt in front of him. "What are you doing in the trash can?"

His eyes filled with tears and his chin started quivering. The desperation on his face was like a shot through the heart.

"I'm hungry!" he wailed and fell against me. "I was trying to find the apple you ate at snack time."

Pain shot through my heart and I fought back my own tears as I held Mason to my chest. My agony was quickly replaced with blazing fury.

A six-year-old boy was eating garbage. His clothes were dirty and his body was filthy. This could not continue any longer. This *would* not continue any longer.

The social worker had been given months to help Mason. She'd had her chance. Now it was my turn. No matter what it took, I was getting inside his aunt's house and proving it was no place for this child.

But first I needed to calm Mason down and get him some food.

"It will be okay, darling. Take some deep breaths," I said, rubbing his back. "Do you want to take a special trip to the teacher's lounge with me? I'll make you a peanut butter and jelly sandwich. And I think there's some brownies in there too."

He nodded and pulled away, wiping the tears from his eyes.

Ten minutes later, I had raided the lounge cupboards and sat with Mason while he inhaled his sandwich, a bag of chips and two brownies.

"Mason, didn't you have lunch today?" Usually when

I pressed for information he would shut me out, but I was hoping today would be different and he would open up.

He shook his head.

"You live with your aunt?" I asked.

He nodded.

"Why didn't she pack you a lunch?"

"Her boyfriend ate all our food. She said I would just have to wait until Friday when she could go to the store."

"Did you have dinner last night?"

He shook his head. "She said I could just get the hot lunch," he mumbled, "but she forgot to pay for my lunch ticket."

Today was Wednesday. Was his aunt actually expecting a child to go days without food? My blood was boiling. I wasn't a violent person but I wanted nothing more than to kick the hell out of his aunt.

"Next time just ask the teacher on duty to put it on my charge account, okay?" I said.

He nodded and went back to his chips.

Clamping my jaw shut, I closed my eyes and took in three calming breaths. They didn't work, but at least I managed not to curse in front of my student.

"How do you get home after school?" I asked.

"I walk."

"Okay. This afternoon, I'll give you a ride. Tomorrow, I will bring your meals to school for you."

He slumped into his chair. "Are you going to get Aunt Kira in trouble? She said if I told anyone about her, the police would come and send me to jail with Mommy."

That manipulative bitch had scared Mason into silence. My temper just kept on rising. How did the social worker miss all of this?

"Mason, do you remember a woman coming to your house and looking around?"

He nodded.

"Did she ask you some questions about how you liked living with your aunt?"

He nodded again.

"Did you tell her the truth?"

He shook his head and his eyes filled again with tears.

"It's okay. You're not in trouble, darling. Go ahead and finish eating. I need to make a phone call."

Stepping into the hallway, I pulled out my phone to enlist reinforcements.

"Ms. Robertson?" I called, pounding my fist on her door.

Kira Robertson's home was a run-down trailer on the edge of town with a rusted white Toyota parked on the lawn. I hadn't been in this neighborhood before but it was reminiscent of my days spent volunteering in the rougher areas of Manhattan.

The trailer's exterior paneling was dirty and coming off in a few places. When I had pulled on the screen door handle, it had nearly come off.

The knot in my stomach tightened as I continued knocking without an answer. But I wasn't chickening out. Mason needed me.

He was currently safe at the Fan Mountain Inn with Maisy and Coby. When I'd called Maisy and given her an abbreviated summary of the situation, she had been more than happy to help, though she had been a bit concerned about my plan. She'd thought I should enlist Jess's help instead of going to Mason's house alone to confront "Aunt Kira." I hadn't called Jess but promised that a visit to the sheriff would be my second stop.

Kira hadn't answered the door for any of Jess's visits and it wasn't like he could force himself inside. My chances of getting through her door would be much greater if I wasn't with a cop.

"Ms. Robertson!"

My plan for this confrontation was simple. Get inside, use the camera on my phone to sneak some video footage of the house, and, if I was really lucky, trick Kira into admitting her care for Mason was lacking.

Having dated a lawyer for years, I knew that recorded conversations fell into a gray area where admissible evidence was concerned. But I was willing to risk it, figuring a judge would be lenient since this was about a child's survival.

"Hello? Ms. Robertson!" I shouted. "This is Ms. Austin. Mason's teacher. Do you have a moment?"

When the door finally swung open, I expected Kira. Instead, a greasy man wearing a dirty white tank top and gray sweatpants answered the door. "Who the fuck are you?"

"Oh. I'm sorry. I'm looking for Kira Robertson? Am I at the wrong house?"

"She's busy," he said, trying to shut the door in my face.

Thrusting my foot into the doorjamb, I yelled, "Wait! I just want to talk to her about Mason. I'm his teacher."

This guy had at least fifty pounds and six inches on me. With minimal force, he could have shoved my foot aside and shut the door on me.

But he didn't push me away.

He reached behind his back and pulled out a black

handgun, pressing the barrel right into my forehead.

Consumed with pure fear, I froze. "Please don't. I'm just Mason's teacher," I whispered.

My plea evoked a menacing grin. This man was completely devoid of goodness or compassion. His glassy stare was nothing but evil. He was a psychopath. All he had to do was squeeze his finger and I was dead.

But I didn't want this to be the end. I wanted to go to my mother's wedding. I wanted to see Mason's dimple again. I wanted to kiss Nick and fall asleep in his arms. I wasn't done living my life.

"Please," I pleaded again. Tears flooded my eyes.

He pressed the gun further into my skin, forcing my head back an inch. "Get the fuck outta here."

The instant I had permission to leave, I scrambled backward. My heel caught on the cracked cement step and I flew to the ground, landing on my ass. While the man laughed and sneered, I fumbled back to my feet and ran to my Jeep.

Clutching the steering wheel with white knuckles, I made good on my promise to Maisy and drove immediately to the police station.

"You and Georgia both need to calm the fuck down and let me do my job. Christ, you women are difficult," Jess said.

"What? Gigi isn't going over there, is she?" I gasped.

"No," he said. "Georgia knows I'd lose my shit if she pulled a stunt like you did. She's threatening to make me sleep in the garage if I don't bring Mason home with me tonight. Rowen told her on the drive home today that she needed two lunches tomorrow so Mason could eat. I hung up the phone with her two minutes before you came running in."

"Oh good," I sighed. The last place I wanted Gigi was at Kira Robertson's trailer.

When I had arrived at the sheriff's department, the dispatcher had taken one look at my ashen face and shuffled me into a conference room. Minutes later, Jess and Sam had huddled around me, listening intently as I'd reported the incident. Sam left not long after I had finished to collect Mason from the motel.

"I'm sorry." It was all I could think to say. I'd known that I was stepping on Jess's toes before I'd gotten to Kira's trailer, but my temper had gotten the best of me and beat out my common sense. Besides, how was I to know that a crazed, gun-wielding man would be living with Mason's aunt?

"I get where you were coming from, Emmeline," Jess said. "Your timing sucks though. Mason was getting pulled from that house tomorrow morning."

"He was?" I asked with wide eyes.

"Yeah. I had a deputy staked out at her neighbor's, watching Kira's place every night for a week. Last night he saw the boyfriend sell drugs to a couple of known users. Busted the users this morning and they gave up the boyfriend as their dealer."

My stomach felt nauseous and my muscles weak. Closing my eyes, I took a few long breaths, trying to keep my emotions together. But it was all too much. I was relieved that Mason was getting out of that place and I was elated that I had survived the afternoon.

Tears started streaming down my face.

Jess slid his chair next to me and pulled me into his

shoulder, using his free arm to dig his phone from his jeans pocket. "Slater. Brick. Better come to the station. Emmeline's here."

Jess's shoulder was soon replaced with Nick's, and as he held me tight, Jess gave him a recap of my afternoon. The more Jess talked, the tighter Nick's grip became.

And I was grateful that Jess could explain the ordeal to Nick. I didn't think I could recount the story again.

"What's next?" Nick asked Jess.

"Need to have Emmeline sign a few papers to officially press charges. We'll add that to the possession and distribution counts and bring the boyfriend in. He's fucked. With his existing record and this added on top, he'll be sent down for a few years."

Nick let me go and stood from his chair, pacing along the window and raking a hand through his hair.

"Fuck!" he yelled and I winced. "How the fuck did the social worker not see any of this, Brick?"

Jess shook his head. "After we got the boyfriend nailed dead to rights on the drug charges, I started digging into who he was. Moved here a couple years ago. Got family in town. Guess who his little sister works for?"

"Greenfield," Nick said.

"Yeah. She's one of the secretaries at town hall. Bryant brought her in a couple hours ago. He's still got her in interrogation writing up her statement. Admitted to tipping off Kira when Greenfield was coming over. Said her brother was taking the state money the aunt was getting for Mason."

"Who's Greenfield?" I asked.

"The social worker," Nick answered.

So that's why Kira's house was always clean and the boyfriend was never there. And probably why neither of them ever answered the door when Jess stopped by.

"What's going to happen to the kid?" Nick asked.

"Called Jack and Annie Drummond. They're on their way down. We'll see how Mason does around them," Jess said. "Hope to send him to their farm tonight."

"Good place for him," Nick said.

"Emmeline, if you could stick around and help that introduction go smoothly, I'd appreciate it," Jess said.

"Sure," I said. "Who are the Drummonds?" The name was familiar and normally I would have been able to place it. But less than an hour ago, a gun had been pressed against my forehead, so I was a bit off.

"I'll let Nick fill you in," Jess said. "Give me a few to get papers together for you to sign. That way when we're done with Mason, you two can go home."

When Jess left, I turned my attention to Nick. He was still standing at the room's large glass window, staring into the station with his back to me. "Jack and Annie Drummond have a farm outside of town. Their son, Wes, was killed last year."

Now I remembered. Wes Drummond was the drug dealer who had been murdered by the same people that had kidnapped Gigi and Maisy. Were his parents really the best people to take care of a little boy who was likely scared out of his mind?

"Is that the best choice of foster families?"

"They're good people, Emmeline," Nick snapped.

"I'm sorry," I said. "I'm not trying to be judgmental. I just want Mason in the best possible place he can be."

He blew out a loud breath and turned to face me. "Jack and Annie were good parents, Emmy. Wes just chose a dark path. They did everything they could to pull Wes out of that life. He just didn't want to let go. They've been through a lot but there's not a lot of better places for Mason than on their farm."

Not long after I'd signed my statement, the conference room filled with people.

Sam came in with a very freaked out Mason. Jess had called the social worker, Mrs. Greenfield, and she arrived to facilitate the meeting. She shook my hand but did it scowling. I guess she wasn't too happy that I'd inserted myself into her case. Jack and Annie Drummond rushed in last, looking both nervous and excited.

Nick had finally stopped pacing and sat down next to me, but he had stayed quiet, not speaking to me or anyone else in the room. My attempts to visit with him while we'd waited had gone unreciprocated.

A horrible sick feeling had settled in my stomach. I hated that he was mad and I wanted nothing more than to hash it out but I reminded myself to be patient.

First we needed to deal with Mason's living arrangements.

June Greenfield did her best to talk to Mason but he was firmly shutting her out. We all watched for thirty minutes while she spoke to him without a single word muttered in response.

I'd finally had enough and decided to jump in. The social worker already disliked me for my interference this afternoon. I could live with angering her even more. Especially if that meant Mason came out ahead.

"Mason, can you look at me?" I asked, swiveling his chair so he was facing me instead of Mrs. Greenfield.

He ignored me and continued staring at his feet.

"You're not in trouble, Mason. We're not here to send

you to jail. Okay?"

His big brown eyes shot up to mine and he looked hopeful for the first time all day.

"We were all thinking that you might like to have a little vacation. Mr. and Mrs. Drummond over there," I said, pointing to the couple, "they have a farm and they'd like you to come and check it out. Doesn't that sound like fun?"

He nodded and for a second I thought we were getting somewhere. But then his eyes returned to his shoes. "Is Aunt Kira in trouble?"

"Yes," I told him. "She was supposed to take good care of you and she didn't."

His eyes flooded and his chin quivered.

"What is it?" I asked. "What's wrong? Did you like living there?"

He shook his head violently.

"Then what is it?"

"What happens when my vacation is over? I don't want to go back to Aunt Kira or Mommy!" he cried and flung his little body at mine.

Pulling him into my lap, I pressed my cheek into his dirty hair and held him close.

"You don't have to go back to your aunt or mother's houses ever again, Mason," June Greenfield said.

I smiled and mouthed a thank-you. I had assumed he wouldn't go back but it was nice to hear her say it.

Holding Mason, I spun my chair so I could look at Jack and Annie Drummond. "Mr. and Mrs. Drummond, do you have animals on your farm?"

"Jack and Annie," Jack said. "And yes we do. We've got a few horses. One milk cow and her calf. And Annie has a chicken house full of hens."

"And we have a dog. Boxer," Annie said.

"What kind of dog?" Mason asked quietly.

"He's a black lab. His favorite thing to do is lick your face," Annie told him.

"Do you think you want to go check out their farm? Meet those animals?" I asked Mason.

"Okay," he muttered.

"I'm going for a run."

We had just gotten back to his house and the first thing Nick had done was go upstairs to change. He'd come down wearing black track pants and a skintight gray T-shirt with bright red tennis shoes on his feet.

"Is it safe to run in the dark?" I asked.

He scoffed as he crossed the main room. He didn't bother looking at me before he walked right through the front door and slammed it shut.

Shit.

I needed wine. And candy.

Two bottles of wine, a bag of Skittles and three-quarters of a Milky Way bar later, I was livid with Nick.

And drunk.

And my stomach wasn't feeling so hot.

How could I possibly have predicted all this? That a visit to Mason's home would end with a gun to my forehead, a sworn declaration of criminal threat and an evening spent at the sheriff's station?

Nick was acting like I did this on purpose. That I had knowingly put myself in harm's way. How dare he be mad at me? And how dare he leave me?

He was mad and his first instinct was to leave.

The sound of footsteps on the porch had me staring at the door as Nick strode inside. His T-shirt was covered in wet splotches and his hair was dripping sweat. He came to me on the couch and bent to kiss the top of my head.

"I'm going to grab a quick shower," he said gently. His anger must have burnt out while he was running. Too bad for him I was furious.

He was delusional if he thought we were going to have a rational discussion now that he was settled. The time for that was earlier. He should have stuck around when we got back to the cabin and not left me alone.

The fight we were about to have was his fault. And if I had a hangover tomorrow, that was going to be his fault too.

I was steaming on the couch when his bare feet padded across the wood floor. I kept my eyes pointed straight ahead toward the fire because he was likely wearing only a pair of flannel pajama pants. The way they hung from his hips. Seeing his naked chest. If I looked at him, my resolve would weaken. Sometimes he was just too sexy.

"Emmy," he said, sinking into the couch next to me.

"Nick," I snapped.

"You're pissed."

"You're right."

"Why?"

"Why?" I said, jumping up from the couch as fast as my drunk ass could move. As in, not fast at all because I stumbled and almost face-planted into the coffee table.

"Easy," he said, reaching out to steady me. "Are you drunk?"

"Yes!" I shouted. "I had to get drunk. How else am I

supposed to cope with all this? It's not like I could talk to you. You left me to go *running*."

"I needed the air."

"What the hell do you think I've been breathing for the last hour? There's air in here!" He bit his lower lip. "Don't you dare laugh at me."

My threat made it worse. The room filled with the sound of Nick's rich laughter.

"Urrrgh!" I growled, clenching my fists by my sides. Apparently, that was funny too because his laughter got so loud, my ears started to hurt.

"Sleep on the couch!" I shouted, stomping across the room and up the stairs. Of course he didn't listen to me. When I stepped out of his master bathroom five minutes later, he had shed his pants on the floor and was propped up in bed.

My upper lip snarled at the arrogant grin on his face. The bastard knew I wouldn't evict him out of his own room.

"We're going to start sleeping at my house," I said, throwing back the covers. "Then I won't feel bad for kicking you out of bed."

"Not happening," he said. "You're wearing pajamas."

"And you're observant." I huffed and flopped on the mattress until I was comfortably resting on my stomach with my face turned away from Nick.

"Don't go to sleep mad, Emmy." His fingers reached across the bed and started tracing light patterns on my shoulder.

"You got angry with me for doing the right thing. For trying to help a child. Then when you had your chance to talk to me about it, you left. Someone pointed a gun at me today. The metal was touching my skin, right here," I said, touching my forehead. "There was thirty seconds today when I thought I was going to die. And you left me."

My voice cracked as a fresh batch of sobs tore through my chest.

Nick pulled me into his lap and cradled me while I cried. And even though I was mad, I clung to his neck. The reality of the situation settled in and I was scared. My body shook with suppressed terror as my chest heaved. But safe in Nick's arms, I let the emotions out and gave my fears to him. It took a while but when my sobs turned into soft whimpers, he started talking.

"I got angry because I was fucking scared, Emmy. When Jess told me that fucker had held a gun to your head, I wanted him dead. But I couldn't drive to that trailer and kill the motherfucker, so I got pissed. And I took it out on you. I'm sorry."

"I didn't know that would happen. I just went there to talk to Mason's aunt. He was starving today. He was digging through my trash to find food. I had to do something."

"I get it. Why you went there," he said. "I shouldn't have left when we got back but I needed to let off some steam. It wasn't about you. Forgive me?"

"You can't leave me when things are bad, Nick," I said. "It brings back too many old feelings. Maybe someday we can get in a fight and you can run through the woods to cool off. But not right now. You have to talk to me first so I know you'll come back."

"I'll always come back. But I won't leave again when we're fighting."

"Promise?"

"Promise," he said. "Just don't pull a stunt like that again."

"Okay." I nodded.

He could rest assured that I would never go to a student's house unannounced again. And I wouldn't be meddling in Child Protective Services' business either.

"And we don't wear pajamas in this bed."

I smiled against his chest. "Okay."

CHAPTER 18

Nick

COME ON, EMMY. PUT YOUR BACK INTO it. Quit fucking around."

Keeping a straight face while I watched her was nearly impossible. Her feet were sliding backward over Costco's concrete floor as she tried to push a flatbed cart loaded with over three hundred pounds of pancake mix, syrup, chocolate chips and peanut butter. Her face turned nearly as red as her hair every time she held her breath and pushed against the handle bar. The cart would rock an inch but move no further.

"Fine! You were right. I can't do it," she huffed. "I'm too small."

Pouting with her arms crossed, she looked more like one of her kindergarteners than a thirty-two-year-old woman.

It was adorable as hell.

If we had a daughter one day, I wished she would get her mother's redheaded temper. Emmy usually kept it in check, but when she let that fire go, I was hard within seconds. Even when I was pissed at her.

"Told you so." I smirked, hoping to get her eye roll.

She didn't disappoint.

"Move over, Wife. Let a man take over," I said.

"Shall I wait until you thump your fist on your chest and let out a caveman roar? Or are you ready to go now?"

"Funny." With one hand, I set the cart in motion. From the corner of my eye, I didn't miss another eye roll.

"Do you think you can manage the cart?" Eye roll number three. I was going to try for seven today, a new record.

"What else is on the list?" I asked.

"Eggs. Bacon. Sausage. Coffee."

"Let's get the coffee first and put in on the flatbed. Then the meat. You can take all the eggs in the cart."

Tomorrow was the Prescott Fire Department's annual pancake breakfast. Every year, the fire station put on a huge fundraising breakfast the Sunday before Easter. Even though it was a fuck load of work, it was one of my favorite things about my job.

The whole community would turn out to support the station and our volunteers. And for the last few years, we'd raised a ton of money. The proceeds always went toward upgrades that I couldn't fit within my normal operating budget, which was already stretched too thin. This year I was hoping to collect enough to get four new sets of gear and at least five new top-of-the-line radios.

So after morning sex, I'd loaded Emmy up and driven to the closest city, Bozeman, to buy bulk breakfast supplies.

"How much money do you want to raise?" she asked me as we meandered through the warehouse aisles.

"Ten grand would go a long way."

She whistled. "That's a lot of pancakes."

"Yeah. We might not make it all this year but every little bit helps."

"You may recall, Chief Slater, I once had a career in fundraising."

"Yeah? I had no idea," I teased.

"It's true. This isn't raising money for political candidates, but I'd be happy to help brainstorm ideas. Maybe think of a few things that could make you some extra cash."

"You don't mind?"

"Not at all." She smiled.

I'd thought to pick her brain for ideas earlier but I hadn't known how she'd react. Anytime she talked about her former career and working for her father, she sounded hurt and bitter. But now that she had volunteered, I was going to take advantage.

She could have just offered to donate a big chunk of change. Ten thousand was probably nothing for her. And it meant a lot to me that she didn't throw her money around. Instead, she was using her time and talent to help me reach the goal.

We finished our shopping and over the next hour, Emmy tossed out ideas as we drove home.

Her intelligence astounded me. Her ideas were creative and smart. And when she landed on a good one, the belt barely kept her in the passenger seat. I loved that she'd nix an idea before I ever had a chance to respond, telling me, "Never mind. Never mind. That won't work in Prescott," while she flapped her hands in the air.

By the end of the trip, we had come up with two fund-raisers in addition to the breakfast.

One was a raffle to win what she called a "restaurant tour." She was going to get in touch with the local restaurants and arrange for a winning couple to have a multi-course feast, each course from a different chef.

Her second idea was a photo contest for a Prescott Fire Department calendar featuring local businesses. Though no money would be collected right away, she thought announcing the contest at the breakfast would create a buzz of excitement.

"I love these ideas, Emmy," I said. "But how are you going to pull all this together for tomorrow?"

"Don't you worry. I've done last-minute things like this for years. Usually it was because my father ordered me to do it. At least these are my ideas and I have a clear vision of the end product. This is going to be perfect!"

I loved her enthusiasm. The way her beautiful gray eyes danced with excitement. How she'd flip her hair around her shoulders, sending the faint scent of coconut floating through the air.

I bit my tongue before I could tell her that I loved her. I'd loved her for a decade and she'd never heard me say the words.

But today wasn't the day. I had too much I needed to do. When I did tell her that I loved her, and I prayed she'd say it back, I wanted it to happen on a day when we could spend all of it in bed.

No. Not today.

But soon.

Emmeline

Nick was in his element.

We had been up since four a.m. prepping the fire station for breakfast. Not long after we'd arrived, Nick's volunteer firefighters had followed. He'd held a quick meeting to outline the plan for the day and then everyone had split to do their assigned tasks.

The fire truck was moved outside. The center of the station's floor was filled with round tables and folding chairs. The furniture in the on-call pit was moved to the back and a food station set up in its place.

Griddles and camp stoves were lined up on two long tables in order to cook pancakes and scrambled eggs. Outside, one of the volunteers was manning a huge barbeque, cooking bacon and sausage links.

Nick had told me yesterday that the station couldn't hold all of the breakfast's attendees, so a couple of years ago they'd started breaking up the flow in waves. All week, Prescott residents had been buying tickets for one of three breakfast servings. They were expecting nearly five hundred people today, nearly two-thirds of Prescott's entire population.

While Nick and his volunteers prepped the breakfast, I set up my raffle station on the front ticket table. Every restaurant I had called yesterday had been delighted by the idea of a restaurant tour. I'd happily spent hours at Nick's office computer, making signs and printing tickets.

"Looks great, Wife. Do you need anything else?" Nick asked, surveying my setup.

"I think we're all set," I said. "What else can I do to help you?"

"You don't need to help, Emmy. Just enjoy the breakfast."

"You've got more than enough work to do. Let me help."

"Do you want to stick around here and help Michael take tickets at the door?"

I smiled. "I can do that. It will give me a chance to promote the raffle too."

He leaned in and gave me a soft kiss. When the catcalls from his men started ringing through the air, I blushed.

"Get back to work, you lazy assholes!" Nick shouted over his shoulder with a grin.

At eight o'clock, the first breakfast attendee walked through the doors. By noon, the food was nearly gone, my raffle tickets had sold out, and I needed a nap.

"That was something else," I told Michael.

Michael was Nick's newest volunteer firefighter and also Maisy and Beau Holt's youngest brother. He wasn't nearly as large as his brother but I could see the family resemblance.

"No shit," he said. "I've only ever come as a guest. That was crazy. I don't know how Nick stays so calm."

I had been so proud to watch Nick this morning. With masses of people all trying to get his attention, he had never once gotten flustered. He'd talk while cooking, effortlessly visiting while flipping hundreds of pancakes.

He was a natural leader. Inspiring. Steady. Genuine. Hardworking. If my house was on fire, I wouldn't want anyone else in charge of putting it out.

"Thanks for your help, Emmeline," Michael said when the table was stowed in storage.

"My pleasure."

"It was cool of you to watch Coby so Maisy could eat without him on her lap."

"I was glad to. He's such a sweet little boy," I said.

"I'm not so good with babies. Beau is better." Michael frowned.

"Don't worry. He won't be a baby for long. You can aspire to be the uncle that teaches him how to fish or takes him camping." The frown on his face turned into a happy grin. Apparently, I had just turned on a light bulb.

"Right. My work here is done. While you guys finish tearing down tables, I'm going to catch a nap on Nick's couch."

"Thanks again, Emmeline. Nick's lucky to have such a nice wife," he said.

Wife.

Since the beginning, Nick had only ever called me by two nicknames, "Emmy" and "Wife." I liked that I wasn't his "baby," "sugar" or "darling." I was "Wife." He was "Husband." Though, I hadn't called him that since Vegas. I wasn't sure what, but something was missing now. A part of me felt that using that nickname disparaged the word's true meaning in a way. Made it less special.

So I hadn't said it.

But I didn't want Nick to stop calling me "Wife." That endearment was only for me. No other woman had fallen asleep in his arms with that word ringing in her ears.

I flopped down on his couch and closed my eyes but couldn't find sleep. There was too much noise outside Nick's office and doubts were swirling in my mind.

We needed the divorce to start over. Right? Besides, even if we ended the first marriage, it didn't mean we couldn't try again someday.

If I could just find a way to explain it, Nick would certainly understand my position. That I didn't feel married.

And even though I loved hearing Nick call me "Wife," I

was willing to give it up.

For a little while. Because when I got it back, nothing would be missing.

"Hello?"

"Put Nick on the phone," a rough voice ordered. I sat up in bed and forced myself awake.

Shit.

The phone in my hand wasn't mine. "Nick," I said, shaking his shoulder.

I was surprised that he hadn't woken up when his phone had started vibrating on the nightstand. He was normally such a light sleeper but we'd had an incredibly long day and were both exhausted.

Four a.m. alarm. At the station by five. Pancakes. More pancakes. Again, the pancakes. Cleanup. Dinner at the café. Sex. When we'd fallen asleep at eight o'clock, we'd been dead to the world.

"Here," I said, handing him the phone. "Sorry I answered it. I thought it was mine."

"It's okay, Emmy." He rubbed a hand over his face and sat up against the headboard. "Hello," he rumbled. Nick came fully awake the second the voice on the other line started speaking.

I reached over and turned on a lamp. Nick's face had turned to stone and his eyes were trying to burn a hole in the footboard of his bed.

"No," Nick clipped.

I heard the man's voice through the phone but was

unable to make out his words.

"Don't call me again," Nick snapped and hung up.

I stayed quiet, propping myself up next to Nick and staring into the room.

In the far corner of the room was the door leading to the master bedroom and walk-in closet. Across from his bed was a wide dresser. Next to his watch and a few pieces of my jewelry was a picture of him and Dash when they were younger. Nick had his arm around Dash's shoulders and they were both leaning against the open hood of a car.

Next to that photo was a new addition. A picture the pilot had taken of Nick and me on our hot-air balloon ride. Nick was at my back, leaning down so his chin rested on my shoulder. His arms were banded across my chest. Our noses and cheeks were pink from the cold air but our smiles were warm and bright.

"Are you okay?" I asked Nick after a few minutes.

"Yeah," he muttered.

"Do you want to talk?"

"No."

"Okay." I turned out the light and shifted under the blankets. I trusted Nick would tell me what was going on when he was ready. And I was much too tired to push him tonight. Not long after he tucked me into the curve of his body, I fell asleep.

It didn't last long.

A pounding at the front door woke us up a few hours later.

Nick bolted out of bed while I rushed to the closet to pull on pajamas and my robe so I could join Nick downstairs in finding out who was at his door at four o'clock on a Monday morning.

"What the fuck are you doing here?" Nick said from downstairs.

"Told you on the phone, we needed to talk."

I didn't recognize the man's voice but it had to be the same one that had called a few hours ago. When I hit the main room, three men were standing across from Nick.

"And I told you that wasn't happening," Nick snapped.

The men shifted their eyes to watch me walk down the staircase. Nick looked over his bare shoulder as I came straight to his side.

All three men were dressed entirely in black, wearing leather vests full of patches. Dash had worn a vest when he had visited weeks ago but before I could inspect it, he had stowed it away in his duffel bag. But it didn't matter. Those vests meant these men were from a motorcycle gang.

"Is this my daughter-in-law?" the man in the center asked.

Not *a* motorcycle gang. Nick's *dad's* motorcycle gang. And this was Draven Slater Sr. himself.

On his head he wore a black bandana covered with white skulls. The curls poking out from under the rag were dark gray and matched the color of his beard. Nick and Dash must have inherited their hazel eyes from their mother because his dad's eyes were solid brown.

"You don't talk to her," Nick growled, standing in front of me.

"C'mon, Nick," one of the other men said. "We're just here to talk."

"Stay the fuck out of it, Stone," Nick said.

Stone was the oldest of the three. His head was bald but his face was covered with a long white beard braided at his chin. His cheeks were leathery and wrinkled.

"Hi. I'm Jet," the third man said, peering around Nick's body to give me a small wave.

Jet was an attractive Native-American man, probably close to my age. His athletic build was similar to Nick's and he had a wide white smile on his face. He was either oblivious to the tension in the room or he just didn't care.

"Hello, I'm Emmeline."

Jet strode right between Draven and Nick and plopped down on the couch. "Emmeline. Sweet name," he said. "And fucking rad robe! My girl would love that. Where'd you get it?"

"Thank you. I got this at a spa in Italy."

"Nice! Do you have any coffee?" he asked. "I'm wiped. The drive here took for-ev-ver."

I had no idea what to say so I just stared at him until he winked at me. I looked to Nick, who shrugged, my cue to get out the coffee. "Sure."

But before I could move to the kitchen, Draven thrust his hand out toward me. "Draven Slater."

"I'm Emmeline Austin," I said, then shook Stone's hand as well as my manners took over. "Nice to meet you both. Coffee?"

"Yeah," Draven said. "We're going to stick around for a bit." His last sentence was for Nick.

"Fuck, you are stubborn, old man. Let me put a shirt on," Nick said and jogged upstairs.

I busied myself with coffee until Nick came back down and we all sat in the living room.

"Would you like to explain why you drove three hours to talk to me when I told you on the phone it wasn't going to happen?" Nick asked. He was sitting next to me on the arm of the chair with his arms crossed over his chest.

"I wanted to meet your wife," Draven said.

"Now you've met. Bye, Dad."

"There's something else."

"Figured," Nick muttered.

"Emmeline. This isn't a conversation for you. How about you make yourself scarce?"

"No," Nick said, placing his hand on my knee so I wouldn't rise. "If you have something to discuss with me that you don't want my *wife* to hear, then you should have picked a better time to visit. I think I was pretty fucking clear on the phone."

The room went silent. Draven's eyes narrowed at Nick before they came to me. I steeled my spine and held his gaze with equal intensity. Determination coursed through my veins.

Draven sneered, expecting me to fold, but I wasn't going to give him the satisfaction. When it came to people I didn't like, I never backed down. And I did not like Draven.

He was rude.

First, he called in the middle of the night. Then he barged into Nick's house before dawn. Now he was telling me that it wasn't my place to sit in the living room of the house where I had basically been living for months.

And this stare-down was just an intimidation tactic.

But I wouldn't let him bully me out of the room, not when Nick said I could stay. In a lot of ways, Draven's behavior reminded me of my father. And though I'd always had a difficult time standing up to Trent Austin, pushing back against Draven wasn't all that challenging.

"Fuck. She's got a backbone, this one," Draven finally said, breaking away.

"She reminds me of your mother." Stone chuckled.

"They're a lot alike," Nick said before looking at his dad. "Emmy can stand up for herself. But I'll warn you once. If you ever stare at her like that again, I'll fucking beat you within an inch of your life."

I swallowed a gasp at Nick's statement.

Draven looked to the floor and nodded. "I apologize, Emmeline."

"What do you want?" Nick clipped.

"Shit's going down with the Arrowhead Warriors. It's getting out of hand and we need to put a stop to it. Something serious. We're looking to send a message. The Gypsies need a favor," Draven said.

"What kind of favor?"

"Need you to help us start a fire."

CHAPTER 19

I CLAMPED MY MOUTH SHUT AND LISTENED AS NICK, his father and his father's men had their conversation. I stayed silent but that didn't mean my mind wasn't racing.

"No," Nick said to Draven's request.

Start a fire? Nick put out fires. He didn't start them.

"I wouldn't ask if I had someone else to do it," Draven said. "Need this done right. No trace."

"Not happening, Dad. I'm not getting involved in your shit."

Draven sat calmly on the couch and stared at Nick, his brown eyes keeping his son's as he refused to give up. "Just need you to come down and give us some tips, help us figure out how to torch this place without it getting back to my men."

"No," Nick repeated, his stance firm and unwavering.

"Why not?" Stone asked. "This shit is serious, Nick.

Show some fucking loyalty."

I was surprised at the older man's sudden anger. If anyone in the room was going to lose their cool, I had expected it to be Draven. Even Jet was now wearing a serious look. But not Draven. His expression remained impassive.

Holding up a hand, Draven immediately silenced Stone's protest. "This deal with the Warriors will not end well if we don't have your help."

"Don't fucking talk to me about bad endings. I've seen firsthand what can happen to the innocents caught up in a rivalry between motorcycle gangs," Nick said.

"What happened with the Travelers and your mother was tragic," Draven said. "I underestimated them and I won't do the same with the Warriors. You of all people should understand my need to strike first, keep the damage and casualties contained."

At the mention of his mother, Nick's already-tense body became rock solid. The muscles of his forearms pulsed as his hands formed tight fists.

"She'll be safer if you help us," Draven said.

"I seriously fucking doubt that," Nick snapped.

"She" must be me and I had to agree with Nick. Helping his dad's motorcycle gang would only court trouble.

"Think about it," Draven said casually, like he was asking Nick to consider dinner plans, not go against everything he stood for as a firefighter.

"My answer won't change," Nick said.

"We'll see," Draven muttered and stood from the couch.

Jet and Stone followed. All three moved toward the door without another word. With their backs to me, I got a good look at the embroidery on the backs of their vests.

In Old English lettering, *Tin Gypsies* arched above

an intricately stitched skull. Beneath it read *Live to Ride. Wander Free.* One half of the skull's face was a gypsy with a colorful head wrap and sugar skull stitching around the eye, mouth and nose. The other was stitched entirely with silver threads, making it look like metal. Behind that half of the skull was a wave of red, orange and yellow flames. On a canvas, I would have considered the artwork beautiful. On the back of their vests, it was chilling.

From the doorway, Nick and I watched the men climb inside a large black truck and drive away.

"Have you helped them before?" I asked when they were out of sight.

"Once."

I sucked in a sharp breath and closed my eyes.

"Not something I'm proud to admit, Emmy," he whispered and walked to the couch.

"When?" I asked.

"Right after Vegas," Nick said. "Dash was hell-bent on joining the club and my friend had just gotten killed. I figured if I helped, then maybe things would settle and Dash could learn how to protect himself. So I helped Dad burn down the Warriors' clubhouse. I had just finished my training up here with the previous fire chief. I made sure the fire was untraceable when it got investigated."

"Did anyone get killed?" I asked.

"No." He shook his head and sank into the couch. "I told Dad I wasn't helping unless he could ensure the building was empty." His frame deflated, his shoulders hunched as his head turned to the floor. I was certain that Nick had punished himself thoroughly over the years for helping his father.

Meanwhile, my head was still spinning as I tried to

process the fact that Nick had aided his father in committing a serious crime. "I'm not sure what to say."

"Say you won't leave me now that you know about my past."

My answer was automatic and true. "I won't leave you."

"Say it again."

"I won't leave you."

Nick pushed himself up off the couch and came right into my space. He brushed his lips against mine, then nuzzled his bearded cheek into my neck and kissed the hinge of my jaw.

A quiet moan rolled from my throat. The jaw kiss was a new thing. He'd been doing it for a few weeks now, and each time, tingles would explode on my cheek. This man knew exactly how to make me shiver.

Nick's mouth hit mine and I let out another moan. His tongue dominated my mouth and I had no choice but to slant my head and give him full access. Spanning my ribs, he hoisted me up into his arms and carried me into the kitchen, whipping off my pajama shorts before setting me on the counter.

When my ass hit granite, it was only covered with satin black panties. And then it wasn't.

"Close your eyes, Emmy." He placed a palm at my chest and gently pushed me back so I was lying on the counter. His hands traveled slowly to my knees, caressing the bare skin on my legs.

Starting with my right side, he trailed kisses along my inner thigh as he gently pushed my knee to the side. Then he did the same on the left.

That beard was going to be my undoing.

I wanted to open my eyes but I knew better than to

ignore his orders. When we were fooling around, he was in charge. And since that had always worked out really, *really* well for me, I didn't protest.

Waiting for Nick to touch me was agony. I was thoroughly primed and ready for his mouth, but it never came. Moments passed without any noise, not even his breathing. My pounding heartbeat and labored pants were the only sounds in the room.

The way Nick could anticipate and read my body always baffled me. The second before I was about to crack, his breath was against my center.

One long stroke of his tongue, and my back arched off the counter.

"My sweet Emmy," he whispered before a second stroke, this one moving all the way up so he could flick my clit with the tip of his tongue.

I gasped when he gave up the strokes and latched onto my clit, gently sucking and nipping until every muscle in my body was shaking.

Nick normally brought me up and down a few times before finally making me come. But not tonight. He kept at me until my orgasm swelled.

When it burst, I screamed Nick's name, writhing on the counter as the sensation rocked my body, his tongue diving inside my pulsing sex.

"So good," I panted when my orgasm finally stopped.

"We're not done yet, Wife." I felt the tip of his cock at my entrance, spreading my wetness onto the condom. He slid inside, pausing for a moment to let my body adjust, and then he let loose.

His hands gripped the back of my knees, keeping them spread apart wide, while his hips pounded forward. Nick fucked me rough and hard. The sound of his skin slapping against mine echoed in the kitchen.

White spots broke out behind my closed eyelids as I clawed my hands against the granite surface, seeking a grip as another intense orgasm ripped through my body. Every muscle in my core pulsed around his thick cock.

Nick's pounding became desperate as he raced toward his own release. I opened my eyes to watch him come. His head was tipped to the ceiling. The cords of his throat tightened just before his mouth fell open with a deep groan.

Wrapping my legs around Nick's hips, I pushed myself up from the counter so I could press my chest against his. His hard cock was still twitching inside me as I threaded my fingers through his beard and pulled his mouth down to mine, tasting myself on his lips.

I broke our kiss to inhale some much-needed oxygen and collapse against him. The spicy smell from Nick's sweat filled my nose as I breathed heavily against his neck.

"Say it one more time," he whispered.

"I won't leave you."

By the end of the day, I was wiped and glad to be back at Nick's for the night. The first thing I did was shed my work clothes for a pair of wool socks and one of Nick's flannel shirts. Then I joined him in the kitchen, sipping a glass of wine while he whipped up us some dinner.

"How was your day?" Nick asked.

"Long," I said. "I'm exhausted. Work was good though. I can't tell you how good it feels to see Mason come to school clean and well-fed. He's really coming out of his shell too."

These last two weeks at the Drummonds' had done Mason wonders. Since the incident at Kira Robertson's house, I'd had a few nightmares but Nick had been my savior those nights, pulling me close and telling me everything was all right. Seeing Mason happy today made every nightmare worth it.

He was finally able to act like the six-year-old kid he was. I just hoped that his time with the Drummonds could last, that maybe they would find it in their hearts to make him a permanent part of their family.

"I'm glad," Nick said. "That kid deserves some happiness."

"Absolutely. How was your day?"

"Brutal. I'm fucking wiped," he said. "I ran around town picking up cash boxes from the breakfast tickets, which was probably a good thing for me to do today. I would have fallen asleep at my desk. We're going to bed early."

"You won't hear me argue. So did you count the money?"

He nodded and grinned.

"And?" I asked, poking him in the chest.

He laughed, clutching his pec. "Ouch!"

I rolled my eyes. "Nick! Tell me!"

"Nine thousand, two hundred and fifty dollars."

"Yes!" I shouted, raising an arm in the air. "We should easily make the rest from the calendar sales."

"Raffle sales were big. I can't tell you how much I appreciate you helping out."

"No thanks needed. I was happy to."

Working side by side with Nick to reach his goals had been fun. Sure, I could have just written him a check for the ten thousand dollars but I hadn't wanted to use my money to help him, I'd wanted to use my mind. And the end result was worth all of the added work.

"So, any word from your dad?" I asked.

He nodded. "Yeah. But let's talk about it after dinner."

"Okay."

The troubles with Draven had consumed most of my headspace today. Mostly, I had been worried about how Nick was feeling. If he wanted to wait until later to talk, that couldn't mean good things.

We ate simple but delicious club sandwiches for dinner and retreated into the living room to relax before bed. Nick worked to start a fire as I lounged on the couch, enjoying the pops and crackles as the fire came to life.

Home.

My house was five minutes away. But here with Nick, this felt like home.

It would be so wonderful to live here together someday. That was, if I didn't completely alienate him by asking for a divorce. And the longer I put it off, the more likely that was to happen.

But with all the drama from his dad today, it wasn't the time to bring it up. Nick didn't need any more stress than he was already dealing with so I'd delay our conversation, yet again.

The fire was roaring and Nick settled next to me on the couch. "Jess called me today and gave me an update about Robertson's boyfriend."

"And?"

"The boyfriend pleaded guilty to all of the charges. We won't be seeing him around again for a long time."

No trial and an extended stay at a correctional facility

meant the chances of me seeing that whacko's face ever again were nil.

"And it gets better," he said. "Guess who packed up and moved to Wyoming this weekend?"

"Aunt Kira?" I asked hopefully.

"Oh yeah."

"Good-bye." I smiled and waved my hand in the air.

"That was the good stuff, Emmy," Nick said.

My nose scrunched up.

"Dad called me all fucking day. Even had Dash try a couple times. He's putting on the pressure for me to help."

"Are you considering it?"

"No," he said. "But phone calls and visits are just the beginning. Dad's fucking stubborn and rarely doesn't get his way. He'll start to escalate his persuasion techniques."

"What does that mean?" I asked.

"Threats. He'll probably find some way to use you against me. Force me into it."

"Oh my god," I whispered.

"Don't freak out yet," he said.

"Too late."

"He won't hurt you, Emmy."

"You just said he would threaten me."

"Yeah, he will. But not with physical violence. My guess is he's already done some digging and found out you've got money. That's probably where he'll start. I can see him blackmailing me. He'll probably threaten to hack your bank account and empty it."

"Good luck, Draven."

My father was paranoid about security and cyber-attacks. He had spent hundreds of thousands of dollars keeping all of us physically safe. But Trent Austin had spent millions protecting his fortune and those of his children. Even though he hadn't personally inherited the fortune from my grandfather, he had always made sure my money and my brother's were secure.

"His hacker is good. It could happen," Nick said.

"It's doubtful," I said, "but they're welcome to try. In fact, I hope they do try and that when they hit up against my father's security blocks, it pisses them off."

"If he gets in, you'll never see that money again."

"If that's what it takes so you don't have to commit a felony, fine by me."

"Honestly, Emmy? I don't know if I can let it come to that, to risk you losing everything just for me."

"He's a manipulative asshole. Don't you dare give into him, Nick," I said. "It's not right. And if you don't stand up to him, he'll never quit and leave us alone."

"I know." He let out a long sigh and his shoulders fell. Nick carried so much on those shoulders. I wished his family would stop adding to the load. I hated to see him like this, defeated.

"I despise your dad!" I shot up from the couch and started pacing in front of the fireplace.

"He's not my favorite person either."

"What else? Other than going after my money, what else would he do?"

"I don't know," he said, raking a hand through his hair. "He'll get creative."

"Is there anything we can do to get him to back off?"

"Not really. When I talked to Dash today, I asked him to help explain to Dad why I'm not doing it. I think he understood but at the end of the day, Dash is always going to be loyal to Dad and that fucking club."

"Then we'll just have to deal with whatever comes. I'm not scared of Draven. He can push as hard as he wants, I'm not giving in. And neither are you." I continued pacing, mentally noting everything I was going to say to Draven the next time I saw him.

"Come here, Emmy," Nick said.

"No. I'm too angry to sit."

Nick grabbed me by the wrist and yanked me across the space between us, directly onto his lap. "I love that temper, Emmy. I love that it's for me. I'm telling you all this so you'll be prepared. But I don't want you getting yourself worked up and worried. We'll do like you said. Deal with it as it comes. Okay?"

I nodded.

"It means the world to me that you'd give up your money just so I can avoid adding another black mark. But I don't think—"

Pressing my fingers to his lips, I silenced his argument. "It's just money. It's not what matters. This is," I said, placing my hand on his heart. "Please don't give into him."

"I won't."

"Promise?"

"Promise."

Easter Sunday. A day that reminded me of pastel frilly dresses. My father had always insisted I wear some elaborate little-girl ensemble for the annual brunch my family hosted at our New York estate. Our staff would spend the week preparing the gardens with hidden treats. All of the children, including my brother, would race outside to see where the Easter goodies had been hidden.

All of the kids except me.

I had been forced to remain on our veranda with a pre-filled basket of candy so that my dresses wouldn't risk damage. The egg hunt had lost its appeal in my teenage years, and college students wouldn't think of partaking in such a juvenile activity.

So this year I was finally free to do something I had wanted to do my entire life: crawl around in the grass and dirt, searching high and low for plastic eggs filled with candy.

And I had enlisted Nick to help. He was currently outside hiding eggs while I stood by the dining room window, spying.

We were spending a quiet holiday together. A glazed ham was currently in the oven along with an amazing potato dish Nick had created. We were also having a layered salad that I had made last night. Gigi had given me the recipe and assured me that I couldn't mess it up.

"Emmeline!" Nick shouted, scaring me away from the glass. He was pointing at me through the living room window. "Stop cheating!"

I stuck out my tongue and abandoned my post to get another Diet Coke. Why had I thought this would be enjoyable? The anticipation was killing me.

While I waited for Nick, his phone rang. Draven.

"Decline!" I told the phone, pressing the red button.

It had been a week since Nick's dad's unwelcome visit and Draven had not backed off his phone calls. Every hour Nick's phone would ring and go unanswered. By Friday, Draven had decided to start calling my phone as well.

And sure enough. The second Nick's phone stopped

ringing, mine started. "Oh for the love . . ." But it wasn't Nick's father calling my phone. It was mine.

I hadn't spoken to my father in months, not since he had called to berate me for ending my relationship with Logan. Our only communication had been via email and updates through Steffie. I'd sent him a note congratulating him on his engagement. He had forwarded me the receipt from paying Fred Andrews for my divorce papers.

"Hello, Father."

"Emmeline. Hello."

"Happy Easter. Steffie texted to say that your annual brunch went well."

"It did indeed. Have you plans for your holiday?"

"Nick and I are having a nice dinner soon. Then I imagine we will relax."

"Of course. Your husband," he said. "Exactly the reason for my call. Fred Andrews told me he has yet to receive your divorce papers. When do you plan on ending this ridiculous marriage of yours?"

I steeled my spine and took a deep breath. It was time to tell my father to stay the hell out of my life. Nervous energy was running through my body but I reminded myself to keep a steady voice.

"That isn't any of your business, Father. And before you interrupt me, I want to make myself clear. I will not discuss this with you. My relationships are exactly that. Mine. What I decide to do about my marriage is not your concern. Now I am happy to visit if you have other topics you wish to discuss. But this one is closed. Understood?"

"I'm surprised at you, Emmeline," my father replied in his icy voice. "Your stupidity. That you would dare speak to me this way. I could ruin you."

"Do what you must, Father. Destroy my reputation amongst your friends. I don't care. I won't be returning to New York. My life is here and nothing you can do will change that."

"I don't understand you," he snapped.

"No! And you've never even tried!" I shouted. "I have always wanted a relationship with you. Always. But living on your terms isn't an option for me anymore and I won't continue to have you threaten and berate me just because I'm living a life that finally makes me happy. Good-bye, Father. Happy Easter."

I ended the call and tossed the phone on the counter.

I did it. Finally. I put my father in his place. I should have done it years ago instead of always running away from him and avoiding the confrontation.

I walked quickly outside. My heart was pounding and I was still shaking but there was pride in my steps.

I hopped down the porch steps and headed straight for Nick. He was bent over a tree but stood when he heard my footsteps. By the time I was a few yards from him, I was running. He stood and braced, opening his arms as I launched my body at his. My legs wrapped around his waist. My arms at his shoulders.

"What's wrong?" he asked, holding me tightly. In the outside light, the sage-green centers of his vibrant eyes were fiercely bright.

A huge smile spread across my face. "For the first time ever, I didn't hold back and I just told off my father." My arms flew into the air and I threw my head back. "Yes!"

Then we both started laughing.

Thirty minutes later, there was dirt under my fingernails. My jeans had grass stains on the knees. There was a twig in my hair. And the smile on my face felt permanent. I had found every one of his hidden eggs but one.

"I give up," I told Nick.

"Right there," he said, jerking his chin to the porch. And sure enough, a bright yellow egg was hiding in plain sight.

"Thank you."

"Whatever your heart desires, Emmy."

My cheeks turned pink. I really loved it when he said that.

With the Easter egg hunt complete, Nick and I worked together in the kitchen to prepare our holiday dinner. With plates loaded, we sat at the dining room table and dove in.

"So what did your father want?" Nick asked.

I had been so elated by my own personal victory that he hadn't asked while we were outside. But now that he had, it was my chance to tell him the truth. That I thought a divorce would be a good thing for our relationship.

I'd found the courage to talk to him about it last week but had gotten distracted when he'd told me his dad was pressuring him to help the club. Since then, I hadn't found the right time to bring it up. But now I wished I had forced it earlier. Having this conversation today was sure to ruin our Easter.

Here goes.

I opened my mouth and then clamped it shut when his dispatch radio upstairs kicked on. It was followed by a shrill beeping from his fire station pager and the chimes on his cell phone.

"Fuck," he muttered, rushing to his pager.

"Is everything okay?"

"The movie theater is on fire."

CHAPTER 20

"**G**ET YOUR COAT, EMMY. HURRY.**" NICK was scrambling to find his keys while pulling on his boots.

"You go. I'll just be in your way," I said though I was still rushing to the coat rack.

"I don't want to be worrying about you up here alone, not with Dad's shit going down. I need to concentrate on the fire and won't be able to with you here."

The ten-minute trip to town took three. While Nick sped down the road, he took call after call, giving orders to the men who had beat him to the fire station.

When we hit Main Street, I could see smoke coming from the theater's front doors. Jess's bronze truck was parked, blocking the road, with his police lights flashing.

Nick took a sharp right off Main, maneuvering through the side streets to avoid the blockade. When we pulled back onto the highway, two deputy's cruisers streaked by, heading in the opposite direction.

Sliding to a stop in front of the station, Nick jumped out and sprinted inside. I shut off the truck, grabbed my purse and rushed after him.

Most of the volunteer firefighters had already arrived and the ones dressed in their protective gear were climbing on the truck. The others were by the lockers, pulling on coats, boots, gloves and hats. Nick threw on his gear in seconds.

"Lock the door!" he shouted, running across the concrete floor and hopping onto the truck as it pulled out of the station. The minute the fire engine's wheels hit the drive, the siren shrieked as it went flying down the road.

I checked my watch.

Seven minutes.

It felt like we had been eating dinner hours ago, not minutes. I just hoped that it was fast enough and the men could save the theater.

The sound of the siren disappeared and was replaced by an eerie silence. The excitement around me was gone but my brain was still whirling.

When the doors were locked, I wrapped my arms around my stomach and made my way to the on-call pit. Sinking into one of the tattered couches, I let myself panic.

What if Nick got hurt? Or worse? The mental image of him running into a burning building consumed my mind.

Nick had a dangerous job but for months nothing had happened. I had fooled myself into believing his work was all volunteer trainings, pancake breakfasts and kindergarten demonstrations.

Now I was faced with the crippling reality. He could be seriously injured in a fire. Firefighters died. What if he didn't come back?

"Stop freaking out," I told myself. I had to stop these negative thoughts. I was losing my mind. And the quietness of the room was making me even crazier. I was proud of Nick for fighting fires. It was heroic and brave. But right now, in this moment, the worry was consuming. I needed a distraction. Something to keep my mind occupied while I waited. And I had just the thing.

For the next three hours, I sat at Nick's computer and researched the cost of starting up a garage. By my calculations, three hundred thousand would buy Slater's Station.

It was too late on a Sunday evening to transfer any money out of my trust, but tomorrow morning I was calling my financial manager. By the end of the week, that money would be available at Jamison Valley Bank. If Draven did end up coming after my fortune, I wanted Nick's garage fund in cash.

I was shutting down the computer when the garage door started to creak open.

Prescott's firefighters slowly piled off the fire engine. They were all covered in dark soot and sweat. I nearly fell to my knees as Nick walked toward me.

"You're okay," I sighed, running my hands over his dirty coat. I didn't care if my hands got messy as long as I could touch him.

"Yeah. We're all fine," he said.

I closed my eyes and willed myself not to cry. For hours I had been anxiously imagining the worst possible scenarios.

"I'm okay," Nick reassured me.

I nodded and inhaled another calming breath. "What can I do?"

"Nothing. We've got to unload the truck. Get equipment

prepped and put away. I'll probably catch a shower here, get some of the smell off before we go home."

"Okay. I'll stay out of the way," I said.

Reaching for his bearded cheek, I tipped my chin so Nick could bend down and lightly brush his lips against mine.

He did smell bad. Like burnt popcorn and campfire smoke. The stench would stick to my hair and I'd be catching whiffs of it all night. But I didn't care.

It was dark when we pulled away from the station.

Nick had taken a quick shower but he was still a mess. His hair needed at least two more rounds with the shampoo, and the soot ground into the rough skin of his hands was likely going to be there all week.

"Is it bad?" I asked as he turned down Main Street. I didn't know if I could stand seeing the theater in ashes.

"No. It looks the same on the outside. The inside is a fucking mess but the good thing is we got there early. Most of the damage was isolated to the concession area. The owners should be able to get it fixed back up."

"That's great. Do you know what caused the fire?"

"Fucking kids. One of the high school kids that works at the theater decided to go in today with his girlfriend."

"On Easter?" I asked.

"Yeah. Theater was closed. They needed an empty place to go have sex."

"What makes you think that?"

Nick didn't answer but instead started chuckling. After a few moments, his chuckles turned into full-blown laughter. His belly was heaving and his hands slapped the steering wheel as he roared.

"Nick!" I shouted. "Tell me!" His smile was contagious.

His laughter died down by the time we passed the theater. One remaining deputy cruiser was still outside but all the spectators and other officials had gone home.

"This kid was stupid enough to stay inside. He comes rushing out of the bathroom, coughing and hacking in the smoke, with two Coke cups filled with water. I grabbed him by the shirt, ready to yank his ass outside, when I looked down to see his tiny pecker hanging out."

Nick started laughing again.

"Pecker?" I asked.

"Yeah. You know? His junk."

"I get it. No need for further explanation. I just don't think I've actually ever heard someone say the word 'pecker.' " I laughed.

"I might have to say it more often then."

"No, thank you."

Nick did not have a "pecker." He had a cock. It was big and thick. It brought me immeasurable pleasure, and if he ever called it a pecker, I was taking away Friday-night blow jobs.

"So what did he do that caused the fire?" I asked.

"Turned on the popcorn machine. He must have put in too much oil. Him and his girl went into the theater and forgot the damn machine was on. It burned too hot and caught on fire. It pretty much destroyed the concession area. One of the walls will have to be taken out and replaced."

I was so relieved that I held Nick's hand in silence for the rest of the drive. I was exhausted but so happy everything had ended well. As soon as I set the dinner dishes to soak, I was going right upstairs to bed.

Maybe next Sunday we could go the whole day without drama. I would love nothing more than to head into a

Monday with a full night's sleep.

"Emmy?"

"Yes?"

"Next Sunday we're shutting off all our phones and locking the door."

He wasn't going to hear any arguments from me.

Nick

"I need to go to my house tonight," Emmy told me over the phone. "It's been a month since I cleaned and I'm sure there's an inch of dust everywhere."

"Okay. I was thinking of getting my bike out of the garage. It's pretty warm today. I wanted to take it for a quick ride, find out if there's anything I need to tune up before summer."

"You have a motorcycle?" she asked.

"My dad's the president of a motorcycle club."

"A club you don't like."

"I don't like the club. I never said I didn't like the bikes," I said.

"Right. So you'll do your riding thing while I clean?"

"No. I'll help you clean and then we do my riding thing together."

"Me on the back of a motorcycle? No. No way. It's not happening."

I opened my mouth to dare her but stopped short. Emmy had told me that she'd forgiven me for Vegas but she also winced whenever I did something that reminded her of our wedding night.

Maybe in time we could get to the place where she enjoyed the reminders, when she'd like reminiscing about how special that night had been. But not right now.

I was finally getting her to a good place, the place where we acted like husband and wife. All I had left to do was get her permanently living under my roof and get my ring back on her finger.

Fuck, I hoped she still had our rings. That by some miracle she'd kept them for ten years.

Getting them back on our fingers would go a long way toward easing my mind. Toward healing the wounds I had inflicted upon us. If I had to buy us new ones, I'd do it, but I'd hate it.

My second biggest regret from Vegas was leaving my ring behind. I had set it on top of my one-word asshole note and then walked out the door. Five steps down the hallway, I had turned to get it back but the room had been Emmy's and I hadn't had a key.

For years, I'd touched the spot where it had rested. I'd only worn it for hours but its weight had always been there. I could still feel the brush of Emmy's fingertips from when she'd slid it on my finger.

And at times, that spot had hurt like a son of a bitch. Any time I had been with another woman, not that there had been many, the area had burned and itched. But I'd deserved that punishment for betraying my wife.

"Nick?" Emmy called, pulling me away from my thoughts.

"Yeah. Sorry."

"Do you need me to let you go?"

"No. Let's plan to meet at your place around five thirty.

I'll swing home and get my bike. You can pick us up some takeout."

"Okay. What do you feel like eating?"

"Whatever. And Emmy, you do not go into that house without me. Wait in the Jeep."

"Right," she said.

I couldn't see it but I was fairly certain I got an eye roll.

The second I hung up with Emmy, my dad called. Again. "Fuck, you're stubborn."

Mostly I had been ignoring the calls these last ten days, but I was getting sick of them and wanted to reiterate my point. Under no circumstances would I be helping the Tin Gypsies in their war against the Arrowhead Warriors.

"Then you're a chip off the old block, Son," Dad rumbled.

"I'm not helping you."

"Not the reason for my call," Draven said.

"What is?"

"Just a heads-up. Shit went down last night. Watch your back."

Before I could ask what had happened, I was listening to dead air.

Fuck.

"That's your motorcycle?" Emmy asked with wide eyes.

"Yeah."

My bike was fucking sweet. Last year I had upgraded and bought a new Dyna Low Rider, then tricked it out. Chrome. Matte red paint with matching rims. The color was almost exactly the shade of Emmy's hair, the color I'd seen in my dreams for nine years and now got to breathe in every night before I fell asleep.

"I like it," she said breathlessly.

Yeah. She liked it all right. The flush of her cheeks and the way her shoulders shuttered told me that she liked it a fuck of a lot.

My dick jerked in my jeans. Before dinner, I was getting her naked in the living room.

Then after cleaning, I'd take her for a ride. I couldn't wait to get her on the back of my bike. I wanted to have her thighs pressed against mine. Her chest against my back. Her small hands wrapped around my middle.

"Inside, Emmy," I said, taking the bags of Chinese take-out from her hands.

Sex. Chinese. Cleaning. Ride. Sex.

Not a bad way to spend my night.

"Where's your kitchen cleaning stuff?" I shouted to Emmy upstairs.

I had given up searching after opening five cabinets, including the one under the sink, to find only coffee mugs.

"By the fridge!"

"By the fridge," I muttered. "Because when I'm looking for a glass to get some water, the most logical place to start is under the sink. Certainly not in the eye-level cabinet right here next to the ice and water dispensers."

I found the cleaning supplies and got to work. Not long after I started, the countertops were dust free and the stainless appliances wiped down.

"Fuck, she gets a lot of junk mail." For weeks, I had watched Emmy pick up her mail and shove it in a drawer. Now the drawer was overflowing and a huge stack was piled on the wet bar.

"Can I throw out your junk mail?" I shouted.

"Okay!"

Catalogs. Holy shit, my woman got catalogs. Home decorating catalogs. Swimsuit catalogs. Clothing catalogs. More clothing catalogs. I was going to need another recycling bin just to keep her damn catalogs after she moved in.

I worked my way through the pile and decided to start on the drawer. My eyes caught on a large manila envelope stamped *URGENT*. The postmark was dated the end of January, nearly three months ago.

I grumbled and pried open the seal.

Emmy was so organized normally. I was astounded that she was so bad about going through her mail. I just hoped that whatever was inside wasn't actually urgent.

The first words that caught my eye were *Divorce Decree*. The second were my name and Emmy's, both spelled out in full.

I got so light-headed, I nearly toppled over. Gripping the counter with both hands, I let my head fall between my arms while I tried to pull in some air.

Why did she still have these? Did she want a divorce? After everything we had gone through these last few months?

I racked my brain, trying to figure out where we had been in January. She had gotten back from Italy. We had gone to Gigi and Maisy's ridiculous kidnapping anniversary party.

Was it before or after she'd promised to give our second

chance a real shot?

Before. It had to have been before, so at least that was something.

She hadn't stopped her attorney from drafting them but maybe that was just because of timing. She wouldn't want to divorce me now, would she? How could she want to end our marriage when we were finally putting it back together?

This all had to be a misunderstanding.

But that didn't ease the ache in my chest.

Emmeline

"I thought you wanted to go for a ride?"

"Not anymore. Besides, you said there was no way you were getting on the back of my bike. So, no. No ride," he snapped.

Sometime between sex on my living room couch, Chinese food and cleaning, Nick had gotten pissed at me. I just wasn't sure why.

I had warmed up to the idea of riding with Nick. His bike was so big and shiny. And when I had pulled up and Nick had been straddling it, I'd flushed at how hot he looked.

"Okay," I said. "If you're sure."

"I'm sure. Let's get the fuck out of here."

The drive to Nick's was tense and stressful. What could I have possibly done to make him mad? Was it the cleaning? He had offered to help, otherwise I would have been happy to do it myself. It didn't make any sense that he would be mad, but I still got that dreaded sick feeling in my stomach.

He pulled his bike into the garage while I parked and waited for him at the front door. His long strides around the side of the house and up the steps were done without eye contact.

"What's wrong? Why are you mad at me?" I asked when we were both inside.

He stomped to the living room and reached behind his back and under his coat. From the waistband of his jeans he pulled out a manila envelope and waved it in the air.

Shit.

He had found the divorce papers. Probably when he was going through my mail. Why hadn't I thought of that?

Shit. Shit. Shit.

It was time for this discussion. Overdue, really. I just wished I hadn't been a coward and had brought it up myself. I might have stood a chance at keeping Nick from getting enraged but there was little chance of that now. I could practically see the heat radiating off his body and the steam coming from his ears.

"I've been meaning to talk to you about those."

"Why?" he asked. "Why do you have these? Tell me it's just because your attorney doesn't know that we are together."

"Will you let me explain?" I asked, sitting on the couch. "Sit down. Please."

He huffed but sat.

I'm sure there were better approaches to this conversation, and had I been the one to bring it up, I would have tried one. But now it was too late so I decided to get straight to the point.

"I think we should get a divorce."

He shot to his feet. "You're fucking shitting me!"

"Please sit down so I can explain my reasoning." I was trying to remain calm but my voice cracked.

"I'm not fucking sitting down. Why? You said you wouldn't leave me because I didn't have money. Or because of my family. So, why?"

"I'm not leaving you," I said. "I just don't want to be married."

"That doesn't make any fucking sense. How can you not be leaving me if you want a divorce?"

"I want to stay together. To keep dating. You'll be my boyfriend."

"Your boyfriend? We're not sixteen years old!"

"We'll still be together, Nick."

"And what? We date forever?" he asked.

"No. Maybe. I don't know. We date like other couples. If we decided to get married again someday, we can. This would just be a fresh start for us. Like hitting the reset button."

"A fresh start? What and the fuck do you think we've been doing since you moved here if it wasn't starting from scratch?" He raked his hands through his hair and rubbed his face.

"I don't feel like we're married," I admitted.

"What?" His hand rubbed his heart and the look on his face cracked mine.

This was not going at all like I had hoped. Yes, I had expected Nick to be mad. But hurt? I didn't want to hurt him.

"How can you not feel like we're married, Emmy?" he asked. "Did that night in Vegas mean nothing to you that you'd throw it all away?"

"That night meant everything to me! Everything! I want to get rid of the nine years *after* that. That's what I want to throw away. Nine years of us being apart. Nine years of heartache. Nine years of you fucking other women. For nine years, I pretended that maybe one day I could settle for someone else because the love of my life had crushed me."

"We'll never get past it," Nick said. "You don't forgive me."

"I do forgive you and I'm not blaming you or holding Vegas against you. What I'm saying is that I don't want to look back at our married life together and have a gap. I want a real first anniversary. Not one ten years later." Tears were now streaming down my face. Nick's eyes were filled with anguish and pain. "I'm not doing this to hurt you. I'm doing this so we can have a real chance."

"The night I found you," he said, "the night we got married, was the best night of my life. I locked every moment in my heart so I'd never forget a single one. Now you're taking them away from me."

He was right. I was taking Vegas away. But I was taking the nine years away too. We couldn't have one without the other.

"I don't want you to leave me, Emmy."

"I'm not," I said. "I told you I wouldn't. That's not what I'm doing."

"Then why does it feel like I just lost you?"

Wow, that hurt.

I sucked in a ragged breath and thought about what I was asking. Was it worth the pain?

No, it wasn't. If this idea of mine was going to drive us apart, I wasn't going through with it. I didn't need a divorce to be happy. I just needed Nick.

But before I could tell him any of that, the front door flew open.

In stormed Dash, followed by another Tin Gypsy I hadn't met. Dash walked right into Nick's space and stood nose to nose with his brother. "You're fucking helping us."

"Get out of my face," Nick growled.

Dash stepped back a foot and pulled at his hair with both hands. His friend had an equally frazzled look.

Nick and I had been so consumed with our own drama, neither of us had heard the motorcycles outside approach.

"You ever barge into my house like that again, I'll put you on your ass, Brother. What are you doing here?"

"Shit went down last night. Warriors attacked. A few of us were drinking at a bar, watching the playoffs. They grabbed Stone and took him outside. Before any of us even knew what the fuck was happening, they shot him. Fucking execution style, man. Just like Mom."

I gasped and slapped a hand to my mouth to keep from screaming.

"Fuck," Nick hissed. His hands fisted at his sides and his entire body tensed. "Fuck!" he roared. The noise was so loud and gut-wrenching I flinched.

"Let's go," Nick ordered Dash.

"Nick, no," I gasped. "Don't do this." He wouldn't forgive himself if he crossed that line. Enemy or not, this would torture him.

"I'm going," he said, following Dash and the other man to the door without looking back.

"You promised you wouldn't leave if we were fighting. And you promised you wouldn't help them," I told his back.

He paused and turned his chin to his shoulder. "I promised my wife. You're just my girlfriend."

CHAPTER 21

To SAY THAT THE LAST FOUR DAYS OF MY LIFE had been miserable would be a titanic understatement.

After I'd watched Nick speed away on his motorcycle, side by side with his brother, I had lost it. Crumbling to the floor, I'd had a complete breakdown.

A part of me had thought Nick would come back when he got some space. After he had cleared his head and put a few miles between us. Maybe when he had realized that he'd just left me again.

But hours later, I had still been alone and crying at his house. So I'd picked myself up and gone home. For the rest of the week, I had gone through the motions.

I hadn't heard a word from him since our fight. My calls to his phone had gone directly to voicemail and all my texts had gone unreturned. I didn't know where he was or if he was being safe. His absence left me constantly nauseous.

And on top of it all, I'd caught the cold that was traveling around my classroom.

But despite my stuffed nose and hacking cough, I had gone to work every day. Staying home hadn't been an option. I'd needed my kids to help me through.

Now it was Friday and I was home. Alone. Stripping off my clothes, I took a hot bath, letting the hot water soothe my aching muscles.

My head was fuzzy and my minor cold had taken a serious turn. Breathing was a struggle and I had a scorching fever. The cold medicine I had taken was starting to make me drowsy but I still couldn't shut down my mind.

It was consumed with thoughts of Nick and our fight.

I had completely *fucked* up.

I was the only person to blame for how I was feeling. Sick. Lonely. Depressed. This was all my fault. I should have talked to Nick about the divorce a long time ago. And though his parting words had been harsh, I had deserved them.

The more I'd replayed our argument, the more I'd understood why he had been so hurt.

He'd left me in Vegas so I could be safe. He'd sacrificed his heart for mine and I had asked him to ignore all of that. And for what gain? So that we could just do it all over again?

I didn't need another wedding. Our ceremony at The Clover Chapel had been a dream. What we needed was time. Time to settle into a life with Nick. Time to build new memories that would outshine the years of being apart. Time to love one another.

My actions had very likely taken away my possibility of getting that time.

The bath water started to cool so I slipped out, shrugging on one of Nick's flannels and going immediately to bed.

Without the distraction of my students, I had no idea how I was going to make it through the weekend. My outlook was fairly bleak.

Maybe if I kept myself loaded up with cold medicine, I might be able to sleep through it all.

I heard the crash of breaking glass before the alarm.

My head lifted up off my pillow but my mind was frozen, unsure of what to do. The NyQuil/Theraflu cocktail I had taken was doing its job and my head was fuzzy.

The noise in my ears stopped just as soon as it had started.

Strange.

I must have been having a nightmare from the first break-in. The sounds of breaking glass and the alarm were all just a dream.

It was a struggle to keep my eyes open so I let them shut as I face-planted back into my pillow. I forced myself to stay awake for a few more seconds while I listened for other noises, but the house was dead quiet.

Moments later, I had almost drifted back to sleep when my phone started buzzing on the nightstand. This time I rolled over and scrambled to sit, desperately hoping the call was from Nick.

But before I could reach the phone, all of the lights in my bedroom came on. I winced, throwing my hands over my eyes to protect them from the blinding light. My head swung to the door and my body jolted.

I hadn't dreamed the alarm. It had been tripped.

Two dark-clad men came strolling into my room. Both were wearing black leather motorcycle club vests, but these were not Tin Gypsies.

Panic consumed me as I tried to untangle my legs from my bedsheets.

In a flash, one man jumped on me. My wrists were trapped above my head and his body smashed me into the mattress.

"She's a pretty one," he said.

He reeked of stale beer and cigarettes. I squirmed and twisted beneath him, hoping to get free, but he was too big. "Let me go!"

"Quiet," he said, adjusting his grip.

He kept my arms secured against the headboard and started groping me with his free hand, yanking at the buttons on Nick's flannel that I had worn to bed. With some of them coming loose, he grabbed my breast and squeezed so tightly I cried out in pain.

"No! Please don't," I begged. I bucked and rocked my hips, trying to get free, but I couldn't get any leverage. My feet, covered with huge wool socks, couldn't get friction against my sheets.

"Jinx," the other man snapped. "Get the fuck off of her. Alarm tripped when you broke the glass, you stupid motherfucker. Cops will be here in a minute. Grab her and let's get the fuck outta here."

"You're no fun, Wrecker," Jinx said, then sat back on his knees, still pinning me to the bed with his hips but letting my arms go.

Then, in a flash, his hand came down, backhanding me across my cheek.

Pain exploded across my face as it whipped to the side.

My hands flew to my face, clutching my cheek as the sharp sting spread from one side to the other. The white spots started to clear and I had just opened my eyes when Jinx's hand came down again. This time his fist pummeled my ribs.

The air vanished from my lungs. Heave after heave, I struggled to suck in some oxygen as he laughed above me.

Jinx climbed off the bed, talking to Wrecker about my jewelry box, while I rolled to my side and clutched my stomach. Tears poured down my face as the pain intensified. I had never been hurt like this. I had no idea just how much physical pain one person could inflict upon another.

Then I was moving.

One second I was writhing in pain on my bed, the next I was being carried out of my house over Jinx's shoulder.

"No! Help!" I screamed, kicking and punching at his back. The pain in my ribs and face got worse with every one of my movements but the adrenaline running through my blood was spurring me to fight.

The phone call must have been from my security company, meaning a deputy was on their way. Maybe if I could delay long enough, I would be rescued. But nothing I did slowed their escape.

Jinx carried me outside with haste. I squinted in the dark, hoping to see lights coming down my driveway, but all I saw was an upside-down black van.

The cold night air nipped at my bare legs but I didn't let the chills stop my fight. I kept screaming and fighting. If I could squirm free, maybe I could run into the woods and hide.

"Let me go!" I wailed, using all of the energy I had to hit Jinx. But my struggle was in vain.

"Enough," Wrecker shouted from my side.

I lifted up my head just in time to see his tattooed fist coming straight toward my temple.

And then everything was black.

Nick

This was the worst fucking week of my life.

I had royally fucked up with Emmy and left her. Again. The one thing she had asked me to do was stay, and instead, I'd run.

And why? Because she had been honest with me about our marriage? Because she felt differently about it than I did?

Of course she would want a fresh start. Our nine years apart had been spent thinking entirely different things.

I had thought she'd be happier and safer without me. I'd spent my time remembering her with longing. With love.

She had thought I'd abandoned her because she wasn't good enough and that I didn't care. She had spent nine years remembering me with pain. With hate.

I hadn't even listened to her explanation. I'd been so enraged that I had shut her out and said cruel and unforgivable things.

I was a motherfucking asshole.

At least I'd kept my promise not to help Dad start an illegal fire. Even though I was in Clifton Forge, I'd made it clear I was here for Stone's funeral and nothing more. Well, the funeral and to get smashed each night. Drunk was the only way I could deal with what I'd done to Emmy. What I was still doing to her.

Emmy had called these past few days but I had ignored the phone. Her voicemail messages had pleaded with me to call her back. Her texts were much the same. I longed for the sound of her voice but dreaded what she would say.

I didn't want to hear her tell me that we were over.

She would never forgive me for this. And when she left me, it would be completely justified. The end of our relationship was my fucking fault and she had every right to divorce my stupid ass.

"Drinking already?" Dash asked, walking into the Tin Gypsy party room.

I grunted. Yeah, I was drinking already. It was only six o'clock in the morning but today I was getting plastered and passing out. Hopefully before ten.

The party room was where the Gypsies entertained their guests. It housed a fully stocked bar, and for the last four days, it had been my home.

The three-hour trip to Clifton Forge on Monday night had cooled my temper. The minute I had shut off my bike, I'd thought about climbing right back on and going home. Getting on my hands and knees while begging Emmy to forgive me.

But I had been too much of a coward. Too afraid she would say no. So I'd gone straight into the Gypsy clubhouse and had gotten drunk.

A beer was tipped to my lips when my phone rang. Digging it out, I was surprised to see Jess's name. I had expected Emmy.

"Shit," I muttered.

Emmy and Gigi had probably gotten together this week and now the Clearys knew all about how much of a prick I was. Jess was probably calling to ream my ass for treating her so badly.

That or something was wrong at the station. I had called a couple of my volunteers and told them I had a family emergency. They were all taking shifts covering the station until Monday.

"Brick," I answered.

"Where the fuck are you?"

"In Clifton Forge."

"Get home. Now," he clipped.

"Why? What's wrong?"

"Your wife was almost abducted at four o'clock this morning."

The second the words registered in my brain, I was off the stool and my beer bottle was flying across the room. It crashed against the brick wall. Glass and foam sprayed over an old worn couch.

I wasn't drunk but I swayed on my feet and dropped to my ass. Sitting on the concrete floor, I put my head between my knees and tried to breathe but the air wouldn't stay in my lungs. The pressure in my chest was too tight.

In the background, I could hear Dash talking on my phone to Jess but I couldn't make out their conversation.

The sound of my heart breaking was too loud.

Standing outside of Emmy's hospital room, I clapped Jess on the shoulder. "I don't know how to ever thank you."

"No thanks needed. I'm just fucking glad it turned out this way and not worse."

I wouldn't let myself even think about what could have

happened had Jess not saved her.

"Here," Dash said, handing me a cup of coffee as he joined Jess, Dad and me in the hall. "She still sleeping?"

I nodded. "Yeah."

I didn't want to be away from Emmy for too long but I had to get some answers. The one-minute update Jess had given me when I'd sprinted through the hospital doors wasn't enough to appease all of the questions racing through my brain.

After I'd collapsed in the party room, Dash had pulled me off the floor and punched me in the face. I was going to have a shiner but I was glad he'd done it. I'd needed that hit to pull myself together.

Never in my life had I felt so scared or helpless. One phone call and my whole world had come crashing down. I'd spent years running into smoking buildings and burning forests. The fear I'd felt then paled in comparison to the terror of almost losing my Emmy.

That terror had fueled my race back to Prescott.

The three-hour trip from Clifton Forge had taken me two. My bike had never been run that hard. Dad and Dash had been right on my heels the whole way.

It wasn't until I saw her settled, safely sleeping in a hospital bed, that my panic had started to subside and the questions had rushed in.

"All right," I said to Jess. "What happened? With details this time."

He nodded, taking a long breath before recapping the events of the morning. "Rowen brought home a cold from school and gave it to Ben. Georgia and I were up all night with him and, at about three thirty, we ran out of Tylenol for his fever. So I left the farmhouse to hit the store. I was just getting ready to pull off the highway and head home when my radio went off. Dispatch got a call from Emmeline's alarm company again. Since I was only a mile away, I decided to check it out."

The bottom fell out of my stomach. Nothing but pure luck had put Jess on the road at just the right time to save my wife.

"Pulled up to the house and saw a van barreling down the drive. Managed to swing my truck in just in time to cut them off. The two guys both jumped right out of the van. The driver bolted immediately. The other guy pulled a gun and took a couple shots at my truck. I took cover, then fired back but with it being so dark, I lost him the second he hit the trees."

"Any idea who they were?" Dad asked.

Jess shook his head. "Didn't get a good look at their faces but I'm hoping her exterior cameras got 'em. Both were decked out in black. The driver looked to be wearing a vest with a patch, kind of like the one you got on." Jess's accusation was clear. He knew this mess was somehow linked to Dad.

"Hey, it wasn't us," Dash said. "She's family."

"I'll let her security footage confirm that," Jess said, crossing his arms over his chest.

"Then what happened?" I asked.

"Then I pulled Emmeline out of the back of that van. She was out cold. One of those fuckers took a pretty hard swing at her face. I put her in my truck, then hauled ass here. She's been awake on and off, but just for minutes at a time. But she's been asking for you."

And I hadn't been here. I hadn't kept my vow to keep her safe.

By all rights, those men should have been able to take

her. Emmy's rescue this morning was nothing short of a miracle. I should have been here.

Fuck!

How could I have been so stupid? I hadn't considered that it was my connections that had been the cause of Emmy's troubles. We'd been so focused on her life that I hadn't once thought maybe it was my father's enemies that had targeted my wife.

Fucking stupid.

The minute she had set foot in Prescott, she had been in danger. I'd been so focused on getting her to love me again that I hadn't made sure she'd be safe first.

"I gotta get to the station," Jess said, pulling me from my thoughts. "I want to see that camera footage and I need to check in with my deputies. They've been combing the area, and with any luck, one or both of those fuckers is now in a cell. I'm hoping we find some evidence in the van we impounded."

"Thanks, Brick. I don't—"

"Don't worry about it. Just take care of Emmeline," he said, clapping me on the shoulder and turning to leave.

"Do you know who it was?" I asked Dad and Dash once Jess was out of earshot.

"Had to be the Arrowhead Warriors," Dad said.

"We'll take care of it, Nick," Dash said. "They'll pay." Dad and Dash shared a look. The chances of the cops finding Emmy's attackers before the Gypsies did were slim to none.

"I've got to get back to Emmy. Bye." My tone was clear. They weren't welcome to stay.

Both nodded and turned to leave. They knew as well as I did that nothing would have happened to my wife had they not dragged their shit into my life.

"Dad?" I called and he turned. "She's my everything."

He nodded and looked to his feet. Message received. Given the choice, I would always pick Emmy. Even if that meant I severed all ties with him and Dash.

"I'm sorry, Son," he said. "For everything. Your mom. Emmeline. I'll make it right."

I nodded and pushed inside Emmy's room. Only time would tell if Dad would make good on his promise. But I couldn't worry about that right now.

I needed to focus on my wife.

Emmeline

I woke up to the smell of hospital.

My eyes felt huge but I managed to crack them open, giving them a minute to adjust to the white panel light above my bed.

Blinking hurt. Breathing hurt. The pounding rhythm in my head caused new waves of pain with every thump.

"Emmy?"

I turned to the sound of Nick's voice at my side. Anguish and heartache were etched on his face but he was still a beautiful sight to see.

"You're here." The words sent pools of tears to my eyes.

"I'm here." His eyes were glistening too.

"Hi, Husband."

"Hi, Wife."

I smiled before my eyes fluttered closed and I went back to sleep.

CHAPTER 22

"Emmy?" Nick's gentle voice was at my side.

I forced my eyes open and tried to remember where I was. The hospital. I turned toward Nick's voice. He was leaning on the edge of my bed with my hand pressed between his.

"How are you feeling?" he asked.

I took a moment to breathe and assess. "Sore. Tired. Thirsty."

He helped me sit and eased a plastic cup to my lips. It hurt to swallow but soon the water eased some of the tenderness in my throat.

"Better?" he asked.

I nodded and looked around my room. The TV was turned to a basketball game and the bathroom light was on. Though the curtains were drawn, I could tell it was dark outside.

"What time is it?"

"About ten," he said.

I had spent the entire day sleeping. I remembered Jess bringing me here this morning and a brief conversation with the doctor, but after waking up and seeing Nick, I couldn't remember anything else.

"Has Dr. Peterson been back in?" I asked.

He nodded.

"What's wrong with me?"

"You've got pneumonia." He frowned.

I wasn't surprised. My cold was the worst I'd ever had and my stress levels during the last day had been off the charts. It had been the perfect recipe for pneumonia. "How long do I have to stay here?"

"Three or four days. You're on an antibiotic and Dr. Peterson said it can take some time to work. You were pretty dehydrated too so they're pumping you with fluids. And he gave you some pain medicine. You've got two cracked ribs, which will hurt for a while. He wrapped them up but they're slow to heal."

"And my face?" It was pure vanity, but I really hoped that there wouldn't be permanent damage to my cheek.

"Just swollen. It should fade to a nice purple, green and yellow color in a few days."

I smiled and sagged with relief into the bed.

"It's kind of cute. We have matching black eyes," he said.

My smile fell as my eyes snapped to his face. In the dimly lit room, with my swollen eyes, I had missed his injury. But now that I was looking closely, the red welt edging his right eye was obvious.

"Who hit you?"

"Dash," he grumbled.

"Why?"

"I didn't handle the news of your ordeal so well. Punching me in the face was his way of telling me to get my shit together."

"Oh." On top of the guilt I felt about our fight, now I felt horrible for putting him through this misery. "We need to talk," I said, looking at my lap.

There was so much to be said. So much we needed to work out. What was I going to do if we couldn't?

"Not until you're well, Emmy."

I looked into his eyes and begged. "Please. I can't leave things the way we did."

Kissing my hand, he said, "I don't want to hash it all out while you're sick. We need to focus on getting you better. Then we can talk. For now, let's just be us. Okay?"

"Okay," I said reluctantly.

We both stared at the TV for a while and my eyes started to droop not long after the nurse came in to check on me. I'd been awake for less than an hour but was exhausted.

"You should go home and get some sleep," I said.

"I'm not leaving."

"Why not? That chair can't be comfortable."

"It's not, but I don't care. I'm not leaving you."

A happy feeling spread through my heart. I was elated to have Nick back. Yes, we had a lot to talk about, but for now, I was going to savor his comforting presence. I needed him close. So I took a deep breath and braced for pain.

With one strong push, I slid my body to the far edge of the bed. Pain shot through my side and I sucked in a sharp breath.

"What are you doing?" Nick said, jumping from his seat.

"Moving over."

"Why?"

"So you can sleep with me."

"No. Get back in the middle," he said, reaching to pick me up.

I swatted at his hands and gave him a frown.

"Emmy," he growled.

I rolled my eyes. "Don't argue with me. I'm sick. I want you to get up here. I'm still cold and you can keep me warm."

He huffed out a breath and muttered, "Fuck," but then he started kicking off his boots.

Gently, he folded his big body next to mine, then eased an arm beneath my neck so I could rest my head in the crook of his shoulder. It wasn't as nice as spooning, but I'd take it.

Two women were outside my hospital room whispering to each other. Or at least they thought they were whispering. They were actually speaking at a normal volume because they were whisper-yelling at one another.

"I'm going in."

"No, you're not."

"Yes, I am."

"Don't touch that door! You'll wake them up!"

"Shut up!"

"Don't tell me to shut up!"

"Shut. Up!"

"Both of you shut the fuck up," Nick said. "You make any more noise out there and I'm locking you out."

"Effing try it!" one of the voices hissed.

Gigi.

I started chuckling against his chest.

"You two woke up Emmy," Nick snapped.

"Oh, good! You're awake," Gigi said, waltzing into the room, followed by Sara Phillips.

Unlike Gigi, who didn't feel any shame for waking us up, the pretty strawberry blond I had met at Gigi's garage party was blushing and averting her eyes. She carried a huge bouquet of yellow and peach roses along with a bundle of balloons. Both women were wearing scrubs, likely to start working after their visit.

Gigi had flowers too, gerbera daisies in every color. In her other hand was a huge white box.

Nick gently slid his arm from behind me and sat up on the bed, swinging his legs over the side. "What are you two doing here?"

"We're the welcoming committee!" Gigi said. She emptied her hands and came to me in the bed, gently caressing my sore cheek. "Yikes! I'm sorry, Emmeline."

"Thanks. What are you welcoming me to?"

"The Kidnapped Club." She grinned.

"Oh, fuck me," Nick muttered as I laughed.

"Ooh! Ouch. Don't make me laugh. It hurts too much," I said, clutching my ribs, which were now on fire.

"Sorry," she said. "Oh, don't look at me like that," she told Nick.

He was currently scowling at her while hovering over me to see if I was all right.

"I'm okay," I said.

He grumbled a bit but sank down into his chair. "What did you bring us from the café?" he asked, jutting his chin toward the white box.

"Breakfast. We love hospital food," Sara deadpanned. "But we thought you might want something special."

For the first time since my ordeal, I actually felt hungry. It was Monday morning and I had spent almost all of the weekend sleeping.

"We called Tina at the café and she whipped up a special batch of cinnamon caramel rolls," Gigi said. "Usually she only makes them on Sundays but she feels so bad for what happened to you that she made an exception."

"Tell me you brought more than two," Nick said.

"Six." Sara smiled.

He clapped his hands together, rubbing them back and forth. Gigi held out the box but before he could reach it, she snatched it back.

"We stay as long as Emmeline wants," she said, narrowing her eyes.

"She starts to get tired, you're out," Nick said.

"Agreed."

I'd never had one of Tina's famous rolls before and I wasn't able to eat much, but every bite was delicious. The rolls were warm and gooey with the perfect mixture of cinnamon spice, sweet caramel and flaky bread.

Nick demolished the other five rolls. When he stuffed the last piece in his mouth, I looked at him with wide eyes.

"What?" he said with a mouth full of food.

I chuckled and winced. "Don't make me laugh."

"Wa-rry," he apologized.

I rolled my eyes and looked to Gigi.

"So what's the Kidnapping Club?"

"Exactly that. You, me and Maisy are the only members. Maisy really wanted to see you but she won't set foot inside this building so Sara is her club proxy. We're here to do your initiation." Gigi smiled.

"But I wasn't really kidnapped."

She waved a hand in the air. "Close enough."

"Okay," I drawled. "There's an initiation?"

"You're freaking her out, Gigi," Sara said. "Don't worry, Emmeline. I was there when she and Maisy invented this 'initiation' twenty minutes ago. It's nothing serious."

"Your initiation to the club requires only one thing. You have to sign our contract," Gigi said.

Out of her purse, she produced a folded piece of paper and handed it to me while she fished for a pen.

> We, the official members of the Prescott Kidnapped Club, do solemnly swear to do the following:
> 1 – Every year attend or host a party for all club members to celebrate the anniversary of your kidnapping (or attempted kidnapping). Invitations are not limited to club members.
> 2 – Attend, at a minimum, six club meetings to be held at the Prescott Spa.
> 3 – Promise to lean on each of your fellow club members whenever you feel scared, sad or alone.
> 4 – Hold up your fellow club members when you see them starting to fall.
>
> *Gigi Cleary*
> *Maisy Holt*

At the bottom, Gigi and Maisy had signed their names.

For the few moments I had been trapped in the back of Jinx's van, I had been certain that I wasn't strong enough to survive an abduction. That it would break me. I realized now that I didn't have to be strong enough to endure it on my own. I could rely on my friends for support.

My friends.

Not just Nick's. These women had fully embraced me and pulled me into their lives. For that, I was grateful.

"May I have the pen, please?" I scribbled my name next to theirs.

Gigi leaned down to give me a hug. "The next month will be the worst. Lean on Nick. And me. And Maisy. We'll be here. Don't try and go it alone."

My nose stung as tears pricked my eyes. I sniffled and nodded.

"All right, we have to get to work," Sara said.

"Thank you for the visit. And the beautiful flowers."

"And breakfast," Nick said.

"You're more than welcome. We're just glad you're back safe and sound," Gigi said.

"These flowers are from us," Sara said, pointing to the roses.

"And these are from your class," Gigi said, nodding to the daisies. She dug around again in her purse and produced a bright orange card. "They wrote you a card this morning. And because I always take opportunities to brag about my baby girl, Rowen's penmanship is by far the best."

"She's very talented." I smiled. "Who is teaching while I'm in the hospital?"

"Garcia," Nick said. "I called him at home yesterday and told him you were out for the week. Maybe next week too. He said he'd take your class and not to worry."

I let out a sigh of relief that my students wouldn't be negatively impacted by my absence. Rich was not only a good school administrator, he was also a remarkable teacher. My kids were in good hands.

"Do you need anything, Emmeline?" Sara asked.

"No, thank you."

"Okay. Well, I'm working up here today, so if you do, just ring the call button and I'll be right in."

"And if she doesn't answer fast enough, press the emergency call button behind you and I'll come up from the ER." Gigi winked.

More hugs, more banter and more good-byes followed until my friends finally shuffled out. A few minutes after they left, Dr. Peterson came in to assess my injuries.

"You're improving," he said.

"Can I still take her home tomorrow?" Nick asked.

At the word "home," I closed my eyes and grimaced. How was I ever going to walk into my house again?

Nick saw the wince and grabbed my hand, squeezing it tightly.

"Tomorrow should be fine," Dr. Peterson said. "Call if the pain gets worse, Emmeline."

"How are you doing?" Nick asked after the doctor left.

"It's been a busy morning. I'm getting tired."

"Jess needs to come over and get your statement. He said he would bring us some lunch. How about you sleep for an hour before he gets here? I'll keep all the visitors out."

"Okay," I said, relaxing into my pillow and closing my eyes.

I felt his warm breath before his lips pressed against

the tip of my nose. "Sleep well, Emmy."

An hour later, Jess and Nick were sitting in chairs next to my bed. My nap had been short but I felt rested.

"Sorry to bother you," Jess said, "but I've got to get your statement."

"It's no problem."

"We'll make it quick," he promised.

For the next twenty minutes, I walked Jess and Nick through the events at my house. Nick got so angry when I told them about Wrecker's and Jinx's physical assaults that we had to take a break so he could walk the hall and cool down.

"You got anything to add?" Jess asked Nick. "Like who those men were? Your dad and brother seemed to have a pretty good idea when we were talking on Saturday."

"On the record," Nick said, "I have no clue."

"Off the record," Jess said.

"It's a long story," Nick sighed.

"I've got time. How about you fill me in while Emmeline eats her lunch?" Jess asked.

Jess had brought Nick and me food from the deli downtown. The restaurant owners had packed up a huge meal. Nick had a large sub sandwich and I'd gotten home-made chicken noodle soup.

Nick started explaining and didn't hold back any details from Jess. He told him about his childhood in Draven's motorcycle club, his mother's murder and how he'd once committed felony arson. I think it helped him process it all by talking it out with a friend. Nick had been carrying these heavy burdens alone for a long time.

When he recounted how he had spent the last week, I was overjoyed when he said that he hadn't helped the club

306

like Draven and Dash had wanted. Instead, he'd just gone to Stone's funeral and hung around the Clifton Forge garage.

"At least now we know who was breaking into your house," Nick said when he finished his story. "Just wish I would have thought about the Warriors as a threat before it escalated so far."

"It's not your fault," I said, reaching out a hand toward him.

He took it and kissed my palm.

Nick was blaming himself for my kidnapping. It had been because of his family's affiliations but it wasn't Nick's fault. And I certainly didn't hold him responsible.

I wished that he hadn't left during our argument. That the Warriors hadn't found me alone. But if they had been breaking into my home for months, it had just been a matter of time. Nick couldn't be with me every second, and since the Warriors had clearly been determined to get me, eventually they would have. It was just too bad that it had happened after our fight.

"All right. I'm gonna take off," Jess said. "Emmeline, let me know if you think of anything else."

Both men stood, but instead of shaking hands, Nick pulled the sheriff in for a brief hug. Jess clapped him on the back and then came to my side. He bent low and gave me a gentle kiss on the forehead. "Get well, Emmeline."

I fought back tears. Jess had saved me from an unthinkable ordeal. Who knew what the Arrowhead Warriors would have done had they made it out of my driveway? I would forever be indebted to Jess for coming to my rescue. "Thank you. For everything," I said.

He nodded and ducked out of the room.

"Thank you too," I told Nick. "For coming back."

"Don't thank me, Emmy." Pain and guilt were etched on his handsome face.

"It's not your fault," I whispered.

"It is."

"It's not. Please don't torture yourself for this. I am fine. I will be fine. And I won't be able to get past this if you blame yourself."

Nick's head dropped to the edge of my bed and his shoulders started to shake. My strong, brave and honest man was breaking down.

"I almost lost you," he whispered. When he looked up, his eyes were wet. "I can't live in a world without you."

Tears dripped down my cheeks too. "You don't have to." I reached out my hand and placed it on Nick's cheek, my thumb gently stroking his soft beard.

"Knock, Knock!"

Our visitor had bad timing. Swiping the tears off my face, I pulled in a few calming breaths. Nick did the same.

"Hi, Silas," I said as he walked into the room.

"Is this a bad time?"

I shook my head while Nick stood to shake his hand. "No. Come on in."

"Brought you both some stuff to wear home tomorrow," Silas said, swinging a large duffel bag from his shoulder.

"Thanks," Nick said, rifling around in the bag. The first thing he pulled out was one of his flannel shirts. "Can you lean forward?" Nick asked me.

I nodded and crunched forward as best I could with the tight wrap around my cracked ribs. Nick eased the shirt over my shoulders and onto each arm. Then he tucked the back behind me and helped me snap up the front.

When I pulled in a deep breath, I smelled Nick and instantly felt better. The pain in my side eased and the aches in my muscles lessened.

Magic.

CHAPTER 23

"WHY ARE YOU DRIVING BY THE school?" The direct route to Nick's house was straight down the highway and through Main Street. Going by the school was blocks out of the way.

"I wanted you to see that," he said, pointing out the front window.

On the school's sign, the black lettering had been rearranged to read *Get Well Soon, Ms. Austin!*

"I love Prescott," I said.

It was Tuesday afternoon and I had just been discharged from the hospital. I was relieved to be out but nervous at the inevitable conversation to come. Nick and I hadn't talked about our fight, about the divorce papers or about him walking out on me.

We had both rested and I had healed.

My ribs were still tender but I could move again without

feeling sharp pains. I was enjoying the sensation of taking in a full breath without wheezing or coughing. And my eye was now a beautiful greenish yellow that matched Nick's.

As we weaved through town and left for the hills, the knot in my stomach tightened. My anxiety peaked the second he turned into his drive. The time for us to ignore our issues was over.

Nick helped me inside but I froze in the entryway. I stood by the door and stared at the place where I had watched him leave and had crumpled to the floor. My eyes found the manila envelope of divorce papers still lying on the coffee table. The door closed behind me and Nick stepped into my space.

"We can't put it off any longer," I said. "We need to talk."

"Yeah. We do," he said quietly. "Come in and sit."

I shook my head and bit my lower lip to stop my chin from quivering. "I don't think I can."

Walking inside meant I could lose Nick from my life. He might not forgive me for the divorce papers. For hurting him. If standing in the doorway would prevent that from happening, I would gladly stay here for the rest of my life.

He laced his fingers through mine and leaned down to kiss the top of my hair. "Come on." He gently tugged me behind him to the couch.

I opened my mouth to apologize but he beat me to it.

"I'm sorry, Emmeline. I'm so fucking sorry. I don't know what else to say."

The emotion swelled from my chest to my throat, nearly strangling me. "No, I'm sorry. This is my fault."

He reached out and grabbed the divorce papers. "I'm going to sign these. And then I'll let you go."

My heart plummeted into my stomach. I started

shaking my head but he was so focused on the papers he didn't notice. His broken voice filled my ears.

"I'm sorry I let you down," he said. "That I didn't stay. You deserve someone who can keep his promises. I'll sign the papers and you can be free."

Tears streamed down my face. "Stop. Please," I said, pressing my fingers against his lips. "It's not your fault. It's mine. I should have talked to you about how I was feeling a long time ago."

"No. No, Emmy. I never should have left you in Vegas. And for me to do it again when you asked me not to? None of this would have happened to you if I had stayed. It's all on me."

"I don't blame you," I said.

"You should."

"I don't."

He shook his head and leaned forward, grabbing a pen from the table. Then he quickly pulled out the divorce papers and started thumbing through the pages.

"What are you doing?" I gasped.

"I told you I'd sign these," he whispered. "If we're over, let's get it done. You can move on. Let's sign these and then I'll take you wherever you want to go. Home. The motel. The airport. Wherever."

Why wasn't he listening to me? I said that I felt bad for not talking to him about a decision that affected both of us. He wasn't giving me the chance to forgive him. He was just giving up. How dare he let me go without a fight? My sadness and confusion turned to anger.

"That's it? End of discussion? You hardly let me speak! How do you know I won't forgive you? You just assume that I can't and that's it? Now you're just making the decision that we're over?"

"I thought that's what you'd want," he said.

Jumping to my feet, I yanked the divorce papers away from him and waved them in the air.

"I want you to stop assuming that I can't and won't forgive you. I want you to stop thinking so little of yourself that you think I could possibly be happy with anyone else. Because I can't. I knew that the night we got married. Thinking a divorce would make this easier was just a stupid mistake. If anyone should be sorry here, it's me. I hurt you and—"

My rant was immediately silenced by Nick's mouth. His kiss was full of passion and intensity. Of hope. Of forgiveness. We were going to put this ridiculous argument behind us. Neither of us needed any more words to move forward.

Well, maybe just a few more.

Nick broke away from the kiss and framed my face with his hands. His sparkling eyes saw straight into the center of my soul.

"I love you," he said.

To hear those words—finally! The feeling was better than any I'd had before. "I love you too."

A crooked grin spread across Nick's face. "Fuck, it feels good to say that."

Nick erased the smile on my face with another kiss.

"Would you build me a fire?" I asked.

"Now?"

"Yes. Please?"

He reluctantly let me go and went to the fireplace. When the wood was burning hot, I knelt next to Nick and tossed in the divorce papers.

We both watched the white paper turn brown at the

center and catch fire at the edges. When they were fully black and curled into a disappearing crumple, I smiled.

Good riddance.

Sitting at the kitchen counter, I smiled while folding up the newspaper and tucking it beneath a stack of mail.

The local newspaper had written a front-page article about my attempted kidnapping and subsequent illness for this week's edition. Considering that neither of us had given an interview and Jess's official statement had been extremely brief, I'd been surprised at how much the editor knew about my ordeal.

I hated how public my life had been in New York but nothing about the Prescott Gazette's bulletin bothered me. It was the first time in my life I hadn't cringed after seeing my name in typed font. The article wasn't nosy or critical. It was caring and sweet. The community was simply concerned about their kindergarten teacher.

I had gone back to work this week, and though I'd come back much sooner than Nick had liked, being with my students had done a lot to help me get back to normal.

It was Friday afternoon and I'd left work early, rushing back to Nick's house, ready to start the weekend.

"Hey," Nick called.

I glanced at the clock. He was home early. I hoped everything was okay because I didn't think I could take much more drama.

"You cooked?" Nick asked, walking into the kitchen.

"Don't sound so shocked. Or skeptical," I said. "I used

the Crock-Pot. I've decided it's going to be my specialty."

"Considering all you have to do is dump everything in and turn it on, you should be able to handle it."

I poked him in the chest and rolled my eyes. "What are you doing here anyway? You're early and ruining my surprise."

"I'm not ruining your surprise," Nick said. "You're ruining mine."

"You have a surprise for me?"

"Yep."

"And? What is it?"

"How attached are you to those meatballs?" he asked. In the crockpot were Thai meatballs I was going to serve over jasmine rice.

"Considering that it's the first edible meal I've ever made you? Pretty attached."

"Okay. We'll eat and then you can have your surprise."

I scrunched up my face and pouted. "Can I have it now?"

"No."

"I hate surprises," I said.

He grinned. "I know."

We ate dinner and then Nick loaded me up in his truck. I figured he was taking me to a movie or for ice cream so when he pulled off the highway and into my driveway, I started having a mild panic attack.

"You're taking me to my house? That's not a surprise. That's torture. I'm not ready yet." My skin was clammy and a wave of nausea rolled through my stomach.

"You have to go in sometime, Emmy," he said, taking my hand. "I'll be with you the whole time."

"I don't think I can."

He stopped his truck in front of the garage and turned to me, taking both of my hands. "Did you know that Maisy was a nurse?"

"Yes. I read it in an article about their kidnapping after I moved here."

"So then you know that her and Gigi were kidnapped and held in the basement of the hospital."

I nodded.

"Maisy hasn't set foot back in that building since it happened. She gave up her career because she couldn't overcome those fears. I don't want that for you, to be scared of a building. This is just a place. It's got good memories and bad. But it can't hurt you."

I chewed on my lower lip. He was right. Avoidance could only last so long. It was my house. But acknowledging the facts didn't make me feel any less anxious.

He lifted one of my hands to his lips and then got out of the truck.

As we ascended the stone stairs, my hands started shaking. In my mind I could hear myself screaming for help as Jinx carted me into the night.

"You can do this. I'm right here," Nick said. He pushed open the front door and led me inside. I clutched his hand with both of mine. "You're doing great. Let's rip off the Band-Aid. Straight upstairs and to your room."

I followed him up the stairs and down the hallway. As we got closer and closer, my feet turned to lead weights.

We crossed the threshold and I stared around my room.

He must have come over this week because the bed had been made and everything was back in its proper place.

I took a deep breath and reminded myself that this was just a place. Nothing in here was going to hurt me. The fears were still in my head, but they were linked to Jinx and Wrecker. My room was just a room. "I'm okay."

"I knew you would be," he said and wrapped me in a tight hug. "Now you get your surprise."

"It better not just be sex because we could have done that at your house and avoided all of this drama. And if it is just sex, you'd better be planning something big to make this up to me."

"Oh, it's big, Emmy," he said, pressing his growing erection into my hip.

I rolled my eyes. "That's not what I meant." Though, he was right. It was big. Very big.

He chuckled. "Sex isn't the surprise."

"Then tell your pecker to calm the hell down."

"My dick is not a pecker."

"I don't like surprises and you've made me wait for hours. You have exactly thirty seconds to produce said surprise or any and all future references to your manhood will include the term 'pecker.' "

Fifteen seconds later, we were in the kitchen.

"You were going to make me fajitas?"

"Yep. And scotcheroos," he said.

I loved that he had planned to recreate the meals from our first cooking experiences in this kitchen.

"We should have put the meatballs in the fridge and eaten over here," I said.

"This will all keep for tomorrow."

"Thank you. It was a lovely surprise."

"The food is not the surprise, Emmy," he said.

"It wasn't? Then what is?"

Nick hoisted me up onto the island and stood between my legs. Fishing in his pocket, he pulled out a key chain with a single silver key.

"Dinner was a good-bye. I thought we could eat here one last time and then you could come home. For good."

My heart fluttered and my breath hitched.

Home.

"This is my key?" I asked.

"If you want it."

I didn't delay in snatching the key from his hands. "Absolutely."

It continually amazed me how much my life had changed for the better in less than a year. Was this all real? Fate had brought me back to Nick. There was no other explanation for us finding one another again. We were destined.

My whole body shivered when he sucked my earlobe between his lips.

"Before we leave we're going to celebrate."

"How?" I panted.

"I've always wanted to have sex on that huge couch thing you have outside."

"Outside? No way. It's too cold."

He gave me a crooked grin that soon turned into a huge smile. "I dare you."

Turns out, it wasn't all that cold.

It was the Saturday after Nick had asked me to move in and we were having a moving party. We'd spent the morning packing up my house with help from Beau, Silas, Maisy and the Clearys, and now we were back at the cabin to unload.

"I think you might have to build me a larger closet one

of these days," I told Nick. He was standing in the living room, rummaging through one of six boxes filled with coffee mugs.

"Done."

"I was kidding, Nick."

"I'm not. I just spent an hour packing your clothes. Closet space is priority one."

"Funny," I said. "That box goes to the garage for storage."

He gave me a quick kiss and turned to the door, then froze. "What the fuck are they doing here?"

I followed his gaze to see two motorcycles approaching. One carried Dash, the other Draven.

Shit.

Nick's hands fisted at his sides and his jaw clenched tight. It was too soon. He wasn't ready to see his dad yet.

"You can always ask them to leave," I said. "I'm sure they'd understand."

He shrugged. "I'm not sure what to do. Dad's been trying. He's called me every day to check on you and apologize for getting you wrapped up in his shit."

That was news and it softened my feelings toward Draven. "Well, whatever you decide, I'll support you."

He pulled me into his arms. "I know," he whispered into my hair. "Let's go out and see what they want. Take it from there."

Hand in hand, we strolled out to meet Nick's family and our friends all congregated by the trucks packed full of my boxed belongings.

"Dash," Nick greeted. "Dad."

"Hey, man," Dash said, giving his brother a quick hug. After they did their manly back-slapping thing, Dash walked right up to me for a hug. His arms pinned mine to my sides as he wrapped them tight and then picked me a foot up off the ground.

"Hey, Sis," he said.

"Put her down, Dash. Her ribs are still sore," Nick ordered.

"Shit. Sorry, Emmeline," Dash said, immediately setting me down.

"I'm fine." I smiled.

"Nick," Draven said, extending his hand.

Nick eyed it for a minute but finally shook with his dad.

Just like Dash, when Draven was done with greeting Nick, he came right into my space. His hug was less exuberant than his son's but just as warm.

"Emmeline. Glad to see you up and around," Draven said.

"Thanks."

"What are you guys doing here?" Nick asked.

"We wanted to come see how Emmeline was feeling," Draven said.

Nick nodded. He was obviously struggling with what to do. With our friends all standing around us, he wouldn't ask his family to leave.

"Are you moving?" Dash asked, scanning all of the boxes.

"Emmy's moving in," Nick said.

"Nice! We'll help." Dash lifted a box from Jess's truck. "Where should I put this?"

My eyes darted to Nick's. He was staring back, silently asking me what he should do. I gave him a small smile and shrugged. If Draven and Dash were trying to repair their relationship with Nick, I wouldn't stand in the way. It was Nick's decision how far to let them into our lives.

Nick's shoulders relaxed and he smiled at his brother. "That box goes in the kitchen. Would you like to stay for dinner? After we get everything unloaded, we're having pizza."

"Fuck yeah!" Dash answered.

And with that, Dash and Draven joined my moving crew. With the added hands, my boxes were soon unloaded and Nick and a few of the guys went into town for pizza and more beer.

"How are you feeling, Emmeline?" Draven asked me as he helped unwrap coffee mugs.

"Better. My ribs are a bit tender but nothing I can't live with."

"Your eye looks better," he said.

"It is. I can cover up the bruise's remaining color with makeup."

"Are these all coffee mugs?" Dash asked as he opened another box stacked on the dining room table.

Maisy and Gigi, who were playing with the kids in the living room, started laughing.

"Emmeline has quite a collection. And they're all totally hysterical," Maisy told him.

"Those ones all go out to the garage," I said. "I'm only keeping the ones in this box inside."

"Maisy, you feel like showing me the garage? I've been known to know my way around a tool bench." Dash winked.

"Dash! No hitting on my friends," I scolded.

"Fuck," he said. "You're no fun, Sis."

"I think I'll like having you at our holiday dinners," Draven said. "It will be nice to have someone on my side to keep the boys in line."

I gave him a small smile and went back to my mugs. I had no idea if we would be sharing holidays together. Nick and I both had a lot of hard feelings toward Draven, but I had to give the man credit. He was genuinely trying to heal the breech.

Hours later, I was officially living with Nick. Every box was unpacked. Artwork now adorned the walls, the guest bedroom had new bedding, and my clothes were stuffed in every available nook and cranny we could find.

I was exhausted but happy.

After a fun evening of pizza, beer and wine, everyone had gone home except for Draven and Dash. While Dash had been shamelessly flirting with Maisy, despite my warnings, he'd convinced his dad to get rooms at her motel in town and spend the night. But before they left us, they wanted to have a private conversation.

"The Warriors won't bother you again," Draven assured us as we sat in the living room.

"You're sure?" Nick asked.

"Positive," Dash said.

"You know we don't normally share club business with outsiders," Draven said. "But I'll make an exception, given your word to keep it quiet."

Nick and I both nodded.

"Change is coming for the Gypsies," Draven said. "We've voted to start getting out of the drug trade. It won't happen overnight, probably within the next year, but border patrol is locking down tight and none of us want to risk spending a decade in prison. Dealers aren't paying us as big of a cut as they used to anyway. So we're done."

"We made a deal with the Warriors for our protection routes coming from Canada. They're buying us out, and we get the guys that killed Stone and the ones that tried to nab Emmeline," Dash added.

"And you think they'll leave us alone after that?" Nick asked.

"If they don't, they're dead," Draven said, sending chills down my spine. "Their president knows they crossed a line by going after Emmeline. I think he's running scared. And they'd be stupid to push back when we're shifting focus to our more legit businesses."

"Dad and I've been talking about expanding the garage. Bringing in more money to offset the lost protection routes," Dash said.

Nick nodded. "That's smart. You guys have a good reputation. If you capitalized on the custom route, you could make some good money."

"You two feel like moving to Clifton Forge to run the garage?" Draven asked.

"What?" Nick asked. His eyes were wide, much like mine.

"I'm retiring," Draven said.

"What about you, Dash?"

He shrugged. "You'd be better at it. Besides, I like working as a mechanic. I don't feel like dealing with the hassle of running the place. If I was the manager, I wouldn't get to work on as many cars."

Nick took my hand. "I appreciate the offer. But I'm not coming back. We're good here. Happy. Emmy's got a great job. We've got our friends. It's not for me."

"Figured it was a long shot, but I had to ask," Draven said and stood. "We'll get out of your hair."

Draven shook Nick's hand before coming to me and leaning down to kiss my cheek. "You're good for him, Emmeline. He's happy. Thank you for that."

"We're good for each other."

"I'm truly sorry about all this. I never meant for that to happen," he said.

"Apology accepted. It's just nice to know it's over. And it's a relief to know who has been breaking into my house."

His eyebrows knitted together. Did he not know about my break-ins? He shook off his confusion quickly and leaned in for a brief hug. "I hope we can put this behind us."

"We don't know each other well, Draven, but you should know I'm not skilled at holding a grudge."

"I appreciate that."

Nick and his father had a long road ahead of them to heal their past wounds but today they had taken that first step. And though a part of me was still angry at Draven for putting my life in danger, I was willing to let it go. His apology was sincere and the real persons at fault were Jinx and Wrecker.

With forgiveness in my heart, I stood by Nick's side and waved good-bye to Draven and Dash.

And the four coffee mugs I had sent with them.

CHAPTER 24

"IS THIS PLACE REAL?" I WHISPERED.

My eyes were glued to the beautiful scenery in front of me. Crystal Lake. Aptly named because the water was crystal clear.

Nick had just led me down the path from our campsite so I could see the lake before it got dark. He was standing at my back with his arms wrapped around my chest while his chin rested on my head.

"It doesn't seem real, that water in the middle of the forest could be that clean," I said.

At my feet, I could see every stone beneath the water's surface. Further into the lake, tiny fish were swimming amongst the green, swaying grasses.

"I love it up here," Nick sighed. We had only been here for ten minutes but I felt the same. "I haven't gotten to travel much, but of all the places I've been, it's my second favorite."

"What's your first?"

His arms hugged me tighter. "The Clover Chapel."

Pure, golden happiness swelled in my heart.

Nick eventually let me go, hooking his pinky with mine to tug me away from the lake. "Let's set up camp. Then tomorrow we can take the canoe out on the water."

"One more second," I said. The setting sun was beautiful as it bounced off the mirrored water. I took one last moment to enjoy the dimming light before I walked up the gravel path behind Nick.

Our campsite was an open gravel circle surrounded by tall trees. There was a ring of rocks at its center plus an old wooden picnic table off to one side.

"What can I do?" I asked.

"Set up those chairs," he said, pointing to the collapsible camp chairs. "And then plant your ass in one."

"You realize that I could help."

"I've got it, Emmy. Sit down and relax. If you want a glass of wine, I put a bottle in the blue cooler. Cups and corkscrew are in the plastic tub."

"Okay." I shrugged.

If he wanted to haul all the stuff around while I enjoyed the scenery, fine by me. And by scenery, I meant him. It was no hardship for me to enjoy ogling his behind covered in those damn tan canvas pants. Especially if I got to sit and drink wine this time instead of hiking up a mountain.

The night air cooled quickly once the sun had set and I bundled up in a warm sweater while Nick started a campfire. Then he blew my mind by cooking steak, potatoes and roasted asparagus on the open flames. I had never been camping before and had assumed we'd be eating snack foods and cold sandwiches.

"So what's our plan for tomorrow?" I asked after dinner.

My belly was full, I had a glass of an amazing malbec in my hand, and Nick was making me a s'more. I loved camping.

"A few miles up the mountain are ice caves. I thought we could hike up there in the morning and come back before lunch. Then we could canoe around the lake," he said.

"Excellent."

"Here," he said, handing me my dessert.

I'd only ever had a s'more at fancy New York restaurants. For a year or so, it had been all the rage. Chefs had made their own graham crackers and served them with ridiculously extravagant chocolate. Then you'd roast a marshmallow over the flame of a candle before assembling the sandwich at your plate. They had cost a fortune.

The s'more Nick had made me, with a dollar milk chocolate bar, boxed graham crackers and a real campfire, was second to none.

For the rest of the evening, we sat in the darkness, side by side, staring at the fire. Every now and again we'd visit but both of us were content to sit and enjoy the peaceful silence while the fire crackled and popped, shooting sparks into the black night sky.

"I'll never get over how many stars you can see," I told Nick as I tipped my head to the sky.

"You don't see that in the city."

I hummed my agreement and yawned.

"Come on, Emmy. Time for bed." He led me to our large tent and lit a gas lantern so I could climb into our air mattress.

I drifted off to sleep while Nick went outside to put out the fire and do whatever else you did at night while camping. When he slid into the bed next to me, I turned so he could curl into my back.

"Are you awake?" he whispered into my hair.

"No."

"Then wake up." He chuckled.

"No."

"Please?"

When I rolled, he shifted the hair from my face. "I found something this week. Something I've been hoping to find for a long time."

He brought a hand between our faces. On the tip of his index finger were two rings. My Gatsby hexagon and his platinum band.

"How'd you find those?" I gasped. I'd made a special point to hide them both in a box with our wedding photo and I had personally moved them to Nick's. Then I'd stuffed the box behind a stack of my clothes in the closet.

"I was in the closet, trying to figure out how I could make it bigger."

My cheeks felt hot. I was embarrassed that he'd found something I had always hidden away.

"I've missed this ring for a decade," he said. "I hated that I didn't have it to hold when I missed you. That I could still feel it on my finger but when I looked down, it was gone. And I hated that I thought I'd never get it back."

How many times had I been tempted to donate them to charity? I was so glad that I hadn't, that I'd kept them all this time and had never given in to the urge to give them away.

"I was going to wait until tomorrow to bring these out, but I can't," he said. "It's been three days since I found them and I feel like they're burning a hole in my pocket. Emmeline Austin, love of my life, would you do me the great honor of wearing my ring on your finger? Of staying my wife?"

I nodded frantically. "Yes."

A wide, white smile filled my vision. The golden-brown flecks spread through Nick's sage-green irises.

"Hi, Wife," he said as he slid my ring on my finger.

"Hi, Husband," I said, doing the same for him.

When it was settled against his knuckle, Nick leaned forward and placed a soft, sweet kiss against my lips. Then he raised my hand and kissed my ring finger.

I slipped my hand from his and into his beard, gently stroking his lower lip with my thumb. "I love you, Nick."

"I love you, Emmy. Always."

Tears flooded my eyes. The happiest tears of my life.

I hated that Nick and I had missed so much time together but that sting was nearly gone. There was no guarantee that we would have stayed together, that we would have made it. We had both been so young when we'd married. I had been naïve. He had been learning how to put distance between himself and his family. Those nine years had changed us and made us the people we were today.

Who we had become was who we were meant to be, two people who would hold onto one another until the end. Who would savor every moment together. Nick had my heart completely and I had his.

He rolled me onto my back and captured my mouth. Then his hands began wandering. When my body started shivering, I pulled at Nick's clothes.

"Condom," he said, breaking our kiss and reaching over to his bag.

"No," I said, grabbing his hand and bringing it back to me.

I wanted my dreams. I wanted a family with Nick and I didn't want to wait.

"You're sure?" he asked.

I nodded.

It didn't take long before our kissing became frantic. His lips broke from mine so he could peel off my clothes.

"Hurry," I pleaded. I was soaked and throbbing.

Nick didn't delay in lining up his cock and thrusting inside. His hips stilled when he was planted deep.

"More," I pleaded.

"Tell me you love me," Nick ordered, pressing even deeper so his cock was against my womb.

"I love you."

"Tell me you want my baby."

"I want your baby. So much."

"Christ, Emmy. I want that too," he said.

Then he started moving. Hard and deep. His pace wasn't rushed, and after each thrust, he ground his hips forward so the root of his cock was pressed against me. The pressure focused on my clit.

I was so close to the edge, I was trembling beneath him. When I felt myself build, I gripped the sleeping bag at my sides and held on tight. Hard and long, my orgasm overwhelmed me. A deep moan came from the back of my throat before I screamed with ecstasy.

Nick abandoned his slow pace and started slamming into me, sending another orgasm rocketing through my core. As I came, I opened my eyes to watch Nick pound away toward his own finish. When it came over him, he threw his head back and groaned. The tent filled with his rough and sexy voice.

When Nick's movement stilled, I wrapped my arms and legs around his body, pulling him as close as I could.

"This is going to be fun," he said into my neck.

I giggled. "You are not wrong."

The sound of us laughing together escaped the fabric walls of our tent and rang through the wilderness and into the starry night.

"Favorite part of camping?" Nick asked as we drove home two days later.

"Canoeing on the lake."

Nick had paddled me to every corner of the small lake. It must have been at least twenty feet deep in parts and I could see straight to the bottom. The sunshine above us had cast a shadow of the boat on the lake floor as we'd floated around.

"Yours?" I asked.

"Besides sex in the tent—which, by the way, I'm a bit hurt wasn't your favorite part—probably the food. I love cookout food."

"It was delicious," I said. "And tent sex was a given. I believe I expressed just how much I liked it this morning when I was on top of you."

"Oh, yeah." He smiled. "Feel free to express yourself like that again. Anytime, Emmy."

"So noted."

I had lied to Nick. Canoeing wasn't my favorite. The sex wasn't either.

My actual favorite part was that I could look at Nick's hand and see his wedding ring. And when I walked, I could catch glimpses of mine, glimmering on my hand as it swung by my side.

Standing in front of the mirror, I smoothed out the skirt of my dress. Tonight I finally had the occasion to wear my sexy green dress. The one that I had teased Nick with all those months ago. The one that required I forgo underwear.

The front of my dress was seemingly conservative, made of green fabric with a matching lace overlay. The neck was high and it had small capped sleeves. It was the back, or lack thereof, that made the dress. An enormous cutout started at the nape of my neck and extended all the way to my sides, down to just below my rear.

I hoped that Nick would be so enamored with the dress that he would be in an agreeable mood. Tonight, we were celebrating his birthday. And tonight, I was going to take him to the empty building in town that I had bought for his garage.

I was nervous that he would hate it. I didn't want him to resent the fact that I had used my money for his potential business. On the bright side, my anxiety would be short-lived. I had just closed on the building this morning, and within the next two hours, I would know how Nick felt about my present.

"Ready?" Nick asked as I walked down the stairs. He was standing by the door, pulling on a sports coat.

I had never seen him so dressed up for dinner before. Or ever. He was still in jeans and a black T-shirt, but with the black tweed jacket and the absence of his green baseball cap, he was looking hot. Damn hot. I couldn't wait to slide that jacket off his broad shoulders when we got home.

That is, if he wasn't mad at me for buying him a building today.

"I like your dress, Emmy."

I grinned before slowly spinning around.

"Fuck," he hissed. "We're skipping dinner."

"Patience," I said.

"Have you been waiting awhile to say that to me for once?"

"Maybe." I smiled.

Not long after we left, we were at The Black Bull and I was demolishing the steak in front of me. "This is wonderful. Thank you," I told the waitress as she brought me my second glass of wine and Nick his third beer.

"How's your restaurant coming along in New York?" Nick asked.

"Really well. My project manager sent me a note on Tuesday with a progress update. They have the design done and are just getting bids on construction. My chef is over the moon that the menu is going to be simple. He's going to work on creating some special butter sauces to serve over the steaks but other than that, he's just going to focus on getting high-quality meat and produce."

"When will it be done?" he asked.

"It's scheduled to close at the beginning of July when everyone leaves for the Hamptons, then open back up at the end of August," I said.

"What'd you pick for the name?"

My cheeks flushed. I was proud of the name but embarrassed to tell Nick.

"What?" he asked.

"I asked them to name it 'Nick's.'"

His eyes sparkled as the smile grew on his face. He reached out to hold my hand, lacing his fingers with mine on the table. "Best birthday present ever."

"I may have gotten you a *little* something else."

He gave my fingers a final squeeze and then we both

went back to our meals. "Should we fly out for the opening?"

"To New York?" I asked, nearly choking on a bite of green beans.

"Yeah. If it opens early enough, we could get out there and back before the school year starts."

"You'd go with me?"

"Are you my wife?" he asked.

"Yes."

"Do I love you?"

"Yes."

"Is the restaurant important to you?"

"Yes."

"Then there's your answer," he said.

I guess we were going to New York at the end of the summer.

By the end of dinner, my nerves were making me jittery. We climbed into the truck and I sat on my hands to keep them from fidgeting.

"Can you make a right turn here?" I asked. The building that I'd bought him was located off the highway. It was only a few blocks away from the fire station and two buildings down from the sheriff's department.

"Why?"

"Your birthday present," I said without further explanation.

"Okay," he said and made the turn. Nick was clearly better at enjoying surprises than I was.

"Then a left here," I said. "And pull into that building on the right."

Nothing about the place looked like a mechanic's garage but I'd picked it because it had great potential. The majority of the long rectangular structure was dark red steel, but at the far end, the metal transitioned to wooden fascia where a small office had been separated from the warehouse.

My realtor had told me that it was originally built by an out-of-state furniture maker. He had moved to Prescott from California but the cold winters hadn't agreed with him. He'd jumped at my cash offer, glad to finally sell the place.

I hopped out of the truck and made my way to the doors. Nick's boots thudded on the pavement behind me. Tugging the keys out of my clutch, I unlocked the office's glass door, hitting the light switch as I pushed inside.

"This is where I got my coffee table and the dining room set," Nick said. He was casually looking around the office, running his fingers over the desk that still remained in its center.

His relaxed and easy demeanor was making my nerves spike. How was he able to function not knowing what we were doing here? I would have been a fumbling mess.

I walked further into the building, flicking on the many switches at the light panel. The warehouse came to life under the bright fluorescents hanging from the industrial ceiling.

My heels clicked across the cement floor as I walked to a table on the sidewall. On it was a handful of business cards that read *Slater's Station*. I'd asked my restaurant project manager for a favor, and based on a picture I'd sent him of Nick's sign, he had been able to have a graphic designer build a logo for the garage. The cards were just a mock-up but I thought they were amazing.

I just hoped that Nick liked them too.

I turned around and saw him standing in the center of the room. His arms were crossed over his chest and his legs planted wide.

"In the future, Wife, I'd prefer we make our real estate

purchases together."

My chin dropped. "What? You know I bought this building?"

"Found out this morning. Your realtor had coffee at the café after you two signed papers. Seth Balan was down there with his retired buddies. His first stop after coffee was the fire station."

"I can't believe this!" I yelled. "He ruined my surprise."

The smirk on Nick's face turned into a wide, white smile. "Oh, I was surprised, Emmy. When he told me you were buying this place and wanted to know what we were doing with it, I believe my exact words were, 'What the fuck are you talking about? I think I would know it if my wife was buying a warehouse.' It took Balan nearly five minutes to stop laughing at me."

"That man is a nuisance. He needs to get a job so he can stay out of other people's business," I snapped. No wonder Nick had been so casual on the drive over.

"He's not even the worst of that old bunch. Just wait until you meet Silas's dad, Elliot," Nick said.

Throwing my hands in the air, I blew out a loud breath. "Now what do I do? I had this whole speech planned. But you know everything already so it doesn't matter."

"Tell me anyway."

"No. It's stupid now."

"Please?" he begged.

In a monotone and rushed voice, I told him what I'd been practicing all day. "Happy birthday, Nick. I bought this building for you so you could open up a garage of your own and finally have your dream job. If you decide that isn't for you, that's okay. I just wanted you to have the option. So here are your keys. You can do whatever you want with the space.

I'll support you no matter what. I love you and I can't wait to celebrate so many more birthdays together."

When I finished, I huffed out another breath. "There. That was my speech. All the time I spent worrying about it today was a waste of time. All because of that damn Seth Balan."

With long strides, Nick crossed the room. "I'm sorry you didn't get to surprise me," he said, taking my face in his hands. "And I liked your speech, though you could have said it with a bit more feeling."

His joke triggered an eye roll.

"It's a great gift, Emmy. I don't know that I deserve it."

"Of course you do. You're not mad that I bought it, are you?"

"No. I'd rather you spend your money on yourself instead of me. But I'm not mad," he said.

"I can't make that promise," I said. "That money isn't just mine anymore. It's ours."

I had already made the decision to add Nick to my trust and my attorney was currently drawing up the amendment papers. Nick was a permanent part of my life. My money wasn't mine anymore, because we were a team. He had the right to use it just as much as I did.

Not that I thought he would. I doubted he'd ever take a cent.

"That's a conversation for a different day," he said.

"Okay. I'm willing to stall the money talk since it's your birthday," I said. "But soon we need to discuss it."

"All right."

"Here," I said, handing him the business cards. "I had these made for you. They're not real. I just wanted to throw out the idea."

Nick lifted the cards to his face and studied them intently. "'Owners Nick and Emmeline Slater'?"

"We can change that," I said quickly. "I don't need to be a part of the garage, and if you'd prefer to do it on your own, I completely understand. But if you want my help with office work or bookkeeping, I'd be happy to help. Whatever you want."

"I like your name on there, Emmy. Especially followed by my last," he said.

"Oh," I said, looking to the floor when my cheeks flushed. "It's just, I always thought I would take my husband's name. I guess I'm traditional in that sense. Does it bother you?"

He bent down and brushed his lips against mine. His tongue darted out and teased my lower lip. I pushed forward, hoping for more, but he leaned back.

"Does that answer your question?"

"What do you think about starting a garage?" I asked.

"Balan didn't know why you bought this place, so when he left the station, I racked my brain, trying to figure out why. I had some other guesses but figured this was the mostly likely. It was probably good I had the day to think about it."

"How come?" I asked.

"My first thought was that I couldn't do it and that you wasted a shitload of money. But then I got to thinking about starting a custom shop. If I could build up a name for myself across the Northwest, I wouldn't be taking business away from the garage downtown."

"You're a good man, Nick, to be worried about someone else's business."

He shrugged. "They're good people."

"What about the fire station? Do you think one of your volunteers would be interested in your job?"

"Maybe. I need to think on it some more. Run the numbers and talk to Dad and Dash. I don't know if it's smart to open my own business if we're trying to have a baby."

"Why?" I asked. "I think it's the perfect time. Think of how much you could teach our kids. They could work with you here, just like you did with your family."

A small smile tugged at his mouth. "I'll call Dad and Dash later," he said. "Maybe talk to Ryan at Jamison Valley Construction too. See how much it would cost to renovate this place."

"Oh. About that," I said, scrunching up my nose. "I may have already discussed that with him. And the money for the remodel is in the office desk. That's the next part of your present."

"I'm thinking that money conversation needs to happen sooner than I thought," he said.

"That's probably not a bad idea."

"Thank you, Emmy. For believing in me."

"You're easy to believe in."

"Let's go home, Wife. I want birthday sex with you in that dress and those heels. But I'm not fucking you in this cold garage. At least, not yet."

I shivered as I walked through the room, and not because it was cold.

CHAPTER 25

"C AN YOU BE MY TEACHER NEXT YEAR?"
"Bye!"
"Will you come to my birthday party this summer?"

My students were taking turns hugging me as they shuffled their way out of the classroom and into their summer break.

The kids were excited to be moving up to first grade and I was looking forward to a whole new group of children to teach, though I would miss this bunch. My first class would always have a special place in my heart. Especially Rowen and Mason.

But the wonderful thing about Prescott was that the kids would never be far. I would run into them on the street or at the café. In the school hallways, I would get to watch them grow from kindergartners to seniors in high school.

Prescott was my home and it would be for the rest of my life.

When the line ended, I scanned the classroom and found the student I had been waiting for. It was no surprise that Mason had held back. He wasn't one to move with the crowd.

"Are you excited for summer at the farm?" I asked, kneeling in front of him.

He nodded, returning my smile and giving me his dimple. "Jack and Annie said I could change my last name from Carpenter to Drummond. And that since I was going to be a Drummond now, the farm would be mine too. I don't have to leave my vacation."

"Wow! That's awesome, Mason!" I said, feigning surprise.

Annie Drummond had asked me to write a recommendation letter when she and Jack had decided to officially adopt Mason. She had been worried a judge would object due to their age but it had gone through without delay. The judge had agreed to an immediate adoption with the condition that Mason's biological mother sign away her parental rights. Jack had chosen to visit the woman in prison, and no sooner had he pulled out the papers than she'd signed them and walked away.

"Will you come and visit me?" Mason asked. "I could show you around. And you could meet my dog."

"I would love to. Now, you'd better get going. I'm sure Annie is outside waiting for you. I think she mentioned something about ice cream to celebrate."

He darted around me and sprinted through the door. He didn't get too far before his footsteps came back my way. Mason ran through the door and straight into me, throwing his little arms around my hips as he hugged me tight. I bent low and did my best to hug him back.

"I'll miss you, Ms. Austin. I mean, Mrs. Slater," he said, remembering my new last name.

"I'll miss you too, Mason Drummond."

As quickly as he had come back, he was rushing out again.

My nose started to sting and the tears weren't far behind. I had known that today would be emotional for me. In a lot of ways, these kids had pulled me through the year. How many times had I thought about moving? I doubted that I would have stayed in Prescott if it hadn't been for them.

So in a way, without my students, Nick and I might not have made it through. I might have given up.

When my phone rang, I wasn't surprised to see Nick's name on the screen. Even from across town, he could tell when I needed him.

"Hi," I answered.

"How are you doing?"

"I'm sad."

"Don't be sad, Emmy. You'll see them again."

"I know you're right. But I'm still sad. I'll miss seeing their little faces."

"You'll be okay. Are you done for the day?" he asked.

"Just about. I need to put a few things away and drop off my grade sheet in the office. I'll likely need thirty minutes."

"Okay. When you're done, meet me at the building," he said.

"*Your* building."

"*Our* building. See you soon."

It didn't take me long before I was walking into the

warehouse. Nick was standing in its center with two other men, Ryan from the construction company and Jess.

Jess bent to give me a quick hug and Ryan shook my hand. Then Nick secured me to his side and explained why we were all here.

"We've been brainstorming different layouts for the garage. I thought we could cut out two big doors on the front and then one at the back, add a couple of lifts in the middle of the floor, benches and tool cabinets around the walls."

The sadness in my heart vanished. Did this mean he was going to do it, quit the fire station and start his own garage?

"Whatever you think is best." I smiled.

"We were talking about building a paint booth out back. Maybe extend off the office? Keep that wooden siding so that it looks nice. That would save me room in here so I could fit two, maybe three cars at a time."

"Okay." I was so overjoyed that I had a hard time coming up with anything else to say.

"This place is gonna be great, Nick," Jess said.

"Thanks, Brick. Appreciate you coming over and checking it out," Nick said.

"Any time." He reached out for a handshake. "I'm taking off. Georgia wants to celebrate Rowen's last day of kindergarten."

"I'm going to miss her," I told Jess.

"She's gonna miss you too."

"I'm heading out too," Ryan said, also shaking Nick's hand. "I'll get the original bid I did for Emmeline updated this weekend. Shoot it over to you on Monday. I've got extra hands right now. A couple of the kids that worked for me last summer are home from college. Maybe start at the end of June if you want."

"We'll talk about it tonight and I'll let you know. Thanks, Ryan."

When we were alone, I looked up at Nick with a hopeful smile. "Does this mean you're considering a career change?"

"Yeah."

"Yes!" I yelled, the sound echoing throughout the empty room.

Nick picked me up and spun me around. I threw my head back and watched the room twirl around me.

Things just kept getting better. It was hard to even process this much happiness.

"I love you, Emmy," he said, looking up at me.

"I love you, Nick."

We were finally getting our happy ending, starting the life that we had both longed for all those years ago.

It was a shame that the devils from the past wouldn't let us live in peace.

I detested summer.

Which was unusual, considering it was my second favorite season behind spring. It had only been a month since school let out and I was bored out of my mind.

I struggled to find enough activity to occupy my time during the day until Nick got home each night. I lived for our weekends, and because they had become so precious, I was in a particularly grumpy mood today since Nick was at work.

Today was one of the Saturdays each spring that his volunteer crew did all-day field training. With forest fire season starting soon, they were doing extinguishing drills in the foothills outside of town with Beau at the Forest Service.

Rather than wallow inside alone and watch the clock, first thing this morning, I had jumped in the Jeep and driven to the garden center. I was going to liven up the front porch with flowers.

Did I have the first clue about planting? No.

Were the flowers likely going to die within two weeks? Definitely.

"You realize they make other colors of flowers, right?"

"Ahh!" I screamed, jumping up to my feet and whirling around. Dirt and a large petunia went flying through the air.

"Sorry!" Nick said, holding up his hands. "I thought you heard me pull up."

"I did not," I gasped. The music filtering from the house had been too loud and I had been concentrating on my task. "You scared me half to death!"

He sucked his lower lip in between his teeth and tried to stop his chest from shaking.

"It's not funny, Nick! I nearly had a heart attack!" I crossed my dirty arms over my dirty shirt and glared at my husband as he burst into hysterics.

"I'm sorry. You look adorable," he said, crossing the yard.

"I'm a mess."

"An adorable mess." He picked at the dirt and leaves stuck in my ponytail.

"You're home early," I said. "How did your training go?"

"Awesome. The team rocked the course in record time. I see you've been busy," he said, surveying the porch.

"They're probably all going to die within a week." I frowned.

"Then you can just replant them all again," he said,

kissing my forehead. "That should give you something to do at least."

"I'm going crazy," I said. "I've never been this antsy before. What's wrong with me?"

"Nothing. You're just adjusting to a new routine. By the end of the summer, you'll love the slower pace."

"Doubtful."

"Ryan called me while I was driving home," Nick said. "They're ready to start on the garage next week. I told him that you were going to coordinate everything."

"Thank goodness. I can't wait for a project."

Nick grabbed my hands and pinned them behind my back. With his chest pressed up against mine, he looked down at me and grinned.

"Got some more good news today too. Michael Holt is looking to quit his job so I talked to him about replacing me at the fire station."

"Really? That would be great! What did he say?" I asked.

"He was a little intimidated at first but I talked to him for a while. I think he'd be a good fit," Nick said. "As long as I stay on as a volunteer, the rural council should sign off on him. He's pretty young but I think he'd do a good job."

For the last couple of weeks, Nick and I had been talking a lot about the garage and how we'd run it together. Every day he'd gotten more and more excited, but he was hesitant to leave the fire department completely.

He had built his life as a firefighter and if he wasn't going to run the department, he felt he should at least stay on as a volunteer. It scared me a little but mostly I was proud of his courage and dedication.

"I'm glad it could all work out," I said.

"Me too. You realize I hate the color yellow, right?" he whispered.

"What?" My mouth fell open. If he hated yellow, then the plethora of flowers I had on the front porch was a gigantic mistake.

"Kidding," he teased.

I rolled my eyes.

"That's what I was going for," he said, which got him another eye roll. "Two in a row."

"Quit teasing me."

Nick bent down to brush his lips against mine. "Never. I love that eye roll."

And just because it would make him happy, I gave him one more.

For the next hour, I finished planting my yellow flowers while Nick kept me company. We talked about the garage, his design ideas and thoughts for getting new business.

The minute we walked into the house, my phone rang.

"It's my father," I grumbled. I hadn't talked to him since Easter. I had made the decision not to share the details of my attempted kidnapping with him or my mother. Mom would just worry whereas he would blame the entire thing on Nick and use it against him in the future.

I scrunched up my nose but decided to take the call. "Hello, Father."

"Emmeline!"

"Steffie?" I said. "Is everything okay? Why are you calling me from Father's phone?"

"Oh, he's here too," she said. "Say hi, Trent."

"Emmeline. Hello," he muttered. Clearly, this group chat wasn't his idea.

"We're coming to visit you," Steffie announced.

"Uh . . ." My tongue felt too big for my mouth. Seeing Steffie would be nice. But my father? In the same state as Nick? Nothing good could come from this visit.

"Hello?" Steffie said. "Did you hear me?"

I shook my head a bit and regained control of my speech. "Yes. When will you be here?"

"Monday," she said.

"What? You mean the day after tomorrow?"

"Yes. You're not working, right?"

"Um, no."

"Okay then. We'll be there Monday."

I racked my brain, frantically searching for any excuse to delay their trip—better yet get them to cancel it altogether—but I couldn't come up with a thing.

"And we'd like to stay with you."

No. They could absolutely *not* stay here. I hadn't spent an entire day in the same confines as my father for years. "Well, I haven't had a chance to tell you, but Nick and I actually moved in together. You'd probably be more comfortable at the motel."

"Don't you have a guest bedroom?" Steffie asked.

"No, it's just a little crowded right now. I, um, haven't unpacked," I lied. "How about you both stay at my house?"

"Your house will be fine," she agreed. "I don't want to stay at the motel. Now that that's settled, Trent has a few things he'd like to say to you."

"Yes, Father?" I asked, mentally preparing for his inevitable criticism.

"Emmeline, I'd like to apologize for my behavior these last few phone calls. I understand I should have handled the news of your *marriage* differently."

This phone call was absolutely Steffie's idea. The apology

too. The word "marriage" sounded like it had caused him physical pain. But I decided just to accept it and move on.

"Thank you. I appreciate your apology."

"Very well. Now that we've settled that, let's discuss our vacation plans. Steffie has convinced me to spend some time getting to know your *husband*." There was that tone again. "Please plan something for the two of us do alone while you girls catch up."

"I'm sure that can be arranged," I said.

"Fine. Now we have other news."

"Yes?"

"I'm pregnant," Steffie announced.

I reached out a hand, swiping it in the air, trying to find anything to hold onto. My legs were giving out and I was light-headed.

"Fuck. I've got you," Nick said, rushing to catch me. It was a good thing he had been standing close or I would have hit the floor. "Breathe, Emmy."

I nodded, pulling in a few breaths to stop my head from spinning. "I'm okay," I said, steading myself.

"Emmeline?" my father called out. "Are you all right?"

"Yes. I'm fine," I said, putting the phone back to my ear. Completely shocked, but fine. "Congratulations."

I swallowed down a familiar nausea. It was the same one I'd gotten when I'd walked in on my father screwing Steffie. Not that I wasn't happy for my friend, but the entire situation was just so . . . weird. Steffie had told me that she never wanted children. It was one of the reasons why she was content dating my father. She had said that with him, there was no risk she'd get pressure from her husband to procreate.

"Thanks," Steffie said flatly. She sounded about as

excited as a woman getting a pelvic exam.

My shock from earlier was replaced with concern for my friend. "I'm excited to see you," I told her.

"Me too."

"Call my assistant if you need any of our travel information," my father said. "I've got to go."

I said good-bye and hung up, staring at my phone for a minute, trying to figure out where to start with my recap for Nick. *Can you please take off a few days from work last minute? My father, a man who will likely hate you no matter what you do, is coming in two days. Oh, and, I am going to be a big sister.*

I decided to start at the beginning, and five minutes later, he was as stunned as I was.

"Are you sure you're okay with them visiting?" Nick asked.

"Do I have a choice? I'd like to see Steffie but this is all so awkward. My father is fifty-eight years old. He's having another child. With my friend and college roommate."

I paced through the room and took calming breaths, trying to ease the knot in my stomach. It wasn't uncommon for older men to father children, and they were getting married, after all. But this rushed visit, their pregnancy announcement, it all felt off.

"Your dad and I are going to have problems if he's an asshole to you. He'd better watch his attitude," Nick declared.

"Let's hope he decides to come here with an open mind," I said. "I'm shocked that he apologized to me, though I suspect it was Steffie's idea. Regardless, I've never heard him admit he was wrong before. Maybe he's decided to mend some fences. What do you think?"

"I think he's a fool for the way he's treated you, but if

he's genuine, I'm sure you two could work things out. You're the most forgiving person I've ever met. You'll make the right choice."

"I'm not so sure about that," I said.

"Your capacity to look past people's faults astounds me. I've never seen anything like it before. I left you the night after our wedding and you still found it in your heart to forgive me. I don't know if anyone else would have done that."

"That's because I love you."

"Yeah? What about my dad? His club got you kidnapped and the first time you saw him after getting out of the hospital, you hugged him. That's amazing, Emmy. You give people your love freely and don't hold their mistakes against them. It's what makes you a wonderful teacher. A great friend. The perfect woman. Your dad won't have to do much to right his wrongs. All he has to do is open that door and you'll let him in."

His words warmed my heart. He always knew what to say to boost my spirits.

"I'm nervous," I said. "I'm a different person around him. He makes me feel weaker. Less confident. What if you don't like that version of me?"

"I love all versions of you. And you don't have to be strong when he's around. That's what I'm here for."

"Stop cleaning," Nick ordered.

"I just want to dust above the fireplace."

I was rushing around my old house, doing some last-minute cleaning before my father and Steffie arrived. It was the second time I had cleaned in two days and the place was spotless. I just couldn't help myself. My nerves were getting the better of me.

I didn't want drama between Nick and my father. I just wanted everyone to get along, for my father to see I was happy here and to stop judging me for my choice to stay.

"Relax," Nick said, grabbing me by the waist before I could step up on the fireplace.

"I can't," I said, squirming to get free.

I reached again for the ledge but right as my duster touched the mantel, I was flying through the air. Nick had picked me up and tossed me onto a couch.

"Oh for the love . . ." I said with an eye roll.

I pushed up on my elbows but Nick was on top of me in a flash, pinning me down. "Let me up. I need to finish cleaning."

"It's clean," he said. "You could eat off any surface here. Enough."

"But I—" Nick silenced me with his mouth.

While his tongue tangled with mine, his hips pressed me deeper into the couch. I managed to wiggle a leg free so I could wrap it around his ass and pull him even tighter into me. Pressing my hips into his, I worked to create some friction to ease the throbbing between my legs but with both of us wearing jeans, it wasn't happening.

"More," I pleaded.

"Later," he said, standing up off the couch quickly.

The doorbell chimed throughout the house.

"Come on, Wife," Nick said, grabbing my hand and pulling me up off the couch. He took the lead and strode to the door. I stayed behind him, waiting to greet our guests as they stepped inside.

The moment Nick opened the door, Steffie's voice filled the foyer. "Whew! I forgot how hot you were. How about a hug? I'll warn you, my hands have a tendency to wander."

I laughed and stepped out from behind Nick to greet my friend. I had expected no less dramatic of an entrance. "Just like I tell my students: hands, feet and other objects to yourself."

She laughed and pulled me in for a tight hug. Maybe it was due to the pregnancy, but her boobs had grown a size or two since I'd seen her last. They were squeezed tightly into the green blouse she had paired with skinny jeans and six-inch stilettos.

"Welcome to Montana!" I said. "Come on in." I peered around her hesitantly, expecting to see my father.

"He's just finishing a conference call," she said. "He'll be up in a minute."

"Sure." Austin Capital ranked above all else.

"So this is your house?" she said, walking through the foyer and looking around.

"It was. Nick and I live further up in the mountains." Hopefully, it wouldn't take too long for a realtor to sell this place for me. I had plenty of time to check on it during the summer months, but once school resumed, I didn't want the burden of an empty, furnished house to maintain.

"Emmeline," my father said, striding through the door. He gave Nick a sideways glance but came directly toward me.

I looked so much like my mother, it was difficult to find any resemblance to Trent Austin. The shape of our mouths was our only likeness. Maybe that's why he didn't like me much. I was nothing like him.

"Hello, Father," I said, giving him a brief hug while he

bent to kiss my cheek.

"You look well," he said.

"You too."

My father looked the same as he had during my childhood, except for the gray streaks in his brown hair and a few wrinkles around his eyes. I was glad to see that he had dressed casually and had left his signature gray suit and blue tie behind in New York.

"Let me introduce you to my husband," I said. "Nick Slater, meet my father, Trent Austin."

"Nice to meet you," Nick said, shaking his hand.

"Pleasure," my father lied.

"Trent, isn't this place just so charming? And woodsy?" Steffie asked, sliding into my father's side.

He gave her a skeptical look before sliding his hand down to palm her ass.

Steffie and my father had always flaunted their highly sexual relationship. I wished, just once, they'd remember how awkward it was for me to witness.

"We've made reservations for dinner out tonight," I said. "You've got time to get settled first. I've opened a bottle of wine if you'd like some, Father. Or Nick has beer."

"Wine," he said.

"Fine. Please come in and sit," I said, leading them to the living room.

"I'll help you in the kitchen, Emmy," Nick said when my father and Steffie were squished together on a couch.

"Emmeline," my father corrected.

"Emmy," I said. "Nick calls me 'Emmy.' "

My father muttered something under his breath but I was already walking away so I missed it.

"That could have gone worse," Nick said.

"Really?"

"We just have to make it through dinner and then we can escape," he said.

"Right. Dinner then home."

I could endure.

Nick and I had survived but dinner had been a disaster.

"How are we going to make it until Wednesday?" I asked.

"It'll be okay," Nick said. "We just have to get through the hike and then another dinner." Nick was taking my father on a hike tomorrow for the man-date Steffie had requested while us girls were spending the morning at the Prescott Spa.

"He was so rude!" I shouted as I threw my purse on the dining room table. "His behavior tonight was awful! I wanted to snatch that phone from his hand and dump it in my water glass. And did you notice how every time we touched, he would glare at us?"

"I noticed," Nick said. "Why do you think I started touching your leg under the table? It was either that or cause a scene by telling him to fuck off."

"Obviously this whole trip was Steffie's idea. He does not want to be here and couldn't have made that more clear."

"My favorite part of the night was when he started talking about your ex," Nick said. "I really enjoyed listening to what a shame it was that you didn't make it. Oh, and how well-bred your children would have been."

"I'm so sorry, Nick."

"Don't you dare apologize for him." He crossed the room and pulled me into his arms.

"Okay." I sagged further into his chest, giving him my weight.

"This fucking sucks."

I nodded in agreement as my stomach churned. "I think I'm going to be sick."

Draven

When my fist connected with the man's cheek, I felt the bones break before the loud crack echoed through the room.

"One more time, Wrecker. How many times did you break into my daughter-in-law's house?" I asked.

Wrecker was currently duct taped to a metal chair in the basement of the Tin Gypsy compound.

The Warriors had honored their agreement to hand over Jinx and Wrecker. Jinx was history. Wrecker would be too, but not before I found out if the Warriors had been the ones breaking into Emmeline's house.

"Just that once," Wrecker mumbled through a bleeding mouth full of broken teeth.

"I think he's telling the truth, Prez," Jet said by my side. "Yeah."

When Emmeline had mentioned that her house had been broken into more than once, I'd gotten an uneasy feeling. Motorcycle clubs like the Gypsies and Warriors rarely made mistakes. Fuck-ups meant jail time. Or death. It didn't sit right that the Warriors would mount two failed break-in attempts before finally grabbing her on the third.

Now I knew why I had been feeling so uneasy.

Nick and everyone else had made the wrong assumption. The Warriors weren't the only ones that had gone after Emmeline. There was someone else.

I had promised Nick I would make things right. For once, I wanted to follow through on a commitment to my son. I hadn't been able to keep his mother safe. I could make damn sure his wife was out of harm's way.

Someone else out there was threatening my family and they would pay.

I just had to figure out who.

CHAPTER 26

Nick

"**A**RE YOU SURE YOU'RE OKAY? I CAN cancel the hike," I told Emmy.

"I'm fine," she said, waving me out of the bedroom.

"You've been sick all night."

"It's just stress and nerves. As soon as I get to the spa and can relax, drink some cucumber water, I'll be as good as new. And I'm looking forward to catching up with Steffie. I've missed her. We need some girl time."

"Cucumber water? That sounds disgusting," I teased.

"It's delicious." She smiled. "Now get out of here. I need to jump in the shower and you can't be late to pick up my father. Let's not give him any more ammunition."

"Fine," I said. "I'm taking him up the same trail I took you on. The cell coverage is good so if you need anything, just call."

"Okay. Love you," she said, climbing out of bed.

I bent to kiss the top of her head as she walked to the bathroom. "Love you too."

I felt like an asshole for leaving my sick wife. It was this entire visit from her father. She was as tense and anxious as I'd ever seen her. I doubted Trent wanted to go on this hike any more than I did but the bastard would probably hold it against me forever if I canceled.

At least it would give us a chance to talk without Emmy around.

I'd seen it in his eyes last night at dinner. He had some things to tell me. Fine. I had a few choice words for Trent myself. Today we'd both get the chance to speak our minds, and Emmy, hopefully, would be none the wiser.

So it came as no surprise that the minute I picked Trent up, he didn't beat around the bush.

"I don't approve of your marriage to my daughter," Trent said.

"I don't give a fuck. Neither does Emmy."

"You'll never get your hands on our money."

I scoffed. "This may surprise you, Trent, but not everyone is like you. I don't give a fuck about your money. Keep it."

"All people want money."

"Not me. I've got everything I need," I said.

"Forgive me for not believing you," Trent said. "I find it much too coincidental that after years of estrangement, you decide to rekindle a relationship with my naïve and stupid daughter just a year after her trust was released into her charge."

My blood started to boil and I clutched the steering

wheel, fighting to keep control over my temper. "I didn't convince Emmy to move here in some elaborate scheme to get her money. The only coincidence here was that she randomly chose to move to the town where I'd been living for almost a decade."

"That's quite a coincidence. Surely, you can understand my skepticism," Trent said.

"It's crazy but true. You might as well accept it. I'm not going anywhere so you're stuck with me."

"We'll see."

"Yeah, we'll see," I said. "Oh, and if you ever call Emmy naïve or stupid again, or any other insult for that matter, I'll break your fucking nose. Watch how you talk about my wife."

"She's my daughter. I'll talk about her any way I see fit."

"Not anymore. Last warning, pal. Don't fuck with me on this."

Trent sank back into his seat but wisely chose to keep his mouth shut.

I fucking hated this guy. All of Emmy's goodness must have come from Collette and her grandparents because her father was a piece of shit.

How could Trent have so little respect for his own daughter? Emmy was smart and funny. She loved completely and forgave easily. Her warmth and beauty drew you in. Five minutes in her presence and you never wanted to be without her again.

It's why Gigi and Maisy had so quickly added Emmy to their girl squad. Why my friends had never given me shit about spending all my free time with her. They knew how special she was and how lucky I was to have her.

"Why are you even here?" I asked Trent.

"Steffie insisted we visit Emmeline and I give you a chance."

"You didn't want to see Emmy?" I asked.

"Why would I? Eventually she'll come to her senses and move home. I can see her then."

"She's not moving back."

"She will," Trent insisted.

This guy was fucking delusional. He actually thought Emmy would be back in New York soon.

All of the things I had wanted to tell Trent were pointless, so I kept my mouth shut. He had no clue what kind of person his daughter was and he didn't seem to care that she had found happiness in her Montana life. All he cared about was making sure I wasn't after his fortune.

Change of plans. I passed the turnoff for the trailhead I had planned to take.

I wasn't going to give Trent the easy hike that I'd planned. Instead, I was taking the fuckwad up the steepest trail I had ever hiked. I couldn't punch Emmy's dad but I could make his life miserable for the next three hours.

"How much farther?" Trent panted. He had stopped again on the trail and was bracing his hands on his knees, trying to catch his breath.

I checked my GPS watch. "About half a mile. Let's go."

Trent groaned but pressed on. The trail was rocky and narrow. The steep inclines were long and the flat spaces between them short.

I had to give the man credit, Trent was in fairly good

shape and was doing better than I had expected. And since we were about the same height, he had been able to keep up with my long strides.

If not for Trent's presence, this would have been an awesome hike. The morning air was still cool and fresh. The sun shone brightly in the light blue sky.

Emmy would love it up here but it would be a tough hike for her short legs. The trail was actually close to the cabin I had rented for our anniversary.

I looked over in its direction. I couldn't see the building through the trees so I tipped my head up to the sky, hoping to catch a glimpse of an eagle or a hawk, but I jolted to a stop when I spotted a thin stream of smoke coming from the direction of the cabin.

In the winter, I wouldn't have thought twice about the smoke. But this was the middle of summer. Seeing smoke this time of year meant trouble. Why would someone start a fire when it was forecasted to get into the low eighties today?

I stared at the smoke for a minute and took a few deep breaths. There was no smell, which was a good sign.

I looked back to my GPS. We were closer to the cabin than I had originally expected. I'd been pushing Trent up the trailhead hard and fast.

"What?" Trent said. "Are we done? Can we turn back?"

"No." I took in a few more breaths, searching for the slightest scent of burning wood. But all I got was evergreens.

Then I listened. Forest fires, even small ones, gave off a unique roar as trees sizzled. All I could hear was a light breeze rustling the trees and a woodpecker carving a new home in the distance.

I tipped my head back again and studied the smoke. It wasn't getting any heavier or darker so I decided to continue hiking and keep an eye on it.

"Let's go," I ordered Trent.

Five minutes later, I stopped again and looked to the sky. This time the smoke was thicker and turning gray. "Something's wrong."

"What? What are you talking about?" Trent panted.

"See that smoke?" I said, pointing to the sky. "We need to check it out."

"I'm not moving *toward* a fire!" Trent said. "Are you insane?"

"Fine. You can find your own way back."

"Wait!" Trent grabbed my arm before I could run off the trail. "You can't leave me alone. What if I get lost? What if I get attacked by an animal?"

"You've got two choices, Trent," I said, shaking off his grip. "You can either follow the trail back down or you can come with me. But I'm not fucking around here. You come with me, you keep up. I won't stop and wait for you to catch your breath. I will leave your ass in the middle of the woods. You've got two seconds to decide. What's it going to be?"

"I'll keep up." Trent nodded.

"Hope you're in shape, old man."

Jogging through the trees wasn't easy. The rough ground was covered in pine needles and fallen branches. Occasionally I would stop and look for the smoke, checking to make sure we were running in the right direction, but other than that, I ran with determined silence. Trent crashed around behind me but kept up with my fast pace.

"You okay?" I called over my shoulder.

"Yes!"

I slowed up a bit. I didn't want to give Emmy's dad a heart attack by pushing him too hard. And I just might need the extra set of hands, depending on what we found at the end of that smoke plume.

As we got closer, the smell I had searched for earlier filled my nostrils. Something was definitely on fire. I just hoped that it was the cabin and not the forest. The house could be rebuilt quickly but the destruction from a forest fire took years to repair. And there were other homes in the area. A forest fire threatened them too.

The air in the trees became hazy. We were close. Ten yards in front of me was the clearing.

I pushed my tired legs, sprinting the remaining distance, and burst through the tree line.

Fuck.

The cabin where Emmy and I had spent our fantastic anniversary weekend was burning down. Smoke was pouring out of the windows, and flames were visible through the open door.

A coughing noise had my head spinning toward the shed off the driveway.

An elderly man was dragging a hose toward the house. His face was covered in black soot and he was struggling to stay on his feet.

Rushing to his side, I helped him stand. "Is there anyone else inside?"

"My wife!" the man yelled. "I need to get her. She's trapped upstairs!"

"I'll get her. Stay here." I helped the man sit on the ground and spun around to the house. "Here!" I shouted to Trent who had just cleared the trees. "Use this and call 9-1-1. Tell them we're at the cabin up Old Haggerty Trail. Got it?"

Trent scrambled to catch the phone I had tossed him. "What are you doing? You can't go in there!" Trent shouted.

I ignored him and took the front steps two at a time. The second I crossed through the door, a wave of heat assaulted my skin. Smoke choked my throat and burned my eyes.

I had just run into a wall of flames.

Emmeline

A white stick, two minutes, one word, and my entire life was different.

Pregnant.

"Oh my god," I whispered, tears falling from my eyes.

I started laughing and crying at the same time. Was this real? It was such a profound moment in my life that I had a hard time believing it was true.

The dread that I'd felt earlier at the prospect of dealing with my father had vanished. He could criticize as much as he wanted for all I cared. It was inconsequential.

I had much more important things to concern myself with.

Like how I was going to share this amazing news with Nick and how I was going to decorate the nursery.

"Good morning," I told Steffie.

"Hi," she muttered.

I had just let myself into the house and found her sitting

on the living room couch, typing something into her phone.

"Do you want to get some breakfast at the café before we head to the spa?" I asked.

"No. I want to stay here." She set down her phone and stared out the living room window, refusing to look at me.

"Okay."

I sat quietly for a few minutes while I waited for Steffie to say something. It wasn't like her to be so quiet. She was always so outgoing and wonderfully loud. She hated silence. In college, I'd had to study exclusively at the library because our apartment had always been bustling with activity.

"Are you okay?" I finally asked. Maybe her pregnancy was troubling her. I was glad Nick and my father were busy on their hike so I could talk to her about how she was really feeling about becoming a mother.

If it weren't for Nick not knowing yet, I would have told Steffie about my own exciting news so we could celebrate together.

"I'm fine."

"You don't seem fine," I said.

She turned to me and snapped, "You're right. I'm not fine."

"Let's talk about it. I want to help."

She laughed dryly. "You want to help? That's ironic."

I held my hands up in surrender and resumed my silence.

"Oh, look, she's pouting. There's a surprise."

"Steffie," I said, hurt. "Why are you acting like this? What's wrong?"

She looked down at her phone and a twisted grin spread across her face. What was going on? She had never looked so cruel.

"Steffie?"

"Shut up." She dismissed me and went back to typing on her phone.

"Okay," I said, standing from the couch. I didn't need her attitude on this special day. "I don't know what's wrong with you, if you're just hormonal or mad at me for something, but you're being mean. So unless you want to explain to me what's going on and start acting like my friend, I think it would be best if we skipped the spa."

I turned to leave but stopped when she called my name.

"Do you remember that guy that was stalking you at NYU last year?" she asked.

My body jolted as every muscle tensed. "Yes."

"He's coming over."

"Excuse me?" What was she talking about? How did she know my stalker? *Why* did she know my stalker?

"He's coming over," she repeated, "to kill you."

I blinked a few times and replayed her words then I relaxed and rolled my eyes. "Funny, Steffie," I deadpanned, "though I'm worried that your sense of humor is becoming a little morbid."

"No, really. He's on his way here right now. I hired him to kill you and make it look like a burglary gone wrong."

The tension immediately returned to my body. Her tone was undeniably serious. Before I could react, Steffie shocked me again by standing from the couch and pulling a small black pistol from the waistband of her jeans. When she aimed it at my chest, my hands instinctively wrapped around my belly.

"Do not move," she ordered. "You're going to stay right where you are until your biggest fan gets here."

My head started whirling. This had to be some kind of

prank. I had to be in one of those nightmares where, even after you wake up, it haunts you for hours. This had to be a dream. My friend was pointing a gun at me.

"I don't understand," I said. "What's going on?"

"It's not complicated, Emmeline. You have what I want." My blank stare made her sneer. "Money."

"You want my money?" I asked, still completely confused.

"Well, it's not like you're going to use it," she snapped. "You're worth over one hundred million dollars, Emmeline. You might be willing to let all that money sit untouched in the bank, but I'm not. Your father isn't as rich as he likes everyone to think. Did you know he put me on an allowance?"

What the *fuck* was happening? I stared at her frozen with shock. Did she actually think my death would get her my fortune?

"How is killing me going to get you money?" I couldn't believe I was even asking that question.

"Simple. You die. Trent inherits your trust fund. I take it from Trent."

"But Steffie, my money goes to Nick." Now that I had poked a gaping hole in her logic, I hoped she would stop pointing her gun at me and my unborn child.

"Wrong, *Emmy*," she hissed. "Fred Andrews didn't make your beneficiary change. He's been stalling. It's still listed as your father."

My mind just kept spinning. How could she possibly know that? Had she bribed him with my millions? Or had she used some of her other more personal "assets" to get information from him?

"Do you actually think you're going to get away with my murder, then marry my father?" I asked, again stunned by this conversation. "This is crazy. You can't be serious. Tell me you're joking."

"I'm *dead* serious." Her desperate and insane eyes locked on mine. "I've spent too much time planning for this to fail. I've sacrificed everything to get here and I'm not stopping now."

This rushed vacation suddenly made sense. She had to commit my murder before Nick became the beneficiary of my trust.

My mind raced through the last few years, seeing things from a new angle. I had once confessed to her that I had been considering donating my trust to charity. She had adamantly talked me out of it. I had asked her once if she loved my father. She had just smiled and said he was what she'd always planned for. Not loved. Not wanted. Planned for.

And when I'd told her that I was being stalked, she had never once encouraged me to go to the police. Instead, she'd asked me to point him out to her.

"My stalker? Were you behind him all along?" I asked.

"Oh, no. He's genuinely obsessed with you. And back then, I doubt he would have caused you harm. But after Logan had him tracked down and nearly beaten to death for stalking you, his obsession turned a little . . . uglier. When I approached him with a big fat wad of cash, he was more than willing to cooperate."

What? I had no idea that Logan had done that. It didn't matter. Not when Steffie had a gun aimed at my chest. Not when my oldest friend was paying someone to murder me.

Pain lanced through my heart. All of my precious memories with Steffie had just been tainted by her insatiable greed. Now I knew just how much she valued our friendship and my life: less than one hundred million dollars.

"You're my friend," I whispered. "Does that mean nothing to you?"

She shrugged. "I'll buy new friends."

My sadness was quickly replaced with anger.

Hadn't I been through enough this year? Personal struggles aside, I'd had a drug dealer press a gun to my forehead and a rogue motorcycle gang attempt to kidnap me. Now my friend, my father's fiancée, was threatening to kill me?

"You'll rot in jail," I hissed.

"I won't," she snarled. "The cops will get here and find me tied up and helpless, sobbing over your lifeless body. Your stalker will be on his way to Canada with the money in my purse, never to be seen or heard from again. Just another break-in gone wrong. You've had such bad luck with those after all. Only this time I'm here to make sure he doesn't fuck it up."

I gaped at her for a moment, letting it all sink in. There would be no pleading for my life, no softening her heart with anecdotes from the past. She would not change course. Determination was etched all over her pretty face. The friend I had always loved was just a phantom. A cloud of lies veiled the brunette stranger in my living room.

She was counting on her gun to keep my feet rooted but I wouldn't just stand here, waiting for my executioner to arrive. I had too much to live for. I would fight fiercely to save this baby inside me. And I was banking on the fact that Steffie's gun had been shaking in her hand since she'd pulled it out of her purse.

So I summoned all the courage I could find and took a breath. *One. Two. Three.*

The second Steffie looked back to the window, I whirled

around and sprinted to the door. A loud crack had me ducking my head. It echoed in the room a split-second before one of the large windows next to me shattered.

She missed!

Steffie bellowed a frustrated scream and yelled my name.

Taking one glance over my shoulder, I expected to see her aiming the pistol again. Instead, she was pulling herself up off the floor. She must have tried to follow me but tripped on the wrinkle in the living room carpet. Her falling was likely the reason that the bullet had hit the window instead of me.

That wrinkle, the one I'd cursed a hundred times, had just saved my life.

Now all I had to do was make it outside before she fired again and I could escape into the trees. The adrenaline pumped in my veins and propelled me faster and faster. When I hit the tile in the foyer, I scrambled a bit but was able to stay on my feet and throw open the door.

"Get back here!" Steffie screamed.

Two steps outside and I thought I was home free. But a strong arm banded around my stomach, pulling me backward at the same time a hand clamped over my mouth, muffling my scream.

"No!" I yelled, fighting and clawing at my captor. But despite my hitting and kicking, he was able to drag me around the side of the house.

"Quiet, Emmeline."

I stopped fighting and the hand at my mouth loosened. I craned my neck and saw a familiar face.

"Dash?"

He pressed a finger to his lips and shushed me. Then he

released his hold, grabbed my hand and pulled me behind a large tree near my house.

In the distance, Steffie raved like a lunatic.

"What are you doing here?" I whispered, crouching close to the ground to hide.

He shook his head, signaling for me to remain quiet.

I nodded and turned, peering around the side of the tree. I was so relieved to be out of that house but more confused than ever.

Minutes went by as we hid and listened for any sign of Steffie. She had stopped screaming and I had no clue where she could have gone.

Movement at the corner of my eye made me flinch. I watched with wide eyes as my stalker emerged from behind the house, creeping slowly toward the front with a sizeable pistol in his hand. He looked just like I remembered, ginger hair and a scrawny frame. His eyes were beady and set too close to the bridge of his nose.

A shiver ran down my spine as he slithered past the tree, thankfully unaware of our presence.

Dash nudged my arm, jerking his chin toward the back corner of the house. Another figure emerged from the same place my stalker had just come from.

Draven.

With cat-like steps, he closed the distance to my stalker. The cocking hammer of Draven's handgun filled the silent air.

"Drop it," Draven ordered.

My stalker tossed his gun to the dirt without hesitation. Then with one swift but powerful blow, Draven slammed the butt of his gun into the back of my would-be murderer's skull, sending his body crumpling to the ground.

"Come on out," Draven called.

"Did you get the skank?" Dash yelled.

"Yeah. She's tied up inside with Jet."

Dash hauled me to my feet and tugged me behind him as we walked toward Draven and the unconscious man at his feet.

"Tie up this guy," Draven said.

While Dash obeyed his president's command, the shock of the situation hit me. I wrapped my arms around my tummy as my shoulders started to shake, but before I could collapse, Draven wrapped me in a tight embrace.

"You're okay," he said.

The shaking turned into sobs and I buried my face in his shirt.

"You're okay, Emmeline," he said. "You're okay. It's over."

"Where is he?" I asked for the hundredth time.

I was in the conference room at the sheriff's station, just like the last time I'd had a gun pointed at me. But this time, Nick wasn't by my side. Instead, I was surrounded by Draven and men from his motorcycle club.

And no one was telling me where my husband was. Every time I called his cell phone, it went straight to voicemail.

It had been almost four hours since Steffie's attack. After I'd pulled myself together, Draven had driven me to town. The sheriff's station, which had been practically deserted when we'd arrived, was now buzzing with activity.

Jess had come in and taken my statement. Shortly

thereafter, he had disappeared.

Milo had come in with bottled waters. Then he'd vanished too.

The only other deputy I knew was Sam and he was currently in an interrogation room with my stalker.

Steffie was locked in a jail cell.

"Something happened. Why aren't they telling me what's going on?" I asked Draven.

"I don't know, kid." Draven's voice was filled with concern.

I was nauseous and shaking, probably from a combination of pregnancy and anxiety. I needed something to eat before I passed out.

"Would one of you mind finding me some crackers? And maybe some orange juice?" I asked Draven's men.

"I'll get it," Dash said.

"Can you talk to me? The quiet is making things worse," I asked Draven.

"Sure. What do you want to talk about?"

"How did you end up at my house?"

Draven had given his statement to Jess but hadn't explained how he had come there in the first place.

"When you told me about your other break-ins, something didn't sit right with me so I started digging. Found out it wasn't the Warriors like you thought, so we looked into your relatives. This morning, my hacker found a couple suspicious emails between that bitch and that guy I clocked. She buried them deep but my guy dug them out. Then he found out she's been pulling cash these last few weeks. Close to a half million in the last ten days. We came down to warn you and Nick that something suspicious was going on."

I let his explanation sink in. What would I have done

had they not been there?

"Fucking lucky timing," Draven said, blowing out a loud breath.

Absolutely. "How did you know where to find me?" I asked.

"Uh, Dash may have swiped your phone the other weekend and put a tracker on it," he said, rubbing the back of his neck.

I never thought I'd be so happy to have my privacy invaded.

If it weren't for Draven, I would likely be dead. I would have escaped Steffie but run right outside into my stalker's arms.

I struggled to believe how fortunate we were. Had Draven chosen to wait until the afternoon to come to Prescott or had the hacker not found Steffie's emails until later, things would have turned out much worse.

"Thank you," I whispered. "For not giving up. For saving me." *For saving us.*

"Glad we could be there," he said, taking my hand.

"Where's Nick?" I asked. My voice cracked and tears flooded my eyes. Something was terribly wrong. I just wanted someone to tell me what it was.

A loud commotion outside the room had Draven and me both shooting out of our chairs and rushing through the door.

My hand flew up to my mouth as Nick jogged across the room. He was covered in ash and soot but he was okay. I lost sight of his face when he folded me into his chest.

"You're okay," I cried into his scorched shirt. Its smell made my stomach roll but I didn't care. All that mattered was he was here and both of us were safe.

"You're okay," he said.

Surrounded by deputies and motorcycle gangsters, Nick and I held tight to one another. The world around us disappeared.

Draven had been right earlier. It was over.

I felt it this time. We'd made it through. Now all that was left for Nick and me was a happy life building our family. Enjoying every moment together.

"Let's go home?" I asked.

"Let's go home."

Even though it was the middle of the afternoon, Nick and I took a long shower and then climbed into bed.

I was emotionally exhausted and needed sleep.

There was a mass of people downstairs waiting to see us, but I didn't care. They'd stay for a couple of hours while we spent some time alone.

Wearing one of Nick's flannels and my winter socks, my back was curled into his bare chest.

It felt like days, not hours, had passed since I'd woken up in this same position. It was hard to believe that just this morning I had learned I was pregnant.

My desire to surprise Nick with an elaborate announcement was gone. Now all I wanted was for him to know.

"I'm pregnant," I said with no fanfare or dramatics. We didn't need it. The news itself was big enough.

His arms pulled me closer and his chest expanded with a deep breath. "Love you, Wife," Nick whispered into my hair.

"Love you, Husband."

His hand traveled from my chest to my tummy. Gently, he lifted up the hem of my flannel and splayed his palm across my flat stomach.

"Love you too, baby."

EPILOGUE

Two years later . . .

"**M**OM, I'M HANGING UP THE PHONE now."

"Wait!" she yelled. "Can we talk about the flowers?"

"It will have to wait. I'll see you in less than an hour. That is, if you'd let me off the phone so I can finish getting ready and load up Draven."

"Fine," she huffed and hung up.

I looked at my baby boy playing on the floor and smiled. Draven Nicholas III was almost a year and a half old, not really a baby anymore. He was an exact replica of Nick, minus the beard.

"Grammy is driving me crazy with this wedding business," I told him.

He gave me a smile that melted my heart and went back to stacking a tower of cups.

My mother and Alesso had gotten married the fall after my ordeal with Steffie. They had come to Prescott and had a no-fuss wedding at town hall. At the time, I had been so impressed by Mom's decision to skip the theatrics. Then that night at dinner, the real Collette had appeared and announced that they were having an enormous wedding reception. She had only wanted to get married quickly so she and Alesso could move into their Montana chalet.

The reception had taken her nearly two years to plan but finally it was all coming together. In a month, we would have the party, and I had vowed never again to get involved in coordinating a wedding.

"Ready to go, buddy?" I asked Draven, picking him up off the floor and kissing his chubby cheek.

It was Independence Day and we were hosting a party at the garage. This was our first Fourth of July gathering at Slater's Station but I hoped it would become an annual tradition for our families and friends.

Tonight, we were filling the parking lot with camp chairs while the men barbequed, the women chatted and the kids played. Then we were all staying for Prescott's fireworks show.

"We're here!" I called into Nick's shop.

Three heads popped up from underneath the hood of a green sports car.

As Nick, Uncle Dash and Grandpa Draven crossed the room, I gave my boy one last hug and kiss. It would likely be the last time I'd get to hold him until well after dark and he fussed for his mama.

"Hey," Nick said, kissing my cheek as Grandpa Draven lifted Baby Draven from my arms.

"Hi." I smiled. "Can you help me unload?"

"Dash and I can take care of it," Nick said.

"Okay. Bring the beer in first, please, and I'll start loading it into the fridge."

"How's my little man today?" Nick asked our son before ruffling his brown hair and walking outside to my Jeep.

Sliding into Draven Sr.'s side, I gave him a sideways hug. "How are you?"

"Good. Glad to be here." He smiled and kissed my forehead.

When Nick had learned that Draven had saved my life, the broken bond between them had healed. They'd built a strong working relationship, and both Nick's garage and Draven's in Clifton Forge were now extremely profitable.

Nick had gotten so busy that I hadn't been able to keep up with the bookkeeping and office work, so the year after they had moved to Montana, Alesso had started managing the office.

"How many cars did you bring with you this time?" I asked Draven.

"Three." He grinned.

I rolled my eyes and gave him an exaggerated glare. "I'm never going to see Nick at this rate. He gets so caught up with one of them that he forgets what time it is. He missed dinner twice this week."

Draven chuckled. "Like father, like son. I remember once, Chrissy got so mad at me for doing the same that she brought ten alarm clocks to the garage and set them to go off one minute apart. By the time the last one beeped, it was so loud that I couldn't ignore them anymore."

"She was a smart woman," I said. Nick's mom's tactic was brilliant and tomorrow I was going alarm clock shopping.

"Yes, she was," Draven agreed with a sad smile.

"Can you keep him while I get the food ready?" I asked.

He nodded before tickling his grandson and heading outside. Draven might not have been the best father but he was a wonderful grandfather. So was Alesso.

They were the only grandfathers Draven would ever have. My father had nothing to do with my life and I wouldn't allow him in my son's.

Trent Austin had refused to believe that his adoring fiancée would attack me. It wasn't until after her trial and she had been sent away to prison that he'd realized just how much she had manipulated him. She hadn't even been pregnant. It had all been a lie to ensure that he married her. I still wondered if she had planned on killing him too.

"Emmeline!" Mom was storming into the garage, pulling my brother, Ethan, behind her.

"Can you please tell your brother that bringing his ex-wife to the wedding reception is completely inappropriate?" she said.

"Hi," Ethan said, giving me a quick hug and kiss on the cheek.

"Hello. Which ex-wife?" I asked.

"I've invited Rachel."

"I like Rachel," I told my mother.

"What?" she yelled. "How could you say that? She started having an affair with your father while she was married to your brother."

"That wasn't Rachel," Ethan said.

"Isn't she the blond one?" Mom asked.

"No."

"Which one was the blond one?" she asked.

"Number Four," Ethan and I answered in unison.

"Then which one is Rachel?" my mother asked.

"The second one. Brunette. Tall. Kind of willowy. I was in their wedding," I said.

"Okay." She nodded. "I like her too. She's invited."

Ethan muttered a curse and then declared he was going to help Nick at the grill. He had been on an extended Montana vacation following his divorce from Number Four.

I wasn't the only member of my family no longer speaking to Trent Austin. My father had started sleeping with Ethan's wife not long after Steffie had been out of the picture. Number Four had taken a chunk from my brother's trust fund and was currently shacked up at the Austin estate.

On the bright side, it was the wake-up call that Ethan had needed to turn his life around. He had realized that his greedy lifestyle was never going to get him the happiness he desired, and I was proud to say that he was becoming a better man.

"What's next?" Mom asked, surveying my food table setup.

The meat was ready and the garage was overflowing with drinks. Gigi and Maisy were bringing salads. Samuel, Mom's chef, had made desserts. It was the perfect summer barbeque.

"Now you can tell me about these flowers and then we'll enjoy the evening," I said, looping my arm through hers and leading her outside.

"Do you miss it, helping with the fireworks?" I asked Nick. "I know how you men feel about blowing stuff up."

When he'd worked at the fire station, Nick had always

helped with the fireworks show. But now that he was just on the volunteer team, Michael Holt was supervising.

Nick bent down to kiss our son's hair and then took my hand in his. "Not one bit."

We were side by side in a couple of camp chairs watching the show. Draven was passed out on his daddy's chest and I was wrapped up in a blanket to keep warm.

After things had settled down the day Steffie had shot at me, I'd learned about the fire that had kept Nick away. He had managed to save the elderly woman trapped in the burning chateau but the building itself had been too far gone to save. Though it frightened me to think of what could have happened to him, I was so proud of Nick.

He was a hero.

"Ryan told me tonight that they're ready to knock out the walls. Did you decide if you want to stay at your mom's or at the motel?" Nick asked.

This summer we were putting an addition on the house. Addition wasn't quite the right term. It was more like building a second house and connecting it to the existing one. When it was finished, we'd have an entertainment room and playroom downstairs with two new bedrooms and another bathroom upstairs. And I would finally get a bigger closet.

"I hate to intrude on Mom for a whole week," I said. "So, the motel I guess."

Nick chuckled and brought my hand to his lips for a soft kiss. "I've got another idea," he said. "We could fly to Vegas for the week."

"Right. Sin City with a toddler would be a blast."

"He could stay with your mom and Alesso."

"I doubt they'd want him with all the activity they have going on."

He grinned. "That's not what Collette said when I asked her."

"You already told her we were going, didn't you?"

"Yeah."

I rolled my eyes. "What about the garage? You've been so busy. Can you afford to be away for an entire week? What if you get behind?"

"Alesso can manage the office. The cars Dad and Dash brought up aren't rush jobs. I'm good," he said.

"It's going to be miserably hot down there."

"Think of it like a honeymoon. We'll just stay inside our room with the air conditioning."

"Honeymoon? More like returning to the scene of the crime."

Leaning over, he brushed his lips across the base of my jaw. I loved it when he did that. "We could see if Clover is still around and renew our vows at the chapel? Maybe get to work on baby number two?" he whispered.

I absolutely wanted to see our chapel again but another baby? "No. No way. It's too soon."

He leaned back and smiled. His vibrant eyes sparkled as the fireworks exploded in the sky above us and in my heart. "I dare you."

I shook my head and gave him a smirk. "That doesn't work on me anymore. You've used up all your dares."

"Fine," he said. "I double dare you."

ACKNOWLEDGEMENTS

Thank you to my family and friends, who spur me on daily with their love and encouragement.

To Elizabeth Nover, the best editor I ever could have wished for. Thank you for the insightful comments, necessary cuts and missing commas. To Sarah Hansen for designing my beautiful covers. To Julie Deaton for your proofreading expertise. To Stacey Blake, formatter extraordinaire. To the crew at EverAfter Romance for the paperbacks I adore. To Nazarea and the team at InkSlinger PR for promoting my stories. Thank you. I am so blessed to have you all at my back.

To all of the bloggers that work so hard to promote books and the passion of reading. Thank you all for your thoughtful words and honest reviews.

And to all my readers and loyal followers. Thank you. From the bottom of my heart, thank you. Your messages keep me going. I hope you've loved Nick and Emmy's story.

ABOUT THE AUTHOR

Devney lives in Montana with her husband and two children. After working in the technology industry for nearly a decade, she abandoned conference calls and project schedules to enjoy a slower pace at home with her kids. She loves reading and, after consuming hundreds of books, decided to share her own stories.

www.devneyperry.com

Facebook: www.facebook.com/devneyperrybooks

Instagram: www.instagram.com/devneyperry

Twitter: twitter.com/devneyperry

CPSIA information can be obtained
at www.ICGtesting.com
Printed in the USA
BVHW061610200120
569971BV00026B/2646